The
Most
Savage
Animal

Also by Hugh Atkinson

The Pink and the Brown

Low Company

The Reckoning

The Games

Johnny Horns

The
Most Savage
Animal

Hugh Atkinson

Rupert Hart-Davis   London

Granada Publishing Limited
First published in Great Britain 1972 by Rupert Hart-Davis Ltd
3 Upper James Street London W1R 4BP

Copyright © 1972 by Hugh Atkinson

ISBN 0 246 10546 1

Printed in Great Britain by
Richard Clay (The Chaucer Press) Ltd
Bungay Suffolk

Preface

THIS novel is little concerned with the politics of the long Vietnam bloodletting. It speaks for those unspoken for, the millions of uncommitted peasants, the tens of thousands of civilian amputees, the devastated bodies, the devastated villages, the devastated hearts and minds.

If this is a novel of protest the protest is an ancient one—the awful history of man's inhumanity to man, which has made an abattoir for twenty-five years of one people, one small country.

There are volunteers of many nationalities staunching the civilian wounds in Vietnam, operating the primitive provincial hospitals where three casualties to a cot are common, bringing comfort to the refugees, those made homeless by battle, those wrenched by the relocations from their immemorial villages.

It was necessary to tell their story in recognition of all forces set towards peace and sanity.

For this purpose, the workings of mankind's one humanitarian international, the International Committee of the Red Cross, has been characterized to represent the organizations of many kinds and creeds whose members work for peace and relief.

This story is entirely a work of fiction, and none of the characters depicted in it who are represented as holding specific positions in the International Red Cross bear, or are intended to bear, any resemblance to the persons who occupy or have occupied those positions in real life. Moreover, the author neither implies, nor intends to imply that the ICRC, its president, members or employees were or ever have been in such situations as described, or that they have acted or conducted themselves or are capable of acting or conducting themselves in the manner described or that any of their decisions have been motivated by any considerations other than the welfare of victims requiring assistance. The use of the ICRC, its status and organization is essentially symbolic. Except for a few figures of international renown mentioned by their real names, no reference is intended in the story to any person living or dead.

There are difficulties and restraints when an author fictions into a great institution. If offence is caused it is unintended and regretted. An author's freedom to make free reference is an essential of his being. Without this, creative writing will soon become stifled to the point where any fictional work not totally devoid of reality, will be incapable of publication.

The material for the Vietnam sections of this novel was gathered on the ground where the story is made to happen.

HUGH ATKINSON

Prologue

In 1859 Napoleon III was drawn up on a battlefield in Northern Italy, in a war to free the Italians from the Austrians. By chance, young Henri Dunant went to Italy in the wake of the battles to petition the Emperor of France for the use of a waterfall, owned by the French Government, to turn the paddles of his mill.

On 24 June in that year, in the little town of Solferino, at three o'clock in the morning, four hundred thousand men fell upon each other in the bloodiest carnage of the nineteenth century.

By nightfall the Austrians had lost some twenty-three thousand men. Napoleon and his Sardinian ally suffered seventeen thousand slaughtered and wounded.

That night Henri Dunant got to Solferino, dressed in a white tropical suit.

The red of the sunrise next morning was rekindled on the bloody landscape. The cries and sighs of the dying and wounded, littered among gobbets of flesh, blew on the air like the outcries of souls in the inferno. In near-by Castiglione, hauled in carts and wagons, the bundled bodies of screaming men packed the hospital, monastery, churches, barracks, halls and homes. Straw that would soon squelch with blood was forked out of barns to bed the cobbles.

Young Henri Dunant in his tropical suit suffered his revelation. For five weeks he worked there, organizing, giving succour, wrenched out of all knowledge of himself. There were French, German, Slav, Arab, Croat, Hungarian and Italian among the wounded.

'The man in the white suit', as they called him, tended them as one human being. The women of Castiglione followed Henri Dunant's example.

'*Siamo tutti fratelli*,' they murmured. 'All men are brothers.'

Before he died, an old man bent under honours, the inspiration and work of Henri Dunant had girdled the globe with red crosses. When he set up his first Permanent International Committee, the word *international* could not be found in the Dictionary of the French Academy.

Geneva

I

THE small château was walled, decently aged, impressively unostenta-
tious. The old stone wore its patina as did Salem his English suits and
the silk shirts tailored in Paris; elegantly, with reserve. It was distanced
from the extravagant villas of the nouveaux riches in unselfconscious
superiority, as Salem himself was distanced by mind and by manners,
and by the name which for three generations had distinguished the
family bank.

A green mohair robe lay on the used bed. The tea service which
Signora Cenci had prepared and which her husband Massino had
punctually served at seven-thirty, together with the newspaper, remained on the bedside table, the newspaper refolded, each piece of the
service used and replaced on the spot from which it had been lifted.

Salem had showered and shaved in the adjoining bathroom, that and
Signora Cenci's kitchen the only concessions to modernity in a house
of antiques, ringing with silence, a palpable breath of the past, which
contrived by perfections of balance, by touches of plush and warmth, to

3

appear lived in and friendly, the place of a family merely gone for the day.

In the bathroom, startlingly inverted, Salem stood on his head, eyes closed, the long, razor-thin body almost hairless, drained of colour, as though no blood beat to tinge or warm the opaque whiteness of skin.

Feet pointed, legs taut and tight in alignment, the body partly shadowed, partly dazzled by the sun streaming from the windows, he looked more like a plant than a man, a white, long-shafted lily.

Like a plant, as the minutes passed, Salem was blanked from thought.

From Lausanne, the château looked down over the mountain to the sheeted blue water of the lake. In the sunshine the rakish white ferry sparkled, frothing its wake as it berthed, shivering its reflection in the water.

Massimo laid the table, flicking his finger at a toast-crumb, checked the time and returned to the kitchen. Signora Cenci took an omelette-pan and warmed it over a flame.

Salem slowly lowered his legs, balanced and thrust himself upright. He brushed the unpeaked brown hair from his eyes and combed it back with his fingers. The striking, high-boned face, as remote as the image on a coin, quested blindly for an instant, then suddenly lit, the skin flushed, the eyes flashed open. Pierre Salem sucked in his breath.

The approaching conflict was by his decision, a charge he had freely accepted. Perhaps it was precipitate, but barbarism had never waited for time. The Chairman, his beloved old Rudi, was ill and aged, his voice had shaken with urgency:

'I am too close to the end of my own road to be concerned except for others,' he had said. 'The weapons are there. We are most fearfully afraid that they will be used. Pierre, the time could be seven minutes to midnight.'

The road follows the lake to Geneva. It comes down off the mountain in a hedging of trees, popping almost audibly from their green grasp into open runs beside the water.

In the front seat of the grey Bentley the chauffeur kept his ordained pace. At nine-fifteen the car departed from the château. At ten it stopped in the President's parking-lot.

Salem leaned in his corner, face turned to the window, the familiar scene unnoticed on his lowered lids.

4

The thing was much too recent to have become ghosted, part remembered, part forgotten. In his routine life of chairing the bank, his interests at the university, his books, his chess, his friends, nothing else imagined or wished for. He had composed a tapestry of life. At first in great pain after his divorce—in more than pain—in utter desolation, unbelieving, agonized by rage and defiance, he had searched all Europe for help. Then came his father's words, touched by embarrassment, his arm warm around the shoulder of his son. 'The bank is a great trust and responsibility, Pierre. It will be yours to devote your life to.' And so he had done. Yet he had said nothing of the bank when old Rudi had come to him; nothing even of needing time to make such a decision. It was as though this thing had waited for him, become realized even while Rudi was speaking, while the others waited, their eyes laid on him, like hands:

'It was our invention, it is at the essence of our nation and people. We have the conscience of the world in our keeping, Pierre. The reversed colours of the Swiss flag are the cross of Christ's suffering, in action.

'Year by year we have seen this symbol debased, the great charter of love derided by the language of political expediency. The grandeur and hope of the Conventions we made here have been reduced to a paper mockery. What do we do? Wither in the dragon's breath, or strike back and slay the dragon?'

The professorial cadences of the celebrated old man who had been born on the other side of the century cracked with emotion. The others, each marked by his own distinction, sat over the ignored coffees and brandies laid out by Massimo in the reception-room, their breathing shallow with waiting.

'We began as professor and pupil, Pierre. The pupil has outgrown his master. This crumbling old body, alas, can no longer provide the strength needed for great undertakings.'

The words continued to come to Salem, seemingly from a great distance, as he watched the face of this old man whom he loved, and the other faces about him.

'When we heard your lecture on the need for a new International Humanitarian Law, we knew that we had found our man,' a committee member said softly. It was the textile industrialist.

Rudi said dreamily, with pride, 'Always my most brilliant student. He was always my most brilliant student.'

Another member spoke, pushing first, at his coffee cup. 'This war is

5

one of unparalleled suffering for civilians. I have been right into it. Unparalleled. I speak as a soldier.'

He had retired as a General. It brought Salem back to himself. A General in the Swiss Army. It resembled the joke about the Swiss Navy. There had been no war for the Swiss in over three hundred years.

The textile industrialist spoke again. 'There are twenty-five of us on the committee. We must have a fighter when the new appointment is made. It is you whom we want. We can't guarantee the support of all, but we do pledge you the majority.'

Then the old professor had said, 'The weapons are there. We are most fearfully afraid that they will be used. Pierre, the time could be seven minutes to midnight.'

The grey Bentley turned off, short of the centre of the city. Ahead could be seen the spume of the Geneva fountain, a single jet leaping from its base at one hundred and twenty-five miles an hour, seven tons of water in permanent suspension, an image of the violence of power.

Salem roused in his corner and stretched. The United Nations building came into sight. They would pass that and take the left turn.

Before, the great building had been a hotel. Before that, a girls' finishing-school. A hundred years into the past it had been a private family château. Monotonously, the green-shuttered windows punctured the façade of the central structure and wings, four storeys of them, in exact, perpetuated alignment.

In the French fashion, rather like a tall, narrow town house unaccountably squeezed on either side by apartment houses, the central feature and entrance rose and abutted from the rest.

An angle-sided attic, flat-topped, with four sentinel chimneys at its corners, bore the wireless and aerial masts of a private communications network. Preceding this metal tangle, stiffened by a breeze, the universal symbol, the red cross on a white ground, streamed on its pole. Stamped on the building's white front in red were the letters CICR. This was the centre of the great organization: the International Committee of the Red Cross.

The grey Bentley was nearing it now, the old château distantly ahead.

'The founder was a banker like yourself,' Salem had been reminded by one of the deputation; 'an interesting coincidence, no?'

'He was well known to my father, and his father to my father's father.'

Jean-Jacques Dunant, the merchant, had apprenticed his son Henri to a Genevese banker. The coincidence might have stretched further. He might easily have apprenticed him to the Salem Bank.

The Bentley swung left into a wide asphalt road to the main entrance at the rear of the Committee International de la Croix Rouge. Salem repeated his thought: *Siamo tutti fratelli*. And then: *perhaps, perhaps*.

2

TED MITCHELL was damned angry. He had waited a long time for an assistant, a nice, tractable work-beast, as he put it. The one he had got was neither nice nor tractable, not anyhow to Mitchell. Damned tractable enough in other directions, he thought, pushing at the thumb tack that added this photograph to the display.

Mitchell hammered the tack with the bowl of his pipe. Tobacco-ash shot out on to his tie. Mitchell brushed at it and inspected the material for damage. The tie had been a gift from Sarah Neveau. It was dull enough to have belonged to her husband.

Mitchell picked up another photograph. His assistant should have been doing this, it was her job, she was cleared for confidential material.

She is going to walk in here bow-legged, he decided, from some upstage, all-night party. Lady Jane Stirling. Some lady. They knew all about it at the Press Club, were falling over themselves to meet her. She had married a queer at eighteen; the poor bastard had shot him-

8

self. She had lived in Tahiti with a young native chemist who had bandaged her leg when she fell off a bicycle, and on that adventure was never photographed in anything but a sarong. Twice she had worked with Schweitzer at Lambaréné, involved herself there with an English surgeon who had taken refuge one night in the river and had all but drowned.

She had told the Press, 'I am a gypsy. I have no hopes and no regrets. I make no plans. I am totally amoral.'

Mitchell continued to pin up photographs. It wouldn't be easy to get rid of her. She was here by influence, her old man was on the committee of the English Red Cross Society. The Earl of Plunk, or some place. Mitchell wasn't Schweitzer, but if she had worked so hard at Lambaréné, he would see that she worked here. If not, there were other Press jobs on the international circuit; it was Mitchell's speciality and expertise. He would hand this lot his resignation and join the World Council of Churches or something.

Martin Neveau saw his visitor to the door, a formal leave-taking of bows and handshakes. They had breakfasted together, alone, baked eggs sprinkled with caviar, a pot of Turkish coffee. The visitor was First Secretary at the Egyptian Embassy, a nervous, gloomy man with the eastern habit of agitating his legs as he sat, which Neveau found disturbing.

The logistics of the ICRC's massive aid to the refugees of the Israeli–Arab war remained a daily concern, a workload snared by Arab pride.

An IRC document headed A SURVEY OF POSSIBLE CAMPSITES FOR DISPLACED PERSONS OF THE SIX-DAY WAR had caused an outbreak of hysteria at the Egyptian Embassy. The Ambassador had telephoned Salem. Neveau, as the Executive director of the International Committee, had been required to visit and excuse the error. The Ambassador, in his own hand, had retitled the document A SURVEY OF POSSIBLE CAMPSITES FOR VICTIMS OF ISRAELI AGGRESSION. Eventually, the document was resubmitted as A SURVEY OF POSSIBLE CAMPSITES FOR REFUGEES IN EGYPT AND JORDAN.

The Arabs disliked being seen entering ICRC Headquarters. At their Embassy, the sullen, capricious mood distressed talks and negotiations. Neveau had suggested the expedient of meeting in his apartment to discuss policy. The arrangement was not an easy one for him. His wife, Sarah, was an American Jewess, a pricking, discomforting accident which her husband had come to feel as a blemish, which he

9

evidenced, if Jewish jokes were told, by a change of colour, and an absorbed interest in his glass, or cigarette.

Fifteen years ago Sarah had been an arrestingly pretty American co-ed, in Europe on a vacation with a girl-friend. She had taken a temporary job as a file clerk in the ICRC Tracing Agency. Martin Neveau had been concerned with Missing Persons then, often visited the Agency's quarters on the grassy hill behind the main building.

Sarah was gay, a little wild, excited by the adventure of being in Europe, by the freedom of it, by the teasing sexual explorations conducted with hard-breathing young men met in cafés, museums, parks and bistros. In the *pension* Sarah shared with her friend they would sit up late at night in their beds, the covers hugged about their knees, comparing experiences, shaking with giggles.

When they returned after their dates they would ask, already abubble, 'Have you still got it?' Referring to their priceless possession, the itching maidenhood, the tyrannous load of virginity; remembering their mothers: *No good man will have you otherwise.*

'Have you still got it?'

'Intact. Who needs it?'

'Have you still got it?'

'Got it. But I had to fight fifteen rounds.'

'Have you still got it?'

'God! I think I've lost it. Pass me the Havelock Ellis.'

'Have you still got it? Mary! Have you still got it? Mary, oh Mary, don't tell me!'

She had been Sarah Stone, Jewess, apostate. Generations ago the Stone had been Stein. Her grandparents had not converted to protestant or catholic or something else, they had simply laid down the burden, for business reasons or social reasons, or out of disgust with the past or fear of it. Perhaps it had been so hard to get to the new country that there was a need to forget, to be new in the new place, if not for themselves then for their children.

It was because young Martin Neveau was so gravely Swiss, so easily dazzled by the sparkling young creature Sarah Stone had been, so easily lit by her and so frankly admiring and awed, that they had gradually come together, Martin so often visiting the Tracing Agency that Mick East, its Cockney director, began referring to him as our Resident Headquarters Representative.

On that day by the water, eating grilled *Féra*, the fish hooked up from the deepest parts of the lake, Neveau had talked about himself: his father had been an export jeweller, with a workshop. On a business trip to Germany during the Second World War both he and Martin's mother had been killed in a bombing-raid on Dresden.

Quite involuntarily, Sarah had reached out and taken Martin's hand. He had looked wonderingly and full at her then, as he seldom did. It was a long moment and there was something else in it, unknown before or unadmitted, or perhaps unrecognized.

At the end of summer, when Sarah returned home to Boston, she had still 'got it'. She and Martin Neveau corresponded intensely for a year. Neveau got a promotion in the ICRC, he had some money his parents had left. He wrote and asked Sarah to marry him. She had still 'got it' when he arrived in Boston for the wedding. Sarah had kept it that way. Only then did Martin Neveau discover that his wife was of Jewish blood. Her father told him. It was hardly necessary. Her parents were caricatures of their race.

Neveau closed the door and crossed the big room off the entrance hall to his study. It had no pretentions to comfort or personal conceits of decoration—the college pennants, photographs, hunting-trophies which American men bestow on what they call their dens.

Years ago, Sarah sometimes forgot and did refer to the room as the Den. It made Neveau coldly angry. 'I am not an animal, Sarah. That is my study, a place of business.'

And that it was, an efficient tool, furnished with a sharp-edged metal desk, typewriter on a wheeled metal table, with papers in wire baskets, metal filing-cabinets, a wall of reference-books and technical works set on metal shelves.

Neveau was filling the big briefcase with its bulky lock and stamped initials ICRC, frowning, when Sarah looked in. She was thirty-five now, four years younger than her husband, a little sunken-eyed, a little thin, perhaps a little apprehensive. But the prettiness was still evident, the flair for clothing, the physical vitality. She looked like a woman only ten pounds and a good holiday away from being very desirable.

Even at this early hour her grooming was perfect, the thick chestnut hair gleaming. It was Neveau rather than Sarah who had altered, aged more than his years, pink crown showing through the dark hair, thickened in face, shoulders and belly, moving slowly and resolutely with the stumping tread of a heavy man.

'Has he gone, dear?'

Neveau did not look up. 'No,' he said, 'as you can see he is here beside me.'

Sarah winced. 'It's just that I did not hear him ... go.'

'I will be late tonight, Sarah. A working dinner at the Egyptian

11

Embassy. I tried to avoid it, they are wretched affairs, but I could make no other arrangement with the First Secretary.'

'Oh, must you? Must you work yourself so hard, Martin? You've hardly had any time to yourself since Salem became President.' She was genuinely concerned. 'Can't he make more appearances instead of loading it all on you?'

Neveau paused for an instant in the scrutiny of his papers. 'His Lordship is above that. The Salems of Geneva, you know. His Lordship is involved in policy. Where that policy will take us, we don't know. Would you call the car, Sarah? And could I have a cup of fresh coffee? That Turkish muck is revolting.'

'I know, dear. I've got a fresh pot perking. You sit on the balcony and drink it while I call the car.'

Sarah had no live-in servants, Neveau said he found it stifling. She had a daily maid and needed no more since Guy boarded at school during the week. He was seven and much too young, Sarah thought, to be away from home at all. Neveau had insisted.

It was the growing Boston inflection in the little boy's English which had caused Neveau to bundle him off; he wanted the boy at a Swiss school where English was taught but not spoken. Despite her struggles Sarah could not master French, and German defeated her utterly.

My wife has no ear for languages, but then what American has? The English used not to learn out of arrogance. The Americans are merely stupid.

There were two telephones in Neveau's study and two more in the bedroom. One of each was a direct International Red Cross line. Sarah took the coffee-tray to the balcony, went to the bedroom and closed the door. On the direct line she ordered a car. On the other she dialled the International's listed number and asked for an extension. She held the receiver from her ear, listening, until she heard Neveau go to the balcony. The receiver clicked.

Sarah said, 'It's me.'

She listened. Her lips opened a little in excitement. She said, 'I can see you this evening. Yes, until late. What time? You won't keep me waiting, will you?'

When she stood up her hands turned and fluttered on her thighs. She nibbled at her upper lip, glanced in the mirror, then swung out of the room.

The conference chamber was simply, almost barely furnished, except for the long table, the twenty-five chairs, the pads, pencils, water-carafes and glasses. The display flats were angled to each other. From the entrance, the table and flats composed the shaft and head of an arrow.

Salem's secretary entered from a side door, a plain, middle-aged woman whom he had brought with him from the bank. Her arms were stacked with documents. A pile which she carried awkwardly, pinned under her chin, head back, moving in short, burdened steps. Ted Mitchell had completed the display; he stood back from it, filling his pipe from a rubber pouch.

'How are you, Fanny?'

She bent to lay the documents on the table.

'Good morning, Mr Mitchell.'

Horrors were notional concepts to Fanny: things which occurred in the disordered world outside Switzerland. It was not necessary, or decent, to think about them. She understood and appreciated the small universe of things that had happened to her own flesh. It was enough, imagination carried her no further. To dwell on these others was morbid.

Now she stood and stared and stared past Mitchell's shoulder. Her tongue licked at her thin rouged lips.

'What do you think, Fanny?'

'It's horrible ... horrible. Fancy taking pictures like that. What kind of people ... would want to take pictures like that?'

'They were only recording the facts, Fanny.'

'They shouldn't do it. Life's enough trouble. People don't want to see such things.'

But she couldn't look away, tongue licking, hands fluttering before her on the stack of stapled papers.

Mitchell lit his pipe and pointed it.

'How do you like that one, Fanny? That's what bubonic plague, the Black Death, looks like.'

Fanny shuddered and turned away, wrinkling her whitened nose with disgust.

There were one hundred and twenty photographs pinned to the display flaps. Each was of a child, or children; some were babies, some were alive, some were dead. The living were naked, posed on wooden stools against a grey backdrop. Each of them, child or baby, living or dead, had been incinerated by napalm or phosphorus. On the living the melted flesh had clotted and cooled the way wax can fix on a candle. These were grotesques of human shape, mutations that might follow

13

the atomic inferno. On the featureless face of a blinded boy, the displaced mouth made a charred hole in his cheek. Babies lay in a group—shapeless, charred black meat, only a hand or heel to tell the difference.

The twenty-five worthy men of the committee—each a Swiss and only Swiss, as ordered in the charter—had begun to enter the building, returning the respectful greetings of the porter inside, checking hats at the desk opposite him, mounting the two short flights of marble steps to the President's reception-room, holy of holies, in its magnificence a breath from Versailles.

Each a Swiss because humanism must exclude politics, race, colour, creed. Who else but a Swiss, bred in the bone out of three hundred years of peace and neutrality, could administer succour to all men, free of the taints of prejudice, vested interest, personal or national involvement? Who else could be trusted?

The conference convened at eleven in the morning. At four o'clock in the afternoon the meeting was still in session.

Mitchell had eaten a good lunch, with a bottle of wine and brandies. At a small table in his room Jane Stirling arranged hand-outs, putting each into the appropriate envelope. She had excused herself to Mitchell. She had a cold and had gone to her doctor, she said, to get a shot.

Mitchell kept looking up from the speech he was editing, to inspect her. Jane was in profile, her blue-black hair pulled back and wound into a bun. When she turned away he could see the warm, shadowed hollow of her neck, the strong, wide shoulders. The nose was small and tip-tilted, it softened the jaw. It was the legs that got him and the wide, welling spread of hips. None of your fashionable, scrawny model's legs, like pipe-cleaners shoved into boots. These were woman's legs, with calves and thighs to them. Legs that could squeeze a man's brains out. He had not seen her hair in a bun before, she usually wore it straight. She looked Spanish, Mitchell thought, very Spanish.

The copied documents put before each chair were divided into two reports. One had been received from the Red Cross Society of the Democratic Republic of Vietnam, the other from the Red Cross Society of the National Liberation Front.

They were captioned: *The Biggest War Criminals of our Time*, and *The U.S. Aggressors' Monstrous Crimes Against the Democratic Republic of Vietnam Health Services*.

Salem and Neveau, President and Executive Director of the International Committee, faced each other from opposite ends of the table.

Between them, on the two sides, smoking, cleaning spectacles, hunched, huddled, pushed back, heads in hands, eyes shut or towards the ceiling, darting glances, depressed, confused, or angry, the twenty-five tired members of the Committee listened as the President read.

Speaking French, his half-glasses low on his nose, Salem's voice continued, flat and remorseless, emptied of emotion or even cadence, a mechanical recitation that somehow further charged the meaning of the words:

'—Soon afterwards, the French colonialists sent their expeditionary corps to Vietnam in an attempt to enslave the Vietnamese people once again. The U.S. ambition in Vietnam was described by the *New York Times* in an editorial in 1950: '*Indo-China is a prize worth a large gamble ... even before World War Two, Indo-China brought an annual dividend estimated at three hundred million dollars.*

'In 1953 U.S. President Eisenhower said, "Let us assume we lose Indo-China. If Indo-China goes, several things will happen right away. The peninsula, the last bit of land hanging on down there, would be scarcely defensible. The tin and tungsten that we so greatly value from that area will cease coming."

'The French colonialists were defeated by the Vietnamese people; and the Geneva agreements were signed in 1954, solemnly recognizing the fundamental national rights of the Vietnamese people.

'From 1954 to 1960, through its puppet Ngo Dinh Diem, the U.S. systematically torpedoed the 1954 Geneva agreements on Vietnam and opposed reunification by preventing the holding of free elections as stipulated in the agreements.

'At the same time, the U.S. imperialists and their henchmen drowned the patriotic movement of the South Vietnamese people in blood. A U.S. military command was set up in Saigon to take direct command of the war.'

Neveau, in great agitation, began to speak 'Mr President, this is propaganda. Mr President, this is no part of——'

Salem continued, over the interruption, the flat voice quacking mechanically: 'Prior to the August revolution the Vietnamese people had to live a life plagued by misery, hunger and disease. After the successful August revolution the Democratic Republic of Vietnam, right from the first, set to itself the task of improving the people's health. One hundred per cent of villages in the Delta and nearly eighty per cent in the Highlands were supplied with medical stations and maternity homes. Smallpox and cholera were wiped out as early as

15

1957. Infantile paralysis had been in the main done away with. In the mountain regions, malaria had been liquidated.

'The fruits of this arduous and humanitarian work have been frenziedly and laboriously destroyed by the U.S. aggressors.

'Up to now, nearly all the hospitals of the larger provinces have been bombed, provincial hospitals are now heaps of ruins, village medical stations and maternity homes have been attacked. Lepers have been chased and strafed while running for cover. Some of these establishments have been attacked forty and fifty times.

'On International Children's Day, 1 June 1966, the mothers' and childrens' health centre at Thanh Hoa Hospital was massively attacked with great damage. The death role from this raid . . .'

Salem's voice cracked. He stopped and filled his water glass. The Committee looked up. Neveau was half turned away, one fist clenched white on the table. Salem asked softly, 'The Executive Director had something to say? Perhaps he would take this opportunity?'

The Committee turned its attention to the other end of the table. It was difficult for Neveau; he was in distress.

'Mr President, gentlemen, I have served the International Red Cross . . . I have served this committee . . . in various posts, various posts, for twenty years. In our unique and responsible role, you and I, we have been privy to the weightiest and most secret negotiations of governments. The ICRC was largely responsible for the cease fire in the Indian–Pakistani war. We were active in Santo Domingo, in the Lebanon, we did what we could in the Yemen. Gentlemen, I beseech you—our charter, our charter, is both precious and frail. The trust that governments of every persuasion rests in us is essentially because of this charter. Above politics. In the twenty years I have served I know no precedent for this conference today. These documents, gentlemen, are propaganda, naked politics, the very corruption which our charter, our trust, is pledged against. I am sorry, but I must reject everything said here today.'

Neveau lifted his glass, hand shaking. Nobody spoke, there was an intense, straining silence.

The old professor kept his head bowed. The others, the deputation which had waited on Salem, remained averted, as though the knowledge of their conspiracy now weighed upon them. He was quite alone. They had chosen him for this, to do what they could not, to be alone, to change things, to help hold back the clock which, as old Rudi had said, now pointed at seven minutes to midnight.

'Hear, hear!'

And again, from the end of the table, with a deprecating cough. 'Mmm, yes. Hear, hear!'

Salem said, 'Gentlemen, the oath I took was to the charter. But the conventions, too, are in our keeping. Every minute of the day in Vietnam the spirit and letter of the Geneva Conventions are being abrogated, trampled on, derided. For how long can we permit this without outcry? For how long will the International endure if we fail this elemental trust? What faith can governments have in us, or in the conventions, if we don't stand fast for their meaning, which is for the civilized instinct against barbarism?'

Near Salem, a committee man shook his head.

'Doesn't apply, President. You know that, you're the expert on international law. The Viet Cong and the North Vietnamese have refused to be a party to the Conventions. The South Vietnamese have reservations because of the unusual type of war they are fighting south of the 17th parallel. The Americans pay lip service to the Conventions but you only have to read the newspapers to know that they do not always observe them.'

'Precisely,' Salem said. 'And that is why I have asked permission of the Committee to publicize these documents. We must do something to draw the attention of the world to the fact that civilians are suffering, prisoners on both sides are being shot and tortured, all because of a technicality.'

'How do you propose to overcome it?'

'Begin with the United States. She is fighting a war in Vietnam. Let her declare so. North Vietnam will certainly reply. Once a formal state of war exists it will be easier to exert pressure to make both sides uphold the Conventions. I see no other way.'

'Not our business, President.'

'Let the United Nations take it up.'

'No part of the charter.'

'Humanism, President, not politics. If we concern ourselves with politics, the world movement will fall apart.'

Softly, sadly, Salem asked, 'Where does humanism begin and end? And by which natural law is inhumanity excused by political expediency?'

'Sorry, President.'

'Couldn't do it. The American national society would withdraw all co-operation.'

'Thin edge of the wedge, President.'

Old Rudi's eyes were upon him now, commiserating, watery blue. A hardly perceptible shake of his head meant: You see? I told you it would not be easy.

Quickly, instinctively, Salem decided not to fight. They were not ready. He had chosen his ground, but he had not prepared it.

'Very well, gentlemen. Can I return your attention to the earlier business of the morning? The report by the National Red Cross of Vietnam on claims of bacteriological warfare and cases of bubonic plague.'

Neveau said, 'We got bitten about those claims in the Korean War, President. By a resolution of the 20th Conference of the Red Cross, it is no longer obligatory for the ICRC to take action on complaints of this nature, except in the absence of any other regular channel, when there is need of a neutral intermediary between two countries directly concerned.'

Salem let it pass.

'According to the World Health Organization, more than two thousand cases of bubonic plague were diagnosed in South Vietnam in the first nine months of 1967. The American journal of military medicine reports: "Bubonic plague cases continue to occur in large numbers in the Republic of Vietnam. Mass immunization programmes are hampered by wartime conditions, disrupted communications and inadequate medical facilities in the mountainous interior. The potential for explosive plague epidemics continues to exist." '

The men at the table relaxed, lit cigarettes for each other, leaned comfortably back. The mood had altered. The nervousness had gone from the room.

3

MICK EAST ended his war with a sergeant's rank in British Army Intelligence. It was a most unlikely posting. He had not the vaguest credential for intelligence. Mick was Cockney, and not merely by the requirement of having been born within sound of Bow Bells, but Cockney bred from Cockney, a London sparrow, as exclusive as a Hottentot or Armenian.

With the usual arbitrariness, the army sent Mick East to Intelligence as a clerk. Oddly, it was a perfect match. Mick's memory was awesome, his capacity for detail unlimited. He was quickly promoted to corporal, and quickly again to sergeant. He would have been, and should have been, commissioned, but none of his commanding officers could face putting a pip and a Sam Browne belt on such an appalling accent.

At the war's end Mick East's unit was responsible for tracing missing British POWs and air-dropped resistance workers.

He was into the concentration camps hard on their liberation, asking

19

his questions of the ghastly, flapping skeletons staggering and gibbering about the troops, entering the huts from which the tough, bearded American soldiers recoiled in horror and nausea. He checked camp files, checked the heaped dead stacked as neatly as cordwood, so ravaged and altered out of human recognition as to be an insult to sensibility.

When the entire documentation of the Buchenwald camp and its one hundred and forty-five sub-units was handed over to the Red Cross, Mick East, civilian, accompanied the records as chief of the ICRC Tracing Agency. Now Mick East sat happy and absorbed at the centre of a web slung across one hundred and thirteen countries, in a temporary structure which had contrived to become permanent, located beyond the car-park at the bottom of the steep dip.

Ted Mitchell's window looked over the parking-lot to the sweep of lawns and gardens and the big, concave sundial, striped in white, like half a globe composed in red brick. From where he sat he could see the Agency building. He had a profitable interest in the Tracing Agency. Interpol and others often petitioned its aid. Mick East's expertise was reinforced by the assistance of Red Cross staff and volunteer workers in every country with a national society. Mitchell checked each day with Mick East. If a good story came up Mitchell made it a feature and freelanced it to newspapers and magazines.

Salem and the committee were still in conference. The building had all but emptied, cleaners at work on the old, polished linoleum of the corridors, sacking waste paper in the offices. Mitchell was waiting impatiently; Salem had advised him that there might be a release for the wires that evening. He decided to have a yarn with Mick East.

' 'Ow are yer mate, orright?'

'Wotcher cock.'

The greeting was invariable, the recognition of each other's singular minority. Mick East was alone, drinking coffee laced with brandy from a large, metal-lipped Thermos. He was pleased with this new possession. A hatch beneath the screw-top opened automatically when the contents were poured. East tapped the Thermos.

'Get yourself a cup, Teddy boy. This stuff puts lead in your pencil.'

Filing cabinets crowded the floor space. IBM punching-machines serviced the one hundred and forty-five million cards of reference on the fifteen million names the agency had on record. Mick East's ambition was for a computer. He constantly harassed Martin Neveau about it. On the wall behind his desk a large chart diagrammed the Red

Cross structure. The International Red Cross Committee topped the chart as the supreme body. A dotted line ran immediately to the Standing Commission whose work it was to organize the four-yearly International Conferences of the Red Cross. Other dotted lines linked the one hundred and thirteen national Red Cross societies and those governments signatory to the Geneva Conventions.

East thumbed back the Thermos's tankard top and filled Mitchell's cup.

'What's doing in the big house?'

'Still at it. Salem is trying to get something across to them. They've been in there since eleven this morning. He's on about these new reports from Vietnam.'

'He's getting up a few noses, our Salem. Neveau's still wearing his arse at an angle. He expected to make President himself.'

'He doesn't have the background. President of the ICRC is big-time.'

'They make me sick, these do-gooders. You take a close look at them, Teddy boy. What they are doing good for is themselves, mate. You know what human beings are? A bloody great nest of soldier ants all chewing on each other. You've got to bite first in this life, Teddy, before some bastard bites you. Here, cop this lot.'

East had taken a bundle of postcards from a drawer. They were glossy reproductions of Indian erotic sculptures, details from the great temple at Karnarak in Bengal. Gods and goddesses were coupled in every possible and impossible configuration. Severe, impassive faces contemplated fantasticized lingams, or reclined for the attentions of moon-breasted females. Group matings from the great frieze joined couples in formalized unions of an ingenuity difficult to translate.

'Get on this one,' East said. 'How is that for a daisy-chain?'

The postcards took Mitchell's mind to the appointment he had made for that evening, awakening heat in him. She had said, *You won't keep me waiting, will you?* He looked at his watch. Six o'clock and they were still in conference.

'Where did you get these?'

'An Indian mate, Jog Chatterji, he comes over to chat up the league. You know, these Hindus are so puritanical they won't have kissing in the films they make, yet you can buy these in the tourist shops.'

Mitchell handed back the cards.

'That's what they mean by the mysterious East, Mick.'

Outside his work, pornography was the only interest Mick East cultivated. He was as serious about it as other people are about money.

'Well, what's new in the web? Anything I could use?'

'The West German deadline for concentration camp compensations is coming up. I have had a request for verification of status from Guernsey. It would be the last one under the wire. There should be something in that.'

'Nazi heirs pay last blood cheque,' Mitchell said. 'How far have you got on the trace?'

'It's with the Agency at Arolsen. They deal there with persons deported and displaced in the homeland and occupied countries. I'll be getting a signal in a week or two. Not to worry.'

East opened one of the manila folders stacked and scattered on the desk. 'Jean-Pierre Koman, guinea pig,' he read. 'Laughing member Krasnerdorf holiday camp, 1942–5. Currently enjoying the best of bad health due to his excesses at the time.'

'What's the guinea-pig bit?'

'Un-volunteer for immersion experiments conducted at Krasnerdorf by Dr Wendel Ludwigshafen who should contact the authorities who have news for him very much against his interest.'

'Anything on this immersion?'

'M. East strikes again with full immersion documentation. Dr Ludwigshafen involved in survival experiments to help Luftwaffe crews shot down in North Sea. Jean-Pierre Koman and others dunked well nigh to death in freezing water and resuscitated by intravenous injections and what-not. One hundred and sixty-three campers failed to respond, naughty Dr Ludwigshafen. Camper Jean-Pierre Koman lucky enough to be put to bed with naked ladies.'

'What's that?' Mitchell asked, unbelieving.

Mick East closed the file, blew on his glasses and polished.

'It worked, too. They'd get a couple of the fatter birds in the camp and put them in bed naked with the guinea pig. Their body heat worked better than the injections. These chaps, three parts dead, were observed to get erections.'

'Codswallop! How much of this is true?'

'It's all true, Teddy boy. Including the last bit. Makes you think, don't it?'

They thought about it. Mitchell got excited.

'This could make a great story, Mick. When can I have it?'

'When I've got it all. When I'm ready. Don't stand over Mick or he'll smack.'

Mitchell fingered his new moustache. It had grown in heavily, more frankly red than the gingered colour of his flopping hair.

'Are you taking a chick to the Neveau's party next week?'

'Mick doesn't have a chick. He's got a crow.'

'I'm taking Jane Stirling.'

'Are you now? Well, well. The scarlet lady herself. How did you crack that? She's supposed to be living like a hermit.'

Mitchell had a small, comfortable service flat in one of the towering new blocks built by Middle Eastern oil sheiks as a compliment to the solidity of the Swiss franc. The apartment had been furnished. Mitchell had added the vulgarity of a circular bed. The bed had a counterpane with synthetic hair and the rosettes of a panther's markings. Mitchell called the bed 'Madame Leopard'. It went with the strong vodka cocktails that tasted only pleasantly of orange, the appropriate music on the record player, the old uncompleted novel, prominently littered on the writing table. It was a depressing commentary on naïveté and the tedious requirement that each generation should learn from the beginning that these creaking approaches should work on the fluttering girls Mitchell got to his rooms.

He did have local advantages. The typists and secretaries employed in the Geneva-based American commercial houses, the encyclopaedia distributors and mutual fund concerns, the girls at UNESCO, the International Labour Organization, the International Press Institute, were often foreign, lonely and bored. The true Geneva citizens remained exclusive. Night life was limited. In the twenty to thirty age group, women outnumbered men two to one.

'It's the easiest place in Europe to get laid,' Mick East had told him. 'There's a status system here, Teddy boy. At the bottom there is the American Mutual Funds. At the top, way up at the top, there's us chaps in the ICRC.'

Mitchell had marked Sarah from their first meeting. She made such a contrast to Neveau, drinking a little too much, febrility in her gaiety, responding so immediately to Mitchell's interest, giving abstracted glances across the party to her husband, returning all her attention to Mitchell whenever Neveau came near, so desperately wishing him to notice her. Sarah had the excitement of a made woman. Mitchell guessed accurately that she could give him four or five years. He marked her nervousness too, the distracted hands and manner.

'... Oh, for ages. I came here while I was still at college. You know, doing Europe? I am an old ICRC girl myself. That's where I met my husband.'

'... Australian? Oh, we have something in common then. I mean,

23

the Swiss are different, don't you think? New World, old world, perhaps.'

'They do tend to think of themselves as God's chosen.'

God's chosen. That had jarred her strangely. Her face blanked for an instant.

'They don't mean it, though. Not really. It's just ... it's just ...'

'It's just that they're not like us.'

She laughed a little.

'Yes, I suppose so. I suppose that's it. Be a dear and get me a drink.'

Sarah had got a little tight. It was the evening of the day on which little Guy had been tearfully installed as a boarder.

Later, startlingly, out of no reference, she had said to Mitchell, 'I suppose you're of English stock. I am Jewish, you know. Not by religion, by blood line.'

When Mitchell was leaving he went to fetch his coat. There was a bathroom off the hall. Sarah had just come out. Mitchell, too, was high.

'Thanks for the conversation,' he said, bent and brushed a kiss on her cheek. Without design, without offence, almost in comradeship, he put out the back of his hand and rubbed her between the thighs.

She hadn't moved. Her eyelids snapped shut! When she opened them they were wet.

'Thank you,' she said.

Mitchell touched his forehead to hers and quickly went to the door.

It began with a very occasional drink together, more meetings at other parties. It was so fated that Mitchell was afraid. Even before Madame Leopard, he had felt the discomfort of Sarah's need. She was going towards it like a sleep-walker, and Ted Mitchell wanted to cut and run.

There was a small arch into the wall near the entrance to Mitchell's apartment. He kept a key there, in a pot. It was not for Sarah's exclusive use. The ghosts of the girls of whom Sarah sometimes jealously felt traces in Madame Leopard, were the defence Mitchell kept between them.

A few drinks at the obscure bar they used as a meeting-place usually lowered Sarah's disturbed excitement. It was less the restlessness of need than the dislocation of shame and guilt, the apprehension of being discovered, that shook her voice and her hands until Mitchell felt his own nerves rasp with irritation.

24

She had taken a drink while she waited. Mitchell was not greatly late. The conference had ended at last, there was no news release.

He entered and closed the door softly. She had her back to him, changing records.

'Look at you, then.'

She pivoted and ran to his embrace, an intense kiss for which he was unrelaxed and unready.

'Steady.'

He pushed Sarah from him.

'How come the fancy dress?'

'Do you like it?'

Sarah moved back, whirled and posed. She was wearing a tight red trouser suit with a short, boxy jacket over a thin white skivvy.

'Mummy sent it to me. I can't think what Martin will say.'

'He will no doubt find it un-Swiss and perhaps a little decadent. Me, I like it. I like what it does for you here.'

He slapped Sarah hard on the bottom.

'I need a drink.'

With the same concern she showed Neveau, Sarah asked, 'Have you had a bad day?'

'Not a bad one, a long one. We've had the committee.'

'Oh dear, and Martin has to go to the Egyptian Embassy tonight.'

'Up Martin.' Mitchell flopped on the couch. 'You look real good. You can make me a very large Martini.' He rubbed his face. 'While you're doing that I think I'll take a shower.'

She was already at the bar.

'Make yourself comfortable, dear. Put on your nightshirt.'

The nightshirt was a joke, a present from Sarah.

'You just want to be wearing the pants.' He unknotted his tie and took his coat off. 'You like it that way, don't you, Sarah?'

'Like what, what way?'

'Me in slippers and a dressing-gown. The two of us here, quietly together. We can pretend we're married, or living together or something. You're a square, Sarah. You're not much good at illicit love.'

'Oh, aren't I? Am I no good at love?'

She was wide-eyed with concern.

'I didn't say that.'

'You said I'm no good at illicit love.'

'I said you're a square, illicit love doesn't suit you. I didn't say you were no good at it. Jesus sake.'

She turned back to the bar.

'I suppose I am, really. It comes of not being very sure of oneself.'
Mitchell was leaving the room.

He said, 'I'll discuss it with Madame Leopard.'

They ate there. A salad of crudités and potato omelettes cooked by Mitchell. It was a conceit of his. He put a dash of Cointreau in the omelettes and served them with cold hock.

They had been to Madame Leopard earlier, Sarah unable to wait, feverish, glazed, slumped against him before they got to the bedroom. There was desperation in it, the need for reassurance. A restatement of her identity and importance, of her womanliness, the simple right to be abandoned without constraint or shame, to cry out from that reeling universe where stars exploded and to seep back to this world free, an American girl and a Jewess.

They lounged naked in the sitting-room, the heat turned to maximum, Sarah's legs across his on the sofa. There was just light enough to see the coffees and brandies beside them, the pink exhalation of flesh.

'Will you find time for me in Paris?'

'I will make time. Are you taking Guy?'

'Little Guy is going to have two weeks in Boston with his grandparents. He's madly excited about it.'

She was silent for a time.

'Martin doesn't get on with my parents very well, actually.'

'Who does Martin get on well with, actually?'

She didn't answer.

'Have you been to an International Conference before, Sarah?'

'Every four years before Guy was born. This will be the first since then. I'm so looking forward to it. It was wonderful in Rome. So gay, so carefree, all the delegations from all over the world, parties and receptions and dinners. I don't know what it is about Geneva, sometimes I want to scream.'

'Here, move your legs.'

'No. Why? I like it like this.'

'I want to get up, stupid.'

Mitchell went to the writing table and came back with a folder. He switched on the lamp.

'If you don't know what it is about Geneva, permit me to instruct you. Listen to this, it's from a guidebook I'm supposed to give our visitors.

' "Can a city be said to have an international vocation? It is con-

26

ceivable that an individual could feel the urge to accomplish a deed normally beyond his power, but it seems incredible that a town, a heterogenous community, should be animated through the centuries by a continuity of purpose comparable to a vocation.

' "There are, it is true, places where the spirit stirs, and for centuries Geneva has been such a place. Geneva's name is written daily in decisions of vital importance for all people. When it is a question of aid to refugees, children, displaced persons, not to mention war victims, when the rights of man must be safeguarded, it is from Geneva that the initiative comes in mitigating the plight of the distressed, in restoring calm. Geneva is consecrated to the service of mankind." '

Mitchell skimmed the guidebook at the wall.

'Have you ever heard anything like it? I'm supposed to hand that thing out. If you wonder what it is about Geneva that makes you want to bust out screaming, I'll let you have a copy to remind you, posted in a plain wrapper.'

Sarah said, 'It's true in its way. You know who it reminds me of?'

'Martin,' Mitchell said. 'I'm bloody well fed up with Martin.'

'What's the time?'

'Nine o'clock.'

Sarah sat up.

'Shush! What was that?'

Mitchell twitched uneasily.

'What? What is it?'

'Somebody's calling.'

He strained, listening.

'I can't hear anything.'

She leaned over and whispered:

'I think it's Madame Leopard.'

4

Salem had dined at the university, on Rudi's invitation, to meet a visiting professor from Princeton. Afterwards, they had walked a few blocks together, the old man on Salem's arm, bundled to the chin in a long woollen scarf visibly eroded by moth.

Salem had felt the need of counsel. He had made the decision to have the Vietnam reports forwarded to the American National Society for the attention of the Secretary of Defense. The further reports of plague were worrying. There had been outbreaks too in Cambodia and Thailand. He would instruct Neveau about it.

'He is a good man, Pierre, a good man. His only wish is for the movement's welfare. Be gentle with him. You must be gentle. He is a man of facts, not of vision. His talents and instincts lie in compromise. He understands the complication of an International which is the sum of one hundred and thirteen nationalistic parts. It is a paradox, this, but then all is paradox, no? Life and death are paradoxes. Without a little suffering, where is the pleasure? Without hunger it is nothing to be fed.'

The weeks had been filled and overfilled. There had been earthquakes in Greece. Cannibalism and mass mutilations had been reported from Africa. A chartered relief aircraft loaded with medical supplies had crashed and burned on the west bank of the Jordan. Two ICRC delegates died in it.

Salem, the banker, had conducted an audit. He had reason for alarm about finance. There was not sufficient money—one bucket of water could only drench so many fires.

Because his own mood was sombre, Salem wanted to be light with his friend.

'I have a story for you, Rudi.'

'Yes?' The old man was pleased.

'We had a collection of blankets for Arab refugees. They were old blankets, they were clean, but many of them had holes. There were complaints. Some of these blankets had been bought from an army disposal dealer in West Germany. The society there protested and a restitution of good blankets was made.'

The old man on his arm looked up, waiting.

'Our own Society received a donation of twenty tons of Emmenthaler. It was good Swiss cheese, Rudi. The cheese went to the same camps that got the blankets.'

Salem paused.

'Yes? So? This cheese is now in the blanket camps.'

'The refugees would not eat it. You see, Rudi, the Emmenthaler, like the blankets, had holes in it. The camp administrator demanded replacement.'

Old Rudi shook on his arm, eyes watering. He wagged his head, wiped at his eyes with the scarf which was holed like the cheese and the blankets.

'Very good. Very good, Pierre. This I will remember tomorrow for my students. The cheese had holes in it. Oh yes.'

They were at the professor's house now.

'Good night, Rudi.'

'Good night, dear boy. Keep trying. We must all keep trying.'

Salem opened the gate and stood aside. Up the road behind him the trailing Bentley surged forward.

He had changed into pyjamas and robe, stood awhile on the bedroom balcony looking down the mountain to the lights about the lake,

29

refreshing himself with deep breaths. It was moonlight, and cold. The cold pierced the clothing, shivered the long, lean body.

Inside Salem bent and adjusted the combination lock on the library safe, withdrew a loose-leafed leather book as large as a ledger. He dipped a post office pen in a brass ink-well, and put on his half glasses. In a small, neat, scratchy hand he headed the letter: *Château Malraux, Lausanne, Switzerland*, and wrote the date.

MY OWN DEAR SON,

The problems continue. One wonders if one deceives oneself, if anything can be done to change the fearful direction of events without recourse to those temporal powers against which we set our face and our spirit.

Perhaps these hopes are arrogant, or romantic, which you know is not my way. When I weaken like this, the thought of you helps sustain me. It is not for ourselves we make the effort, but for you, the new growth, the innocent, the future hope.

There must be, and will be, rule of law. The evil men whose plausibility so confuses us must be brought to book and exposed.

I take comfort in Malraux and the liberating joy of knowing that simple love and Mutual Aid (as the great Prince Kropotkin named it) is at the very essence of man's being, an immutable, enduring natural law as real as nature's red tooth and claw.

I have made new appointments to our Juro-Legal body, it now numbers thirty experts.

This is what I have decided:

Under my direct guidance we will set about a massive task; the drafting of a new code of Humanitarian Law to be the grandeur of all the ages, a monument so unimpeachable, that those who become its signatories will be delivered from evil; and those demented men in whom the forces of darkness clamour for that man-made darkness will be dealt with in righteous wrath.

Oh yes, there is hope yet, even at seven minutes to midnight. The atom that could consume us is also the building block of the universe.

Salem lay his head back, eyes closed, the pen gripped like a spear in his fingers. Then he eased, dipped the pen and wrote again.

Good night, my dear son. My love and thoughts go with you.

30

Salem had personally telephoned Neveau's office and then dispatched Fanny to search the building for him.

He was waiting, prepared, his eyes on the door when Martin Neveau knocked and entered.

'Good morning, President.'

'Good morning, Martin. I am sorry to have chased you. Fanny could get no answer from your office.'

'I've not seen Fanny. I have been giving dictation in records. President, WHO has requested a meeting this morning. It's the plague again. There is great risk in this area. WHO is very concerned. I am having a background typed up. Here is the new material from WHO and our field reports. It would seem the plague has got to Indonesia. At least WHO is satisfied they have traced the infection from Saigon shipping.'

'I see.' Salem frowned at the papers Neveau handed him, and laid them down. 'Martin, I have decided a certain line of action on the Vietnam reports. This is what I intend——'

'Could that wait, President? I took the liberty of giving WHO an eleven o'clock appointment.'

Salem picked up the papers and pushed at his glasses.

'In that case...'

The reports were characteristic. Three weeks earlier a forty-three-year-old Djakarta dock worker had complained of illness. His symptoms were noted as fever, respiratory difficulty and blood-tinged sputum. He was treated with sulphamerizene and dihydro-streptomycin. Two days later, on 12 September, he died.

Subsequently, four earlier deaths in the family were revealed. The first was a thirteen-year-old daughter, who had died on 6 September, after a short illness. The son, aged six, died on 9 September. On the morning of 10 September, a seventy-year-old male and a fifty-year-old female, both members of the family, died.

On 15 September, a fifty-nine-year-old male who frequently visited this family registered with the local health worker. His illness was characterized by high fever, cough and malaise. Three days later he died. Because of his advanced age his death caused no unusual concern.

During this man's three-day illness, six persons either lived in the same two-room house or were actively engaged in his care.

On 22 September, the man's wife, his sister and a neighbour became ill with the same general symptoms. On 29 September, the wife died at home. The sister had returned to her village outside Djakarta and died there on 24 September. The neighbour also died on this day in his room across the street.

Of the next two cases, number five had taken care of the dock worker and returned to his village where he died on 17 September. Case six was a Regional Forces soldier who had returned to his barracks, stayed two days and then visited his parents in the same village where he died on 26 September, after a short illness characterized by fever, cough and expectoration of blood-tinged sputum.

On 27 September, two more cases occurred in this village. The sister's husband became ill and died within forty-eight hours. A boy of seventeen who had visited them became ill when he got home. He died after a three-day sickness. His father became infected while taking care of him and died within forty-eight hours.

This man's sputum had been collected for culture. He died two hours later and a lung biopsy was obtained for examination.

Pasteurella pestis was isolated from both the lung biopsy and the sputum. It was bubonic plague, the Black Death.

Neveau lit a cigarette. Salem was skipping through the reports.

'There have been other cases, on other Indonesian waterfronts. It is very grave, President. The plague can rage like a fire, carry over mountains like the wind. Even with advanced attention, the recovery rate is less than ten per cent. The two thousand Vietnamese deaths reported might be only a tenth of the true figure. There is almost no medical care in some areas. The plague could be killing and growing and spreading there outside any possibility of diagnosis.'

The detached professionalism which Neveau customarily applied to his duties was gone now. There were no politics in this to worry him. His pleasant, stolid face, the skin smooth and boyish, was pinched with anxiety. Perhaps old memories stirred in Neveau, an atavistic reminder of the shadowed past when Europe stank with corruption, and trundling carts heaped with corpses creaked on the cobbles before barricaded houses to the cry of 'Bring out your dead'.

'What does WHO propose, Martin?'

'They have a programme to discuss, we must count it as a top priority. To begin, there must be mass inoculations in Djakarta. We will have to broadcast for an urgent supply of vaccines, there is an acute shortage. It has mostly come from Australia, but it is not enough. Not enough.'

Gently, Salem made his point.

'And how will this vaccine be distributed? How will the inoculations be given?'

'We will supply Saigon through the Vietnamese National League. The Revolutionary Development Cadres are in the field. They've been inoculating against cholera and typhus. The American Combined Action Patrols will also help. WHO has a force out there.'

'Will the few inoculations these people can give make us safe? You said the plague can rage like a fire, carry over mountains like the wind. The cholera and typhus are still uncontrolled. Can we stop the Black Death, Martin?'

Neveau was aware now. He ceased his restlessness, butted his cigarette deliberately.

'Your point, President?'

'It's this war, Martin. That's where we must begin, with the war.'

Neveau said, in a cold voice, 'Switzerland is a neutral country, President. The war is none of our business.'

Salem was satisfied.

'At eleven, then. Shall we meet here in my office?'

It was not until evening, and then only opportunely, that Salem returned to his decision to ask the American Society to forward the Vietnam reports to the American Secretary of Defense. He had left the headquarters late. There was only one other car in the parking-lot. It was Neveau's. A rain squall had drenched the distributor.

'Come, Martin, I'll drop you off. I'm going that way, to the university.'

I will tell him now, Salem decided, it might be better like this, informally, the short journey its own punctuation.

They sat in opposite corners, Neveau hatless, his black, thinning hair raised on the wind, Salem in tweeds and his brown soft felt, the brim upturned in Continental fashion.

He had not expected the response. Neveau had turned to study him with a quirk of amusement, a hint almost of patronage.

'What possible good do you think that will do?'

The mood, rather than the words, unsettled Salem. He had not replied when Neveau continued:

'The American National Red Cross, President, exists by an Act of Congress. It is almost an arm of government. Its building is on government land, it had a coded government telephone number. The books of the Society are audited by the Department of Defense. Its Honorary President is the President of the United States. The American Red Cross is heavily occupied with the welfare of the American soldier. Forwarding those documents is pointless.'

Neveau was frankly smiling. Salem felt chagrin burn him. He had

33

not known. Truly, he was new. It was an unaccustomed feeling, to be humbled. More so because of his deliberation, the weight he had thought to be in this decision.

Neveau had needed this moment, capitalized on it further.

'You were showing concern about ICRC finances, President. I remind you that the American Society will spend one hundred and twenty two million dollars on relief this year. It would hardly be sensible to cause offence in that direction.'

There was no time for debate, Neveau was almost home.

Salem said, 'I intend to include a strong call for the declaration of war and the strict observation of the Conventions.'

Neveau did not answer, he opened the door, flushed now.

'Good night,' Salem said. 'Thanks for your help.' The Bentley moved on. Why had he said that? It had not been intended. It was petulance. It had come out unbidden. Now he must make such a call.

Salem held on to the jump strap, eyes tight. He had permitted himself to be rattled. It was a disappointment.

5

Neveau gave a small cocktail party and buffet several times a year in his flat. It was usually for the entertainment of an overseas visitor not sufficiently important to merit the florid and formal parties judiciously given at headquarters. Jog Chatterji, the Indian member from Delhi, was the honoured guest on this occasion. Chatterji was a rigid teetotaller. Neveau had prepared a fruit cup for him, flavoured with imported mangoes.

The ICRC heads of departments had been invited, a customary gesture in personal relations on the occasions Neveau entertained.

If Salem was President, rarefied and unattainable, the Executive Director was headmaster. An invitation from him caused a small sweep of excitement, like the declaration of an extracurricular holiday at school. Lower-echelon employees who had earned particular notice were rewarded on these guest lists.

Mitchell was pleased. It had been impulse that had made him invite Jane Stirling. She had shrugged.

'Why not? It might be amusing.

Joseph Richter, Second Secretary in the American Embassy, was looking forward to Neveau's party. He had recently announced to the ICRC his appointment as one of the eight State Department representatives to the International Conference in Paris.

He had dealt with Neveau and the ICRC on minor matters of co-operation. That had been at a different level, one of official routine. This unexpected promotion, or at least elevation in responsibility and status, had obviously come to him because he served in Geneva and had personal contacts with the ICRC.

Richter hurried along the footpath, head and shoulders over the others, an eager, gaunt, noticeable six feet five. Richter's best silk suit was with the cleaner. He wanted to wear it that night.

The elaborate buffet which Sarah Neveau produced for these parties was celebrated. A chef was customarily hired from the École Professionalle Suisse por Restaurateurs et Hôteliers, a teaching academy down the hill from the ICRC where the executives usually ate lunch, a *menu gastronomique*, created by the school's trainees.

Neveau had reviewed the food as gravely as a general reviews troops, inspecting each dish, tasting, signifying approval.

'It's past seven. Isn't it time you changed?'

Neveau put his cuff-links and wallet on the tray of the valet unit where, each night, he carefully creased his trousers and arranged his jacket on the hanger. He thought of Salem. A strong call for the declaration of war and the observation of the Conventions! The man was impossible, impractical, without the vaguest grasp of reality. It was too much, it would make trouble, as if there was not trouble enough.

Neveau bent to unlace his shoes, sat there with his elbows on his knees.

Perhaps if Salem were severely set back over this, chastised, made to see the reality, it might be a salutary lesson. Richter was new and keen. Perhaps a few words said to Richter, in confidence.

Why not? It might be amusing.

Jane had not meant that. It would be difficult to conceive of anything less amusing. Mitchell had caught her sprung on a mood, a weariness of her own company, a sickened boredom with the work, the place and the people, and a fear, the familiar feared fear, of the lurching, striding restlessness that pushed at her mind and body.

This had not worked, and it would not, there was no service here to absorb the self with forgetting, to make the escape into others. It was grindingly dull, worse, far worse, than being a salesgirl.

That had at least been novel, worth it alone for the chat in the girls' room, the graffiti in the lavatories which appeared as miraculously as it was expunged, the sub-world of boy-friends at the staff entrance, cafeteria meals, the giggled intrigues with tatty floor-walkers treading their fiefs as loftily as sheikhs.

It would be safe at Neveau's and she found some amusement in that. It would be safe with Mitchell. His knowing good looks did not attract. Mitchell's vulgarity was essentially mean, the synthesized urban product of conceits in bad taste. Mitchell would not understand the attractions of true peasant vulgarity, the pure power of the un-washed, insensitive, demanding male.

Jane touched the skin beneath her eyes. There were tiny lines there, a softening of muscle, like an omen. In detail she scrutinized the reflec-tion. Cheeks, mouth, chin, underchin and neckline.

'You'll do,' she told the mirror.

She wondered what to wear and thought perhaps something prim with no make-up. To hell with that, she would give it the works. They'd be talking about her anyhow.

It was 'Joe' and 'Martin' between them. Richter's harsh, straight hair was severely brushed down. The suit he had collected from the cleaners, despite the expense of its tailoring and the newness of press-ing, seemed to hang on him in folds, somehow shrugged out of shape by his hunched shoulders and the concavity of belly which had become his adopted posture, the attempt to minimize or apologize for the height that lofted him so much above his fellows.

The big sitting-room opened through wide french doors on to a bal-cony. The evening was warm, hushed and still. Neveau's guests grouped and regrouped, cigarette smoke stirring on the ceiling, stream-ing to the balcony where others looked down on the city and appreci-ated the fresh air. The roar of voices undulated as though orchestrated for rhythm. White-coated waiters edged and pushed through the shoal-ing guests, drink trays miraculously balanced.

The Indian guest of honour sipped his fruit juice and goggled with the others at Jane Stirling. She wore a thin black jersey dress, moulded tight, mini-skirted and cut with a neck that exposed small, unex-pectedly pushing breasts. Her long blue-black hair was severely brushed back, pinned with a Spanish comb, an accentuation of the high-boned purity of her features. She wore no jewellery and little make-up. The striking figure she made, the deliberate insolence with which she returned the hot-eyed appraisals of other women, invoked her for the men.

Sarah Neveau had white patches on her cheeks. When she could, her voice hissed in whisper, she leaned to Mitchell in passing.

'How dare you bring her to my house?'

Mitchell made himself innocent.

'What's wrong? It's an ICRC Party, isn't it?'

Sarah snapped her eyes and swept away, arms out and voice loud in a theatrical greeting of the Reuter's Bureau Chief, whom she barely knew.

Little Mick East enjoyed parties, but seldom contributed to the conversations. He preferred to watch from something comfortable and drink and eat as much as he could. He inspected Jane. He had only glimpsed her before, his face steadily reddening, his cheeks bulging with wind, emptying his beer mug as though he were under pressure of time.

Later, much later, out of irritation at being unable to establish any intimacy of conversation with Jane Stirling, Mitchell had insisted on her meeting the head of the Tracing Agency. It was less to impress Mick East than to be advantaged by the isolation around his corner of the lounge. Jane had shrugged and agreed, a concession to Mitchell's status as escort.

Lazily, Mitchell made the introduction.

'Lady Jane Stirling. Mick East, the big brain of the Tracing Agency.'

In the extraordinary tones of Petticoat Lane, long put behind him now, Mick East hoisted his mug and said without rising, 'I fink yer a wight smasher, ducks. Goodenuff t'eat. I'd wavver 'ave you then jellied eels.'

Mitchell couldn't believe it. He turned slowly to Jane.

She put out her hip, pointed one foot and said in tones as Limehouse clear as East's:

'Yer a bitta a'right yerself, wacker. 'Ere, slide up the pew, an' I'll sink a glassa wallop wicha.'

Mitchell stood there, alone in the isolation he had coveted, trying and failing to intrude himself on the raucous Cockney conversation he only in part understood. Mick had to be drunk, dead drunk. He was complimenting Jane Stirling on her breasts, using Cockney rhyming slang.

'That's a righ' ol' pair'a threepenny bits, ducks.'

'I liffs up me tits an' I titters, love.'

Mitchell reeled off. He was stunned. He had no answer for Sarah Neveau when she hissed another whisper.

'Don't tell me you've torn yourself away?'

Joe Richter was crouching more than usual in Neveau's presence, trying to signal to Neveau that their heights should be reversed.

'If President Salem publicized documents like that, I mean propaganda from Hanoi, it would come as a great shock to my Ambassador. He would be greatly shocked, greatly hurt. It would be an embarrassment to the President himself. I mean, Communism must be stopped somewhere. All responsible persons know that. We're fighting for all the free world out there.'

'President Salem is greatly concerned about the bombing. The injury to civilians.'

'Civilians get hurt in every war, one regrets it but it's unavoidable. He must know that every care is being taken. The Defense Secretary has gone on record about this. The bombing is highly selective.'

There was no credulity gap between Richter and policy. Neveau felt a spasm of irritation. He knew that the bombing approached saturation. There were only so many factories and bridges in that tiny country. The bombing was a mess, its further consequences a frightening calculation. Because it was a mess, personally and professionally Neveau deprecated it.

'The Secretary went on record about the Tonkin Gulf attack. I now understand that proved to be a sonar hum from the ships' propellors.'

Richter was distressed and surprised, swallowing on his prominent Adam's apple.

Neveau said carefully, re-establishing himself: 'It's a point made by President Salem.'

Jane Stirling was among the early leavers. She had refused as unnecessary Mitchell's bid to escort her home. He spent the remainder of the evening in sullen dissatisfaction.

6

THE appointment in Paris, the great four-yearly meeting attended by the delegations of one hundred and thirteen countries, had quickened tensions and further burdened the ICRC workload.

The standing committee, whose chief duty it was to organize the conference, anticipated the International with foreboding. Nothing was resolved in the Levant. There would be tension between the Jews and the Arabs, further exacerbated by Israel's petition for recognition of its League. Israel had chosen the Star of David as the symbol of its Society. This would not be acceptable to the Arab Republics, as indeed it was not to the Charter. The Star of David was a religious device, one of the subjectives the Charter denounced. Israel insisted that Egypt's Red Crescent was a device of the Muslim religion and argued in dogged unreason that the Red Cross itself, in addition to being the reverse of the Swiss National flag, was also symbol of the Christian religion. It exasperated and maddened Neveau.

The Communist delegations would bitterly attack the National

Society of America, the war in Vietnam and the ICRC's rigidly upheld discretion. There was rumour that Red China would seat a delegation, with subsequent outcry from the Nationalist Government of Formosa. The delegations of the North Vietnamese Red Cross, the Red Cross of the Saigon Government and the Red Cross of the National Liberation Front would charge the congress with warfare.

Mitchell was beginning to agree with Mick East about the do-gooders. Everything done was palliative, a sentiment that made the outrages tolerable. What was the use of it? If things were going to smash, what could he, or anybody do? Mitchell had heard the rumours about the tactical nuclear and chemical biological weapons the Americans had positioned in Vietnam and Thailand. It had seeped through the entire building. Like the others, Mitchell also felt a hot resentment in the chill of fear.

The Tracing Agency was crowded with file clerks, the IBM machines pecking at long trays of reference, an apparent confusion only ordered in East's mind. He had been at Neveau again about the computer and the need for a bigger building. There were thousands of missing persons in the desert, the documentation wildly inadequate.

Mitchell gave himself a coffee and brandy and sat moodily on a corner of East's desk, silent. East continued to pencil at the stacks of manila folders.

'Cat got your tongue, Teddy boy?'

'I'm fed up, Mick.'

'What's the trouble?'

'I don't know. Too much bloody work for one thing. What's to become to us?'

Mitchell continued to scowl.

'What's going to happen in Vietnam, Mick?'

'Boom, boom. Beaucoup boom boom.'

'No, seriously. You've had the grapevine about these nuclear weapons. Now they're on about risk of an Eastern plague epidemic.'

Mick said, 'I could solve that problem for the Yanks. You want to quote me?'

'Go ahead, solve it.'

Mick put down his pencil and leaned back.

'The Yanks are blasting the country flat, right? They're going to take it all out in order to save it, right?'

'Right.'

'These Charlies are in the forests and jungles and under Westmorland's floorboards and they've got to go buster, right?'

'Right.'

'So, concrete it.'

Mitchell was suspicious.

'Concrete what?'

'Concrete the whole bloody country. Begin at the tip and concrete the lot, clear up to the DMZ. That way there's nowhere for Charlie to hide and no rice to feed him. Make as much sense. Cheaper, too,' Mick East said.

Mitchell put down his coffee cup.

'Get stuffed. I'm going back to work.'

Mick East took a typed letter from those awaiting his signature. It was from Janos Kisch, head of the Jewish Research Bureau, who was in Geneva. Mick invariably called on Kisch in Berlin when he travelled on business to Arolsen, and as invariably Janos Kisch called on him.

They liked each other, had shared many investigations. Between them the two men commanded more documentation than the added files of Interpol, Scotland Yard and the Federal Bureau of Investigation.

They met in Kisch's hotel, Kisch warm and welcoming, already finding reason to laugh, his notable bonhomie and enjoyment of everything the mark of an untroubled man, one whose good fortune it had been to live his sixty years in plenitude and peace.

Janos Kisch was originally a Pole, a schoolteacher from Cracow. He had endured and survived eleven concentration camps. Fifty of his relatives had died and been murdered in others. At Nürnberg Kisch had been a key witness at the war criminal trials.

Years ago he had told Mick East, pleasant, mild, laughing, 'I don't believe in justice, I don't believe in mercy. Everything in life has a price. I have paid a heavy price. Now I am an instrument of vengeance for my people. Vengeance is the purest, most liberating of all emotions. An eye for an eye is a beautiful law.'

Much of their talk had been about the Martin Bormann trace conducted by Mick as a hobby and by Janos Kisch for his own reasons.

Kisch did not believe that Bormann was in the fortified German settlement in South America from where he had been reported. Mick was satisfied that he was. He had his own information that Israeli commandos had tried to penetrate the settlement, approaching it by river. He was sure that Janos was using his waggish disagreement as a cover.

They were preparing to leave when it came to Mick, nagging him.

42

'Janos, this trace you requested on Rudolf Kleinberg. Something keeps knocking on my door.'

Janos Kisch concentrated. He had reason to respect Mick's instincts.

'Let me refresh you. A year ago a former SS officer sold information on the whereabouts of Hermann Hatz, Commandant of Krasnerdorf, and some of his assistants. Rudolf Kleinberg appears as assistant on medical experiments. If he assisted those animals, if he is alive, I want him.'

Mick East dreamed at his glass while Kisch waited.

'No,' he said. 'Nothing comes.'

Janos Kisch sighed and signalled for the bill.

The nag the name Rudolf Kleinberg had raised in Mick East came to him a few days after Martin Neveau's party. He had lit his last cigarette and was absently crushing the packet. Revelation arrived as it usually did, with the sudden clarity that for an instant dislocated reality. It was a different packet he held in his hand, old, dirtied, flattened, blurred words pencilled on it.

He said to one of the girls, his voice edged, 'Bring me the history book, will you, Nell?'

There, among the memorabilia was the curiosity Mick East could not forget. The inside of a cigarette packet, thrown from a death transport to the gas ovens, collected by a railway worker and handed to the Red Cross at war's end. It was a list of names, with places and dates of birth, all that remained left to the crushed, gasping creatures in the cattle trucks.

In faulted, flawed characters that required a magnifying glass to translate, the list ended: *Betrayed—R. Kleinberg.*

7

In the first months of Salem's tenure of office, the insistent punctuality of the grey Bentley's ten o'clock arrival had become a joke to the staff. Now the big car was often parked in the mornings before the door porter got into position.

As Salem's grasp firmed, as the multitude of issues became familiar, hardening into outline and pattern, so did his purpose and confidence harden. There was great energy in the sparse, deceptive elegance of Salem's presence, energy unused since the furious studies of his student days and later dampened in routine—the anodyne of the shock and pain of his divorce, which still lived in his flesh as a sad and wistful memory. Salem's imagination had caught, driving him harder and deeper into the work. The leather-covered book he kept in his safe was heaped with new drafts beginning: *My Own Dear Son*.

The Juro-Legal division had started work on the new Humanitarian Law that would replace the Conventions one day. Daunted at the beginning, the division's experts had caught fire from Salem's fire, borne up by his own considerable reputation in International Law, at ease and excited to be able to exchange with the President the esoterics of legal language.

This was acceptable to Martin Neveau, the massive task would require years. He hoped that it might eventually absorb Salem completely.

The Vietnamese documents and Salem's personal call for a declaration of war had duly been passed by the American Red Cross Society and the Secretary of Defense. The response had been more than Neveau had hoped, for which he privately congratulated Joseph Richter.

The American Secretary of State himself had addressed a reply to Salem. It was a lengthy one, a most definite refutation of the North Vietnamese claims and an implied surprise that the President of the International Red Cross would seriously consider such propaganda.

The call for a declaration of war was treated much more brusquely. A state of war did not exist. The conflict in Vietnam was one of insurgency. The American presence existed at the request of the Government of South Vietnam, a rendering of aid and assistance within the provisions of the South-East Asia Treaty.

A further document was appended, listing Viet Cong atrocities in the south, with a recommendation that the ICRC might be well employed investigating these.

It was, as Neveau had hoped, a salutary lesson for Salem. The lesson was there, but it wasn't what Neveau had imagined. If Salem was shaken it was by the intransigence of the communication.

In 1954 the Geneva Agreements had arranged a Vietnamese settlement. The final resolvement only waited on the free, supervised elections agreed for 1956, unilaterally abrogated with American connivance by the disastrous puppet Ngo Dinh Diem.

If Salem was largely uninstructed about politics, he lacked no instruction about law. The patrician contempt this aroused in him was the beginning of something new. It armed his resolve to fight, to commit the ICRC and to revive the dead letter of the Conventions.

Salem was masked for Neveau; he would add nothing to his present satisfaction.

'I believe we might adopt this advice.'

Neveau wondered whether he meant all or part.

'The last paragraph. The suggestion that a visit to Vietnam might be instructive.'

45

Neveau was wary.

'To what end, President?'

'There will be charges and counter charges in Paris. The chair will be greatly strengthened if it knows the fact from the fiction.'

'I disagree. A visit to Vietnam could be construed as a partisan action. The chair's strength in Paris will depend on political non-involvement.'

Neveau's dogged persistence, his refusal to respond to any friendly overture, his righteousness, had become a burden to Salem.

'I think you disagree with me on principal, Martin.'

It discomfited Neveau a little.

'Not at all. I would not like you to think that. I have worked here almost twenty years. One becomes very aware of the tightrope we walk. The International has only survived to benefit mankind by remaining vigorously neutral. And that, President, means politically, militarily, denominationally and individually neutral.'

'Are you individually neutral in all things, Martin?'

'I am,' Neveau said certainly. 'I have no doubt about my own neutral feelings.'

Salem had the instinct to pierce Neveau's defences, to reach inside, find the man and tweak him.

'Martin, you know that when I first came here I was required to read the dossiers of the heads of departments, including that of the Executive Director.'

'Your privilege,' Neveau said briefly.

'I have no wish to open old wounds, and I was moved by the tragedy you suffered as a boy. I make this point, Martin, because absolute individual neutrality is an abstract concept that does not exist in human life. I make this point in the hope that it may help you better to understand me, whose reactions to most things are only too human.'

Neveau was poised, all slackness departed from the heavy body.

'Well, then?'

'Are you absolutely neutral about the deaths of your parents, the British or American airmen who might have flown that raid? Indeed, about the Germans whose war it was?'

The slightest tremor touched Neveau's lips. His words came roughly.

'That is ... that is something ... about which I had to satisfy myself. I had to satisfy myself about that before, in conscience, I could do the work of this committee. I had to satisfy my conscience and in due course I had to satisfy the then Executive Director that my feelings ... that my feelings were in no way alienated from true Swiss neutrality. I did that, President, and I am, and will remain, individually neutral. I feel nothing but neutrality towards the Germans or the Americans or the British or towards anybody else ... the Jews who started that war ... started Hitler ... started the war in which my parents were killed, I feel only neutrality towards them ... neutrality.'

Neveau's fingers tapped on his chair arm, his breathing had thickened.

'I am sorry, Martin. I have never doubted the truth of your conscience, not in any way. That was a debater's trick I'm afraid, a little exercise in semantics. I had no right. I am very sorry.'

'Quite all right. Quite all right. Nothing to be sorry about.'

Salem sat staring at the door Neveau had closed behind him. Neveau had fought for his neutrality. It wasn't just the charter, it was the man's private obsession. That extraordinary remark about the Jews, it didn't bear examination. What labyrinths the stolid man carried within him.

Ted Mitchell had made little contact with Salem. He was much more reserved than the past president, careful not to go over or under Neveau's head about anything, punctiliously dealing through the Executive Director in all matters except the Humanitarian Law.

Mitchell was surprised and pleased to get a direct call from Salem. He had made it a point on newspapers to be noticed, if he could, by the publisher and had maintained the principle in the internationals where he had worked.

Salem made no attempt at concealment. He said directly, 'Mitchell, I would like you to do me a service. It is a matter of some delicacy and must remain a confidence. I have a statement here, which for certain reasons, I am unable to publicize under the ICRC imprimatur. This statement has been prepared by six hundred and sixty-seven leading American scientists. It says in part...' Salem lifted his glasses: ' "We can see no guide from science, philosophy, religion, sociology or government as they exist today, and time is running out. Therefore, we address ourselves to the International Committee of the Red Cross." ' He put down the glasses. 'The statement is a protest against the corruption of science in Vietnam and the precedents it sets. It draws attention to the repeated outbreaks of plague and the terrifying possibility of a new Black Death in the East. I would like you to, I believe the word is "leak", to leak this statement to the Press. There is, and must be, only one copy. I would like you to read it in privacy, make

47

what notes you think fit and then return the statement. You understand me, I am sure.'

Mitchell took the proffered papers.

'I understand.'

Ted Mitchell had good reason to be pleased. In a matter of minutes he had emerged from comparative obscurity into a private conspiracy with the President. The depression which had earlier gloomed his spirits vanished.

Mitchell began to read the statement.

'... the creation of biological weapons with uncontrollable effects of unknown magnitude which could endanger humanity and disrupt human, animal and plant ecology ... the as yet unmeasured effects in an area where rice is the mainstay of life for eleven hundred million people ... six hundred scientists are engaged in an increasing programme of research on bacterial diseases as potential weapons at...

'Attention is focused on the development of disease organisms that make them suitable militarily ... among them anthrax, dysentery, viral diseases such as denge fever, encephalitis, yellow fever, botulism toxic and,' Mitchell read, with a shiver, 'bubonic plague...

'The journal of the American Association for the Advancement of Science had documented massive research in chemical and biological warfare ... budget in excess of one hundred and fifty-eight million dollars ... eastern university split over secret project to develop defoliants, rice damagers and crop destroyers ... testing ground for assessment and proving of chemical and biological weapons, presumably on animals...

'Secret arsenal reportedly producing nerve gas, mustard gas, incapacitants and anti-crop weapons ... Six chemical compounds already used in South Vietnam include tear gas (CN), nausea gas (DM), vomiting gas (CN–DM) and irritant gas (CS) ... aerosol infection of monkeys with fever organism ... pneumonia plague, bubonic plague...

'Here was the death wish, the lemming syndrome, the Hitlerite paranoia which could still scream at the end, *Is Paris Burning?*'

Mitchell was unaccustomed to these concerns, resented this new depression. If he could find a tax-free international of topless dancers, or a united world order of bird-seed manufacturers, he would turn in this job immediately. He would take this load of valentines up to the Press Club and leak it. He was going to get so full himself he'd be leaking at every pore.

In the foundation-laying of his Humanitarian Law, Pierre Salem had found fulfilment. The dead place inside him, the ash and clinker as dry and grey and sharp as something swallowed, which he had accepted as a condition of his being, was forgotten.

Salem woke now to the tea-tray Signora Conci served him, shivered by excitement and impatience for the day.

For the present he had plotted a strategy. He would continue to apply pressure in all meetings with the committee, choosing his words carefully, unemotional about it, raise wings of warning to a judged point of contention and then fold them suddenly.

It had Neveau unbalanced, and the uneasiness that Salem sought was already evident in the committee.

There were more than enough alarums with which to salt the strategy. The petition of the American scientists—their concern over biological warfare in principle, and over the outbreaks of plague that might spread throughout the world—competently leaked by Mitchell, had been carried on every wire service. Several of the committee had invoked the newspaper reports in worry.

'I know, gentlemen, but my hands are tied. In the absence of a declaration of war...'

Vietnam

8

ADAM THOMSON opened his eyes and stared with hatred at the ceiling fan. Something in the mechanism had been jarred by the mortar shells that had exploded on the roof and in the compound. The fan would not adjust for speed. On each revolution it groaned, tormenting Adam in his restless sleep with hallucinations of the hospital. His hair was sticky with sweat, sweat ran on his neck and dampened his armpits. He wiped at it with the curdled sheet and reached for eyedrops.

The fan groaned. God only knew when an electrician could be got to fix it. In the next room the mortar hole was still patched with canvas and God alone knew when something would be done about that.

Adam got up and walked in his shorts to the mess room, took a can of Coca-Cola from the stacked refrigerator, punched it and drank. The others had eaten and gone. The fizzy drink rumbled his empty stomach, hardly cutting the thirst. He must remember to be regular with the salt tablets.

'Borgia!'

An elderly Vietnamese looked out of the kitchen, wiping a plate.

'Breakfast. Cereals and coffee. Have you put out the salt tablets this morning?'

Borgia looked quickly to the condiments, jams and sauces that remained from the earlier meal.

In the characteristic, grinding English of which the old man had only a few words, although his understanding was reasonable, he assured Adam that the salt tablets had not been forgotten.

A Red Cross field worker had named the cook Borgia because he was trying to poison them. Borgia had been stubborn about spicing his dishes with the Vietnamese delicacy of Nuoc-Nam sauce, leaked from putrid raw fish. A visiting correspondent who had eaten in the mess likened the smell of Nuoc-Nam to a fertilizer truck involved in an accident outside a tanning factory in a whaling town.

It was agreed by those who had eaten his cooking that Borgia was at least Viet Cong.

Adam went to the door and looked out, pressing at the weight in his eyeballs. The sky was low, scummed with grey cloud, a turbulent, palpable pressure. He could feel the charged load of the coming monsoon on every muscle. It crackled in the clouds, each day pressing down more heavily, a bated, breathless waiting that tore nerves, glistened the skin with dank sweat.

Adam wished it would break, get it over.

Artillery whumped in the distance, pulsing the mosquito screens on the opened windows. He was used to it now, only heard it if the concussion was unusually strong. Three months ago it had brought him off his bed, mixed and contorted into the bloody dreamings that pursued him from the day.

Mark Hatton, officer in command of the American advisers compound, had noticed. 'They're ours. The big ones you hear are ours. You'll get to feel good, Thomson, each time you hear a big one. Quong Lo is secure now.'

The Viet Cong hit secure Quong Lo three days before the elections. The mortar shells slammed in at two o'clock in the morning, probing for Hatton's compound and provincial headquarters. While fires lit and Vietnamese shouted and searched for cover, the guerrilla forces breached the Quong Lo jail and released twelve hundred prisoners. On the way out they fired a petrol station and dressed their wounded in the hospital.

The Americans had sheltered in the bathroom until dawn, mattresses stacked against the door. It was the most protected place in the villa which had once been the home of a French administrator.

The shells that exploded inside the walls and holed the roof had hit in a bracket, three shattering crumps that had bulged the mattresses, spewed plaster and dust, struck at their ears and eyes. The great steel-sheeted protection gate had been blown into holes, the sandbagged sentry-box ripped. The Vietnamese who should have kept vigil was asleep behind the villa, his life saved by this customary dereliction of duty.

Sam Jarra, a refugee camp organizer, consulted the damage in the sullen first light, an M16 on his arm.

'This is a goddam chickenshit pad to make a civilian mess. We got the adviser's compound one side of us, Gook headquarters the other. Charlie's going to blow our asses off one day.'

Adam Thomson stretched his legs over the sandbags, switched on and listened anxiously to the starting motor. The jeep was worn out, starting or stopping according to an arbitrary arrangement of its innards. All civilian transport in Quong Lo had the floorboards sandbagged now. A USAID staffer had been blown to pieces in the bazaar when his booby-trapped Renault exploded.

Adam backed out, the steel gates swinging shut immediately. The jagged holes through which sunlight beamed in early mornings reminded the guards of the tenderness of flesh.

Tanks were slewed off the road, the Vietnamese crews squatted smoking in their shade. A line of personnel carriers, engines vibrating, lay ahead. Adam wondered if this could be an armoured patrol or part of a bigger operation. The likelihood worried him. The hospital was like a slaughterhouse, it would be impossible to handle more civilian casualties.

The town was strung along the main highway south, a motley of small shops and a few solid, two floored buildings. Bicycles were everywhere, bells constantly ringing. Army trucks bullhorned along the asphalt that striped the middle of the road, lurching into the rutted edges, churning up stifling dust. A few American troops wandered in a slouched desperation of boredom, cuds of gum in their cheeks, giants among the tiny Vietnamese who quietened and moved to let them pass.

Quong Lo was capital of the province, an administrative headquarters established by the French, an ugly, rickety leaving of colonialism, crushingly humid in summer, a squelched and sucking quagmire in the rains.

It was also an island into hard-core Viet Cong territory.

Farther into the Central Lowlands, in the fishing villages on the South China Sea and in the mountain longhouses of the Montagnard tribesmen, the VC had ruled undisturbed since before Dien Bien Phu.

Adam turned off the asphalt on to the holed and battered dirt track to the airstrip, face and arms set against the jolts from seat and wheel. He had made this detour for days. Medicines dispatched from Saigon had gone astray at one of the stops on the Air America schedule.

The transport was coming in, making a sudden plummeting drop at the extreme end of the strip. A 'sorry about that' landing the pilots called it. Aircraft had been hit making longer, lower approaches. The 'sorry about that' evasions were noticeably hard on the passengers.

Mark Hatton had returned his driver's salute and walked towards Adam, pegging a little on his stiff right leg, fatigues pressed crisp, fair hair cropped in combat fashion, the thin face clean and hard, its tan untouched by perspiration. Hatton carried a grip and a holstered ·45 pistol wrapped in a webbing belt.

'You travelling, Doctor?'

'No, Major. Just checking supplies.'

'Uh—huh. Thought I might have had your company.'

They watched the aircraft drop steps to unload the shaken passengers. A Beechcraft ran up engines and took off, pulling up as steeply as the transport had let down.

He's going for another medical, Adam decided. He's still trying to get back into action.

It was known that Hatton was grim about this convalescent posting. He exercised the wounded leg each day with a sack of sand across the foot.

There were Vietnamese civilians among the disembarking passengers, air-sick as was customary.

'Another stinking ride. These people shouldn't be on our transport. Why don't they make them travel Air Vietnam?'

'No room, I suppose, Major. They have to travel somehow.'

'Do they?' Hatton said.

The pilots were out of the aircraft, making for the transport hut to check the manifest and drink something cold. The crewmen bounced boxes through the door, in cheerful disregard of possible fragility.

The southbound passengers began to cross the tarmac. Two were correspondents, one with camera gear. They saw Hatton and waved. He barely nodded.

'Newspapermen?'

'The worst kind. Bleeding hearts.'

A jeep and trailer collected the cargo and sped away to the huts. Fighter bombers screeched overhead and disappeared, jet trails expanding in tattered wisps.

Hatton lifted his grip.

'Be seeing you, Doctor.'

Adam was halted at the main road, waiting to cross, when he heard the whump of bombs. It was air strike, probably the jets that had barrelled across the strip. It reminded him of the heavy armour and APCs making up earlier. He worried again about the prospect of more civilian casualties.

The surgeon Adam replaced had served in Quong Lo a year. He was fifty, looked sixty, ill with exhaustion and the recurrent fevers that had boiled the flesh off his bones.

'I got malaria in New Guinea, the last war. Spleen shot. I shouldn't have come out here.' He had screwed his eyes at Adam and offered a cigarette. 'I understand you had a New York practice. Never got into the big-time myself. Country man, mid-West.'

They stood on the verandah. Watching Adam he hitched his head at the ward they had just left.

'Don't let it get to you. You'll get used to it, son.'

'That's all there is? That's the only operating theatre you've got?'

'Why, it's good now. We got our own generator. When I started here the power used to cut maybe four, five times a day. I'd be in there, blood and guts to the armpits and wham! Blackout.'

'How do you cope? How many are in that ward?'

'Ninety-six, this morning's count. Ninety-six for thirty beds. You don't cope, son. You sew 'em up and you saw 'em up and you do the best you can. Pretty soon you don't know much else. If you want to stay healthy out here you make up your mind damn quick you're not going to let it get to you.'

But it had got to Adam. The loneliness of responsibility, the pressing corruption of death, the inability to do more than patch and dismiss the awful traffic in peasant bodies, had tormented his sleep with nightmare.

He had had no preparation for this brute reality. He had volunteered to work the three months relief, more out of self interest than devotion. Adam's senior partner had agreed that the surgical experience could be useful, a possible asset to the practice.

The three months had passed, and passed with them was most of the man Adam Thompson had been.

The hospital was set back from the road in a deep and dusty compound. A few pepper trees gave shade, Adam switched off, and felt sick. There were litters on the galvanized iron verandah, the Vietnamese nurse bandaged a child's leg. There had been a new intake. Adam closed his eyes and then swung out of the jeep.

The long, low, dung-coloured building might have been a shed, or a stable, in another country. Four women, two men and three children lay on the verandah, flies buzzing the bloodied bandages.

'When did these come in?'

'An hour ago, Dr Adam.'

'Has Dr Pedro seen them?'

'Yes. He's in reception.'

'More in there?'

'Twelve. We wait for you.'

'I've been at the airstrip. The supplies arrived, they're in the jeep. Is the theatre ready?'

The little nurse nodded, speaking in her own tongue to the gasping child she bandaged.

'All ready, Doctor.'

'Can you manage here? Where are they from?'

'Transfers from Chu Lai. Big fight. Much can-non. These be okay, I think.'

It was always cannon. Whatever hit them, whoever hit them, it was always can-non to the villagers.

A tall American soldier with an interpreter's identification on his shirt pocket walked out on the verandah. He saw Adam and paused.

'Hi, Doc.'

'You working?'

'We've got a VC in back.'

'Is he wounded?'

'Wounded some, I guess.'

The interpreter looked uneasy.

'Did Dr Darder clear you to interrogate that man?'

'Well, he bandaged him. I'm not interrogating. They just sent me along to listen. The Arvins have got him in back.'

'You get in back and tell them I'm coming to examine that man.'

The interpreter was aggrieved.

'Don't kick my ass, Doc. I'm just here to listen.'

The reception-room was a windowless concrete cave between wards. Water-pipes were mounted in the floor as rests for the litters. There was only this provision for six. The other casualties lay on the concrete. Dr Pedro Darder, the Spanish volunteer, was injecting an old woman with morphia. He looked up at Adam, shook his head, pointed at the corner and put his thumb down. A middle-aged man lay on the nearest raised litter, bloody hands on his stomach, a toddler, naked except for a shirt, asleep beside him, cuddled in.

Adam touched the man's leg, smiled, nodded and gently moved the clasped hands. The belly was holed. Edging the bloody plug of gauze, the steaming entrails worked.

There were three litters in the corner Dr Darder had indicated with his thumb. With the old woman, that made four inoperables.

Darder said, 'The child's not hurt. That's the father.'

'How many have we got?'

'Three majors. That belly wound and two amputations. Three patch jobs I could do.'

Adam said, 'I'll take the belly wound first.'

9

Elsewhere, the monsoon breaks in a single act of violence, unpreceded by the rehearsal of showers. Here, there were harbingers of the deluge, short, steamy cloudbursts that made the humidity soar.

The downfalls collected in buckets on the sagged hood of Adam's old jeep. Forgetting, out of habit, he would catch there to swing himself in, receiving the dump on his shoulders with calculated inanimate malevolence.

The early rains had been a discharge of the pressure condensed in the clouds, the mornings cooler now, less oppressive on waking.

It was easier too at the hospital. The rains had slowed the search-and-destroy operations that had packed the wards with gunshot. The dying shed and the napalm ward had been cleaned and made more comfortable. In orthopaedic, the floors were still crowded, beds pushed to rest three and four, but there was time now for attention, time to work the wards, time to take better care of dressings and progress.

The USAID chief of the province had bullied through a consignment of cotton mattresses. Adam had watched with satisfaction as the used ones burned. There was something essentially clean about fire. Something essentially good about the fierce flames that lit on the putrid mess to lick it from memory, consumed into powder to blow on the wind. There had been days when some of those mattresses had exuded blood the way a pressed sponge exudes water.

It was a measure of the distance Adam Thomson had travelled in four months at Quong Lo, that this respite from extreme should seem a holiday.

There were four on the Quaker team, three men and a woman. The new hut was towards the road, on the boundary of the compound. It was cheerfully white, concrete floored, roofed in galvanized iron, with the luxury of ceiling fans. Half the hut was for therapy, half a workshop for artificial limbs.

The Quakers were hardly settled, exclusive and careful. Authority regarded their presence as a test of private relations. Saigon was unforgiving about the Quaker ship chartered out of Hong Kong that had carried medical supplies to the North and the Quaker team that had worked it.

She was at a fixed table, massaging the stump of a girl's leg amputated below the knee by Adam, a handsome woman in her thirties in a wrap-on grey cotton cover. A raised umbrella was conveniently jammed in a split in the fixed table, against the rain leaking through the roof.

'They would have to put the table here,' she said, 'under a leak we can't stop.'

A boy of five or six was trying a raw wooden peg, using a tiny set of parallel bars. Another girl, stick-legged, stick-armed, lay on her back, exercising weakly with weighted pads. A young man hopped on a crutch.

Adam examined the ceiling.

'It's a seam. The rain is coming through the overlap.'

'That, Dr Thomson, is a diagnosis I had managed myself.'

Beyond the low divider, Vietnamese trainees were busy in the workshop. The turning and buffing machines brought by the Quakers were against the front wall, benches behind them. Crutches ferruled in cut-outs from motor tyres hung on pegs. Timber limbs, almost all small, stood on the benches, children's sandals painted roughly on the inflexible feet, some with knot holes like disease in the wooden flesh.

'Dr Thomson?'

'Nurse?'

'Understand me, I have no wish to make trouble. But is there no hope of getting some kind of hostel for these children? It's heartbreaking. You discharge your amputees long before we can give them effective therapy. Most of them are orphans, or lost. Their villages have been burned down in the relocations. They have no homes. There are so many of them, so many.' She continued the massage, the strong clean muscles lifting on her brown forearms. 'This unit is producing two hundred artificial limbs a month. Two hundred. And it's not enough. This child is doing well, but you've discharged her. She will have to beg in the bazaar and hobble out here to get the treatment she needs.'

'You've seen the hospital, Nurse. We haven't got room to walk the wards. If they can get about, we have to push them out.'

'It wouldn't cost much. Just a shed like this with some mattresses and food. It would make such a difference.'

'There have been recommendations. Why don't you get your team leader to take it up with USAID?'

She frowned.

'It's difficult. We're not very popular, you know.'

'I know. This is just one provincial hospital in forty-eight, Nurse. It's worse in some of the others. There's just not enough money to go around.'

'There's money enough for killing.'

Adam said wearily, 'The annual American budget for medical aid equals one half-day's expenditure on the war. You work it out. Don't let it get to you. Just do the best you can. You'll get used to it.'

She looked fiercely at him.

Don't let it get to you, do the best you can, you'll get used to it. These were almost the words the old surgeon had used to Adam. They came back to him now as though across years and deserts.

He was leaving, had just begun to say that she didn't need the umbrella, that the rain had stopped, when the awful scream struck them still. They were fixed, staring at each other, when the screams tore the air again.

'What——?'

Now there were other screams, shouted voices, figures running in the compound.

The man had gone amok. He wasn't badly hurt. That morning Adam had removed grenade fragments from his ribs and elbow. He had risen from a stretcher on the floor, screaming, tearing at the dressings. Screaming, lurching, he had run for the door, trampling the other bodies in the corridor, hurling the little Vietnamese nurse away, reeling off the beds, screaming out a frothy vomit.

A compound worker was grappling with him, Darder jumping the floor patients scrabbling for shelter when Adam leapt the steps to the verandah.

Briefly, his eyes bulging, lips snarled off the vomit in his teeth, the man struggled, and collapsed backwards, rigid.

'Reception. Get him to reception.'

The two doctors lifted the small, bleeding body and pushed through the gapers crowding the verandah.

Inside, they lay him on a raised litter. He was in rigour, body muscles twitching, tongue protruding, dry and swollen. Adam shouted for new dressings. The man had torn off his bandages.

'What happened?'

Darder shook his head.

'Don't know. Pulse very fast, very shallow. Temperature high. He's burning up.'

'He was all right this morning.'

'Feverish. He was feverish.'

'He would be. He'd had those wounds for days. What do you think?'

'I'll put him under intra-muscular streptomycin.'

Adam nodded.

'We'd better keep him here and lock the door.'

Sam Jarra put in a twelve-hour day in the camps. He was tough, fortyish, a Red Cross professional, expert in disaster relief. He had worked cyclones in Florida, earthquakes in Greece, floods in South America, landslides in Italy, malnutritions on Indian reservations and, he said, a serious outbreak of sexual frustration among the wives of the Washington Headquarters staff.

Sam carried a ·45 pistol in his jeep and a box of grenades under a sandbag.

'The goddam VC come in that Ten Kilometer camp at sundown every day. They knock up more women than their husbands do. I got enough creepers and crawlers in that camp already. If I get a reliable transport to drag my ass fast out of there, I'm going to lay for Charlie with a Red Cross Fourth of July.'

Sam Jarra had served his time in Quong Lo, had requested an extension. He was sexually hung-up on Vietnamese girls.

'You ever see anything so small and cute? You ever see anything so pretty as these Au Dais? You ever see other women play and laugh that way? Man, those Saigon girlie-bars, you're up to your armpits in the highest grade stuff in the world. I tell you, I've been all over. Sam's Number One down there.'

It was for this he had stayed, for the visits to Saigon or Da Nang for which he contrived frequent reasons.

Sam Jarra was the only civilian in Quong Lo to make friends with Major Hatton. They sometimes played poker together. When Sam could no longer suffer Borgia's cooking he ate in the army compound with the Major.

'So he's got a chip on his shoulder. What do you want? He's a career man. It's the leg. It put him out of business. He could be making colonel somewhere instead of wiping snotty Arvin noses. That Hatton is something else. If they fight the war his way, they'll wrap it up in a year.

'I was down to the compound. Here came these six, eight draftees. Not even shaving yet. Hatton lines 'em up. "Any of you heard an angry shot?" "A shot, sir? No, sir." "You listen to me and you listen good. From this minute on, until they fly you out of here, there's no Gook too young or too old or too sick or too pretty, they can't kill you. There's no place so far or so near or so safe, you can't die. From this minute, until you cross out that last day on the calendar, and you're in the air or on the ship home, it's you against everything that moves. You got it?" "Yes, sir, we got it."'

Sam had got the ·45 and grenades from Major Hatton contrary to army regulations. He carried them contrary to his own.

Adam was on his bed reading when Sam Jarra knocked and entered. He had a fifth of bourbon and two glasses.

'You free a few minutes, Adam?'

Adam put his legs over the bed and pushed a chair at Sam with his foot.

'This the real ol' sour mash, Adam. The fly boys brought it in.'

Adam took a glass.

Sam asked, 'How are things out to the slaughterhouse?'

'We're killing as many as we can, Sam.'

Jarra nodded understandingly. 'Don't get much better, does it? This light at the end of the tunnel's a helluva long time coming. You know what I heard today? The Koreans are moving down with two thousand refugees they relocated from An Ho. Sweet Jesus, we got no place

64

to put another two thousand. We got to double up Number Two camp. Another two thousand in Number Two camp, we're going to be up to our asses in crap.'

It was unusual for Jarra to visit Adam. At the end of the day he usually played poker on the mess-room table.

'See Major Hatton lately, Adam?'

'Some time ago, at the airstrip.'

'That the last time he goes to Saigon?'

'I think so. He was flying the schedule.'

'You know what they gave him down there, about his leg, I mean? They gave him the black spot, Adam.'

'No good?'

'In spades. It's not the muscles. It's some goddam nerve's the trouble.'

'Why doesn't he take an exploratory op?'

'He's a hard-nosed bastard. He don't want any more cutting on him. He figgers they'll get him to Japan, or a hospital stateside, and start cutting on him again, some bright bastard board him out.'

'There's a few hundred thousand in the country who'd change places with him, Sam.'

'I know it. Hatton's something else.'

Sam Jarra shook the ice cubes, his long-nosed face intent. He inspected the big, blotched freckles in the sandy hairs on his hand. 'These Quakers out to the slaughterhouse, Adam. They're physiotherapists aren't they?'

'Three of them.'

'There wouldn't be much they wouldn't know, I guess.'

'One of them has written books about it, Sam.'

'Is that right?' Jarra was pleased and impressed. He laid down his glass. 'I'll level with you, Adam. Hatton took this on the button. He doesn't talk much, but this he took on the button. He'll make a deal with the Quakers. That scout car they got is bushed. Hatton will give them a jeep and a driver if they go to work on his leg.'

Adam was astonished. 'Hatton will make a deal? Major Hatton will make a deal with army property?'

'Why not?' Jarra said. 'That goddam leg's army property.'

Adam smiled. Jarra watched him urgently. 'The thing is, you can set it up, Adam. You take a look at that leg and lay it on the line for the Quakers.'

Adam continued to be surprised at the sentiment and urgency in

65

Jarra. 'Can you imagine Major Mark Hatton taking his pants down for me?'

Jarra gripped Adam's arm. 'We talked about it. He wants it. I told him I'd get you down there tonight.'

Jarra had telephoned the compound. At the guardhouse they showed identity cards and signed in. Adam was moved by more than curiosity. He was thinking of the Quakers. They could do with the friendship of Major Hatton. They could certainly use decent transport.

Hatton waited in his office in the pre-fab administration hut. He had drinks and glasses on the desk.

'You know Doc Thomson, Mark?'

'That I do. How are you, Doctor? Sam, you know where the freezer is. Get a little ice in here.'

When they had their drinks they sat and talked, mostly about Saigon.

'Nothing's changed. The city's full of Viet fat cats. The blackmarket looks like a stateside PX. The correspondents get liquored up every night in the Continental or the Caravelle.'

'You hit the girlie-bars, Mark?'

Hatton smiled. 'Not this time, Sam. I didn't have the steam.'

'Well, Doc, you want to see the leg?'

They used the adjutant's office.

Hatton had been hit eight times, between the hip and the knee, six times by rifle fire and twice by grenade fragments. He had a hole in his flank like a cup. There was a steel pin in the bone.

'I went down in jungle country. Charlie couldn't see much of me. But he kept right on sending it in at the little patch of cloth he could see. It was hard to take it without jumping the leg. Charlie didn't know which end of me was which. When the choppers hit the co-ordinate I crawled out of there.'

Adam left Hatton to dress. When he followed, jaw muscles tight, he poured a drink before speaking.

'What do you think, Doc? Don't mind Sam.'

'It's a remarkable job, Major. You've had a fine surgeon. I think they're right about the nerve.'

'Is it reversible or is it not?'

'I can't say. Mind you, this is not my speciality. At the risk of being irresponsible, I would think it is.'

Hatton's face did not change. He thrust out his hand. 'I want to thank you, Doc.'

The casualty locked in reception remained mostly in coma the next day. Dr Darder continued injecting streptomycin every four hours, more out of habit than hope. He would have moved the man to the dying shed except for fear of another insane outburst.

Darder was helping in the operating theatre, the nurse arranging instruments on the trolley.

'I forget,' she said, 'that mad one die.'

Darder nodded. 'So much for streptomycin.'

It was because he had been locked in reception that the body was not removed. Darder looked in and cursed. He was about to shout when he noticed the lump in one armpit. Darder moved closer. Both armpits were lumped. Under the smooth, brown skin of the corpse a tinge of blackening showed. Darder pushed at it with his fingers, making white dimples.

They stood at the litter, the door shut behind them.

Darder said, 'Look here, under the dressing.'

'Could be bruising from the wound.'

'It's too new. What do you think, Adam?'

'I don't know. Have you seen this before?'

Darder shook his head.

'Where did he come from? Was he one of the Chu Lai transfers?'

'No. He walked in. I saw him arrive. He can't have come a great distance.'

'Maybe nurse will know something.'

'What should I do with the body, Adam?'

'Have them burn it. Get his mattress and burn that too. Burn this litter. Have the room fumigated. I will talk to the nurse.'

The dead man had been a charcoal burner. His village was fifteen kilometres into the hills. That evening Adam and Pedro Darder sat up over copies of Military Medicine. Next morning, a WHO man left for the hill village with two Vietnamese and a heap of bamboo traps.

They made the autopsy, Darder using the knife. Diagnosis was the Spaniard's speciality. He had opened five of the rats trapped in the village. On the sixth he looked up, tightened a clamp and let out his breath. He began to cut again.

'Subcutaneous congestion, diffuse ... Occhymosis ... enlarged lymph nodes ... blood-stained fluid in serous cavities ... spleen enlarged, deeply congested ... congested lungs.'

Darder laid down the scalpel. 'Diagnosis: Pasteurella pestis. It's the plague, Adam.'

67

IO

In the next two weeks thirty-six men, women and children from the charcoal burner's village died in the jungle quarantine they had been removed to after their homes were fired. Immediately after the autopsy on the infected rat, Adam sat all night at the telephone trying to make contact with Saigon. The VC had cut communications. Late the next afternoon he reached the director of the Pasteur Institute. They had little comfort for each other. Plague had been reported in twenty-two of the twenty-nine provinces north of Saigon. The Institute dispatched vaccine and an observer.

Day after day, wobbling with fatigue, the volunteers worked the camps, inoculating for plague. There were forty thousand refugees crowded into shelters around Quong Lo. Night after night, in red-eyed exhaustion the men tossed in apprehension of tomorrow. If the plague should reach the camps, breed there in the fetid hooches where families barely had body room, there could be no remedy. The entire province would become a dying shed.

Sam Jarra said, 'I've seen goddamned rats as big as Alsatians. Up in the Highlands in this village I was in after a firefight, you couldn't goddam hear yourself talk for these rats crunching on the John Does. The stink's fit to lift you out of your boots. If you slapped a saddle on some of these rats you could run them in the Kentucky Derby. They're so full of raw meat and spunk they get up on their hind legs and fight. Man, if the plague hits these camps the war's over. Here goes the whole goddam country.'

The plague did not reach the camps at Quong Lo, although there were many deaths in the hills.

Sam Jarra said it for them all. 'The only way you can figger it, somebody up there likes us. It ain't on account of me, man. I never lived right in my life.'

The rains came and submerged Quong Lo, turning the refugee camps into new misery. The Viet Cong and the guerrilla forces came out of their holes, ranging the countryside, raiding outposts, protected from air strike by the swirling grey clouds. The American forces turned to defence. Day and night the artillery lobbed shells into the free fire zones cleared of civilians in the big relocations. From the helicopters that crabbed beneath the cloud cover and emerged out of mist, the familiar whack of the motors strangely muffled, the countryside was seen as an endless spotting of shell and bomb craters, the few standing remains of villages and hamlets stuck in the mud like bones.

Respiratory infections and the endemic skin, ear and eye diseases stalked the huddled bodies in the camps. Gutters choked on muck and spilled into the bamboo-framed hooches. The packed earth of pathways greased and ran. The paddy patches used as latrines, encrusted by the sun before the monsoon, lifted layers of human dung under the hammering of the rains and floated the mess over the crumbling earth walls.

Sam Jarra left his rubber boots at the door of the villa and walked in, his toes poking through holes in the socks. He sat down and wiggled them, rubbing his face.

'If I don't get to Saigon or Da Nang I'm going to explode. What are we trying to do out here? We trying to kill these people or save them? Like Hatton says, it's a half-assed war. First you blow 'em up, then you sew 'em up. You hear what happened last night in the Catholic camp? The VC comes in and burns about seventy hooches. I'm short a hundred hooches already out there. How they get them to burn in this weather I don't know. I can't light a goddam cigarette.'

On the thirty kilometres to Chu Lai, where Task Force Nebraska waited out the rains in the sand hills on the coast—a conglomerate of huts and tent cities, of artillery emplacements and rocket batteries, of ammunition dumps, tank squadrons and the stilted looming watch-towers striding the wastes to the battalions on the perimeter—the VC again and again cut the road.

In the first light of each morning, armoured patrol carriers and tanks rumbled along, searching for mines to destroy. Three times in three weeks troops were killed and wounded by claymores set a little off the road and exploded by remote control.

In the hills a small settlement was struck in the first stirrings of dawn. An outpost of South Vietnamese, a pacification unit, left their bunkers and ran. The VC destroyed the village in a sweep, kicking open doors, spraying bullets at the dark, rolling grenades into the huts and trenches. Many of those who survived the killing died afterwards in the hospital. Dr Darder believed they were weakened by terror of the strange surroundings.

Hatton came each day, late in the afternoon, his reserve a little broached now. Adam recognized that it was hard for Hatton to admit need of weakness, and had suggested his use of the operating theatre. It was contained and private there. The bearded Quaker who admini-stered the therapy remained taciturn, perhaps uneasy in his conscience to have a professional soldier under his hands.

Adam had been in the jammed orthopaedic ward on the day that Hatton first arrived. The Major had asked for Dr Thomson and stood in the door. Adam went to him, stepping over the litters.

Hatton said tensely, 'What happened here?'

'What do you mean, Major?'

'This.'

Adam was puzzled for a minute.

'This? It's always like this. Like this or worse. Haven't you been here before?'

'No.'

Hatton's smooth hard jaw bunched in muscle.

The Vietnamese on the jammed beds and litters stared at the uni-formed figure, eyes wide and fearful, the small-boned men and women seeming more child-like than ever because of their huddling for com-fort, the tattered variety of their clothing, their slant-eyed, staring apprehension. Relatives squatted, cooking in tins on tiny spirit stoves. At the ward's far end a very old man leaned over his daughter, clearing her tracheotomy with a rubber tube. The air stank with sweat, corruption and medication.

'This is the other side of your war, Major. For every casualty the army takes there are a hundred or more like this. Perhaps a quarter, or a third, ever get to a hospital. Hospital is the courtesy word we use for places like this.'

Hatton looked up, face and eyes hard. 'Show me the rest of it.'

The little boy was perhaps six or seven. He had been brought in with an elder brother. Adam had amputated the brother's arm, high up on the shoulder. The stump became infected. For a week the smaller child shared his brother's litter. When his brother died, at night, there was difficulty next morning separating the living child from the cold body. From that moment no voice, no sense, no response could be got from him. He refused the Vietnamese nurse's persuadings, but would not leave the compound. The nurse named him Ho and saw that he was fed.

Adam was pulling at the hood of his jeep, lashing it tighter to the frame with gut and a surgical needle, the dumb boy beside him, when Mark Hatton walked out from his first treatment.

'Still here, Doctor?'

'Last operation for the day, Major. This thing just gave me another shower.'

Hatton came up.

'It's shot. You need a new hood. Maybe I can get you one.'

Ho had turned then. Suddenly, with croaking whimpers, he rushed to Adam's legs, pulling at the trousers, burying his head, pushing and shaking.

'What's up?' Adam said. 'What's the matter? Ho, what's got into you?'

He spoke the few Vietnamese words he had learned to quiet and comfort. Then he frowned. Half carrying the boy, half walking him on the leg wrapped with both arms, Adam struggled up the verandah steps and turned into the building.

Mark Hatton flexed the old wound. It was probably imagination, it had to be, but the leg felt better, less bound in some way, more alive. When Adam returned, Hatton smiled, 'You got some kind of problem there?'

'He's dumb. Shock I think. That's the most noise I've heard him make in a month.'

'Something sure spooked him.'

71

'I think it was the uniform.'

Hatton was about to nod. His face chilled. He turned his eyes on Adam. 'You mean this uniform?'

'I'm afraid so. It sometimes happens with the young ones after a relocation.'

Hatton continued to stare, his face dead and cold. 'You believe that? It was the uniform?'

Adam stared back. 'I believe it.'

He could hear Hatton's breathing, feel the rise in his own pulse, feel the threat of something unidentified prickling on his skin. Then Hatton turned away.

'Good night.'

Adam had tried for an hour to answer the letter, tearing off pages, beginning again, trying to find a way to say it. It was hard because it was not certain in him, because decision was swung on a pendulum, because he did not understand it himself and lacked energy for the effort. He knew that something had changed. He could feel it as distinctly as a physical dislocation, like an organ repositioned.

How could he explain this reality to the make-believe he had known? It got into a man like calcium into the bones. It shrunk the horizon to one battered strip of Asia, one province, one miserable, ugly town. If he left now, it would be looking over his shoulder; he would stumble on the future out of involvement in the past.

Adam lay on his cot, the fan groaning above him, and re-read his partner's urgent letter. The practice had been everything to him. But there was something here that he had to know, something final, something he could sense but not grasp. He would wait a little longer.

Distant explosions whumped the mosquito screens. The letter fell from Adam's fingers.

Hatton woke in darkness. Immediately his hand was on the leg, fingers clamped.

I think it's the uniform.

There had been no anger in the dream. Thomson's face was clear and hard, his long hair rising and streaming, as Hatton had seen hair stream on corpses under water. He smashed it with his fist, feeling no bone, leaving no mark on the image dissolving. Sobs of frustration shook him.

They had been caught in the open paddy. The point man was

72

signalling, hitting the ground, when his body exploded in puffs of flesh and cloth. Orange flames sprayed at them from the tree-line. Hatton could not hear the commands he shouted as men splayed and jerked in the dust. The weapon shattered in his hand. He was on his side behind the dyke, saw machine-gun bullets eat the earth. He twisted and shouted, dirt in his mouth, but his throat made no sound in the iron clamour. They were running for the dykes, twisting, bent, their own bullets discharged without aim. Mortars gulfed up the earth. Huddled figures in the open, arms clasped about their helmets, uncurled, crawled, broke to bend and run, slumped, screamed, cartwheeled over.

The ·45 was under him. He scrabbled a hole in the dirt, searching for the butt, pressed on the earth with all his weight. A body hit the dyke beside him. Hatton wrenched himself over, got the ·45 free. He could only distinguish the soldier's rolling eyes. The face was a pulped mess of blood. Silence rushed in his ears like another awful explosion. The man beside him pointed, his teeth shining in the blood as he struggled to speak. Bolts of lightning streaked the paddy, fire-balled in the tree-line. The first helicopter emptied its rocket pods and shot away. Hatton was on his knees, shouting for a move.

The village the jungle had hidden was laid bare. Thatch burned. Bodies, intestines, bits of bodies smoked on the ground, hung on the limbs of smashed trees. A few women, old men and children, crawled and screamed in the wreckage, stripped naked by concussion, parts of them incindered and smoking. A young man ran on the edge of the village, clutched his gut and fell. A soldier fired his carbine into him.

Did he want to go back? The Communists had started the killing, and they had to be stopped. Somebody had to get the job done. It was his job. He was good at it and proud, it used all of a man to be good. There were no lies, no self-deceits you could allow yourself and live. It was real the way nothing else in the world was real. You laid yourself square on the line and your buddies laid it there with you. You took your lumps and knew yourself to be a man beyond most men.

Hatton rubbed in the dark at the wound. If he could get over this one, get back to combat command, he'd make rank. He'd make rank because he was good.

On how many drops had he led his team to verify strength and location? He'd left his dead. He'd never left his wounded.

Had MacQuaid been dead? It was hard for MacQuaid to do what had to be done to stay alive. Hatton had got them out, half dead, but out. MacQuaid could have got them *all* killed.

Geneva Two

I I

As the Paris conference approached, Sarah Neveau saw little of her husband. It had been his habit to lunch occasionally at home, for relaxation, and to walk afterwards with little Guy in the public gardens near by. When the child began boarding, Neveau discontinued the custom. He was more frequently late in the evenings, preoccupied and edgy.

There was little in the apartment for Sarah to do. The elderly maid was unconceding about the mistress's efforts in French. She went about the work her own way, a routine which did not heed suggestion. If Sarah made a small rearrangement of furniture, the maid altered it back.

Sarah had met Molly Best at a coffee morning. The American women gave them for each other. She had accepted the invitation out of loneliness and a need to be among her own kind. But it was hard to share their talk of leaves spent at home, postings hoped for by their husbands, letters from children grown up enough to be in American schools and colleges.

'I'd like you to meet Sarah Neveau. Her husband is Swiss. Sarah lives in Geneva all the time.'

Molly Best was older than Sarah. They discovered that Sarah knew her husband. He was the Reuter's correspondent she had welcomed so warmly at Neveau's party.

'Why wasn't I there? Because that bastard Barney didn't tell me. He's at two and three cocktail parties a night when he isn't propping up the bar at the Press Club. If I ask him, darling, Barney's working.'

They had liked each other. Molly Best got her handbag and looked about for the hostess.

'I can't stand this another minute. If it isn't children or their husbands' salaries, they've got nothing, but nothing, to talk about. I'm going to get me a drink in some low bar.'

She had stopped and considered Sarah.

'You're a bit lost here yourself, aren't you? Why don't you cut-out with me?'

The Carousel was new, two plush bars and a small restaurant. Molly Best was known. She mounted a bar stool and waved at the men.

'Hi there, troops.'

It was glossy and strange to Sarah, daring to be drinking like this at midday, in the full flush of sunlight from the street. Men came and spoke, asking Molly if Barney was away on a job.

'They get a good crowd here. Most of them are Americans, UNO and the Embassy, a few visiting firemen.'

She questioned Sarah directly about herself. Where had she met her husband, how long had she been married, did she have children.

'I wanted kids once. Now I'm glad. I couldn't handle kids by myself. Barney's away eight months of the year. If Pompidou opens his big mouth, Barney's on the plane to Paris. If something happens in Poland, Barney's gone for a visa. If the Pope gets the cramps praying, Barney's off to Rome. For the last month he's been in Israel. You don't know how lucky you are to have a husband in bed every night.'

It was such a change, so easy and friendly. Sarah sipped her drink, the sunlight warm on her cheek. She felt lighter and younger than she had in ages.

'You're not happy, are you?'

Sarah was surprised, nervous.

'Happy? Yes, I think so.'

'Not. I can tell. It's something I always know about. Something's wrong. A woman like me can tell about another woman.'

Molly lit a cigarette clumsily.

'That bastard Barney. Away eight months of the year. What do you think Barney does? Goes to bed with a book? What am I expected to do?'

Sarah grasped for something to say. Molly Best seemed suddenly drunk.

'I'm built, you know. I'm built where it matters. If you see me naked I've got a girl's legs and hips. The only place my skin's not like silk is the face—wouldn't it have to be? I've spent more money on this face, with these thin lips. I should have a mouth like yours, the way I feel. That bastard Barney away eight months and I've got this face I don't feel like. Men, they're stupid. The first thing they look at is the face. Not her, her skin's bad. Where it matters I've got no bad skin. Where it matters I'm furnished like a divan with cushions. I'm built. You should see me.'

Molly Best drank her double whisky and reordered. She seemed to have forgotten Sarah. When the older woman spoke again her voice was knowing and sad.

'I know what you're thinking. Forget it. You're thinking I'm some kind of lesbian. Maybe it would be easier that way.'

She looked around her.

'You know why I come here, Sarah? I come here to make friends with a man. Maybe have dinner. If it's a young one, a kiss in the car and a pat on the head. If it's a hard one and he knows how to work me, it's a motel and heels in the air. Don't be shocked, kid. We're all women. All of us, we've got the same problems. I'm telling you this because you've got trouble. No, don't tell me no. You've got a husband who comes home. You've got your little boy. Stay with it. Make it work. The other thing is for the birds.'

In the apartment that evening, alone after Neveau's secretary had telephoned, Sarah continued to hear Molly Best, see the sudden desolation that had touched her. She dabbed at her cheeks and hair, wandered, lit cigarettes and forgot them. She had never heard a woman speak like that, she was unaccustomed to female confessions. How had she known and what had she known? It was inconceivable, terrifying, that she might know about Ted Mitchell. If she did, if something was known, God, others must know.

If it's a hard one and he knows how to work me, it's a motel and heels in the air.

She flushed at the image. It wasn't Molly Best, it was Sarah herself. It wasn't a motel, it was Madame Leopard. Sarah shivered with shame.

79

But she could not deny the lick of heat that further frightened and confused her.

If she could have Guy back, have him home the way it used to be, the vivid little face and chatter that she sometimes desperately missed, it could be mended. If only Martin would help. A little comradeship, tenderness, sharing. If he'd only unbend, be human. If only he would let her love him.

Sarah Neveau broke with Ted Mitchell, a disordered conversation from a coin telephone to his flat.

'You're being hysterical, Sarah. What has happened? Something has happened.'

'Nothing. Nothing has happened.'

'Sarah, what has happened?'

And then, coldly: 'Have it your own way, then. There's no reason for this. You're being silly. But have it your own way.'

Mitchell dismissed it. For weeks he hardly thought of Sarah Neveau. Nervous women like that were risky. He was well quit of her. But then unexpectedly he missed her. It irritated, then angered him. He had let her play house, that was the trouble. He had let her get too damn close. He had talked too much and let her talk too much. He wouldn't make that mistake again.

Years ago, Sarah used to call Neveau every day. Pointless little conversations with an item of news about something she had bought, or heard in a letter, or to ask what would please him for dinner. She tried again now. At first Neveau was a little surprised, even pleased, but soon there was no response to her banter. He was busy and yes, Sarah, what is it? What is it you want to say, Sarah?

She began to study French again, spending hours at it, struggling with the accent she could never get right, playing the records over and over only to hear the triumphant, ineradicable, flat Bostonese make a mockery of her efforts.

She tried a few phrases, casually, as though they had just slipped out. Neveau looked pained. 'What language is that?'

They slept on single beds, a small table between them. Neveau usually read before turning out the light, Sarah lay on her side, a little make-up under her eyes, a touch of rouge on her lips, eyes open, smiling at her husband when she caught his attention. It worried him, distracted his concentration. He turned a little, for privacy.

The weekends, with little Guy at home, full of stories to tell, had been the happiest times. Now he had become almost gravely adult, stern about his homework, wanting to wear his school blazer on outings to the lake or the cinema. He had made great progress in French and German. His father spoke to him in these languages, correcting his grammar, encouraging the child with praise. Desperately, Sarah tried to enter their conversations. Guy would shriek with laughter. No, Mama, like this, in the throat.

She was in a pit. The walls were sand. The sand was slowly sliding beneath her.

When Neveau did approach her she took him wildly, doing new things, uncaring that he might wonder, uncaring of his tiredness, fierce to rouse him again. He did wonder at her and in his way did respond.

She was falling asleep when it startled her awake. As she had heaved at him, eyes shut, teeth gritted, wishing for destruction, the clear image of the man she held and entwined had been Ted Mitchell, not her husband.

Neveau and Sarah had eaten dinner. He was considering an inspection of the Arab Refugee Camps. The Israelis had lodged a fierce complaint that the camps on their border had become centres for terrorist raids, that Red Cross medical supplies were used for the dressing of terrorist wounded.

Neveau had bathed after dinner and changed for bed, he was tired. Now he sat in a robe before the television set and waited for the nightly news review. In the apartment above them a tap splashed steadily. The new building had been ill-designed for acoustics. The plumbing was loud in the walls. Neveau turned up the volume.

Later, when he switched off and was about to drink the hot milk he took as a night-cap, an unplugged bath began to gurgle, sounding the sitting-room wall in its fall.

Neveau banged the cup on its saucer. His raised voice brought Sarah from the kitchen.

'Did you call, Martin?'

Neveau was in his study, complaining on the telephone to the concierge. It was well past ten o'clock. Twice this week the bath above them had been used after ten. The concierge would see that it did not happen again.

Sarah was distressed.

'Oh, Martin. Did you have to do that? What will they think? They're such nice people.'

'If they were nice people they would have more consideration. They know the rules.'

'Rules, the rules. It's always the rules. Have you no tolerance or charity?'

Neveau looked at her hard. She was frankly angry, white, her hands shaking.

'You might live like that in America, Sarah. But here we have civilized rules, rules of consideration for others.'

'I'm sick of your rules, do you hear? I'm sick to death of them. You don't live yourself, and you won't let anything around you live.'

Neveau was shaken now. He said, uncertainly, 'Control yourself, Sarah, you're shouting.'

'I want to shout. You know why? It's the American in me. The vulgar American. It's the emotional Jewess in me.'

She couldn't stop now. She was choking on sobs. She didn't care what happened.

'Sarah, that's enough. What's wrong with you?'

'You know what's wrong with me. I'm not Swiss. That's what's wrong. Why did you ever marry me?'

He had no precedent for this. No precedent for the realizations that suddenly churned in him, strange and unwelcome and confusing. He wanted to shout back, a sudden heave of passion to match hers. Yes, you're one of them. One of the trouble-makers of the world. You're right, yes, you're right. Why did I ever marry you? For an instant he was powerful with hostility, a liberating rush that focused other frustrations. He wanted to leap at her, beat her down, feel her claws on his face. Then it sagged in him, dropped off his body like a weight. He went to her, speaking softly, his voice sad and tender.

'I'm sorry to have upset you, dear. Here, Sarah, let us forget it.'

But it was too late for that.

'Don't touch me. Don't touch me. Let me alone.'

She wrenched herself away and ran sobbing to the bedroom. For a long time Neveau stood in the silence, his bland face worried by confusion and revelation.

Pierre Salem had witnessed the change in himself with an almost detached interest. There were two of him now, one over the other, blurring both images like photographs imposed. The reserve which he had compounded by will years ago had thawed. He could feel it distinctly, as a melting. There was a pleasure now and even a need in the human contacts of the day. An excitement of involvement that touched him physically. Not the dead part, not there, but on his skin and his step and his voice.

Salem had never known the yearning or spur of ambition. It was in him now and it was the most awakening thing he had known. It was more than ambition for objective achievement. It was ambition for himself, a demand from the ego that had at first shocked him.

A dinner party had been given for a visiting member of the Nobel Prize Committee. He had remarked the long association of their two institutions. The first Nobel Prize, in 1905, had been awarded to Henri Dunant, the Red Cross founder. The only Peace Prize announced during the First World War had been conferred on the ICRC, and again in 1944. In the year of the Red Cross Centenary the Nobel Prize had been jointly awarded to the International Committee and the League of Red Cross Societies.

Salem had tingled. A Nobel Prize. A Nobel Prize for the Humanitarian Law. Salem's Law.

For a month Martin Neveau had been uninvolved with Salem other than on matters of routine. They were easier now with each other. Salem's lightened manner helped. Neveau was absorbed in liaisons with the Standing Committee on questions of the Paris Conference.

The League of Red Cross Societies had been founded in Paris, immediately following the First World War, at the initiative of the chairman of the American Red Cross war council. In the years since its founding in 1919, the League had launched hundreds of international appeals for the victims of natural disasters, alerting its member societies, co-ordinating operations, arranging a vast logistic of food, clothing, shelter, bedding, medicine and simple human solace. Out of its Geneva headquarters the League co-ordinated the work of its society members, answered to the International Committee and represented its one hundred and thirteen national members at the United Nations and its related agencies, spoke for them to governments.

For weeks the ICRC, the League and the Standing Committee had been drafting an agenda for the 21st Congress. Requests and suggestions from the National Societies were passed to the ICRC by the League. Neveau had met that morning with Robert Collins, the American Negro who was the League Chairman. The Israeli Red Cross membership petition had again raised the question of its symbol.

Collins was a big man, light-skinned, with a small moustache, a graduate in law. He had been a distinguished civil rights worker and an administrator of President Kennedy's Peace Corps.

'Now, Martin, as I understand it, the International Conference of 1863, in Article 8 of the resolutions, chose as the distinguishing mark of

83

voluntary medical personnel a white armlet with a red cross. The authors of the Geneva Convention later adopted the red cross on a white ground. Is that right?'

Neveau said, 'Will this never be settled? The Israelis have been told time and again that the Red Cross had no religious significance.'

'This is a new approach. They accept that the symbol does not imply the Christian cross directly, but it has the association because something similar was worn by the crusaders.'

'Damn and blast them. They've worried us about this for a year. Nobody is absolutely sure what the founders had in mind. It is believed that the 1906 Convention adopted the reversal of the Swiss flag as a compliment, but nobody knew if the founders intended that in 1863. All this nuisance began with the breaking of the rules laid down in the Charter. The Turks changed the symbol to a red crescent during the Russo-Turkish war. They said the red cross offended Muslim soldiers. The 1929 diplomatic conference recognized it, but stressed the absence of any religious significance. Then Iran wanted a red lion and sun, because they're Muslims of the Shia branch, to be distinguished from Turkey. I won't permit this to be debated. The Shield of David is an overt religious symbol. We can't have it and we won't have it.'

Collins wore a pearl stick pin in his tie. He had the habit, when in thought, of rolling a finger-tip on it. He mused for a time.

'It's very awkward. There's a lot doing out there. We need the Israeli chapter in the League. It would mean some kind of *rapprochement* between them and the Arab societies. They're emotional about this.'

Neveau had withdrawn his attention. Sarah had never burst out like that before. Her individuality had been submerged in his. She had never displayed such emotion.

'Emotion won't do,' Neveau said firmly, 'we have to go by the rules.'

'I expect so. Well, we can only try to reason again.'

The manner of Salem's presentation of the Vietnamese documents to the chairman of the American Society, the personal and peremptory call for a declaration of war, had caused anger and upset in Washington, as Martin Neveau had expected. The photographs of the burned children had so offended the American League that only a mention was made of 'photographed propaganda' when the documents were forwarded to the Department of Defense.

Questions were asked in important places about the new ICRC President, his background, his history, the manner of his election.

By a resolution adopted at the International Conference of the Red Cross in 1921, it had been declared 'that the Red Cross, feeling it is not enough to work in time of peace, intends to work for peace'.

In 1946 the board of governors stated that 'a most important task of the league and the National Red Cross Societies lies in everyday effort to preserve peace and in gathering all forces and means together in order to prevent future world wars.'

A resolution of 1965 appealed to all governments to reach agreement on the ban of all nuclear weapons and on general and complete disarmament under effective international controls. The International Committee of the Red Cross was encouraged to undertake every effort likely to contribute to the settlement of possible armed conflicts, and to be associated, in agreement with the states concerned, in any appropriate measures to that end.

Most governments subscribed to these pieties. The ICRC had been frequently used as an honest broker in secret manoeuvres. It was there as are priests, its function understood and ordained. It existed by discretion, absolute impartiality; any initiative implied politics.

In agreement with the states concerned. Did Salem's note implicate the ICRC in a covert agreement? Political noses that let nothing pass quivered a little and wondered.

The Ambassador handed Joseph Richter a file.

'This came in today's bag. Since you're on the team for Paris, you might study it. Have you met President Salem?'

'No, sir. He's rather exclusive.'

'But you have the ear of the Executive Director. How do you judge his relations with the President?'

Richter wasn't sure, afraid to make a mistake. 'I think, in general opinion, they might not be in sympathy. In some ways, not altogether in sympathy about policy.'

'Richter, when Neveau mentioned that President Salem had considered publicizing that Hanoi propaganda, do you suppose he might have intended you to report it back?'

Again, Richter was unsure. Confidences with his Ambassador were unnerving. If Neveau, for his own reasons, had used him would that make his position laughable or would it not imply a confidence? That he had made the report and it now seemed important, was not that proof of alertness of judgement?

'To be frank, sir, I don't know. In retrospect it seems likely.'

The Ambassador gave a tiny smile. Richter's reply had pleased him.

'I'm not sure myself, Richter, what all this involves. There's a suspicion that the unfavourable publicity that emanated from here, the scientists' protest about bacterial and biological weapons, their concern about the plague, might well have been inspired. Our Government is in a very sensitive position just now. It's as well we should know our friends. Keep your eyes and ears open.'

Joseph Richter's looming figure strode the corridor at full height. It was happening. He had only been in Geneva a year. He was on confidential terms with the Ambassador.

The Ambassador considered his own formal meetings with Salem. He had thought him a cold fish. An old school European, inclined to look down his nose. Perhaps he would bear watching.

12

FOR twenty-five years the narrow strip of Asia had been steeped in blood and suffering. The wreckage of bodies had become a mountain too awful for conscience to excuse. Japanese imperialism, French colonialism and now strategic political interest had exploded in steel on two generations of an illiterate peasantry for whom there was nowhere to hide.

Weariness and doubt, pity, fear and outrage, coalesced in a loudening protest that broke violently around the world. In the National Societies, at the League headquarters and the ICRC, from individuals, unions and institutions, came calls and demands for action.

Immovably, in committee debates, Neveau refused to consider any suggestion of unilateral initiative. He had made an estimate of the members' attitudes, had taken his private soundings. He had shrewdly identified Salem's support and calculated its minority. These men were finally concerned with the strength and survival of the movement; it was laid in their charge, the unique creation and pride of their country.

They had no need to answer Salem as they pushed back their chairs.

'I wonder if one day, gentlemen, we might keep the ICRC and lose the world?'

It was on Neveau's motion that a resolution was carried to call for talks that could lead to peace. The ICRC offered itself to all parties in any role that might be useful as an intermediary. The past history of its successful interventions was recalled. The resolution satisfied and relieved the committee.

Salem recognized the disparagement implied in Neveau's motion. It would give him less time to spend on the Humanitarian Law.

In all the world's areas of civil conflict, the Geneva Conventions were as dead in letter as the mandates of the old League of Nations. In Vietnam the terrible arsenal of doomsday weapons incinerated troops and civilians without restraint or conscience behind the pretext of an undeclared war. For the first time in centuries, honour in arms was not even a pretence. Man, the most savage animal, ran blood-crazed on earth while his science manufactured pestilence and sought the secrets of the destruction of the environment.

In two world wars of unparalleled slaughter the Conventions had reaffirmed the distinction between man and animal. In the great works of charity and mercy there had been hope for the future in the present. There was nothing now, no bridle or curb, save the isolated demonstrations of protest. Worse, in the dead letter of the Conventions was the complacent belief that they lived. The necessary comfort good people take to blank their eyes to horror.

Now, Salem knew, there could only be one alternative to conflagration. The monolithic law he laboured at, a law with penalties, not a set of conventions to be debated at will. Salem's Law. A law to end war. When he thought about it his heart hammered. His eyes burned and his spirit leapt.

But meanwhile there was now. Something had to be done in the now.

It was many, many years since Château Malraux had been opened for entertainment. When he came back to live there permanently, as a young man after his divorce, Salem had moved into a suite of four rooms. The remainder of the house had not been shut away. Signora Cenci and the maid dusted there each day. The doors to the main receiving room and the big lounge were always open, the heavy curtains drawn for light. Salem often walked there, among the

88

antiques and paintings, the reminders of his parents, all the house and all that was in it an unbroken connective to childhood.

When he had returned he had been unable to bear the shrouded furniture, the deadness of bolted doors. It had been too much like the deadness inside him.

Salem had twice given dinner parties in the big house on the hill. When he first instructed her, Signora Cenci had gasped and thrown up her hands. Her wits deserted her in excitement. She couldn't remember where the good service of plate was stored, or the brandy goblets or the special table linen. She dithered for days over menus. Massimo was measured for a new white jacket and four pairs of cotton gloves to serve in. The maid was set to cleaning and polishing. It was impossible not to be infected by the bustle and fuss of preparation. Salem spent an entire evening with Massimo in the cellar he had not entered in almost twenty years, coughing dust, sweeping aside cobwebs, hunting the bins for long-forgotten storings.

The dinner was to be for eight guests. Signora Cenci repeatedly rehearsed the dressing of the table, changing the plate and silver for Salem's opinion. He had left the dining-room when he realized that Signora Cenci had set ten places.

'For your guests, Signor, yourself, and the signora.'

'But there will be no signora.'

'It is not possible. It lacks grace. A house must have a hostess. There is the question of withdrawing, the question of wraps, the question of coiffures. There can be questions of pins, questions of elastic. It is too delicate to discuss.'

Signora Cenci was determined, even a little shocked. Salem had not provided for this, the thought had not existed.

'You could advise the ladies, surely, on the question of your questions, Signora Cenci. Hedda can take the wraps.'

'Impossible. It is not my place. I will be concerned in the kitchen. Hedda is for cleaning, not for the wraps of the ladies. An arrangement must be made. It is expected.'

There was no arrangement Salem could make. In all Geneva there was not an unattached woman whom he knew well enough to ask her to receive his guests. The two wives of old friends with whom he was at ease were attending the party with their husbands. Fanny, the secretary who had accompanied him from the Bank, was not remotely possible.

It had reminded Salem of his singularity, disturbing him again, invoking the need to retreat, an impulse to withdraw the invitations.

Hedda had done well enough with the wraps, but it was more difficult at table, and afterwards there was nobody to lead the women's conversations, to provide them interest and entertainment of their own.

It had distracted Salem from his purpose of the evening, which was to interest the eminent German philosopher in the new Humanitarian Law. He and old Rudi had discussed with excitement a world seminar of great minds, a resource of the rarest intellects and spirits for whom the law would be the crown of mankind's achievement.

On that occasion, Rudi and his wife had stayed behind the other guests. While Salem and Rudi talked before the drawing-room fire, his wife dozed there, a small, motherly woman some few years younger than her husband, her hands clasped on a velvet evening bag, a pearl necklace looped to her lap.

'He sees it all, Pierre. He sees it as clearly as we do. Do you know what he told me? He said, "I have waited long for this." We can depend on him. Oh yes, there are great things happening. Great things.' The old man turned the brandy in his glass, bent to the bouquet.

Salem's face shone with excitement, his eyes fixed on the fire.

'Great things,' Rudi said again. 'This brandy is one of them. There is much to be said for moderation. A good wine, a good brandy, I have taken pleasure in these all my life. I continue to do so, perhaps because of moderation.'

The old man looked fondly at his wife.

'Look how gently she sleeps, like a child.'

He mused and gazed about him.

'This is a beautiful home, Pierre. I well recall your father before this fire.'

Old Rudi was not far himself from sleep.

'What this house needs, it needs small children in it, Pierre. How well I recall the happiness we had when our children were small. Small children are like flowers in a house. I have always liked the German word *Kindergarten*. A garden of children. Pierre, why did you never remarry? You should have remarried and brought this house small children.'

Salem had turned as grey as death.

'Martha and I have often wondered about it. Young Pierre Salem, with a great name and everything to offer that a good woman could desire.'

Salem's lips moved to speak. He said nothing.

The old man frowned. 'What is it? You don't look very well. Surely I've not caused offence?'

Salem rose and took his goblet to the sideboard, answering with his back turned. 'Of course not. How could you? I do feel a little upset. The sauce, perhaps. I don't believe I will take more brandy.'

'My dear boy, pour yourself a glass of mineral water. It is excellent for the digestion. In any case, we should all be in bed. Poor Martha is sleeping like a child.'

Salem said, still turned, 'Shall I have the car called then, Rudi?'

The Chairmanship of the League was a prestigious one. It had been mooted for Collins soon after the early distinction of his work with Kennedy's Peace Corps. Now, he had served a term in Geneva, with that authority about him, the administration had other plans for him.

The bullets in Dallas had taken that as they had taken so much else. Collins watched the agony at home in bitterness and frustration. He waited, chafing, for the Paris Conference, his resignation prepared.

Salem sensed the tensions in him, not out of political or racial understanding but through his intuition of deformity, of the vague unease of the big Negro's presence on the two occasions they had met on formal gatherings at the American Embassy.

Salem needed Collins's support, freely given and freely understood. He needed a sympathy between them. The Humanitarian Law could be a beginning of that. The Law would provide for racism. Salem resolved on an entertainment at Château Malraux.

Robert Collins's wife was with him in Geneva. She was a quiet woman, awkward in company. It posed the difficulty about which Signora Cenci remained unsatisfied. If Mrs Collins should prove ill at ease, it would be difficult to relax her husband. Salem was resentful of this absurd complication in his life.

Neveau said, 'The Earl's visit is informal. But as a member of the British Committee it is customary that he should pay a call. His daughter is with us, you know. She has been working with Mitchell.'

'I did not know that.'

'It was arranged.'

'I presume you have met the Earl, Martin. No? Could you not lunch him? With perhaps one or two of the Committee, the Chairman of the League?'

'It is customary to be received by the President.'

Salem said, 'Very well, then, if that is the custom. Perhaps a cocktail before you lunch.'

It struck him then that this could be a beginning with Robert Collins. An informal gathering in a public place, without the constraints of office or business. 'Perhaps, after all, I might join you. Would that be in order?'

The final arrangement was thoroughly unexpected. Salem had supposed a private room perhaps in the Hotel Belvedere. On the way, in the Bentley, Neveau tried to explain that the Earl had insisted on giving them lunch. Neveau was nervous about the address. It was not in the favourable quarter.

'Can this be it? Surely not.' Neveau inspected the fishing nets and crossed oars arranged about the entrance.

The chauffeur said, 'This is the address, sir.'

There were more nets inside, with glass floats, lobster pots, corks, a skiff filled with green plants. Fish swam in a tank, a landing-net against it. There was another smaller room with a bar at the end, decorated with sea shells. A large balding man with side-whiskers stood at the bar talking with two women, Robert Collins, a member of the International Committee and a stout little man strange to Neveau and Salem.

'Ah, Neveau, there you are.' The big man with the whiskers walked towards them, his hand out. 'And this is President Salem? Honoured to have your company, sir. I knew your predecessor well.'

Neveau said weakly, 'President Salem, allow me to present——'

'Peregrine Stirling. Perry for short. Now, you must meet the ladies. This is my daughter Jane, who tells me she knows you by sight. This is Phoebe Rutherford, who does something or other at the United Nations. President Salem, ladies, and his Executive Director, Martin Neveau. Tubby Williams, First Nonsense at the British Embassy. And these other gentlemen, of course, are your colleagues.'

He turned to the bar. 'Now let me order you a drink. For my part I recommend the Black Velvet. Tubby and I were rather late to bed. We find that a drop of Guinness and Champers knits up the raddled sleeve of care.'

Neveau's discomfort spared Salem his own surprise. They both accepted the stout and Champagne pressed upon them. Neveau put the tankard to his mouth, flushed and dabbed his frothed lips with a handkerchief.

'Hope you enjoy seafood, President. I've known this place for ages.'

Robert Collins looked at Salem, who stood a little stiffly. Then he smiled, his big brown face lighting, the rich voice amused. 'The food really is good, President. The fera is the best in the lake.'

Jane Stirling left the bar. She spoke to Neveau, using French, addressing him as 'Monsieur le Directeur'.

'I apologize for being here. I hope it is not too awkward. My father simply telephoned and ordered me to lunch.'

'Of course,' Neveau said, without conviction; 'perfectly proper.'

Jane turned to Salem, smiling.

'I am sure you would be much more comfortable if I took your hat, President.'

Salem was grateful.

Jane added softly, 'Please don't drink that if you'd prefer something else. Daddy is convinced that all the world shares his tastes.'

There were others in the restaurant. The waiters moved in a cheerful clatter. The plump English First Secretary talked easily with the committee member. The sun beamed a dazzled light through a roof panel over the bar, addling the wisping cigarette smoke.

For an instant, Salem felt young, unconcerned. The taste of other times rose in him. The elegant carriage, always constrained, eased a little. There was curiosity and frankness in his smile as he thanked Jane Stirling. 'The drink is very pleasing. In this much I do share your father's tastes.'

The Earl said loudly, 'I was just telling the League Chairman I had a long talk with his countryman, Dr Luther King, in Washington. Not a difficult chap at all. Got on together splendidly. Shall we have the other half before we sit down?'

The small room was reserved to themselves. There was no menu. Jane's father had ordered for everybody. 'If you have preferences, gentlemen, discuss them with my daughter. She's mother today. My French is abominable. Tubby will assure you on that score.'

There was talk about the civil war in Nigeria, where the English League had been active. Jane's father said she knew Africa, had been out there with Schweitzer. It caused a general interest. She and Robert Collins talked seriously about it.

'He wanted nothing changed,' she said. 'He wanted to keep it the way it had always been. He was a very inflexible, overwhelming man. He disapproved, for instance, of electric light.'

When the fera was served, after clam soup and langouste, and the Earl's choice of wines with each course, it had become a pleasant party. Jane Stirling had seated the Earl and Salem at opposite ends of the

93

table; Salem had Jane and Robert Collins at his left and right. The Earl had Neveau and the First Secretary on his. The girl from the United Nations sat opposite the Committee member, a retired diplomat of grave habit. This atmosphere, more effective perhaps for the surprise of it, the Earl boisterous and blandly unaware of possible incongruity, made it easy for Salem. He was able to mention his Law, and advise Collins that he would welcome his view. The Negro was warmly interested. It was understood that Salem would explain at a more suitable time and place.

Neveau had recovered and eaten well. When they rose for their leave-takings, a little formal again, he was almost gay, suggesting that Jane might stay with her father and that he would answer for Mitchell.

In the Bentley he wound down the window.

'An excellent lunch I thought, President. A surprising place to choose, perhaps. But I thought the man himself surprising. How did he recognize me? We had never met.'

'I imagine his daughter described us. What exactly does she do for the Press Officer? She's a most accomplished young woman.'

13

MICK EAST had forgotten about the cigarette packet after he settled the nag in his memory. He had his own pride in his powers. The documentation had been added to Rudolf Kleinberg's file and left open-ended. Janos Kisch had been informed in Berlin. Mick East had other webs to spin.

He was surprised to receive a note from Kisch announcing another visit. Mick judged that he might have uncovered a wanted Nazi. Mick himself had turned up a hunted man operating a garage in Geneva.

They met in the Tracing Agency later in the afternoon. Mick sent for a fresh Thermos of coffee and laced it from the Cognac bottle in the locked cabinet where he kept the trace on Martin Bormann.

Janos Kisch sat over the coffee, beaming, laughing, after he had embraced Mick East. A jolly uncle with cheerfully plump jowls and an unexpected vanity of moustache.

'Perhaps, perhaps,' he said, laughing, to Mick's shrewd suggestion that he had other business in Geneva. 'Who knows? Who knows?'

He wanted to see the cigarette packet in the Tracing Agency's history book. Mick had it brought. Kisch studied the worn scrap through a magnifying-glass and wrote the listed names in his notebook.

'But I gave you the names before, Janos.'

'Ah yes. But there can be much in the spelling of names. Already I find you in error. Here, and again, here. This is not an *i*, it's an *e*. This is not an *e*, it's a *u*.'

Mick East made his own note.

'Have you got something new on Kleinberg?'

'Not exactly. But Wiesenthal is interested.'

Mick popped his eyes and whistled. 'Wiesenthal! Is he, now? Why is Wiesenthal interested?'

'I told you about the SS man who provided information on Hermann Harz ... and others.'

'Yes. Others including Rudolf Kleinberg.'

'That information was given to Wiesenthal,' Kisch said. 'I merely sat in. It was the first and only time I have ever seen Wiesenthal lose his self-possession.'

Simon Wiesenthal was a legend, operator of the Jewish Documentation Centre in Vienna, the man who had traced Adolf Eichmann. Mick East had exchanged information with him, they had not met. The whereabouts of his office was secret. Mick had heard that it was disguised as a cold storage room fronted by a refrigerator door.

Before the war, Wiesenthal had been an architect in the Polish city of Lvov, now Lemberg. There had been one hundred and fifty thousand Jews in that city. There were now five hundred. Wiesenthal had survived thirteen camps, including Mauthausen, where he had attempted to take his life. He wore the badge of that in great scars on both wrists.

Mick saw a pattern. Wiesenthal had been in a concentration camp. Had he known Rudolf Kleinberg?

Wiesenthal had stated that he held twenty-two thousand five hundred dossiers on Nazis yet to be arrested, including Hitler's deputy Martin Bormann, Dr Joseph Mengele, the doctor who commanded Auschwitz, and Heinrich Müller, the chief of Gestapo.

'They live,' Wiesenthal had said. He had spoken his fears bitterly in a rare press interview, after the Israelis at Department Zero Six had kidnapped Adolf Eichmann. 'My fear is that the Nazis will come back. Listen, let me tell you what has happened. Twenty per cent of all the judges in Germany are Nazis. Nazis fill the police force, the civil service. In many towns in Germany and Austria the leading men are ex-Nazis. If the Nazi movement comes back ... I try to get these men exposed and put on trial. In South America they want to live out their lives in safe luxury. In Spain they are waiting for the Fourth Reich, there is a possibility that the country will change after Franco's death. But in Cairo they are *working* for the Fourth Reich. That is the way it is stacked.'

Simon Wiesenthal wore a licensed pistol in a shoulder holster. Kisch had told Mick East that he carried photographs of Bormann, Mengele and Müller in his wallet, with pictures of concentration camp horrors.

Kisch appreciated East's coffee. 'Mmm. Very good. You're interested, no? Everyone is interested in Wiesenthal. Very well, my friend, I will tell you this little story. It had been arranged. We collected the informer from a café. For a long time we drive. Then we blindfold the man and sit there. Are we being followed? No. Very well, we lead him. Oh, we lead him here, there, up, down. We lead him in circles, squares, straight lines.'

Kisch laughed at the recollection. 'Now there is a chair. Sit down. We take off the blindfold. There is a room. A desk. Behind the desk is Simon Wiesenthal.

'Immediately, as always, this creature told us he was forced to join the SS.

'We ask him, where is Harz? More talk. He was forced, he is innocent. There is no blood on his hands. Where is Harz? Now there is a difference. The creature licks his lips, swivels his eyes. Yes, he knows where Harz is, but he needs money, his family, we understand. It will cost money for Harz.

'How much money? Twenty-five thousand dollars! We haven't got it. Then fifteen thousand dollars! No. Ten thousand? No. How many Jews did Harz kill? We don't know. At Krasnerdorf? Seven hundred thousand. More perhaps.

' "All right. I'll make you a special price. Seven thousand dollars. It's a bargain, really. One cent per dead Jew." '

'That is when Simon lost his self-possession. The one and only time I know of.' Kisch smiled cheerfully, drinking his coffee.

Mick East had been there, he had seen it, he had walked in those places, and after that one would never be gulled again about what men are. But he felt cold in him now.

'What happened, Janos?'

'An interesting thing. This man, this creature, waited and then asked, "Do you want to moralize me, or do you want Obersturm-führer Hermann Harz?" '

They had got Harz, in a Volkswagen factory in São Paolo, working under another name as a mechanic.

Mick gave himself more coffee. 'Did he get his one cent per dead Jew, Janos?'

Kisch spread his hands, looking waggish, bending. 'That you must ask Simon Wiesenthal.'

When Kisch had gone, Mick decided to reactivate the Rudolf Klein-berg file. He would signal the International Tracing Service at Arolsen to keep contact with Janos Kisch. East was interested to see what was to happen in the matter of Rudolf Kleinberg and Simon Wiesenthal.

The stink of the concentration camps was very much in Mick East's nostrils. There had been much to do lately on traces and authentica-tions. Jean-Pierre Koman in Guernsey had been mistaken about the statute of limitations on compensation payments to victims. The limitation only applied to 'normal' suffering. There was no time limit for those who had suffered the tortures of the pseudo-medical experi-ments.

The German Federal Republic had turned over approval of these claims to a commission appointed by the ICRC. The International Tracing Service supplied documentation. The commission considered the ghastly injuries and traumatic wounds of the haunted applicants.

The commission and victims met in the ICRC headquarters. In the last convening, seventy-nine survivors of the horrors had been ques-tioned and medically examined. Fifty-one cases had been accepted and recommended to Bonn. Five had been rejected. Four were set aside for further investigation and nineteen decisions deferred until the commis-sion's next meeting.

14

In his sitting-room the Earl slumped and fingered the brush of moustache and side-whiskers.

'Tubby warned me, y'know. Came straight out with it. Right to the last, travelling in the car to the ceremony, Tubby said I should cut for the boat train. Tierra del Fuego, Tubby recommended. Up the Limpopo in a dug-out canoe. It was excellent advice, I've got to give Tubby that much.'

Jane said, 'I must say this one was short and sweet. It hasn't been a year yet, has it?'

'It's been a lifetime, dear girl. A season in hell. I've not known a peaceful day. The woman's a monster. I shouldn't be surprised if some mad scientist assembled her in a laboratory. I told you about her cutting the legs off my trousers? Imagination staggers at such depravity.'

The Earl sniffed gloomily. 'She's American, of course. I must say, I've had the most wretched ill luck with these women. Can't seem to handicap them at all. Stick closer to home in future. Stick to the stables I know.'

There had been times when she had cried for her father, after her mother's death. His comfort had been to pack her off to a school in Paris and remarry in the Argentine. When her young husband committed suicide the Earl had been travelling in Canada. He had cabled Jane to stand fast against his return. She had waited on that for three months.

'You really can't go on this way, Daddy. These marriages will leave you with nothing.'

He looked up quickly. 'In point of fact, old girl, I was coming to that. The thing is, I'm more than a bit short of the ready. Archer and Archer have knocked up some papers on the Welsh farm, and if I can have your signature as guarantor, it would see me out of the wood. I mean, you agree that the woman must go? I mean, cutting off one's trouser legs. The time comes to cry halt.'

When the business was done the Earl ordered Champagne and grew anxious about the time. It was not unfamiliar to Jane.

'And now, how about you? You're happy here, dear girl? And like doing whatever you're doing? Not planning to hare off again?'

Jane said, 'I'm bored to sobs.'

'I see.' Her father frowned at his watch. 'I'm sorry to hear that, dear girl. Why don't you marry? Settle down, what? On second thoughts, I withdraw that remark.' The Earl shuddered. 'The very word conjures evil spectres.'

At Château Malraux that evening Salem informed his housekeeper that he would be entertaining the next week. Signora Cenci reminded him that Hedda would be on leave.

'The questions of the wraps, Signora Cenci?'

'The wraps, among other questions, Monsieur.'

'I believe we might settle that to your satisfaction.'

'A signora?'

'It is possible.'

The housekeeper granted her approval in a nod. 'It is expected. It is proper.'

Salem had spoken without earlier consideration. Standing before the fire, drinking the cocktail Massimo had brought him, he convinced himself. Jane Stirling had got on well with Robert Collins. She would no doubt greatly help in putting the wife at ease. Her French was impeccable. She was handsome and accomplished. He was not sure about the propriety, the possibility of misunderstanding. He would think about it further.

'Jane is being analysed! Jane is being analysed!' It had been fashionable, the fun thing to do, all her friends were in analysis.

'Oh God, I'm so bored with my man. Is your man Freudian, Jane? The Freudians are so tedious. Everything, but everything is sex, darling. Max brought me tea in bed. I was so overcome I knocked over the teapot. Max was furious, of course, the poor lamb had the most awful hangover. My man said, yes, you see the spout on the teapot is a penis symbol. You are sexually dissatisfied with your husband. Knocking the teapot over was an unconscious rejection of your husband's penis. Can you believe it? But, really! At nine o'clock in the morning I am unconsciously rejecting Max? Darling, I can't even see at that hour.'

Jane's man had been a Freudian. He said that her adventures with men, which were beginning to frighten her, were a search for a father-substitute. Her block against satisfaction was because of her disappointment in her father, and her underlying contempt for men.

She had been too young, too headstrong then, to take that, or anything, very seriously. But the block against satisfaction persisted, even though she raged at it. Always, she thought that this time she would be made whole.

Jane Stirling had been at the end of something when she came to Geneva. She needed that backwater, to be alone there. The silence of the rooms which she cared for herself, keeping the windows curtained, was an anchorite's cave of retreat. Her weariness and fear for the future which scarcely appeared on her face, were turned inside to burden and chill her.

The striding restlessness had returned as she recovered; the familiar rise of defiance, an urge to hurl herself upon something. She had felt it in the presence of her father, the old reckless mix of anger, appetite and emptiness.

Salem had rehearsed it, an unaccustomed difficulty with words. He was worried that she would think it strange, but the advantages pitched him forward.

'Miss Stirling, I'm giving a dinner party for Robert Collins and his wife. A small gathering. I wonder if you would consider attending?'

He had halted and then plunged on. 'Quite truthfully, I can't manage the ladies. I would greatly appreciate your help.'

'It would be a pleasure. Shall I get the details from your secretary?'

It had happened in a minute and she was gone. Salem looked happily forward to making the announcement to Signora Cenci.

Jane did think it strange. She was thoughtful when she returned to her room. She had answered quickly, out of Salem's uneasiness and her total surprise. Why had he chosen her?

15

Iт had been a lonely year for Robert Collins, the most isolated he had
known. He was doubly at war because his nation was at war and his
own people at war within it. He was further at war in himself because
of the sensitivity of his position, the need to dissemble in public the
emotions that grieved him at home. In the rioting summer of the fire
next time Collins withdrew from the few Negro friends he had made
in Geneva, avoided when he could the social connections with the
Embassy. For now and until after the Paris Congress he was Chairman
of the League, representative of many colours, creeds and nations.

Collins had grasped at President Salem's talk of a Humanitarian
Law, at first with legal curiosity, a professional wonder at the grandeur
of the undertaking. As Salem continued, the long-boned hands gesturing intensely, building in imagination, Robert Collins had restrained
his excitement. There could be true involvement for him in this, now
and beyond the present. He could carry it home with him when he
returned, contribute a study on civil rights.

The two men, so unalike in all that life grants, had met in perfect understanding.

The initiative had come from the League. The dangers and miseries of the Vietnam conflict were too overwhelming to suffer any longer the confusions that waited on political action.

Salem had privately shown Robert Collins intelligence ordinarily only seen by the International Committee. The movements of protest and concern heard everywhere in public demonstrations had been translated into action by uncommitted governments. Responsible envoys from Sweden, Holland, Poland and France had been conferring clandestinely in Hanoi. The stopper was out of the bottle. The secret diplomatic pressures of European governments were beleaguering the American administration throughout the world. The most stubborn intransigence could not for ever resist the bloody stalemate, the heating fires of opposition that alienated governments once friendly or at least neutral. The American President's repeated declaration that his representatives would go anywhere, any time, to talk peace, was being brought home to Washington with increasing temper and insistence.

Robert Collins had canvassed his National Societies to contribute to a massive programme of Vietnam relief. 'We must take this action now,' he had said, 'before the human wreckage becomes uncontrollable.'

The programme was based on a round-the-clock air-lift of comforts, medicines, hospital equipment and food. Volunteers were requested from every National Society. Help for the civilian victims of American bombing was to be dispatched to North Vietnam at the insistence of member countries. Consignments were to be shipped via the Trans-Siberian Railway.

Almost immediately on the League's announcement of the plan the Polish Minister of Welfare quoted it in a television interview, pledging his Government's support as a signatory to the Geneva Conventions. Other statements of support and welcome followed. In Geneva, the League and the ICRC were clamoured at by the Press.

Martin Neveau was horrified.

'This must be stopped immediately. How could Collins make such a mistake? He has made the League a platform for communist propaganda. You must instruct him at once, President, to refuse any further comment. You know what the Press will do with this—it will interpret the League's programme as a world-wide criticism of America's presence in Vietnam.'

'There is such a criticism, Martin. It is not our place to deny it.'

'It is not our place to share in it, directly or by implication. Can you imagine how the American Society will react to this publicity?'

Salem had a keen remembrance of the instruction Neveau had given him about the American Society's attachment to its government. 'The American Society is only one in ninety-eight national members, Martin.'

Neveau struck the arm of his chair. 'The American Society is one of the strongest. It has two and a half million members. It was on the initiative of the American Society that the League was formed in 1919.'

'What do you suggest I do? What authority does the ICRC have in such matters?'

'On matters of policy, matters of politics, matters concerning the charter, we have every authority. And every responsibility, President. Every responsibility.'

'Very well, Martin. We will discuss it with Robert Collins. I do feel this reaction is exaggerated. You surely don't argue the need of League action in Vietnam?'

'I'm sick of Vietnam. There's altogether too much emotion about it. We looked after two million Algerian refugees in Tunisia and Morocco. After 1948 we looked after a million more in Palestine. That was managed without emotion or reporters crowding the corridors. There's more than one war in the world. Every day something new happens. We have so little to go around. If the League organizes this programme in Vietnam, what will we have for Biafra?'

'Biafra? Has something new happened?'

Neveau answered in the same tired, low voice, his face turned. 'The Nigerian Society has appealed. Things are desperate.'

For the second time in a few months the news services based in Geneva had broken unfavourable stories.

'You make it pretty damned clear to Collins, Richter. There's too much being made about this.' The Ambassador lit a cigarette irritably. 'Collins was a Kennedy man and he probably still is, but you damn well remind him he's an American. You'll be speaking as a State Department delegate to Paris, right? Not on behalf of this Embassy.'

Robert Collins had not been prepared for the stir which had followed the League's call. He quickly estimated the danger. But the text of the declaration was out, he could only move to modify the implications.

He had told the Press: 'The League of Red Cross Societies gives comfort in all the world's areas of conflict. In this work the League of Red Cross Societies does not ask, and is not interested in knowing, by which side a victim of war was made to suffer.'

Collins had made his statement, and declined further comment, on the morning Richter applied for an interview.

In the time since his appointment to the International Conference in Paris, Joseph Richter had briefed himself on the history, humanities and politics of the Conference, the ICRC and the League. He went with confidence and curiosity to the meeting. He had never had to deal on equal terms with a Negro.

Richter had learned to manipulate his height. It was a drawback when he wished to grant an advantage to another, as he had with Martin Neveau at his party. But he could also dominate with it. When he presented himself at the League, Joseph Richter stood at his tallest.

He had not met Robert Collins, had not expected the culture of his accent or the authority and muscled bulk of his figure. Collins had stood to shake hands, offered nothing more, indicated a chair and waited.

'I should have called on you earlier,' Richter said. 'The State Department has appointed me as a delegate to the Paris Conference.'

'Yes, Mr Richter, your name was forwarded to the League.'

Richter smiled and offered Collins a cigarette. He declined, and pushed a table lighter over the desk.

'It looks as though we might have trouble there.'

'What kind of trouble, Mr Richter?'

'The communist countries. You know the kind of thing. Martin Neveau at the ICRC expects trouble from the North Vietnam and Red Chinese delegations.'

'There will no doubt be differences of opinion.'

'They will be out to make propaganda. This Polish affair indicates that. Speaking as a delegate, it seems to me we should put the lid on that one.'

'By we, do you mean the State Department?'

Richter laughed again, made himself comfortable. 'Well, no: by we I mean all of us concerned.'

Collins looked directly at Richter. 'I don't think I follow. What is there for us to be concerned about?'

Richter hardened. 'Come now. Surely this Polish provocation of publicizing the League's appeal was a bid to make anti-American propaganda.'

'It seems to have been construed that way. There's a good deal of anti-war propaganda in the world just now. There's a good deal, for that matter, at home.'

Richter had not missed the change of wording. 'Anti-war propaganda is not the same as anti-American provocation.' Richter remembered the Ambassador's words about Salem. 'Our government is in a very sensitive position just now. It is as well we should know our friends.'

The big Negro leaned back, the flat of his hands on the desk. 'What exactly are you trying to say, Mr Richter?'

Richter sat up a little. He did not have the command he had expected. 'I should think the difficulty involved here is clear. It is a simple matter of not handing the enemy ammunition to shoot at us. We are both Americans, we have the same interests.'

Collins said softly. 'You are mistaken. The Chairman of the League of Red Cross Societies, while he does the work of this parliament, has no nationality.'

Richter's long, gaunt face paled. The cigarette burned close in his fingers. 'Does that include giving comfort to the other side?'

He had angered Collins. It was sharp in his eyes and flushed on the brown of his skin. Richter spoke quickly, to cover the mistake. 'Don't misunderstand me. I only refer to the construction some people place on things. The ... er ... unfortunate constructions.'

Collins let out his breath. 'I don't misunderstand you, Mr Richter. Have you any other points?'

'As a delegate to Paris——'

'We are not in Paris yet.'

Richter was strained with temper and confusion. 'As a delegate to Paris,' he insisted, 'I must bring up the invidious position in which the League's appeal has placed the American National Society. You know it is virtually an agent of the Government, concerned with the welfare of American forces. How can the National League support an appeal for the relief of North Vietnam? Our boys are dying over there. What would they think, or the parents who financially support the Society, if it was to comfort the enemy their boys are fighting?'

'Is your suggestion now that the ICRC and the League should abandon their charters and the International, because of the peculiar obligations of the American Society?'

He was like a great brown wall. Richter wanted to shout at him. His voice did louden when he spoke. 'I didn't say that. I'm pointing out that the American Society must disassociate itself from this appeal. I'm pointing out that the other side will make anti-American propaganda out of that.'

Collins got up. 'In the work charged to this League there is no other side, Mr Richter. I'm afraid I'm unable to help you.'

Richter stood at full height. 'You have no intention of doing anything about the present negative publicity?'

Collins picked up the press release and put it into a folder. 'That was done this morning. I hope you approve of the text.'

Richter had walked a block, fuming, before he remembered the folder gripped in his hand.

The ICRC observers posted to Biafra on the first chartered aircraft to unload medicines at Port Harcourt reported the country in shambles. One, who had served in the Middle East, described conditions as a hundred times worse than the Yemen.

Neveau's opposition to the League plan for Vietnam was carried by default in the new emergency. The Nigerian Red Cross had made its plea international.

Robert Collins had lunched off a tray in Salem's office. He was writing in confidence to Dr Martin Luther King, with Salem's agreement, about the racist sections of the Humanitarian Law, asking him to help the International Committee in this great inspiration.

The League's call had stirred other debate than that briefly celebrated in the Press. There had been an indifferent or negative response from the Red Crescent and Red Sun and Lion Societies. The Societies in South Korea and Thailand had outrightly refused co-operation. Laos had countered with its own request for aid. Australia and New Zealand had been wary, their Societies claimed to be already extended in the South.

Salem listened in disappointment. 'What can be done, Robert?'

'There is so much conflicting information. So much claim and counterclaim. We need a report, an authoritative report. With that to present to the Societies it would be difficult for them to run for cover.'

'The President's report?'

Collins put down his coffee cup. Their eyes held. Salem shook his head. 'Don't think it has not been in my mind. The Committee would never consider it. Neveau would shout politics, and that would be the end of it. You have considerably more freedom in your office, Robert, than I have in mine.'

It was Martin Neveau who presented Salem with his answer. A serious pocket of plague had appeared in Cambodia. There had been isolated cases in the South Vietnamese army, more cases in Indonesia, and plague deaths, both suspected and diagnosed, in the city of Saigon.

Neveau came to him with it. 'The most worrying thing, the great worry, is that the infection is not being contained. If it can reach Indonesia where next might it appear? There is a flashpoint in unchecked, epidemics. We have had experience of that. In the south Indian outbreak the area was completely quarantined, there was every resource, a total mobilization. We couldn't stop it. It took seventy-five thousand lives and a year of effort to contain it and stamp it out.'

'How does the World Health Organization review this?'

'WHO is most apprehensive. This is the kind of thing the Chairman of the League should be exercising himself about. Sending mobile hospitals to North Vietnam, this ill-considered programme he put to the Societies, is meaningless in these circumstances, meaningless. The war is in one territory. But the plague doesn't attend to frontiers. With your agreement I propose an immediate seminar.'

The seminar continued for two days. It was attended by executives of the ICRC, the League, the WHO, the United Nations and authorities on plague from the Pasteur Institute in Paris. At the close of the second day, Pierre Salem made his proposal. 'Gentlemen, in view of the agreed gravity of this situation, I propose that I, together with competent men nominated by you, should make an immediate investigation in both South and North Vietnam, in the hope of uniting all parties in a concerted action to fight the plague before it becomes epidemic or threatens other places.'

Neveau had seen the plague before. He had been much younger then, on his first overseas mission as a delegate. The rains had failed for three seasons. There had been famine as well as plague. The sun burned, rheumy-eyed with its own violence. The earth had broken under the hammering, heaved itself up in pain, cracked apart into fissures and gulleys that streamed dust as fine and bleak as ashes. The landscape was dead, as naked as the moon. The wind strummed in the bones and carcasses of cattle. Vultures flapped and croaked on the dry wood of trees or hopped the ground, gorged, too heavy to fly.

The wind blew and it seemed that the black death blew on it, finding out every hut and hamlet, leaping unseen from the dying to the living with a venom that multiplied with its victims.

They had burned the bodies and burned the villages, retreating farther each day before the pestilence, as before an invisible, slaughtering army. In the areas still free of contagion the volunteers established lines of defence, inoculating day and night from huts, tents, the tailboards of trucks.

The sick and dying lay on the floors of schools and warehouses or suddenly staggered and fell in the open. Soldiers mounted roadblocks and raced jeeps over the broken fields to turn back those who tried to flee the terror.

Martin Neveau had helped fight the black death until he collapsed from heatstroke and exhaustion. He had been returned to Geneva long before it snarled itself out in an end of the killing.

He had kept this from Salem, as he kept most things to himself, and because he could still shut his eyes and see that place, smell the stench of the burning and feel the fear in his throat.

Neveau had seen the plague and had felt its ghastly breath. If it was feeding itself now in Vietnam in the cover of the mountains and fighting, if it had already stalked from its breeding grounds where it fattened on the useful bodies, the world could know a reckoning beyond the power of guns and bombs.

Neveau had offered Salem no opposition, moving quickly about the preparations. A press announcement was prepared by Neveau himself. It stated briefly that the President of the ICRC and his colleagues would travel to South Vietnam for routine discussions with the National Society and other welfare agencies in that country.

'Wotcher cock.'

'Have you heard the news?'

Mitchell forgot his share of the greeting. Mick East saw his excitement and sat back. 'No. What's up?'

'Salem is going to Vietnam.'

East whistled. 'Is he now? What brought that on?'

'Officially, it's a routine visit. My guess is that it's something to do with this seminar on the plague. There's a team going. Neveau's handling it all himself. He's got the radio room under security.'

Mick East nodded and looked thoughtful. 'There could be something bigger than bugs in this Teddy boy.'

'What do you mean?'

'It could be peace. He could be using the bugs as a cover.'

'Never. He wouldn't move publicly if it was peace. He wouldn't draw attention to himself.'

'Don't be too sure. Election year in the States is coming up, remember. The cowboy could be making a little hoopla.'

It was a new thought to Mitchell. He poured a coffee and considered the probability. 'No, I can't see it. This is not the way they would play it.'

'If he's going to the North he might have a meet on about the *Pueblo*.'

'No. I overheard Neveau speak about that. The North Koreans are uptight for an admission of spying. If they don't get it they could put the crew up for trial and sentence. It would be within their rights, according to the Conventions.'

'I still think he's got something on,' said Mick East.

'You're a devious-minded little bastard.'

'It's the business I'm in, Teddy boy. If they've got any filthy postcards out there, bring me back a few sets.'

'I haven't been told I'm going yet.'

'Salem will need a Press front. When the President moves it's news.'

Mitchell sat on the desk swinging a leg happily. 'This is just what I need, Mick. I'm fed up with Geneva. From what I hear, Saigon's wide open. The Reuters man was out there. He says you've got to knock back the girls with a stick.'

'Don't forget my filthy postcards. I'm interested in this proposition that it goes sideways.'

Mitchell finished his coffee. 'I'd better get back. If something new comes up I'll let you know.'

Mitchell had continued to miss Sarah Neveau. None of the others had her tension. He could crumple her body with a touch. She was so strung on guilt and desperation that it exploded like dementia in her. He believed that he could bring her back with a call, but he wanted Sarah to come to him. He could break her then, use her as he wanted; it would always be his terms after that.

This was what Mitchell needed, time away, the distractions of a wartime city. Time in which Sarah Neveau could marinate.

In the next days, while Mitchell awaited instructions and continued his self-congratulations, Martin Neveau pondered. Representing Salem to the Press would be dangerous. The President had no conception of procedure or proper discretion. Salem would need a secretary, somebody to organize efficiently.

It was this that brought Neveau to Jane Stirling. She knew the signalling procedures. She had dealt at second hand with the Press. Her French was fluent, she was cultivated and travelled. Neveau was troubled by Salem's austere reputation. He tried to think of a form of words in which he could put the proposal.

She had stayed on because she had nowhere to go, because she had come to the end of something. She had stayed later because he had asked her to hostess his parties, because she had enjoyed that, and out of curiosity about Salem. He had eased and warmed towards her but it had not narrowed the distance. There was something unreachable about him, a void more than an armour. She had taken to watching him on the Château Malraux evenings, the eagerness of his talk, his formalities with the women, the fineness of his wrists and hands and smoothly drawn face.

He was new to Jane, not only by distance but by the sense she had of the long body, of its tenderness. He had caught her eyes once, had stopped in surprise and then turned quickly away.

Jane had thought about making herself available to him, partly out of sensuality for his elegance, but more out of curiosity and the instinct for conquest, simply to reduce him as she had so many others. But the distance remained, and the formality. The Bentley was always summoned for her with the last guests or before them.

When Neveau spoke to Jane Stirling she hardly heard after his first words. Salem must have asked for her. Now she had somewhere to go. Wildness leapt and shook her. She felt free again, unencumbered again, rushing to things unknown.

'Wotcher cock. Hello, hello.' East took off his glasses. 'What's up with you, then?'

Mitchell could hardly speak. 'That bitch,' he said, 'that toffee-nosed nympho bitch.'

'Hold hard,' Mick East said. 'That's no way to talk about me mate.'

'Salem's taking her to Saigon. I've been left like a shag on a rock.'

East put his head back and blew a long, loud whistle. The filing clerks stopped. He waved them back into action. 'What's been going on, then?'

'She must have got at him. That's why she's been so quiet here. She must have got at Salem.'

'At Salem? Not on your nelly. Salem is as clean as a whistle. He's been one jump away from a monastery for years.'

'I feel like packing it in, Mick.'

'Don't go off half-cocked, cock. You're on a feather bed here.'

'I was going to take a trip home,' Mitchell said bitterly. 'It's only a few hours from Saigon to Sydney. I've got the leave coming up.'

'Maybe you should have a word with Neveau.'

'That bastard. It was Neveau who told me.'

'What can't be cured must be endured,' Mick comforted.

'Well,' Mitchell said. 'I'm packing it in for today, anyhow. They can all get stuffed. I'm off to the club.'

'Bang go my filthy postcards,' East said, then brightened. 'Maybe Lady Jane will get some for me. Yes, I like that—her selection would be something.

'You can get stuffed, too,' Mitchell told him.

Later, drunk, Mitchell asked the barman for coins. He would telephone Sarah, and to hell with everything. He would get back at Neveau the best way.

The retired general who sat on the International Committee had offered himself as soon as Salem's proposal was accepted. The French expert on plague from the Pasteur Institute later cabled his willingness to travel. The WHO had nominated a young scientist who had earlier visited South Vietnam. An ICRC delegate, a specialist in epidemics, had been added to the team by Neveau. A date for departure was set.

Kits were readied for the team, armbands, Red Cross passports, flags, doorstickers, language guides in Vietnamese, international driving licences, inoculation certificates, Telexcards, provision for funds in any currency.

Clark Clyde, the big young American scientist from WHO was recalled from a holiday in Mallorca and arrived late in Geneva, hungover and complaining. He had bought a ketch for the summer in partnership and had established himself with a young girl from Manchester who owned an interesting variety of wigs.

When Salem's team finally took off, there had still been no response from the North other than acknowledgment of the request for entry. For three years Hanoi had refused to permit inspection. Neveau had arranged with Robert Collins to apply further pressure through the League's Societies.

Salem would be kept informed of progress while the team travelled in South Vietnam.

Vietnam Two

16

THEY had breakfasted in Bangkok, a stop to refuel, in a squalling of stiff and tired children. Ton Son Nhut, in the Saigon suburbs, was also an American army and air base. Civil aircraft did not delay there, the field was often mortared and shelled.

They had looked for the war, coming in. The transit passengers leaned over each other, pointing at shell holes, wondering at smoke, clicking cameras through the windows. As the aircraft jolted and rolled, fighter bombers nosed up on Salem's window.

They stepped out into a mulch of damp air that immediately swarmed on the skin. The old hands hurried off to the peeling reception buildings. The sky was full of the noise of aircraft, roared by jets and cargo carriers, whacked by the sidling helicopters. Tiny Vietnamese soldiers walked the outbuildings, heavy pistols in decorated holsters. American troops slumped on wooden benches, sleeping, smoking, passing soft drinks, dull-eyed with the boredom of interminable waitings. Vietnamese officials in khaki uniforms handed out currency forms, bumping each other behind a chipped horseshoe barrier, checking passports and visas while American guards chewed gum and reslung their rifles.

The smell of war and the taste of war and the bustle and boredom of it, was as palpable and grasping everywhere as the flannelled damp in the air.

Clark Clyde carried Jane's hand baggage, shepherding the group before him. A man in a flowered shirt waved from behind the barrier. Clark Clyde wagged a briefcase at him.

'One of our chaps. Tom Mix. His name really is Tom Mix.'

The World Health man across the barrier turned and signalled behind him.

They were surrounded now, being bowed at, shaking hands, lost hopelessly in introductions. Press men flashed cameras. 'Which is the President? Where's Pierre Salem? Who's the broad? What are you here for, Pres'?'

A young Vietnamese lieutenant of police shouted for clear passage. The President of the South Vietnamese Red Cross introduced members of his committee. General Thieu's personal representative bowed. A member of the American Embassy made himself known.

The helmeted GI guards stopped chewing to ask each other what the hell was going on.

Pale, surprised, responding in English and French, holding the brown felt hat that suddenly appeared incongruous, Pierre Salem flinched at the physical intimacies that continued to press at him as their hosts backed and beckoned the visitors across the concrete floor to a stairway.

The civilian lounge was set with formica tables and a desolate bar. Deep windows looked over the airport. Fans stirred and cooled the air. A long table under a starched white cloth was laid with Vietnamese, Chinese and Western delicacies, burdened with flowers and decorations. Champagne cooled in napkinned buckets.

Jane Stirling had changed on the aircraft from slacks to a cotton dress and high heels. She was glad of it now. Without instruction she told the correspondents that President Salem's vist was routine, repeating the text that Neveau had issued in Geneva.

Pierre Salem eased in the privacy of the lounge, better able now to connect names with faces, his eyes going to the windows for a sight of the savage shapes of power that snarled in and out across the glass.

The team was to be quartered in the old Continental Palace Hotel, on Tu Do Street, off Constitution Square. It had once been the centre of French privilege and power, on a boulevard of fine restaurants, shops, night clubs and brothels that had made it both the Montmartre and Champs Élysées of the east. The low, yellow-plastered building facing the old Saigon opera house was haunted by its imperial past.

It was understood that President Salem and his colleagues would appreciate a rest after the long hours of travel. They would proceed in a convoy, headed by the police lieutenant, on a route that would touch on the Chinese quarter of Cholon, cross to the docks on the river front and follow Tu Do Street north to the Saigon Basilica, the spired Catholic Cathedral on John F. Kennedy Square. It would provide an idea of the interest of the city before they rested in the Continental. That evening, there would be an official reception in the Presidential Palace.

Salem and his Committee members were to travel with the President of the South Vietnamese Red Cross. The others were divided among the welcoming authorities. There was no difficulty in marking the departure. Except for a few specially licensed vehicles, taxis and private cars were forbidden to approach close to Ton Son Nhut.

Before the convoy swung out of Cholon, watched with impassive curiosity by the pushing crowds on the sidewalks squatting to fry and sell fish, cooking in glinting brass pots in the unceasing din of pedicab bells, the Buddhists had moved about their preparations.

Near a four-way intersection in downtown Saigon, two Bonzes, orange-robed, heads shaved to the ridged bones of their skulls, sat talking softly in a rusted Renault. Behind them, on a corner, an older priest stood head bent, his eyes closed. Two women carrying Buddhist altars entered from a jammed side street and placed them in a clearing near the meditating Bonze. They sat cross-legged at the altars, lit incense sticks among the flower petals and turned up their palms in prayer.

In each arm of the crossroads Buddhist householders appeared with altars. Monks and nuns in orange and grey walked slowly towards the intersection, single file and in couples. A few old cars hooted the pedicab riders and stopped where they could find kerb room. Pedestrians began to walk the gutters, pushed off the crowding sidewalks. The clashing of gongs in the Xa Lai pagoda carried faintly.

The three big American cars that followed close on the braying siren of the police jeep had almost entered the crossroad when the streets ahead filled with bodies—spilling from alleys, kerbs and shopfronts as quick as the slide of earth on a mountain. Behind them cars slowed across the outlets of the intersection and stopped. For minutes everything stilled. The cymbals, muffled before by traffic and distance, clash-clashed in the quiet. The mob began to roar, slogans stamping in their throats.

The police lieutenant had twisted for the field telephone behind him when the mob broke and flooded. The jeep disappeared. In Salem's car his host shouted, hammered his fists on the driver's shoulders, cranked up his window and sprawled across Salem to get at the door lock. They were surrounded. They saw the police jeep go over, wheels spinning. The car windows submerged in bodies and slant-eyed faces. Pierre Salem sat neatly, holding his brown hat, lips white, uncomprehending.

A young Bonze, eyes and nostrils distended, bent and banged on the roof. His mouth worked, shouting. The driver had thrown himself to the floor, crouched under the dashboard.

Placards nodded towards them, sheeted cardboard on batons. The crush about the car spread, waved back by bare-armed priests. The demonstrators held the placards to the windows, ringing the roof with their fists. The placards read in Vietnamese, French and English: *Thou shalt not kill. End napalm barbarity. End American Colonialism. Coalition not Roman Catholic Dictatorship. Stop the Martyrdom of Vietnam.*

The President of the Vietnamese Society wiped his streaming face. He put his mouth to Salem's ear and shouted. 'Please do not worry. It is all right. Please do not worry. Please smile.'

He collapsed back in his corner, head lolling, dabbing his handkerchief.

Ahead, a fierce jet of flame, plumed in black smoke, leaped high over the mob. The police jeep had been fired. Fists continued to drum on the car's roof and bonnet. The placards knocked on the windows. Faces loomed on the glass and vanished. Salem eased, blood burned his cheeks. His lips parted in wonder at the exhilaration that jumped inside him. He turned eagerly to the window, nodding, smiling, waving the absurd felt hat.

Behind the Bonzes, on one side, portraits of the Presidents of America and South Vietnam were bundled forward overhead. A boy dashed forward and drenched them with petrol. Matches were pitched. The painted faces buckled and twisted in a shocking parody of pain as the flames licked the boards, consuming the features and licking them out in blowing flakes of black ash.

The change from demonstration to riot was heard before it was seen. The stamping chant of the slogans altered into a savage rumble. The pack about the beleagured convoy quietened. The tide that had flowed one way broached, stilled and turned. Slowly, then surging, the mob closed around the cars again, a wave of pressure directed towards the crossroads. As they went the placards were discarded, their props shouldered like rifles. In the closed car the air had stifled. Moisture condensed and ran on the glass, their clothing was dark with perspiration, hair soaked. The driver poked his head above the windscreen.

The President of the Vietnamese League was tortured by loss of face. 'So sorry. So sorry. What will you think? So sorry.' He gagged and began to vomit, clutching the sill, glasses slipping down his nose. 'So sorry. Forgive me.'

Salem patted the heaving shoulders.

The capsized jeep was still burning, the hood frame buckled like bones in the white ash of the canvas. Salem found the door lock and got out. Above him heads peered from balconies and windows. A few figures watched from doorways.

Salem walked to the car behind him, worried about Jane Stirling. She stepped out, her arms and face shining with perspiration.

'Miss Stirling. Are you well? Were you troubled?'

She brushed at her hair, unpinned the thick, sodden coil and shook it free. The government man was expostulating, apologizing, in a fever of worry and excitement. Salem couldn't hear her.

'What did you say?'

'I said, that was quite a welcome.'

She was calm, amused, flapping the sticky bodice of her dress with both hands. They were smiling at each other, turning to the other cars when a truck of helmeted police, entered the street from an alley. An officer swung down, shouted instructions, jumped back as the truck ground off.

'We are to wait,' the government representative said. 'They will tell us which road to take.'

There was the smoke of many small fires ahead as the mob thinned and took to the alleys. They could see the lines of uniformed figures, goggle-eyed and snouted in gas masks, prodding and clubbing with rifle butts. Canisters rolled and spilled mist. Figures fell, elbows out, knelt head bent to the trash littered road as though in prayer.

'Gas,' the government man said. 'Vomit gas. Soon it will be over.'

The footpaths around them began to fill with staring, impassive faces, talking softly, looking up the road. An old woman in a coolie hat and black pyjamas walked out of a doorway with baskets and began to set up a food stall. Clark Clyde, stained and dishevelled, pushed towards them, his arms full of soft drink. Salem realized how parched he was.

'What will it be? I've got lemonade or orange.'

Jane licked her lips. 'Anything. You wonderful man.'

'I hope you mean that,' Clyde said seriously. 'Mister President?'

'Lemonade. I'm very grateful.'

'That was quite a compliment to you, sir.' He opened the bottles and passed them. 'The demonstration—from the Buddhists with love to the great white Father.'

'Surely not, Mr Clyde,' Salem said.

'You can depend on it. Ask Mr Thuy here.'

The government man nodded wanly. 'I'm afraid so, President Salem. They were making propaganda. I'm afraid they had it arranged.'

Four trucks, headlight to taillight, packed with armed troops, rocked past and turned into a side street. Clark Clyde toasted them with his bottle. 'Bang goes the Xa Lai pagoda. First they knock the iron gates down. Then they lob in the gas grenades. The monks come to the balconies and beat gongs, anything that makes a noise. The troops go in, break a few heads and toss a holy sample over the balcony. It's a dull town.'

Salem said again, 'Surely not.'

'That's the way it works, sir. Isn't it, Mr Thuy?'

The government representative shook his head miserably. 'I'm afraid so. I'm afraid so. Oh dear, what will you think of us?'

Three police jeeps arrived to guard the convoy until a safe route could be opened. The team was advised to return to the cars. When they backed to leave, Salem noticed that the young police lieutenant who had escorted them from the airport had returned to examine the ruin of his jeep. His uniform was ripped, there was blood on his face. He kicked at a wheel in rage.

They moved again, and Salem watched the long street unfurl. Arvin and American soldiers sprawled behind strong-points of oil drums and sandbags, automatic weapons before them. Jeeps moved slowly. MPs lolling in postures of boredom. Europeans in cotton shirts and cameras inspected the windows of shops. Bars advertised themselves in dead neon. The shade trees hung their leaves inertly in the heat. Everybody moved slowly, like the trance of fish in still water.

Pierre Salem closed his eyes and looked forward to the door he would close behind him, to the splashing of cold water and the safe, familiar place of his thoughts.

The cars drew up before the shadowed patio of the old Continental Palace, watched by the correspondents and USAID staffers drinking among the columns and potted plants. The management came out to receive them.

Jane Stirling stood in her slip, stretched the speckled shell of her armpits at the blowing air conditioner, tested the double bed and flopped there, her knees drawn up, the perfectly rounded legs bare. She pushed the long, black hair from under her head and put it over the pillow. She had laid out the dress she would wear that evening. In a few minutes she would bathe.

The Chinese floorboy had knocked several times. He tried the handle, the door was unlocked. He was inside, in the dimmed light of the curtained room before he saw her, bare-armed, bare-legged, all the pale pink and lilac of the tinted flesh, the swelling thighs, striking his eyes like thunder. He stood there pock-marked, mouth open, one tooth glinted with gold, a skinny little fellow in a ragged white jacket, dumb with the shock of her. Without lifting his eyes he backed away, watching until Jane flung an arm and the door clicked shut behind him.

Tom Mix drank cold beer while Clark Clyde shouted from the bathroom. Nothing much had changed in a year. Clark's Number One girl at the Nations Bar had borne a child to an American sergeant. His Number One at the Melody Bar was still unattached. Prices had gone up. The Mama-Sans asked three thousand piastres to sell out a bar girl for the evening. Major This had gone stateside. Captain That had been hit in the Plieku fighting. Some correspondent had caught the clap, the penicillin wouldn't take for months. Some of the girls had been infected so often that they were breeding a strain almost immune to drugs.

That afternoon, the refreshed team met to discuss plans in Salem's sitting-room. It was agreed that Salem and the General would call on the Vietnamese Minister next morning. An epidemics relief expert would confer with the Society. Clark Clyde would meet with the World Health people. The doctor from the Pasteur Institute in Paris would talk with the Saigon director about plague vaccine.

Free of the formalities he had always known, in this strange place, strange even in its smells, with bougainvillaea climbing from a pot on the balcony, profusely in flower, hot with orange and purple blossoms,

Pierre Salem sat among the shirtsleeved men in a sober tie and jacket.

At the bank and at ICRC headquarters he had always conferred across a table, the severe, polished wood a constraint in itself, the pads, pencils, water carafes and stiff-backed chairs inanimate calls to order and the protocols of procedure. Here, on old cushions, grouped about the worn carpet under a flaked, soaring ceiling, opposite the shock of Clark Clyde's hula shirt and feet bare in sandals, Salem was discomfited.

Dignity and distance could not survive here. The heat of these streets and the indiscretion of sweat, these alone delivered one man to another. The violence of the morning had shaken them. Salem sat with the letters and papers on his knees and he wanted to run from, and run towards, the simple physical intimacies from which he had sheltered so long.

The guards had checked the cars at the great decorated gates and passed them through lawns and flowers to the floodlit Presidential Palace. It had rained earlier. In the sunshot evening that coloured the clouds like watered silk, mixing and fusing the blaze of reds and pinks and orange, the earth rebreathed the moisture. There were lanterns in the garden, Chinese shapes, spotlights on the Palace entrance.

Under the pillared arch, above the wide sweep of steps, the two small, uniformed figures waited, General Thieu and Marshall Ky, President and Vice-President of South Vietnam. Near them, the tall, shrewd-faced figure of the American Ambassador watched. Behind him stood the Diplomatic Corps and other ministers of government.

Formally, as they moved down the welcoming line, escorted by the Chief of Protocol, the meaningless platitudes of pomp were exchanged like objects between them.

Later, when he could, Clark Clyde said to Jane Stirling: 'I never expected to make this scene. The great white father seems to have relaxed.'

'The President is more at home in French. Isn't it strange? After all that has happened, these people speak about France as their second home.'

'Not all of them. There were a few drop-outs at Dien Bien Phu.'

Once again Pierre Salem's shell had been cracked. This time, in the realization of his unique office. Here, in protocol, he outranked the hard old American Ambassador. Neutral, in an institution cleaving to neutrality, he was treated as a head of state. Stateless in office, he was elevated like a pontiff. The infection of pride, the self-regarding ambition the Humanitarian Law had awakened in him, the thought of a Nobel Prize, had its counterpart in this revelation of the universal importance of his office.

The demonstration and riot of the morning was an inescapable topic, joked about by the English, apologized for by the Vietnamese, pointedly invoked by the Americans.

At the banqueting table Pierre Salem, President of the International, sat like a ruler.

In the grounds of the Palace where shadows deepened, guards patrolled softly. In the surrounding streets secret police scouted the sidewalks, squatted to smoke in doorways. Jeeps with mounted machine-guns rolled slowly along the kerbs. A helicopter gunship swung regularly over the rooftops, slicing the night with a searchlight.

The defence of clothing, the need to be covered, had become as habitual with Salem as his manner. At the weekends he customarily dressed in a suit and tie. Only behind the château's wall, in the summer, did he sometimes walk shirtsleeved in the garden.

In the first week in Vietnam, caught in showers, sweltered in villages and hospitals, belted into the canvas seats of helicopters, Pierre Salem shed his jackets and ties, and browned and changed in the sun, hair knotted in the scalp's salty damp, blown by fans and the rush of rotor blades, armpits and chest patched with perspiration—a frankness of flesh which implied and demanded other freedoms.

The shell in which he had lived was cracked further with every day, the abstracts of charity and mercy confronted by the brute evidences of human need, a shattered society that struggled to endure with a terrifying stoicism of purpose.

Against all advice and need, against official hints that worded themselves more strongly, Salem put away the dignity of office, the polite conferences arranged and expected of him, the calculated visits to exhibition areas. He asked his own questions, insisting politely on his own decisions, often sick with shock at what he saw, forcing himself to exposure as though this were a penance for the separated, indulged life that had been his.

In the action signals Jane Stirling filed to Martin Neveau, there were few proposals or suggestions. There were instructions.

Clark Clyde said, after a meeting, 'He's had me in four provinces in seven days. And I don't get a Beechcraft. I'm riding those unlined, side-benched Air American transports. My back looks like a dartboard from trying to sleep against those goddamned fuselage bolts. He's working our tails off setting up this inoculation drive.'

The plague and the spectre of plague was everywhere, despite official denials. Clark Clyde had established that the Government had forbidden the diagnosis of plague deaths on the Saigon waterfront. These were to be ascribed to biopular embolism. It was feared that publicizing of the outbreak might result in the withdrawal of foreign shipping.

The World Health team had begun a flea-count in four provinces. Rats were trapped, the fleas on the carriers counted. The controllable index was three fleas a rat. In numbers above that the fleas began to leave their hosts and directly attack human beings. In some of these provinces the plague rats carried a poisonous population of sixteen, each flea loaded with death.

17

SALEM had been visiting a Save the Children project north of Saigon when he heard about the attack on the Montagnards. It was his second trip to the area. The misery of the orphaned Vietnamese children had become a personal involvement. He spoke bitterly about it, outside the neutrality expected of him. The USAID chief had already instructed his department heads to avoid reference to refugee children in dealing with the ICRC President.

The Viet Cong had been in strength. The tribesmen were defended by seventy soldiers, thirty of whom were part-time militia, under command of a Vietnamese lieutenant. It was a small village, some two hundred and fifty hunters and farmers, the women skirted and bare-breasted in Montagnard fashion.

In the afternoon of the preceding day the VC had threatened men working their crops in cleared jungle beyond the village. They had tried to recruit there before and had been driven off in a firefight. The tribesmen returned to their huts and put out spears and crossbows, watching the heavy green tree-line.

In the latening afternoon they saw the birds rising over the jungle and read the warning of their calls. Mongrels bristled their spines and stretched their necks, the bare-breasted women caught their babies and crouched in camouflaged holes and trenches.

The small-arms fire took the village on three sides, beating the poor defence back into shelter. The tree-line burst into running bodies behind a roaring wall of jetted flame that transformed huts to black cinders and people to blackened stumps.

Two hundred of the two hundred and fifty men, women and children died in the attack, cremated beyond recognition by the flame-throwers.

Pierre Salem, the banker, walked there next day among the few uprights of the longhouses, on the blackened warmth where timbers still smouldered, in the stink of charred flesh and the roar of clouded blowflies. From the bunkers, trenches and other hideouts the army gingerly handed up the screwed black lesions of bodies or offered food to the bare-legged, bare-breasted women who squatted whimpering, heads in their hands. The stiffened bodies of snipers dangled by their strappings in the tree-line, sprung by their weight as the green branches fretted in the wind.

The bile of nausea burned Salem's throat. He leaned on a tree, eyes closed. There had to be a law. There had to be.

She had worked for him, travelled with him and eaten with him, in the urgent climate of war. They had sweated together and dirtied together in the dust blown by armour and trucks and in the sudden drench of rains. She had watched him harden and loosen, redefined by the violence about them, by the tiredness patched under his eyes.

Once, hurrying a back road towards the city at sundown, the Vietnamese driver nervous and anxious to flee the darkness the guerrillas would use as mantle, Jane's head had dropped forward in sleep. Salem had touched her, gently lifting the small head to comfort in the corner of the cushions. She had opened her eyes with his hand on her. He had not moved, face carved, eyes lost as though in memory. She wanted to go towards this strange man, to bury her head and feel his arms about her. He had kept her there with the prop of his hand, eyes awake now.

Then he had said softly, 'You were asleep.' He gripped the jump strap and turned away to the window and the broken masonry, the upset circles of tombs and the shell holes.

128

At the end of two weeks, Martin Neveau had signalled Hanoi's refusal to permit entry to Salem or the team. Instead the North Vietnamese Government called on the ICRC to act on the torture, abuse and murder of the Liberation fighters taken prisoner in the south. The message reiterated the charge that the American forces had used and were using, bacteriological weapons.

Concerned newspaper articles about the programme of Chemical and Biological Warfare, had appeared in the world's press. Six thousand sheep in a remote district of the United States where there was a secret testing ground had mysteriously died after an experiment with nerve gas.

Charges were made that the storage of germ munitions in Thailand were incompetently supervised, responsible for outbreaks of bubonic and pneumonic plague. The Navy Department's answer to the charge confirmed that the stockpiles existed.

At the official level the ICRC team noticed a bleakening response to the growing blueprint for an attack on the pestilence. Salem listened to the reports hard-eyed.

'Would you describe these reactions as obstruction?'

The head of the World Health Organization in South Vietnam fidgeted uncomfortably. 'No, I don't think so. The official position is more that we are overstating the urgency. They are afraid of publicity, of possible panic. It's very difficult. After all, we are guests here, Mr President. We can't force anything on the Government.'

'Do the flea-counts indicate an overstatement of urgency to you?'

The WHO head had his government's interest to serve. But he knew the danger and it forced out the words. 'Hell, no. We've got a classic pattern here for an uncontrollable epidemic, and someone had better believe it.'

Salem nodded. 'I will see that they do, Mr Harris.'

The Press continued their questions. Many of the international corps of correspondents were quartered in the Continental Hotel and in the new Hotel Caravelle on the farther corner along Tu Do Street. Salem remained faithful to Martin Neveau's warning. This was a fact-finding tour. Jane told the Press that the President had met with the Catholic Relief Services, the International Rescue Committee, or the World University Service. That he had visited projects of the Save the Children Federation, or the German Knights of Malta, the American Red Cross, World Vision Relief.

'Is it true that the President is here because of the spread of plague?

How serious is the plague in South Vietnam?'

'The President is interested in all aspects of civilian welfare. His visit is to help co-ordinate the work of relief among the many internationals in the country.'

Jane, too, had been well briefed by Neveau. She enjoyed this importance, the flattering, frivolous jokes the correspondents made about the Red-hot Cross lady press officer.

Jane Stirling worried Clark Clyde. He couldn't forget her striking presence, the physical promise; and yet he couldn't get closer to her than a chaffing comradeship. On his returns to Saigon he invariably tried to arrange a dinner or a night-club party. She would accept nothing more than a drink on the patio, seemingly unconscious of being observed by the old hands who declared themselves surfeited by the slant-eyes, who nodded and smiled from their tables or whispered appreciations to each other. The few European women in Saigon lived in a hot musk of sexuality, courted and complimented wildly past the claims of their attractions.

'I can't figure that one,' Clark Clyde told Tom Mix. 'Look at the way she moves, the small steps she takes, as though she's carrying an apple between her legs. That one's loaded, she knows it and yet she stays as cool as a nun. You notice the way those big brown eyes scum up after she's had a few drinks. That's a signal you can't mistake. She's thinking about it then. That faraway look isn't for the suffering Gooks.'

Clark Clyde was drinking in the American Officers' club on the roof of the JUSPAO building, when the English correspondent leaned forward on his stool.

'Hey, you down there. The big chap.'

'I think he means you,' Tom Mix said.

'You're with President Salem's team, aren't you?'

'He's drunk,' Tom Mix said. 'He's always drunk.'

'Yes, I'm with President Salem. Why?'

'I hear you've got Lady Jane Stirling with you.'

Clyde glanced at his friend. 'There is a Jane Stirling. She appears to be a lady.'

The correspondent tipped his head and growled like a dog. 'She's a lady, to be sure. By title at least. That one could take on all the whores in Saigon. No wonder you look like a fat cat. Wipe the cream off your whiskers.'

Clyde grounded his glass and swung off the stool.

Tom Mix grabbed at his shirt. 'No trouble. Let's not have trouble.'

'Trouble,' the correspondent hooted. 'Where's the trouble travelling with randy Jane? I'm the one with trouble. They're sending me to Biafra.'

Clark Clyde lurched up the bar again, toppling his stool, dragging the WHO man with him. Quickly, two uniformed officers and a civilian barred the way. A man with cameras around his neck pulled the English correspondent to a side table.

'Take it easy, Mac. He doesn't mean any harm. He's just had too much today.'

'He's got a big mouth,' Clyde said, breathing hard.

'Sure, sure. Now he's shut it.'

They went to the double bank of elevators and rode down. Outside the arcaded entrance to the building, white-painted oil drums filled with cement fenced traffic away. Plastic explosives had been tossed inside from motor cars.

Correspondents in unbelted safari jackets, the badge of their trade, the affectation of ball-pointed pens and cigarette packs tucked into the pockets sewn on the half sleeves, dodged the pedicabs, reporting for the four o'clock briefings and hand-outs or to plan field operations.

'What did you make of that?' Clyde squinted at the slanting sun. 'Did that rummy mean that Stirling is really a Lady?'

'That's the way I heard it. A fast Lady.'

'I'm going to find out about this.'

When Clark Clyde learned the gossip of her history it did not shock him, it awed him, he swaggered to be seen buying her a drink. Jane had become a personage of drama. He wrote to his friends in Mallorca about her.

The USAID chief had been a White House staffer on the Vietnam desk under President Kennedy. He retained some of the aura of that administration, frank, friendly, energetic, youngish and deliberately fit. A large photograph of the assassinated President, inscribed and signed, hung behind the desk with others. The room had been made carefully casual, with cushioned cane chairs, settees and low, glass-topped tables. The guards on the gates and inside the entrance, wore only side-arms. The atmosphere was detached from the war, markedly civilian, bustling with a shirtsleeved informality.

While he waited for Salem the USAID chief again reminded his department heads to keep off the subject of the children. 'We'll have him off our backs soon. He leaves for Quong Lo tomorrow. Where are the signals on that? Are they ready for him up there?'

'Air America had laid on a Beechcraft. Tim Frost isn't keen about the visit. They've been under regular mortar attack.'

'Tim doesn't like people poking through his camps. They'll be safe enough in the Guest House. When Charlie mortars, he's looking for Provincial Headquarters or the Adviser's compound. He's not trying to lay them on Tim. The Ambassador has been into this. The Arvins are putting a ranger battalion into Quong Lo for President Salem's visit.'

The secretary looked in. 'They're here, Mr Ross. They're on their way up.'

'I'll receive them first. When we get to the inoculation programme I'll call you guys in with the paperwork.'

It was early evening when Pierre Salem finished his business. The WHO men, the French doctor from the Pasteur Institute and the ICRC delegate who had handled epidemics, remained to discuss and plan further detail. The flea-count made in the four provinces had sobered the sociability the USAID chief had wished to establish. The optimism of his manner returned in the relief with which he escorted Salem to his car. It wasn't easy to be an American in an American war, discussing the wreckage of it with this formally mannered President. The emotional need to defend the war's morality or dissemble about it was a familiar, nagging burden in dealings with other nationals, their volunteered labours of relief and reconstruction in themselves a reproach to policy.

Jane Stirling had arrived in a taxi to be briefed on the movement to Quong Lo. She had waited while hand-outs on the refugee camps were offered for the President's interest. She had been supplied with maps of the Province, details of the relief organizations there, the names and duties of authorities in the town.

Salem's car was at the door when Jane came down the stairs to join the leave-taking.

18

THE district had been a French residential quarter. The roads were wider here, tree-shaded, coloured by the painted plaster of flat-roofed villas behind drives that had once been gravelled. Schoolchildren, marched by nuns, swung satchels in the shimmered sunset. There were few reminders of the violence besieging the city, floating it in a sea of insurgency like an island wild waves could engulf.

Jane Stirling explained the next day's arrangements as the car bumped on smaller roads, crowding again with pedicabs and ramshackle buildings.

They had time neither to protest nor to wonder. A galvanized iron gate swung inwards. The driver wrenched the wheel, sprawling them into a corner, braked, jumped out, the door jammed open on its hinge. They saw a small courtyard, muddied and trash-littered. Figures ran from the darkened doorways of the tenement. Salem looked behind him. The gate clanged shut. Two men dropped a beam across it.

'President Salem, please do not be disturbed. You are in safe hands, President Salem.'

A Vietnamese in an old pith-helmet was at the window, speaking urgently in French. 'I'm from the Liberation Front. You understand? Do not be disturbed, Mademoiselle. We wish to talk to President Salem.'

Other voices repeated the words. 'You are in safe hands. We are from the National Liberation Front.'

A pulse beat in Jane's throat catching her breath. She whispered. 'Are they Viet Cong?'

'Yes.' Salem put his hand on her. 'Be calm. Do as they ask.'

The group by the window waited anxiously.

'Very well, gentlemen. What do you wish to say?'

'All right now?' The man in the pith-helmet bobbed apologetically. 'So sorry to surprise you. Professor Pham Thu has the honour to be President of the National Liberation Front Red Cross. So you see, there is no reason for concern.'

Salem's breath eased. He glanced about the courtyard to establish himself. Already, some of the dim figures had gone back into doorways. The threat he had felt subsided. 'Where is the Professor?'

'Inside. He is inside. Please, we will go to him now.'

On the dropped beam behind them two men squatted, machine-guns on their backs, watching the narrow street.

The spokesman opened the car door, backing and bowing. 'You will come this way, please?'

The sour stink of fish and garbage rose strongly around them. Salem kept Jane Stirling by the hand.

The entrance to the tenement was low. Salem bent beneath the sagged beam, heard the whispers in the darkness, the slapping sibilance of bare feet. A candle peaked a yellow flame, leaping shadows, abruptly lighting the disembodied head of their escort.

'Please follow. Be careful of the steps. See? Here is a handrail.'

The staircase was narrow and awkward. They followed the bobbing candle in an odour of body sweat and damp rot. There was a long gallery, light chinked under doors, another staircase.

'Only a little way now. So sorry for the inconvenience.' He kept bending to look back, nodding and smiling, craning his pock-marked face and battered helmet into the light.

They stood on a small landing, crowded by the pressing walls. A body moved in the dark, like an animal rousing. The candle lit the man as he stood up, gleamed on the gun-barrel, the heavy grenades in his belt. He looked at them once with sullen curiosity, stretched to knock the gun-barrel on the roof above him. There was a scrabble. They looked up to a sudden square of brilliant light, a glimpsed face. A bamboo ladder scraped through the trapdoor.

'Can you manage, President Salem? Can you manage, Mademoiselle?' The guard slung his weapon, braced the ladder with a hand and foot.

It had happened too quickly. He had been swept into it by the nature of events, not knowing what to expect. Salem looked at the brilliantly lit hole above him, all his conservatism protesting. He felt cold on his skin, a revulsion to climb into that entrapment, a need to get out of this catacomb. What was happening to him? What did they want?

The pock-marked face pressed close to his in the candlelight, commiserating and anxious. 'President Salem, can you manage?'

Jane Stirling whispered, her voice catching. 'Go up. Don't worry. We must go up.'

Salem bent his height to the ladder.

The refuge was a long, beamed attic, entirely sealed. Gasoline lamps flared a glaring white light, striking their eyes after the darkness. Hands grasped their arms to help them through. Salem straightened, testing himself against the ceiling. He strained to adjust his vision and mind, images registering unsequenced. Bedding was rolled against a wall. Men sat over an ammunition box, loading bullets into belts. Two young girls cooked on a primus.

'President Salem? I am Professor Pham Thu. This is indeed a great honour.'

The cultured, perfectly accented French seemed unreasonable in Salem's ears. The tiny figure in wide khaki trousers and a shirt stood beside him, a hand limply extended.

'Professor Thu?'

The Vietnamese took Salem's arm and drew him gently away from the trapdoor. 'Come and be seated. You see, we have organized chairs in your honour.'

Easily, gracefully, he turned to Jane. 'You are very welcome, Miss Stirling. My informants have not exaggerated your beauty.'

Jane's face was puckered with surprise, her hands uncertainly clasped.

'I'm afraid this rude welcome has been confusing. You must forgive me. Come, sit and take some refreshment. Do you like China tea?'

There were two canvas chairs at the attic's far end, an ammunition box between them. Thu seated them and crossed his legs on a stool. He clapped his hands and one of the young girls rose and filled a kettle from a plastic can.

He was very thin, shoulders as narrow as a child's, his face tightly drawn, lips full and red. The short hair, bristled off his scalp, was grey, the first two fingers of his right hand livid with nicotine.

'You are fortunate to live in Geneva, President Salem. It is a very beautiful city. I know it from old times. Once I taught Oriental history at the Sorbonne. I was young then. Paris was a city for the young.' He smiled, offering cigarettes, as calm and easy as a man in his drawing-room.

Thu's acceptance of the armed attic, the manner of their being there, increased the unreality for Salem. The weeks in Vietnam had changed him, but all his life had been ordered against surprise. He willed the nerves that pitted his stomach, strove to match the other man's composure. Sheer curiosity strengthened him.

'You are from the National Liberation Front Red Cross, Professor?'

'Indeed, yes. I have the honour to be President. We are much interested in your visit. Since it was hardly practicable that you should come to us, we have, as you see, come to you.'

He sucked in the cigarette smoke, nodded and smiled at them both, raising his eyebrows in a suggestion of humour.

The girl had come up very quietly. She stood with her eyes lowered, flushing, a Chinese pot and cups on a wooden tray. She wore the Au Dai, a dark surplice over coloured trousers, the long, blue-black hair forward over small breasts. The oval of face was perfect, lips and brows as ideal as a sculpture.

Thu indicated the ammunition box. She dropped gracefully to her heels, head bent in shyness and laid out the service. Jane watched her in admiration.

'Her Vietnamese name means Little Flower,' Thu said, noticing. 'She is of an old family that once served the Emperors of Hue. Perhaps this Little Flower is a rose, a blossom on a bush of thorns. She has already fought in three battles, carrying herself as bravely as a man.'

Even in that strange place where men sat loading shells, quiet and watchful, with arms stacked and grenades in boxes, it seemed impossible to Jane. The girl was too young, too tender, too beautiful. She whispered the name, 'Little Flower.'

'Femininity is no bar to patriotism.' Thu sipped his tea. 'There have been warrior queens in Vietnamese history. The English had their Boadicea. The French their Joan of Arc. The Hindus their Rani of

Jansi. There are many Little Flowers in our poor country.'

Thu refilled Salem's cup. He spoke almost dreamily, his eyes on the others in the attic. 'I would have preferred a less irregular way of enjoying your company, President Salem. But we are fish that swim in the water of the people. Out of our element we die. I must tell you that I am also a member of the Liberation Front's Central Committee.'

Salem said, in a dry voice, 'I observed that your quarters are hardly furnished with the doves of peace.'

Thu flicked his bright eyes, jigging his crossed leg. 'Peace is the most elusive of birds. Perhaps that is why it is white, the colour of hope. It is a bird that must be free, Mr President. Peace cannot live in a cage.'

Salem had forgotten his surroundings, intent on the other man. 'What is your business with me, Professor Thu?'

Thu leaned back on his stool, turned up the dark palm of one hand. 'Business. Yes, it is necessary to talk of business.'

They waited on him. He removed a tea leaf from the rim of his cup. 'We ask your aid. Your assistance.'

'What kind of aid, Professor Thu?'

Thu leaned forward, holding Salem with his slick, bright eyes. 'The Americans are going to propose peace talks, President Salem. These proposals will be accepted. We believe it will prove a manoeuvre, that we will be betrayed as we were after the Geneva Accords. We have left much blood on our earth since then. What we ask of you is this, that the International Committee of the Red Cross should make a declaration for peace at the Paris Conference, that it should call on America to halt the immoral bombing of North Vietnam.'

Salem was still focused on Thu's first words, his breath stirred by excitement. 'How is this known? Why should America propose peace now?'

All of the man was changed, his voice and face screwed tight. 'Because they are beaten, as the French were beaten. Because the more of us they slaughter, the more will rise up. Because they can stand booted in our blood, burn us to the earth, and we will reach up and claw at them with our fingers.'

The pulse in Jane Stirling's throat beat wildly. The sudden threat and menace of the frail little man shivered the air.

'You are sure?' Salem asked. 'You are sure of this?'

Thu lowered his head, let his shoulders sag, gestured with his cigarette. 'Consider. The contempt of the world grows for the Americans. Every day governments once friendly to them turn away in disgust. Their country and administration is in dissent. Their economic posi-

137

tion difficult. Why should their young men die here for a policy that could put a torch to the world? Asia has had enough of landlordism and feudal repression. Vietnam has had enough of colonialism and corruption. There are forces, President Salem, which arrogance can't bomb out of being.'

Salem was leaning forward, his handsome face burning. 'When will it happen? When will the proposal be made?'

Thu smiled and lifted his eyebrows. 'Remember, it will soon be election year in America. The gold pool countries have already secretly instructed the administration that the dollar will not be shored up to support America's adventure here. Behind all their wild words, the panic grows. There will be more demonstrations, everywhere, hammering on the doors of American Embassies. Wait and see. Soon there will be blows and more blows to shake them like an earthquake.'

Salem's mouth dried with apprehension. 'Do you mean more war? The Chinese?'

'Come now, President Salem.' Thu wagged his finger, shut his eyes for an instant. 'We are Vietnamese, not Chinese. My people fought China for six hundred years. We are grateful for China's help, but we fight our own wars, our own way. The Chinese threat to Asia is an American superstition, or an excuse. Each time the administration escalates the war, the reason for it is escalated too. Now some of their people say that if they don't fight us here, they will have to fight us in California. Oh dear.' Thu turned up the palm of his hand. 'I doubt if we can get there in our sampans. Please take more tea.'

Peace. A chance for peace. An end to the things he had seen. A resolution which he, Salem, would move, while the world watched. The image of Neveau rose in his mind, face stretched with horror at this conversation, this place, this man. Salem would suffer no more of that.

His face continued to burn, imagination leaping. 'I am not a politician, Professor Thu. There are some initiatives I can't take. If talks do occur, I must know the prospects from your side.'

Thu nodded. 'I understand your position, President.' Again he made the slack gesture with his wrist. 'How else could I talk so freely? The prospect is simple. What is the alternative? War without end? A universal conflagration? No, I do not think so. In negotiation, honour will be met with honour, as fire has been met with fire.'

There was a held silence between them, a mixed sadness of understanding and a difference beyond any meeting.

Salem said carefully, 'I will do what I can.'

'Thank you.'

Thu leaned back, jigging his leg. 'And now,' he said, smiling, almost gay, 'I know of your concern about the plague. I am empowered to offer a truce of four days to permit inoculation teams to enter our areas.'

Salem had forgotten the plague. The little Vietnamese waited smiling, as though he had made Salem a gift.

'A truce?'

'Indeed, yes. A truce.'

Again Salem was whirled by excitement, adjusting to this new possibility. He asked the question for time: 'Is it bad in your areas?'

'There has been plague. How bad it is, I do not know. There are few doctors in the jungle. We are accustomed to plague, President Salem. The French lay on our country like a plague for one hundred and fifty years. I repeat, I offer a truce. It must be arranged by the ICRC, the teams must be from the Red Cross of neutral countries. They must enter and leave our areas six weeks before the festival of Tet.'

Salem had not heard of Tet. 'When is that, Professor?'

'Tet is celebrated from January the nineteenth.'

Salem considered the condition and cooled. 'That leaves little time for negotiation.'

The Vietnamese occupied himself with a new cigarette. 'I understand your flea-count indicates an urgent situation. Let us regard it as such.'

Thu remained occupied. Salem studied him, a little edged. 'You are very well informed.'

'Yes.' Thu smiled gently. 'We are fish that swim in the water of the people.'

The flaring of the petrol lamps, the hard white light, the intent men, had mesmerized Jane. The words sounded without true meaning for her, the quiet movements and whispers at the attic's other end a dreamed reality. Only in the shapes of violence, in the grenade boxes and the dulled weapons stacked against the wall, was there reminder that the issues were of life and death.

Something rapped below them on the trapdoor. The Vietnamese in the attic stilled. Thu was motionless, head cocked. A message rapped out in spaced rhythm.

He was on his feet, no laziness in him now, his movements quick and taut, eyes flicking. Thu gave an order and spoke to Salem. 'It is time for us to leave. The night too is a Vietnamese patriot.'

Thu bent over Jane Stirling's hand. 'You have spirit, Mademoiselle.

Please accept my admiration. President Salem, your car has been returned to your hotel. When you leave you will find a vehicle waiting.'

The guerrillas were wrapping weapons in bedding and mats, belting rice in strips of cloth under their shirts.

He put out one small hand and grasped Salem's arm with the other, looking up to him. 'We depend on you, President Salem. May your life and your work be blessed.'

An emotion, for nothing and everything, filled Salem's throat. 'It has been a strange and memorable meeting. I will not forget it.'

'Nor will I. Now we must hurry.'

They backed down the ladder into the dark. A candle lit and peaked. Jane Stirling paused. 'Goodbye, Little Flower.'

Thu spoke quietly in Vietnamese. The young girl nodded and blushed. 'Goo' luck. Goo' luck.'

They came off the wide sweep of La Loi, busy with racketing motor scooters, food and merchandise stalls, into the neon glitter of Constitution Square. They had made the short ride almost in silence, still there in the tunnelled tenement, with Thu in the attic's white light. The waiting cab which had jerked away before Salem pulled his door shut, turned into Tu Do Street, under the looming mass of two crouched Vietnamese soldiers, bulked as they never were in life, the monument to Unknown Heroes.

The evening was languid, comfortably cool, the girlie-bars and restaurants bustling. On the Continental's patio, correspondents exchanged stories. Soldiers on leave watched the synthetic violence of a Second World War entertainment on American Forces Network Television.

The driver remained bent to the cab's wheel as Salem and Jane got out. Then he turned, grinning with broken, stained teeth.

'Thirty piastres, please,' he said in strained English.

It was the anxious little man in the crumpled pith-helmet.

19

They wanted to be alone with what had happened, to recall it in sharing.

'Shall we eat in my apartment?'

It was a privilege for Salem, offered by the management.

'I must wash. Look at me.'

Jane turned up her hands, blackened by fumbling the walls of the tenement. Salem inspected his own, soiled to the wrists, dirt and cobwebs on the sleeves of his jacket. He brushed quickly at himself, not wanting it seen, as though these traces betrayed them.

The manager met them at the staircase, bowing, handed Salem an envelope addressed to him. It was the briefing for the Quong Lo visit, which Jane had dropped and forgotten in the first disorder when the iron gate closed behind them.

She had let down her hair. It swung heavily from the shower, weighted by the damp she could not towel out of it. The cotton frock touched her neatly.

She had forbidden her own violence, retreated before it, sought an agreement with emptiness. That was unnecessary now. The violence outside her had cracked the pretence. The truth was survival, there was nothing more, a time to fill in as best one could.

Jane Stirling moved slowly about the preparations, touching perfume on her flesh, leaning sleepily to the mirror, her face as bare of cosmetics as Little Flower's, seeing images again of the attic, feeling Salem's hands reaching to help and guide her through the dark.

She went to his apartment, the perfectly cut, rounded chin raised, the wide eyes opaque as Clark Clyde had once noticed them.

Salem had ordered Champagne, because it felt like a celebration to him. The floorboy had uncorked the bottle, hearing Salem in the bedroom. He came out in trousers and shirt, wearing a tie for the dinner, when he heard the cork popped.

He drank and refilled the glass because he needed distraction, an occupation for his hands. There had been no preparation in the anodyne of his life for these experiences. He was as new to them as a child, stirred and shocked by everything, as though most of what he had known had been dreamed.

Salem strode the room, alarmed by the excitement that burst in his mind like the bubbled wine he continued to swallow.

She knocked and he called her to enter. He was across the room and drawing her inside before she had opened the door.

'Jane, I think I should return to Geneva. The others can finish here. There can be nothing as important as what happened tonight. Think of it, a face-to-face meeting, a hard proposal that might lead to anything. This wouldn't be a religious cease-fire, a sentimental pause in the killing. It would be mutually taken for mutual reconstruction, the first signal of sanity.'

She moved with him, watching his face, his hand laid unnoticed on her arm. He filled the glasses, paced again in the room.

'The ICRC made a truce of a few days in Santo Domingo, to return prisoners and wounded. The fighting did not start again. What an extraordinary man. Wasn't it all most extraordinary?'

She smiled a little from her wine, very still in the chair, indulging and possessing the difference of him, broken out of suits, broken into frankness and excitement.

'When will you go, Pierre?' She spoke the name to herself again, she had not used it aloud before, watching him as he had once caught her at Château Malraux. She did not want him to go back there into his armour and distance. She wanted to keep him with her here, sweating and close in cars, shouting in the wind in helicopters above jungles and shell holes. Here, in the reality that mocked at emptiness, reaching out to shake and instruct them.

'Thu has given me until six weeks before Tet. He must feel that if his offer is limited, it won't be allowed to drag. That must be his purpose. I must act quickly. I must return to Geneva at once. I will tell the others I have been recalled. There must not be suspicion of anything else. You understand that, don't you? You must give no hint of what happened.'

She rose and walked towards him and he watched her come. She walked with short steps, arms stiff, her spine pitched back, in the thrall of her body's will. She laid the flat of her hands on his chest and brought herself against him on her toes.

'Yes, Pierre,' she whispered. 'I understand.'

His long body shuddered, his eyes closed, the softness and fullness of her flowed over him. He broke a little towards her, bending his height. The glass he held fell and smashed. He was folded in her flesh and her perfume. She reached a warm arm behind him, tilted his head with her hand. His eyes remained tight shut as she took his mouth, arching herself into him. She sought his trembling lips, his trembling body, found a blundering seeking of his own. Again she felt for his mouth, choking her breath into his, again he gave himself up, blundered against her, his body clumsy in her arms.

Then he stiffened, a shaking that stretched him beyond her. His voice was broken, arresting her. 'No. God, no. No, please, no.'

His arms stretched above him, fists twisted, his chin turned across one shoulder, all the face masked in lines of anguish.

She fell away from him, trying to come back, hearing the gasps that shook him. 'Pierre. What is it? What is it?'

His arms came down slowly, his head twisted away. 'Please. Don't look at me. Please, let me be alone.'

But she couldn't leave him alone, borne on the black tide which had not left her. 'Pierre, what is it? Let me help you.'

She touched him again, sick with passion and tenderness.

And again he cried out. 'No. Please. Let me alone.'

She backed away and she did not know where she was or who she was, searching his face with unfocused eyes. He moved past her to the bedroom's open door and leaned there, his forehead on his arm. After a time he quietened, his voice came lifeless and low.

'Can you forgive me?'

She shook her head, not knowing, more lost than ever. 'I don't know. I don't understand.'

He straightened and faced her. 'I must know that you forgive me.'

'I don't know what forgiveness you want.' Unaccustomed tears had lit in her eyes, her lips shook. 'Is it me? Is it something about me?'

He groaned. 'Oh God, no.'

'Then I don't, I can't understand.' Her voice rose and broke. 'What is it then, what is wrong?'

He shook his head. 'Please go now, Jane. Try to forget this.'

'Go? Just go?'

'Try to forgive me.'

The General had been shopping for his family. He carried coolie hats and Chinese slippers embroidered with dragons and flowers. She was almost running in the dim light of the passage, a fist screwed against her mouth.

'Ah, Miss Stirling. Is the President in? He called us for six o'clock. We waited an hour and then gave him up.'

Jane nodded. 'Yes. He is in.'

The General tipped his heavy, blunt face at her. 'Anything wrong? You look peaked.'

She calmed herself. 'I have a headache. A touch of the sun perhaps.'

'You should watch that. It's a beastly climate. Is everything arranged for Quong Lo?'

'Yes. We leave tomorrow afternoon.'

'Been shopping,' the General said unnecessarily. 'Damned merchants don't use wrapping paper. Had to walk through the streets like this. Felt a damn fool. The VC mortared Ton Son Nhut this afternoon. Did you hear about it?'

She shook her head. I'm afraid I will have to get an aspirin, General.'

'I think you should. Lie down with a cold towel on your forehead. Works wonders.'

He watched her go and called after her. 'Hope there's no damned mortaring out there tomorrow. Don't know what to expect in this city. Whole damned place is thoroughly unsafe.'

She lay face down on the bed and she wanted to cry, but could not. She didn't know what to cry for. It would not be for shame, she felt none. She couldn't cry for Salem, he had frightened her, his arms stretched like a sacrifice, his face twisted on his shoulder.

144

The fervour, the idealism that had reached and moved her during the Château Malraux parties, seemed hollow now. His beauty was meaningless. All of him, all they had shared, somehow meaningless. Jane turned, dry-eyed, gazing into the dark, exhausted by the crowded day, by the decision that had come unbidden and engulfed her.

Try to forgive me.

She would not forgive him his asking for forgiveness, the cheat of him, the meaninglessness of all he had appeared to be and to mean. She felt no shame, but she was bitter for her error, bitter for having believed in him. She drew a hand across the full mouth she had given him, in a spasm of anger and disgust. The tide had gone out and emptied her. Jane fell asleep in the dark.

She started up when the telephone rang, her heart beating painfully, in a confusion of dreams, striving to identify the room, to identify herself, to leave that place into which all the past weeks had tumbled in grotesque dislocation.

'It's Clark Clyde, Jane. I just wanted to say goodbye. I've got an early meeting in the morning.'

She came to herself gratefully, reached for the light switch. 'I'm sorry. What was that? I was sleeping.'

'It's Clark Clyde. I just wanted to wish you goodbye.'

'Where are you going?'

'I'm not going anywhere. I mean I'm going to Quong Lo. I'm not going back with you to Geneva.'

She brushed at her hair, frowning.

'I don't understand, Clark.'

'Are you in bed?'

'On the bed. What's the time?'

'Nine o'clock. If you're not in bed can I buy you a drink?'

She had thought it was the middle of the night. 'You can buy me a dinner.'

Seated together in the Hotel Caravelle, Clark Clyde stared dismally at the menu. He had barely finished a big meal before telephoning Jane.

'We took it for granted you would be going back with him. You've been nursing him like a mother.'

Jane shook her head. 'Mother's staying. I like it here.'

'Can't say that I do. There are rumours about an attack. Did you know the VC mortared Ton Son Nhut this afternoon?'

'The General told me. The General doesn't like war.'

'What happened, Jane? Salem was in a state. He was as nervous as a cat. He kept watching the door as though a ghost might come through it.'

'What did he say?'

'Just that he'd been called back. You do the signals. Is anything the matter? Something has put him in a state.'

'Yes. He's in a state,' Jane said coldly. 'Let's share a châteaubriand.'

'A châteaubriand?' Clark Clyde was miserable. 'Are they very big?'

'Not too big for a big man like you. I'll have shrimp cocktail for a start.'

'I don't believe I'll have a starter.'

'A lady can't eat alone. It isn't manners.'

Clark Clyde shut his eyes. 'Very well. Shrimp cocktail for two.'

The Caravelle was a new hotel, a gay place in the evenings. They were at the end of the meal when they heard the heavy concussions, a muffled whump, whump, whump that seemed to vibrate the air. The chatter quietened. The guests waited, the men's faces suddenly sharpened.

'Artillery?' somebody asked.

Again the concussions whumped the room.

'No. More like heavy bombing.'

A correspondent scraped back his chair, wiping his mouth with a napkin.

'I'm going up on the roof.' He took his wine from the bucket. 'Come on, bring the glasses.'

They watched other hurried departures.

'Do you want to go?' Clark Clyde asked. 'Up on the roof, I mean. There might be something to see.' He emptied his glass and Jane's, and stuffed them in his pockets.

The parapet was lined with figures, bottle and glasses before them, exchanging calls and conjecture. A jet screamed near by, its tailpipe flaring.

'Sock it to them, man,' someone shouted.

There were more whumps, other distant explosions.

'What do you think? Is it Ton Son Nhut?'

'More the other way, near Cholon.'

On the dark horizon the sky lit with blazing streaks of colour, like fierce shooting stars.

'Helicopter gunships. They're putting the rockets in.'

Blazing parachute flares burned holes of luminosity in the dark. Tracer shells rose hotly, bent and expired.

146

'It's Cholon side. Somewhere back of Cholon.'

Again the fierce shooting stars struck at the ground from low on the horizon. The air whumped again.

The shouts and laughter on the roof grew louder.

'Sock it to them. Sock it to the little bastards.'

Jane thought of the attic. The small men in bare feet and sandals, hurrying to wrap weapons in mats, tying rice belts around their waists.

'It looks like cracker night,' Clark Clyde said. 'That's all—just like cracker night.'

Another jet screamed over the city. A woman in an evening dress tried to find it. 'Hurry up. You'll be late for the party.'

Jane thought of Little Flower. Was it possible she was out there? It shivered her skin. She couldn't drink the wine. She didn't want to watch any more. She wanted to get away from these people. She touched Clark Clyde's arm. 'I've had enough. Let's go back to the Continental.'

He was reluctant, looking at his watch. 'I suppose we should. It's getting close to curfew. I'll just kill the last glass.'

At her door he said, uncertainly, 'Are you going to ask me in for a nightcap?'

For a moment she considered it. 'It's late. I have a letter to write.'

He didn't pursue it.

'Thanks for the dinner, Clark. Come here.'

She moved slightly towards him, pulled his head down, arched herself against his big frame. When she gave him up he was pale.

'At least you can kiss,' Jane said. 'Good night.'

He stood shaken, staring at the door.

'Holy mackerel,' he said.

20

THE US guest-house was the most comfortable in Quong Lo, flat-roofed and cream-plastered, practically furnished, with the comforts of an unpretentious motel.

Fronting the two-floored main building, an uncompleted annexe housed a droning crackling radio room. Steel rods bristled in the uncompleted two bedrooms and bathroom above it. Double steel gates with an observation trap armoured the high concrete wall. There was a sitting-room inside the entrance, a homey, chintzy place that partly denied the strewed ammunition, the gas and smoke grenades kept on the flat roof against attack.

A staffer who had been moved from the big building to temporary quarters in the annexe had carried a carbine and grenades with him to signify his dissatisfaction. 'The hell with these visiting firemen. If Charlie hits us you guys will be on the roof, bowling gas into the compound. We'll be out there, likely choking to death.'

Tim Frost had been posted from the State Department to be USAID chief of the province. He usually wore a wide straw hat, the brim curled cowboy fashion, trouser bottoms inside black ankle boots. He was short and tough and hard about the war, strenuously committed to the rightness of the administration's policy. The heavy lensed glasses that covered his eyes magnified the anger that quickly smouldered there at hinted criticism or doubt.

'I've lost good friends up here.' It completed the equation for Frost, as though the killing should be unilateral. The deaths of his friends, of any American, confirmed to him the impossible evils of communism.

Tim Frost had put on a suit for the arrival of President Salem. The big camp of Cao-Dai religionists had been spruced up, rehearsed and readied. He had instructed his staff about the schedule: 'I want this bunch in and out fast, and I don't want any philosophizing. We've got a complex situation here and they're not about to understand it. Watch your mouths when you answer questions. Make it factual and make it short. Remember, President Salem is the most important outsider we are likely to get in this province. The whole Agency is in a sweat about him. We're busting a gut up here. We want it to look as good as it can.'

Adam Thomson left the hospital to shower and change. The suit he had worn to Vietnam was at the back of the closet. He drew it out, staring with dismay at the crumpled mess on the hanger. Grey monsoon mould patched the jacket. The trousers inside it flourished in mould like a culture. Adam wiped at it, shouting for Borgia.

Frost was leaving the guest-house when the signal was brought him from the radio room. He read it, mouth tightening, slammed it down on a table.

'The goddamned man's not coming. President goddam Salem. He's been called back to Geneva.'

Frost's deputy said, mournfully, 'But everything's ready. The rooms, the reception, everything. They've been working in the kitchen all morning. They've put a Ranger battalion into this town for President Salem.'

Frost looked down at his carefully prepared suit, his eyes expanding in anger. 'Visiting Presidents, visiting politicians, visiting lousy correspondents. What are we, a reception centre for every nosy carpet-bagger in the country?'

He picked up the signal. 'Ex-Saigon 1100 hours. They've been sitting on this at Da Nang.'

Frost was more than glad to be free of Salem. He felt personally exploited because he had dressed, because the signal had not been passed according to its priority.

'You get on to Da Nang about holding up our signals. Let them know I want an explanation. Pick up your face. The others are coming. You'll get your party.'

Bumping to the airstrip in his scout car, Frost marked the clumps of troops and armour on the road. Twin-fuselaged spotter aircraft were up, rolling to scan the country. Maybe the army had not been told either. He was mollified by the likelihood.

In the latening afternoon the heat still jumped and shimmered on the airstrip's asphalt. Sam Jarra sat in his jeep wearing shorts and a sweaty shirt. He had driven in early from the camps. 'This Salem's the Big Daddy of my business. I figger I should see him once.'

The shabby, low buildings that edged the strip were fronted by jeeps and scout cars. The civilians laughed and talked, seeking the shade, jackets on their arms to keep them fresh. They felt the importance of the President's visit. Each of their organizations was somehow bonded to the International in Geneva. Salem's coming to Quong Lo reaffirmed the need for their being there. A signal of international solidarity in the loneliness of helping and healing.

Adam Thomson was talking with Mark Hatton. The mould patches Borgia had scrubbed shone mistily in the sunlight. Adam was painfully aware of it.

Sam Jarra inspected him, chuckling. 'Hi, Adam. You off to some fancy-dress ball? That's the first suit I ever saw with leprosy.'

They were all there, invited and uninvited. The Red Cross men from the camps, The West Germans from the hospital ship, the Canadian medical observers, Thomson from the hospital, the Quaker leader, a few correspondents helicoptered from Da Nang.

Frost stared morosely at them. An Australian writer and a Welsh photographer had recently given the camps and hospital a black eye. Their articles had concentrated on what Frost called the 'negative aspects' of relocations. He was sick to death of them all. There was no peace from them. There was always something more they needed, shaking their heads and looking mournful, forever presenting the civilian case. Who were the civilians? Children tossed grenades and ran. Greybeards planting in the paddy whipped up machine pistols to shoot troops in the back. The whole cursed country was booby-trapped and mined by these innocent civilians.

They had turned out like this to reproach him, to demonstrate for the ultimate dove. But the dove had flown back to Geneva. They had put themselves out for nothing.

Frost made himself seem surprised, looking them over carefully. 'What's this? A foreign community convention?'

He was a hard man. They were never sure of him.

'It looks like it, doesn't it?' one smiled.

'We thought we'd beef up the President's welcome,' a Canadian said. 'It's a big day for Quong Lo.'

Frost looked puzzled. 'You don't mean President Salem?'

They were puzzled now. Uncertain, looking for the joke.

'He don't mean LBJ,' Sam Jarra called, and got a hard look for his trouble.

Frost pursed his lips. 'Gentlemen, President Salem isn't coming. He's been recalled to Geneva.'

When the Beechcraft dropped steeply down the sky and taxied to the huts, the welfare workers of Quong Lo waited in disappointment.

In the taking away of the expected, because they had planned and prepared for it, each was hollowed by a sense of loss which awoke other depressions. Salem's visit was to have been something for themselves.

Sam Jarra had backed his jeep and was leaving.

'You want to play poker later, Mark? Or you still going to this party?'

Hatton watched the Beechcraft stop rolling, turn into the wind for take-off. 'I'm an official welcomer, Sam, with or without the President.' He went with the others towards the aircraft.

The door of the Beechcraft opened. Clark Clyde stepped out squinting, pushed on a pair of sunglasses and turned to help Jane Stirling. She wore slacks, tightly fitted, and a sleeveless open-necked blouse.

Sam Jarra pulled himself up by the wheel and stared over the jeep's dirty windscreen. 'Man, look at that fanny. For this I'll give up the slant-eyes.'

The rain squalls that had steamed Quong Lo had ceased abruptly. The monsoon was coming now in earnest, rumbling the heavy clouds that screwed tighter, darting crackled lightning in their bellies, congesting for the burst that would tear them apart and dump their load on the town.

The work of creating free fire zones hurried towards completion. Battalions of Task Force Nebraska made a last assault before the rains on a promontory of fishing villages among the pines and volcanic rock on the South China Sea. At the beginning of winter the marines had fought a bitter battle on the promontory, a confrontation with main force NVA units and entrenched VC.

During the assault Sam Jarra had helicoptered in to examine the suggested site on which the villagers would be relocated after their hamlets were secured and destroyed.

In the Red Cross mess, when he had showered and got himself a cold beer, Sam reported on his two days' inspection. 'There ain't many casualties, Adam. There are these rocky islands off shore where Charlie's hiding. They're blasting him out with air strike. We got six civilian casualties in the paddy this morning—up went this claymore on a trip-wire. You got many transfers out to the slaughterhouse?'

'Not today, Sam. What time was this?'

'Early. Maybe they're all dead, then. I saw this old lady, one leg blasted off, the other kind of hanging. They brought her back to Command in the Colonel's chopper, but she's dead on arrival. Maybe they're all DOA.'

The Red Cross team leader, a big man of German descent who had negotiated relief in Berlin with Hermann Goering for the last three years of the Second World War, took another cold beer from the freezer. 'Is any work being done on the campsite?'

'They got her levelled off, Jim. There's this hill where the battalion's got strongpoints. They want the camp under the guns for protection if Charlie should make a hit. When the rains break they're going to be swimming down there. They've got this camp in a saucer. I found another site on the Colonel's map but the trouble is he can't cover it from his strongpoints. I told him they'll be swimming. So he tells me these are my people—I bring 'em in, I've got to protect 'em. My people, crissake. He's about to blast their villages and he's sweating and worrying about his people. Maybe I've been out here too long. Whole thing's a big funny farm.'

The team leader got up from the couch, rearranged the fan, sat back and sighed. 'Could it be drained? Is there any fall to the land?'

'Like I say, it's a saucer. You ever try draining a saucer? Only thing they can do is build these hooches up. Get the floors maybe half a metre off the ground. If they lift in a dozer, maybe they can do it like that.'

The team leader sighed again, undid the top button of his shorts to ease the swell of his paunch. 'Did you get an estimate?'

'Two thousand, maybe more. They're still going in up there. One

152

thing, it's sandy country—should suck down a lot of water. You should see these tunnels the marines dug Charlie out of last winter. They burrowed that sand like crabs. I was in one got rooms big, bigger than this villa. Some of these tunnels go for miles. They've got hospitals down there as big as Adam's.'

Sam Jarra tipped his long, sandy face and looked shrewd. 'Charlie hasn't got everything in these hospitals. He hasn't got a volunteer like Adam's got, with a fanny that'd make a dead man get up. You been noticing Adam lately, Jim? This big smile, this walking about on his toes?'

The ribbing had not stopped. It was open season on Adam. He found himself embarrassed by it, to his surprise and irritation. 'You've got a one-track mind, Sam.'

The team leader smiled, glanced slyly over his spectacles. 'That's true, Adam. A dirt track.'

Sam agreed, nodding his head with satisfaction. 'It's a dirty old mind and that's for sure.'

Tim Frost had wanted the visitors in and out fast. They only stayed two days. The General had been unwell on arrival and sickened next morning with stomach pains. Pedro Darder treated the upset, which was known as Ho's revenge, but the General kept woefully to his bed, convinced he had contracted a sinister ailment.

The disappointment that had struck at the airport remained to depress the reception. The long, hard weeks had tired Salem's team, it affected them now in his absence. It had been his drive and authority, his concern, that had renewed them. They had been important because of his importance. The General could have helped but did not, refusing food and drink, chewing digestives, being unable to find the bathroom.

Clark Clyde whispered to Jane, 'This is miserable. They're not here for us. I feel like an impostor. I'm going to get myself stoned.'

The Quakers were first to leave. The ICRC delegate had mentioned the Geneva Conventions in conversation with the bearded physiotherapist. Hatton heard it. His voice cut across them, drawing attention. 'The Geneva Conventions are rules. This is a war without rules. We didn't make it that way. The enemy did.'

Silence pooled for a minute. The young woman Quaker talking with Jane Stirling paled and put down her fruit juice.

'Your enemy, Major,' She said tensely. 'We have no enemies here. We have only sick and crippled children.'

There was another, deeper silence. The Quaker leader looked at his watch, coughed nervously. 'I think we should be going. It has been a great pleasure, General, gentlemen, Miss Stirling. Thanks for the hospitality, Mr Frost.'

The others found reason to talk with animation, offering each other fresh drinks. Jane had turned to Hatton. Her voice was cool.

'I presume you are a hawk, Major?'

Hatton returned the appraisal. 'No, ma'am. I'm a soldier.'

'You don't believe in the Conventions?'

'I never saw them. I believe in what I see. The way it is here.'

Adam Thomson had listened. 'I understand you want to visit the hospital, Miss Stirling.'

Jane was slow to break with Hattton. She said, 'Yes, Dr Thomson. If that can be arranged.'

Hatton said, 'I wouldn't advise it.'

Adam began to speak. They both ignored him.

'Why wouldn't you? Why not?'

'It's rough out there. It isn't a clinic in Geneva.'

'Have you heard of Lambaréné, Major?'

Hatton had not.

Jane said to Adam, 'Perhaps the Major has heard of Dr Schweitzer.'

Hatton clamped his jaws.

'Lambaréné was Schweitzer's bush hospital in the Congo. It was rough out there, Major. I nursed and cleaned for two years in that hospital.'

Adam Thomson gaped at her. 'Good Lord! Did you really?'

Tim Frost was working on estimates of needed building materials in the big, gauze-walled dining-room.

'What do you mean, she's staying?'

His assistant shrugged. 'She just said she's staying. She's going to work in the hospital.'

'The hell she is. She hasn't asked my permission.'

'She said the General will make any necessary arrangements in Saigon.'

Frost banged the table. 'I make the arrangements in this province. I don't want her here. I want her on that aircraft with the others.'

He began to write on his pad, carving out angry capitals.

Frost's signal to the Director of USAID was dispatched and replied to by priority. Frost was advised to extend President Salem's aide every co-operation. The signal further said that a confidential report on Miss Stirling's movements and attitudes would be appreciated in Saigon.

Frost's assistant read the message in the radio room. When he delivered it he did not wait.

Big Clark Clyde had been reluctant and depressed saying goodbye. 'It's funny. I didn't want to come here. Now I feel funny about leaving. It's like I'm running away from something. It gets to you, doesn't it, as though this is where it's all happening? Jane, it could get hairy here. Quong Lo's been hit hard more than once. You sure you know what you're doing?'

'Yes, Clark. Come, you must hurry.'

'I'm going to miss you. I don't like this ships-that-pass-in-the-night thing. It gives me a nothing feeling.'

'You're a dear boy. Now you really must go, the car's hooting.'

'I suppose so.'

He was still reluctant, glancing about the chintzy sitting-room as though he needed to fix it in memory. 'Can I write to you, Jane?'

'I'd like that.'

Clark Clyde lifted his bag. 'As the sun sets we say goodbye to Quong Lo. Here goes nothing.'

21

It wasn't a clinic in Geneva and it wasn't Lambaréné. The hospital at Quong Lo was no worse in provision than Schweitzer's collection of sheds. She had nursed fevers, diseases and accidents there, ignorances and superstitions, but the bodies were black, out of another time, their miseries environmental.

'Most of these are gunshot,' Adam told her. 'Have you had experience in dressing?'

Jane looked down the crowded beds and litters, at the stained and bloodied bandages, the stirring watching bodies.

'Not enough for this.'

'Dr Darder will open some. He has his own system for dressing wounds.' Adam was unsure about her. 'Don't try to do too much.'

He wanted to give her other reassurance, sought for a way to phrase it. 'I don't know how it was at Lambaréné, but these people have a high threshold of pain.' He began to stumble. 'I mean, it might get you down to begin. You shouldn't invest too much of yourself.'

Darder helped him, brisk and cheerful.

'It's true. I don't know why it is, but they don't hurt as much as Europeans. Well, Nurse Stirling, shall we begin? A day in the life at Quong Lo provincial shambles?'

It was a strange way to find integration. Within a few days Jane was competent with the dressings, glowing at Darder's approval, particularly lit by the acceptance of the patients, their shy smiling response.

'They're such a beautiful people, Adam. I must learn Vietnamese. Have you any books? I want to start now, tonight.'

She had been a week in the hospital when Sam Jarra returned from the new Relocations. In that time there had been no intake of serious wounds. On the following morning a teenage girl was brought in on a medevac helicopter. There had been a further explosion in the paddy. The girl was injured in one leg. A medic had treated the wound at Battalion, administered morphia and plasma.

Adam Thomson examined the casualty.

Pedro Darder said, 'The pulse is sound enough. She's a strong kid. Will you operate now?'

Adam nodded.

'Clean her up.'

Jane had been rehearsed to help in the theatre. When she had washed and put on a smock and mask she wheeled the trolley to the sterilizer, laid out the instruments. The Vietnamese nurse who customarily assisted Adam checked the trolley and nodded, the gauze of her face mask crinkled into a smile.

'Is good. Is OK.'

She adjusted the big overhead lamp and switched it on, repositioned the trolley and pushed kick baskets close to the table.

Jane asked, 'It's not a bad wound, is it?'

'Not bad. Not good. Ssh now! Doctors come.'

The girl was unusually pretty, her face perfectly moulded, the lips full and delicately drawn in the characteristic Vietnamese fashion. Darder had injected pentathol. The long black-lashed eyes, partly open, faintly veined, lay like flowers on the unflawed skin.

Darder checked the pulse, lowered the rubber face mask. The Vietnamese nurse put the girl's good leg on an extension board, began to swab the mangled flesh of the other with iodine.

Adam Thomson pushed tighter into his gloves. For several minutes he stood unmoving, focused on the wounds. He touched the tender, rounded thigh and pointed. Darder wrapped a hand-towel in a rubber bandage and fixed the torniquet. White towels were laid over the leg.

Adam Thomson stood hunched, his eyes dark under the cap pulled low on his forehead, looking nowhere, almost as though he had forgotten them in some other absorption. Darder checked the dial above the gas cylinders, nodded.

Adam Thomson jerked out his hand, palm up. The Vietnamese nurse slapped an instrument there.

Jane looked away when the scalpel sunk down the flesh, a momentary revulsion at the body's butchering, of the frankness of meat under the petalled skin which the mind knows but rejects.

They were close about the table. There was little she could see, other than the young girl's face, wonderfully at peace, the eyelids and lashes flickering a little as children's do in dreams.

Jane felt fiercely proud of Adam, of them all, of herself, that they should be there to make this young beauty whole. She wished there was more she could do, more share she could take. The nurse slapped a bigger scalpel into Adam Thomson's hand, exchanged it for a needle and cat-gut.

It was unreal for her now, outside the stare of the overhead lamp's reflection, only their breathing loud in the unspoken silence, faintly hissed by the anaesthesia. The light and the green-smocked figures bent in it, hypnotized Jane a little. She let her thoughts float and jumble.

It was a long time before the nurse took the needle and handed Adam the tiny saw. Pedro Darder raised his arms, hands clasped, and stretched himself. He looked over at Jane, popped his eyebrows and bent again to the table.

Because there had been hardly a sound and little movement save the quick passing of instruments, Jane startled at the soft thud, the quick almost violent movement with which Adam Thomson kicked away the basket, stretching to suck in his breath, ease his back, one hand outstretched for ligatures.

Jane Stirling could not bear the shock and disbelief that shrieked in her. Her eyes snapped shut in protest. She clutched her masked mouth with one hand. She would have to see the kick basket if she opened her eyes. She must keep them shut for ever.

The Vietnamese nurse prodded Jane's arm, pointed to a pad of vaseline gauze in a basin. She had to open her eyes, move to pass it. The kick basket was square in the light. In it the young girl's leg gleamed.

Adam Thomson sat on the chipped cement verandah and smoked, watching the dumb boy Ho running to float a kite left for him by

Hatton. The leaves on the pepper tree barely moved in the sweltering compound. Little Ho's face trickled with perspiration. Adam decided to take him to lunch at the mess. He could fly the kite from the jeep.

Each evening, when Hatton came to have his wound treated, he would greet Ho in Vietnamese. If the boy stopped, or ran from him, Hatton pretended not to notice. Sometimes he brought candy. He made no attempt to entice the child, tossed the candy to him, calling, 'Catch this, Ho,' and walked on. Adam had observed that before he left Hatton would look for the candy.

The wrapped bars lay untouched in the dust to begin with. While they exchanged a few words on the verandah, Hatton would see them and his jaw would tighten.

The fright Ho had taken at his uniform had become an issue to Hatton. He did not discuss it again with Adam, but persevered about it as stubbornly as he exercised his leg.

On one day the candy was gone from the compound. On the next, when Hatton called and tossed his gift, Ho dropped a ball to catch it.

Adam, who was repairing the hood of his jeep again, saw it and smiled. Hatton looked stoney, gave up and grinned, then frowned at the old hood to cover his pleasure. 'I'm getting you a new one, Doc.'

It had been a long operation. He appreciated the cigarette and the rest. When the stump had been bandaged and he moved from the table and held out his arms for the nurse to strip the bloodied gloves, Adam had looked into Jane Stirling's streaming eyes. She remained like that, gulping, wrenched off her mask and ran from the theatre.

He would have to face her. It might as well be now. Adam flipped his butt into the pepper tree.

There was a shaded place behind the hospital, with a few deck-chairs and a metal table. They sometimes sat there to drink coffee. He found her dry-eyed, her hands clenched on her knees.

Adam took a chair, tapped up a cigarette and offered it. She shook her head, not looking at him.

'Would you like a drink? Pedro has Spanish brandy.'

She shook her head, did not answer.

'It might do you good.'

Her voice was hard, flat. 'Why did you do it?'

'It was the only way, Jane.'

Now she turned to him, fierce. 'I've seen injuries before. You didn't have to do it. You butchered that girl. You smashed that pretty creature's life.'

Adam leaned on his knees, head bent, hopeless and wearied. 'Jane, I will try to explain.'

'Explain! How can you explain? How can you?'

Adam remained bent, his voice low. 'Will you listen?' He waited.

'Yes, I could have saved her leg.'

He looked up, almost like Hatton, hard and unrelenting. Then he bent again. 'Perhaps there would have been some risk of toxic absorption from crushed muscle, it's doubtful. Given time, three or four months and a series of operations, given asepsis each time and proper after-care, yes, I could have saved the girl's leg.'

'Then why didn't you?' She stuck a fist on the chair. 'Why didn't you?'

'Jane, we don't have three or four months. We don't have after-care. At any time we could be flooded with casualties. There have been weeks when I have stood in that theatre patching and cutting ten hours a day. You can't favour one life over another, allocate one casualty a bed for three or four months which ten or a dozen might need.'

He stopped and spoke toughly. 'These are the facts of life here. I can't change it. If it's too much to accept, you should leave. There are sixty thousand amputees in this country now. God knows how many there will be before it is over. When we take a limb we give back a life. We have to think of it like that. Can't you see?'

The distress was frank on his face. She wondered at him, trying to understand. At last she touched his arm.

'Adam, I'm sorry.'

22

THE clouds voided in a downpour that fell on Quong Lo with the weight of an avalanche. The thirsting earth, once cracked and powdered by the hammer of summer, had already been slaked on the squalls and showers with which the monsoon had experimented. Now the paddy, the roads and compounds, were saturated past further absorption. The torrents struck and the greased surface of the world choked them back in rubbished brown lakes.

In the town's streets the trash of a year was swirled into drainage pipes, damming the outlets, heaping back the muddied tides into which vehicles sprayed, coughed and stopped. The short Vietnamese waded thigh-deep, thrusting bamboo poles into storm pipes, looking like water-borne mushrooms in their conical coolie hats.

Under the galvanized iron of the hospital and annex they shouted down the roar of the rains.

Adam Thomson's jeep had benefited by a new hood as Hatton had promised. In it, wrapped in a poncho, Adam sprayed and skidded between the hospital and the mess as satisfied as another man would have been in a limousine.

With some of the anger gone from its belly, the sky lifted and thinned, settling down for the season. Punctually in the mornings it disgorged, and again in the latening afternoon. In between the sun shone, raising steam, drawing it back for further condensation, drying out those caught in the rains of the morning to soak them again in the afternoon.

In the camps the refugees huddled in the hooches, patching the ceilings and coughing, expressionless in this new torment, reduced past hope into the fatalism and inertia of animals caged.

It was unusual for Sam Jarra to be gloomy. He took off his poncho and shook it out on the hospital verandah, after looking into the orthopaedic ward. 'I tell you, Adam, I'm no bleeding heart, but this place I want to stay away from. How they breathe in there I don't know. That Stirling broad looks like Ava Gardner but she's got a lotta spunk to stick this.'

Sam sucked in his cheeks to light a sodden cigarette, pitched it away in disgust. 'You got a dry one, Adam?'

Adam gave him a packet. 'Have them, Sam. Pedro keeps a few cartons in the sterilizer.'

'That's pretty clever for a bullfighter.' Sam inhaled appreciatively. 'Why I'm calling, Adam, is because I've got nothing but head sores and ear fungus in the creepers and crawlers at Ten Kilometre Camp. Those Krauts from the *Heligoland* are doing their best but what we need bad is that mobile dispensary the ICRC delegate promised. Jim's been signalling at Geneva through Saigon but I get to thinking we've got an ace in this Stirling. If she wants, she can go to the top.'

'A good idea. Why don't you ask her?'

'It's got more muscle if you ask her, Adam.'

It was his turn to rib Jarra. 'Wouldn't you like to get close to that fanny, Sam? You've been talking about it enough.'

Jarra rubbed his long, freckled nose and sniffed. 'You ask her.'

'Sam, you're not shy? Not Sam Jarra. Number One in the girlie-bars from Saigon to Da Nang?'

Jarra pulled a face. 'I reckon I am and that's the truth. It's so long since I've been next to a round eye maybe I'll break out in the sweats.'

Adam shook his head, clapped Jarra on the shoulder. 'She's in the office. You know how small that is. I'll introduce you and shut the door.'

'You do that,' Sam Jarra said. 'And I'll break out in the sweats for sure.'

Sam Jarra had reminded Jane of Mick East. She kept him for coffee, asked about the camps and the new relocation. It was indeed a small room. Jane gave Sam Jarra the chair and perched on the desk.

Adam was setting a woman's broken arm, when Jarra looked in before leaving.

'She going to do it, Adam. No trouble.'

'Good. You break out in the sweats?'

'I tell you, I was goddam near it. She crosses these long legs at me and I can't find my mouth with the coffee cup. You know what she wants me to do?'

'What's that, Sam?'

'She wants to see the relocation when I go next time.'

'Oh?' Adam frowned, fixing the splint. 'That comes under war, Sam. Did you tell her she's not in the army?'

'I told her. So she says she'll ask Hatton. The thing is, I owe her something now. But I don't want it to cross me up with you.'

'Don't worry, Sam. Major Hatton will straighten her out.'

It was a surprise to Adam Thomson when Hatton arrived for his treatment in a check shirt and cotton trousers. The uniform and the holstered pistol had seemed the projection of him rather than the accessories. He looked younger, less resolute, reduced in commitment by the civilian clothing. On the next few evenings Hatton came uniformed and side-armed again. Adam Thomson felt oddly relieved.

Hatton had alternated his dress several times before realization struck Adam. He was doing it for Ho—determined to wipe out the dumb boy's fear of the uniform. Adam remembered Sam Jarra's expression: *That Hatton is something else.* He began to understand Jarra's admiration.

On that first day, at the guest-house party, Jane had felt Mark Hatton's challenge. It was in his carriage as well as his gaze, the particular erectness with which he balanced the stiffened leg. Hatton's fair skin had tanned to a burnished setting for the unyielding blue eyes. The spare, hard-moulded face and the cropped hair added impact to his directness. It discomfited Jane, awakened a challenge of her own, an instinct to be wary.

They had met again during Hatton's visits to the hospital. He was easy and polite, prepared to chat, but she could not accustom herself to his habit of appraisal. The long, level look before he spoke, hard to return or break away from.

Adam Thomson had explained the reason for Hatton's visits, without detail, surprised at his feeling for the other man's privacy. The bearded Quaker was equally reserved, deliberately evading Jane's curiosity.

It was more than a wound to Hatton. They sensed the deeper trauma, the involvement with his idea of manhood.

Jane Stirling had settled after a month at Quong Lo. Tim Frost had grudgingly accepted her. She usually ate alone, keeping different hours. In the evenings she studied Vietnamese, helped by Frost's Eurasian secretary, an educated girl whose officer father had been buried with French colonialism at Dien Bien Phu.

There was no remoteness from the war. The sense of it pressed everywhere, boded in the news broadcasts of the day's fighting on the dining-room radio tuned permanently to the American Forces network. Day and night artillery crumped, lobbing shells into the desolation of the free fire zones. When the grey monsoon skies lifted, the grey cargo aircraft and troopers splashed up from their strips. Armoured patrols formed outside provincial headquarters and Hatton's compound to grind and clank through the puddled streets.

When night fell the steel protection gates were barred. The Europeans took cover and nobody knew what might happen.

Hatton was getting into his jeep, raising the stiffened leg.

'Major Hatton, could you wait a minute?' Jane was laden with dressings. He was walking to the steps when she reappeared, dusting lint from her arms.

He looked levelly at her, smiled and nodded. 'I see the rains haven't washed you away.'

'I'm used to monsoons, Major.'

'Uh-huh. Lambaréné.' He put a touch of derision on the word, and Jane felt again the resistance Hatton aroused.

'Lambaréné, India, the Philippines, North Australia. The monsoon is not unique to Vietnam, Major.'

He nodded and waited, one foot on the steps, a hand on the butt of his pistol.

'Sam Jarra told me he is making a day visit to the new relocation. I would like to see it. Sam says I would need your permission.'

'I would think you'd need Tim Frost's permission. Foreign civilians in the province are his responsibility. It's not secure up there.'

'Sam said the fighting has stopped.'

'Out here, Miss Stirling, the fighting never stops. Now and again it gets postponed.'

Jane brushed her hair back, in a quirk of irritation. 'Very well. Postponed then. If I arrange it with Frost, do I have the army's permission?'

'The army is busy on that promontory.'

'Yes, and a woman would be a nuisance. I won't trouble the army. Sam will look after me. I'm not totally helpless, Major.'

He watched her carefully, then straightened. 'I don't believe you are. See what Tim Frost says.'

Tim Frost reminded himself of his instructions to extend President Salem's aide every co-operation.

'That woman's a damned nuisance. How much longer is she going to stay? She's some kind of spy for Geneva. I watch her mail. A few days ago she sent a letter to President Salem. The flap was sealed with sticky tape.'

Jane had taped the letter she had written for Sam Jarra because the gum had been eroded by damp. Tim Frost glared morosely through his glasses, certain that the taping had been a provision against tampering.

'Have they fired those hamlets yet? They'd only started when the big rains hit. That's probably what she's hoping to see, like those English correspondents. Three pages of photographs, every one showing a GI burning a hooch, with a woman and kids in the background. Black eyes. Everyone tries to give us black eyes.'

Adam Thomson lay on his bed reading. The drum of the rains drowned the groaning of the ceiling fan.

Sam Jarra knocked, put his head through the door. 'You asleep, Adam?'

He was patently awake, the book up in the directed beam of the reading lamp.

'Come in, Sam.'

Jarra carried a green bundle. 'I been down to the MACVEE compound. I got an escort back. There's a bazaar rumour Charlie's in close.'

'There was bazaar rumour last week. Nothing happened.'

'Yes, and there was bazaar rumour when he hit last time. We got

165

this mortar through the roof. This is a chickenshit place to put a Red Cross mess, half-way to Hatton and Gook headquarters.'

Adam said, chanting, 'We'll get our asses blown off one day.'

'You're goddam right. We near got our asses blown off last time.'

Sam sat down, the bundle on his knees. 'Hey, Adam. You're not mad at me?'

'Why Sam?'

'Taking Stirling to this relocation.'

'I'm not mad, Sam. I'm just surprised she fixed it.'

'She'll be all right. It's quiet now.'

'It wasn't quiet when those mines blew.'

'I know how to walk the paddy, Adam. You find a GI with these feet as big as gunboats. You walk in back of him.'

'And if he blows up, with these feet as big as gunboats?'

'That's where it's a science to walk the paddy. You stay in back of him, one mine away.'

Adam Thomson lit a cigarette. He wanted to get back to his book. 'What have you got there?'

'A uniform.'

'What for, Sam?'

'For Stirling. Hatton says she'll be less conspicuous in uniform. How, I don't know. This fanny she's got, it ain't about to be flattened by a uniform.'

Adam said shortly, 'Major Hatton is showing uncommon interest.'

23

THE helicopter had been ordered in from Task Force Nebraska. A few soldiers sat on their helmets on the muddy ground, near the wire, absurdly like men on chamber-pots, smoking, looking with curiosity at the jeep.

'They think you're a lady correspondent some kind,' Sam Jarra said.

One of the GIs stood up, walked over. 'Pardon me, sir, ma'am. You got a chopper coming in?'

'She's due now,' Sam said. 'Where you going?'

'Trying to get to Bien Tho, sir.'

'We're going north, soldier.'

'Oh,' He was disappointed. 'Excuse me.' He walked back to sit on his helmet.

Jane said, 'How young they are. He's only a boy.'

'They better grow up damn quick. Like Hatton tells these draftees down to the compound, if they want to stay alive out here, they're up against everything that moves.'

The Huey passed low across the pad, the fierce wash from the rotors blasting the earth, flattening the grass, streaming the hair and clothing of the young soldiers who bent before it. Jane and Sam Jarra did not hear the jeep stop near them.

Exactly like a dragonfly, the helicopter paused and hovered, dipped and turned in one fluid sweep, paused again and settled.

Sam nudged Jane's arm and shouted, 'She's ours. Come on.'

As June swung her legs out a hand gripped her elbow. It was Hatton, carrying a helmet. She could not make out what he shouted to Jarra, he was pushing her along, his eyes screwed against the rotor wash.

The young machine-gunner was out of his pod, bare-armed in a flak jacket. The pilots looked over their shoulders, like spacemen in their huge white helmets, lips pursed to whisper at the tiny microphones swung across their faces.

Sam Jarra bent under the blades and climbed in. They sat Jane between them, buckling her into the canvas seat. The machine-gunners mounted their pods on either side, pulled on earphones. The Captain twisted to look. The rotors roared, the Huey lifted. The soldiers outside the wire turned their backs and bent away.

Angling, the helicopter soared upwards, turned steeply to fill one open side with a tilted view of the township, straightened and pointed into its course.

The battalion was camped on the beach ten kilometres from the relocation, on a flat place easily covered by the gunships and fighter bombers attached to Task Force Nebraska. The ten-wheeled trucks that lurched and barged over the churned paddy by day, the light tanks and armoured personnel carriers moving on to the promontory, travelled the long white beach in convoy.

At sundown the battalion pulled out of the field to stand watch in the strongpoints above the campsite or return to the tents on the beach.

Where the trucks and armour lined up to be ferried on a landing-craft across a small river opening into the bay, the villagers watched, the children cadging gum and cigarettes, paddling woven-reed boats sealed with pitch in the gently breaking surf.

Fishing nets were slung to dry on poles in the river, sagged there like monstrous hammocks. A few dhow-sailed junks stood in the river's mouth. Behind the beach, in the short, tangy pines, pigs foraged among the huts. Sand-covered humps marked the bunkers in which the fisherfolk had sheltered from airstrike, artillery and firefights.

The helicopter dropped low over the battalion, following the wide ribbon of sand, whacking above the convoys. The children in the boats shouted, waved and spilled, the water around them boiling in the Huey's downdraught.

Sam Jarra touched Jane and pointed to a levelled spot on a hill beyond the river as the helicopter began to bank.

Hatton put his hand out. 'Good to see you, Dave.'

'Likewise, Mark. You still fighting that desk?'

'It's got me surrounded. May I present Miss Stirling from the provincial hospital. Colonel Clagger. You know Sam.'

They sat on a log outside a big bunker, Clagger with a map spread on his knees for Hatton, marking the plastic cover with a grease pencil. Their voices were low. Sam explained the campsite to Jane, both of them dividing their attention to hear the murmured voices beside them.

'There are hostiles in this co-ordinate. They're laying mines at night. We're taking sniper fire here, and here. On a promontory like this they can come in from the sea. It's that or they're in tunnels.'

Below them a bamboo fence wandered the sand and pines. Hatton pointed. 'How much of that have you got?'

'Near enough to five kilometres. We've got spotlights out there at night. It wouldn't stop anything, but it makes for an early warning. My people like it. It gives them a sense of security.'

Sam Jarra said to Jane, 'They'll be through soon. We'll go down the paddy.'

Clagger had called in his command helicopter. It waited for them now in the sweltering paddy close to a field radio from which a young captain instructed his element. There had been a large hamlet here, distributed in the trees. Some of the houses had been substantial, three and four rooms of homemade brick. They remained now in wreckage, walls blasted, roofs caved, rubble spilled across the balconies. The sweating troops, their M-16s slung, shouted and directed the villagers who worked to dismantle their huts, pulling down the thatched bamboo they would re-erect at the campsite. Trucks charged like tanks at the earth walls and hedges, loaded with wall-frames, thatching and matting, sacked grain, tools, cooking-pots, their wide-eyed owners clutching the sides, staring silently, as the big vehicles lurched and roared in the churned, sucking mud.

There were hard-packed paths between the paddy fields.

'Follow us,' Hatton told Jane. 'Stay on the hard ground. Sam, don't let her cross these hedges.'

Sam said peevishly, 'I know how to walk the paddy, for crissake.'

She had screwed her hair under the cap. Perspiration patched her chest, began to run on her forehead. Jane dabbed at it with a sleeve. Most of the troops carried small towels over their shoulders. There was the smell of burning everywhere, a haze of smoke lay ahead.

Clagger stopped at a group being shouted at by a tall Negro. He seemed double the height of the little old man he was shaking by the shirt.

'What's the trouble, soldier?'

The tall Negro was too exasperated to be impressed by his CO's appearance. 'Colonel, suh, Papa-san won't move, suh. I got to carry him from his hooch. All his family gives me a hard time. None of them goddam move.'

The big Negro put his streaming face close to the little grey-haired fisherman. 'You gotta move your ass, Papa-san. This Number Ten, man. Number One like this.'

The Negro bent and hoisted a bamboo wall.

'Where's the interpreter?' Clagger asked.

Sam Jarra said, 'You want me to speak to him, Colonel?'

The Negro soldier waited, shaking his head, mopping his face with a towel. A truck ground down the paddy, and waited, vibrating.

Sam said, 'Papa-san's not about to move. He says the long-noses burned down the villages, that's likely Number Ten Thousand. If they want him out they will have to carry him.'

The old man's daughters and children waited, their dark bright eyes sliding everywhere.

Clagger said, 'Carry him out, soldier.'

'Suh?'

'That's the way Papa-san wants it.'

The Negro shouldered his towel and lifted the old man into the air.

He made no resistance, impassive in the thrust out arms, a frail, wrinkled survivor of twenty-five years of war, defeated at last, his fields ravaged, his hamlet readied for the touch, the tombs of his ancestors tumbled and shattered, his sons perhaps dead or fighting, riding stubbornly in the arms of an American Negro soldier as a last defiance.

Jane looked back. A heavier, darker smoke blew from other hamlets.

170

Through it she saw the Negro soldier lifting the old man's family and possessions into the truck.

The litter of other moving was about her. A charred fish-trap, wooden-soled sandals, shattered pottery, destroyed wells, wooden pens that had once caged pigs and fowl, a broken doll, a clay Buddha.

Her voice trembled a little. 'What happens now, Sam?'

'They burn it.'

'And after that?'

'Anything left, artillery and airstrike takes it out.'

The promontory on which three thousand farmers and fishermen had lived from immemorial times, proceeded to the making of another free fire zone, a churned and charred desolation on which anything that moved must die.

The sweat-soaked, fire-blackened platoon, came out of the smoke, two men helping another between them. Clagger had been wiping his balding head. He jammed back the helmet.

'What happened, Sergeant?'

The sergeant's eyes were smoke-stung. He screwed them in surprise. 'It's you, sir. We ran into sniper fire. Simpson lost his knee.'

Clagger swore. 'Get that chopper in here. At the double.'

A young GI unslung his rifle and ran. The two panting soldiers with the casualty lowered him groaning to the ground.

Clagger had his map out.

'What was your position?'

Jane's eyes were fixed on the wounded man. A towel had been stripped and tied above the smashed leg. She did not see Hatton stride towards her. He grasped her arm and jerked her down, face taut, eyes gleaming.

'Stay there. Stay down.'

'He needs a dressing.'

'Do as you're told.'

Hatton and Clagger huddled over the map with the platoon leader. The others squatted, watching the way they had come, whispering. Smoke curled like mist around them, the breeze on which it carried hot and choking. Their ears filled with the din of the helicopter.

Clagger was at the radio as they put the wounded man inside. One of the platoon crouched beside him, holding him in. The helicopter lifted.

When he could be heard, Sam Jarra uncorked a water-bottle and handed it to Jane.

'It's thirsty work, walking the paddy.'

A near-by soldier wondered at the civilian. Then his eyes stretched in disbelief, his mouth open. He looked away, looked back, grabbed another soldier by the arm.

Jane smiled at them.

Sam Jarra scratched his nose. 'They don't believe it, that's for sure. Get the cap off.'

Jane's black hair, wet with perspiration, swung about her face. The young soldiers braced in astonishment. Then they smiled back, grinned at each other, moved away to tell the others.

Sam Jarra said, 'Wear the cap. If we louse up this war, Hatton will kick our asses clear back to Quong Lo.'

The section which had taken the sniper fire had earlier been cleared out and burned. There was no above-the-ground cover the platoon leader could identify. There had been a lot of blown smoke in the area.

Clagger had ordered a ground sweep, spotter aircraft and a Medevac helicopter to transfer the casualty to Nebraska. He had forgotten the civilians, thought of them only when the command helicopter returned.

Hatton said, 'Sam, you and Jane go with Colonel Clagger.'

'What are you doing?'

'I'm walking in. Get moving.'

He did not wait for comment, he was going through the smoke with the sergeant's platoon before they reached the helicopter.

Sam Jarra leaned to Jane's ear. 'He's walking in. That Quaker is doing a good job on Hatton's leg.'

The helicopter searched the co-ordinate. There was no movement to be seen. Close to the section they had left, the walls of a brick building showed in the pines. It was partly roofed. Clagger noted it for demolition and spoke into his face mike. The helicopter banked and climbed, crossed the promontory and ran down the coast, the machine-gunners leaning out over their weapons. If the snipers had not joined the villagers they could be breaking for the cover of the rocky islands offshore.

The platoon had only advanced a kilometre when the point man signalled and crouched. They went down quietly on the sandy soil, kneeling, peering through the stunted pines and smoke drift. Hatton unflapped his holster.

The point man levelled his finger to the right, drew a slow line across his front. He pumped the flat of his hand above his head. Silently, crouching, they moved towards him, knelt again at the sergeant's signal.

The sergeant was young, thin-faced, uncertain. He had taken a casualty and blamed himself. He came back and squatted. 'Two men. Crossing from the west. Maybe they're villagers walking through from Blue Sector. They do that, Major. Looking for relatives and such.'

Hatton was restless, jaws clamped, squeezing out of habit at his wound. 'It's your command, Sergeant.' He had needed the reminder. 'Let's go.'

The platoon moved forward, the point man ghosting into smoke.

The house must have belonged to a rich farmer, or a landlord, in this isolated position. It was holed but otherwise intact from the front. The back wall had been punched inwards, a heap of brick and plaster.

The trucks and half-tracks evacuating the coastal sectors were heard as an overtone here, as lulling as bees buzzing. The smoke had cleared, the breeze had dropped. The ruined building shone in the sunshine and silence.

The platoon made its approach from the rear, their footfalls soft on the sandy earth, rifles readied, slipping quickly between the pines. The young sergeant checked for covering fire, signalled and moved in.

An instant before he saw the blur of movement, Hatton's senses shrieked. He had slapped the ·45 into his left hand, leaped sideways and was rolling without the need to think. The grenade was in his right hand, the pin bitten out, as he came up and threw it.

They were flat on their bellies, sighting at the ruin from which the explosion wisped smoke, the ragged roof dropping fragments into the silence. There was no sound, no movement, when that stopped.

The sergeant raised himself on one knee, eyes straining, the M-16 loose against his shoulder. A flank man raced, crouched, flattened himself on a corner, head back to calm his breathing. Slowly, he rolled his helmet on the brick, looked in. He edged his rifle around the wall, and held it pointed. Then he stepped inside, over the rubble.

Hatton's grenade must have exploded between them. The bodies were ripped to pieces, streaming with blood. One was a full-grown man, the other a boy, perhaps fourteen, naked except for shorts.

The man looked and looked away, white-faced, trembling a little with reaction. Hatton's burnished tan was grey. He moved the

173

bodies with his foot, jaw muscles humping. The platoon evaded his eyes.

One said, low-voiced, 'They're not armed. They've got no weapons.'

The thin-faced sergeant licked his lips, looked covertly at Hatton, removed his helmet and rubbed at his eyes. It was his command, something had to be said. He could not think of anything.

It was Hatton's law. He had learned it. It's you against everything that moves. There had to be a weapon. What were they doing in that place? They could have hidden weapons, to walk through and join the evacuation.

He could feel their eyes on his back. The sergeant's words sounded in his ears. *They do that, Major. Looking for relatives and such.*

Only the sergeant remained near. The others had hunkered down outside, upending water-bottles, talking softly, bare-headed to rest from the heavy steel pots.

It was Hatton's law. He had learned it and he stood by it. He challenged the sergeant with his hard blue gaze until the young man looked away.

'Should we bury them, Major?'

The sergeant wanted them buried, out of the pooling, stiffening blood and out of sight. Under the earth so it could be forgotten, so that it might not have happened.

'No. Colonel Clagger will want to check it.'

Hatton pushed at the rubble with his foot, sending it tumbling and smoking dust, searched in the broken battens of the ceiling. His eyes returned to the corner: a large pottery bowl was inverted there. It should have been broken. Pottery was strewn everywhere in fragments. It was odd that this bowl had survived the destruction of the house.

Hatton slowly bent the stiff leg and squatted. The corner behind the bowl was clean. There should have been debris, there was no roof above it. He studied the bowl, the edges of it, the walls behind.

'What is it, Major?'

'I don't know. A big bowl like this, why isn't it broken?'

'The grenade missed it.'

Hatton pointed at the walls. 'This place has been hit by mortar fire, fragmentation and artillery. The bowl should have been smashed long ago.'

Hatton got up. 'Ask your men to take cover.'

The automatic blasted twice, the pottery bowl dissolved. Hatton stepped over the rubble, holstering the pistol. He looked down once and then turned, his eyes on them all, hard and fulfilled.

They crowded about the hole, glanced to the bodies, looked back, as though to connect them with the hideout.

Hatton licked his fingers, held them over the opening.

'It's ventilated. There's a tunnel here.'

'You heard the major,' the sergeant shouted. 'There's a tunnel here. Search the area. Gottlieb, Jones, drag these bodies out. Get some dirt over that blood.'

Hatton sat outside the walls on a piece of masonry and slowly stretched his stiff leg. He took off his helmet, lit a cigarette, putting his head back, shutting his eyes to exhale the smoke.

It was his law. He had learned it. It was you against everything that moved. He hadn't made the rules. It was that kind of war.

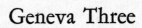

Geneva Three

24

In Biafra the politics of secession had become crazed slaughter, an atavistic orgy in which women waved torn limbs in the streets as tribal trophies.

Neveau had convened the committee to consider a Papal plea for the protection of the black Catholic minority.

'Mr Richter from the American Embassy telephoned twice. He is anxious to know if President Salem will give a Press conference.'

Neveau frowned at his secretary. 'President Salem is in Vietnam. What does he mean?'

The girl shook her head. 'Mr Richter said to be sure and let him know the moment you got out of the committee.'

Neveau took the telephone with half attention.

'You called me, Joe?'

Richter used Neveau's christian name solemnly, to indicate respect for the privilege. 'Ah, Martin. Sorry to trouble you. It was the Press Officer's suggestion. He did not know of the President's return.'

Neveau's mind was still on the committee meeting. It irritated him not to understand. 'What do you mean? The President is in Vietnam.'

Neveau's attention focused on the other man's silence, the prefacing, apologetic cough.

'He's back, Martin. I saw him at the airport when I got in from Paris. Sorry about this. I thought he might be giving a Press conference. You know how it is, we might have missed the notice.'

Richter coughed again and waited.

Spots of white pinched the bland flesh of Neveau's cheeks. He wanted to say that Richter was mistaken. 'What time was this?' he asked, making his voice light.

'I got in on the two o'clock flight.'

Now it was after five. Richter had to be mistaken.

'I was in committee, as you know. If the President has returned, I must have missed a signal.'

'That would be it,' Richter said quickly. 'Sorry to trouble you, Martin.'

There was no signal. He did not expect to find one. Any message from the President would have been brought to him. Neveau checked first with the radio room. The last file from Vietnam was dated two days earlier, announcing the team's departure for Quong Lo.

He wanted to leave it like that because the alternative lacked sense and order. Even had something happened, perhaps a sudden sickness, Jane Stirling would have advised. But he could not leave it, uneasiness pricked him, the flat certainty in Richter's voice unavoidable.

He decided to call Signora Cenci on an excuse.

Salem was there, he was sleeping. It was incomprehensible.

He had asked the Signora to wake him. 'Wake him now,' Neveau had shouted. She would not do that, he was tired. She would wake Signor Salem at eight.

It was unusual for Neveau to drink spirits before dinner. He customarily took wine with his meal, sometimes a brandy afterwards with coffee. He had gone directly to the sideboard, poured a whisky, carried it to his office.

Sarah heard the movement from her bedroom.

'Is that you, Martin?'

'Yes.'

There had been no more, the abuse of a door slamming.

The opened soda was noticeable, busy with bubbles, the cap beside it. She knew he had taken a whisky because the bottle was out of alignment, and thought to get him ice. It was a service they both would once have taken for granted.

Sarah mixed herself a whisky, hardened against his entrance and the slamming office door, aware without grieving of the opposition her husband now so easily aroused. The impulses of Sarah's nature, the vivid, uncomplicated response, was the truth of her. She had constrained and denied it to remake herself for Neveau's approval. It was past that. She could not remake her origins. There would be no relenting from him, ever.

It had come to her, seen and whole, the night Neveau had the concierge threaten the family upstairs for running baths after ten o'clock. The squalor of her affair with Mitchell had come to her that way, on the remembered words of Molly Best: *If he's a hard one and he knows how to work me, it's a motel and heels in the air.*

She had made the decision, hard as a general, when Mitchell drunkenly telephoned to revenge himself on Neveau for Jane Stirling's appointment to Salem's team. She had gone to him for her own purposes, without guilt, because there was nothing to betray. If the destination was squalid, so was the point of departure.

Sarah sometimes visited the cheerful bar used by Molly Best. Molly was there the day after, drinking her double whiskies. She had looked long and closely at Sarah, patted the stool beside her. 'It didn't take, or you didn't listen,' she observed. 'The hell with it, welcome to the club. That bastard Barney is travelling again.'

Sarah had tried too hard for too long and that was over. If the bright eyes dulled on the knowing of it, the will in her was deepened and asserted.

The irregularity of Salem's return, his having learned it from Richter, disturbed and rankled Neveau. It would already be Embassy gossip, conjectured about at the Press Club. Everything the man did or said endangered proper procedure. Neveau walked between the metal desk and the filing-cabinet, watching the time, sipping whisky.

Punctually, at eight o'clock, he telephoned.

'It's you, Martin? Signora Cenci told me you had called.'

Nothing more. As though the man had never been away. As though his privacy had been invaded. Anger rushed in Neveau's ears.

'Why didn't you signal? Why are you back? Where are the others?'

'The others flew to Quong Lo, as scheduled.'

And again nothing more.

Because he wanted to shout, Neveau strained his voice into coldness. 'May I ask what happened?'

He listened to Salem's breathing. He should not have been able to hear it. Apprehension touched his skin. 'Something happened. What happened?'

Salem's fluency, the patrician ease, was disordered. 'There is ... a possibility ... a possibility ... of limited truce.'

'A truce? How? A truce of what kind?'

'A limited truce. The NLF and the North are prepared to permit our inoculation teams into their southern areas.'

'When? For how long?'

'There is a festival called Tet, in January. The teams are to be in and out of their areas six weeks before Tet.'

'How was the offer made? Did it come through the South Vietnam Society?'

'No. It was made to me, by the President of the National Liberation Red Cross.'

The apprehension that had touched Neveau, flared. 'Good God! Not in person?'

'Yes.'

Neveau groaned.

'Is it known about? Does the Press know?'

'Nobody knows.'

Neveau said, steadily, 'We should not discuss this further on the telephone. I will come to you immediately.'

'Don't do that. I am tired. We can talk about it tomorrow.'

'But surely——'

'Tomorrow, Martin.'

'But, President, we must——'

'Tomorrow, Martin.'

Salem hung up. Neveau stared at the dead instrument in disbelief.

It was too new. It had been mixed into his mind on the journey and before that all the fretful night. He could see, smell and feel her against him, on every wincing particle of flesh.

Something happened. What happened? Neveau's words had confused him. It must be the last time. He would face it down, as he was accustomed. He would take this night and tomorrow and face it down.

Salem took the leather-covered pad from the safe and dipped the pen in the inkwell.

'My Own Dear Son.' His hand was shaking.

At ten-thirty the next morning Neveau could keep patience no longer. Mitchell had asked about Salem, there had been inquiries from the Press.

He instructed his secretary. 'See if Miss Bryce has heard from the President this morning.'

Neveau had already plotted a course the truce negotiations could take. If Tet fell in January there was little enough time.

'Miss Bryce is not in the house, sir. She has taken President Salem material from records.'

'To Lausanne?'

'Yes, sir.'

He stared at her, the white patches spotting his cheeks, rasped back the chair.

The records clerk gave Neveau the list of material requested by the President. He saw it was files and delegates' confidential reports on truce and peace missions arranged by the ICRC since the outbreak of the Second World War.

After Salem's return they had worked to a common end. In common, they had been defeated. The gulf remained, a handbridge of compromise across it. For Neveau, it would have been enough to stop the plague. In Salem's imagination the truce was to be the halt from which he would declare a programme for lasting peace.

The difference in Salem, the sharding of nerves and quickness to combat, survived the disappointment. It remained as a bitterness, an obsession about Vietnam and his Humanitarian Law.

On simple matters of detail, Salem would ask Neveau, 'What are the politics of this?' making his voice derisory. 'Will the American League approve our sending milk to Biafra?'

The handbridge was down. The burn the Vietnam sun had put on Salem's skin became the burn of his anger. Neveau's resentment wearied to hostility. The Committee stirred with criticism, baited by Salem in assembly as he privately baited Neveau.

'Before we deal with the Nigerian agenda, gentlemen, here is this month's list of aid to North Vietnam. A million francs' worth of medicines from Belgium. Thirty thousand francs from Switzerland. Eight million crowns from Denmark. A new fund announced by the Congress of Canadian Women's Union. A thousand francs from Guadeloupe. An unstated contribution from the Dutch Women's Union. What are we doing in North Vietnam this month, gentlemen?'

Dryly, from the table's other end, 'The business on the agenda concerns Nigeria, President.'

'I have not opened the agenda. Is the Committee content that others should assume the responsibility of this International?'

In the week that Reuters reported the ICRC President's statement on the abuse of the Conventions in Vietnam, Salem made a speech at Geneva University.

The Nürnberg judgment of 1946, he said, had declared that crimes are committed by men, not by abstract entities. Only by punishing individuals who commit such crimes can the provisions of international law be enforced. If this applied to the Nazi war criminals, it must also apply to present outrage. The Humanitarian Law would declare that nations agreed in advance the jurisdiction over individuals of an international body.

He had been appointed by conspiracy, however innocent. In the stirring criticism and resentment, the counter conspiracy was being seeded.

Pierre Salem had kept from Neveau the strange details of the talk with Professor Pham Thu in the attic. He had kept from him Professor Thu's place as a political force on the Liberation Front's central committee and that he had been forewarned that for electioneering reasons America would propose talks for peace. Above all, he secreted his plans to make a declaration at the Paris conference regardless of resistance or consequences.

In the letters he continued to write to his son, Salem confessed his feelings with increasing emotion. He despised the older generation for he saw they were inured beyond hope in corruption, a devious clique of powerbrokers floundering in lies and cynicism. Manufacturers of monstrous weapons, with monstrous logic that excused them.

They would pass the young a bitter heritage. It would not be so without Salem's fight.

25

RICHTER's small apartment had been passed on to him by the attaché he had replaced. It was cramped and shabby. He had not particularly noticed this at the beginning. His elevated status at the Embassy had made him aware that these surroundings were unsuitable.

Richter brushed his long teeth, rinsed and crouched to lather his long face in the bathroom mirror. He would look for a new apartment now he could afford one. He would buy a bed he could get his feet in. He would fix a bathroom mirror he could shave at without crouching. He would have a cocktail cabinet and a stereo, entertain a little. Perhaps Martin Neveau and his wife would come for a Sunday drink.

The pictures in Richter's head got between him and the mirror. He cut himself. Blood swelled and ran. Richter wiped at it, frowning. He had an appointment that morning with his Ambassador. He would have to sit there with a crust on his chin.

For months, every move that the ICRC and its President had made was known to Richter. It had been hard going. The understanding he had built with Neveau had not helped. The Chairman was as flapped about plague as though he himself was in the midst of it, without inoculation.

It had been a ludicrous proposal. Richter puzzled how a realist like Neveau could suppose that the American Red Cross, the American forces and their allies, the South Vietnamese Government, would agree to a truce to inoculate the enemy.

The South Koreans had been outraged. The Australians had barely replied. One could imagine the headlines at home. TRUCE IN VIETNAM TO INOCULATE VIET CONG AGAINST PLAGUE. Why not rearm them at the same time and distribute vitamin tablets?

Westmorland had announced that his command could soon begin to phase out. The pacification schemes were everywhere successful. Saigon had denied the rumours of plague deaths on the waterfront. There had been a few upcountry, it was normal.

Yet Salem had persisted and with Neveau's support. The ICRC delegate to South America had been flown in to negotiate with Hanoi and the Liberation Front. He had returned with their agreement, according to truce procedures laid down in the Geneva Conventions. It had been hard going, hard to keep it from the Press. When Salem had threatened, even Neveau had wavered. He was flapped about plague, it was his blind spot.

Richter had laid it on the line, put it down hard as the Ambassador had instructed. Under what circumstances, how, when and where had Salem received the offer? Why had he left Saigon so abruptly, his schedule uncompleted? Why had he advised the South Vietnam Government that he had been recalled to Geneva, when his Chairman was unaware of his arrival?

Did President Salem, while the honoured guest of the Government of South Vietnam, treat clandestinely with its enemy? If so, could that be construed as the absolute neutrality which was the condition of the ICRC's existence?

Richter had laid it down hard. When he got it said, he spread his hands, softened his voice into apology. 'I have to say these things, Martin. We both know, if you'll forgive me, that President Salem can be a little indiscreet. He's not, if you'll forgive me again, a professional like yourself. We both have the same interests here. I'm sure you understand.'

Neveau had understood, with some alarm. He felt no resentment. But he did reassess Joseph Richter.

186

It had been the Ambassador's instruction, but it did not end in Neveau's office. The CIA had interested itself in President Salem.

His personal call for a declaration of war in Vietnam, together with the North Vietnamese atrocity propaganda, had been sufficiently irregular to demand attention. The leakage to the Press of the scientists' memoranda on the spread of plague and the manufacture and storage of biological weapons had been traced to the ICRC's press officer. The publicizing in Warsaw of the League's appeal for emergency action in the North and South had been exploited by the dissenters and protesters, propagandized in Russia and Eastern Europe.

Salem's every appointment and movement in South Vietnam was scrutinized. Every signal passed between the team and Geneva had been studied. The shock of the truce proposal, the unexpected aggressiveness of Salem's efforts, were past ignoring. The operators in Saigon rechecked his movements.

It was plain enough. Salem had left USAID headquarters for his hotel at 6 p.m., prepared to fly the CIA airline next day to Quong Lo. He had not returned to the Hotel Continental until 7.30 p.m., a drive of fifteen minutes.

At 6.30 p.m., the car provided for Salem by the South Vietnam Red Cross had been left at the society by the driver who disappeared that evening. The man had no known family, could not be traced.

A meeting of the ICRC team, set by Salem for 6 p.m. that evening in his suite, was abandoned in the President's absence.

Clark Clyde, the WHO member on the team, at present in Mallorca, had been sounded by a retired U2 pilot resident in Palma. Clyde remembered President Salem's very noticeable disturbance later that evening when he announced his recall to Geneva.

No signal of recall had passed through Saigon communications.

Joseph Richter, special attaché in the Geneva Embassy and State Department appointee to the International Conference of the Red Cross in Paris, confirmed that the ICRC Chairman had not known of the President's return.

Something must have occurred to change Salem's plans, between his departure from the USAID headquarters and his arrival one and a half hours later at the Hotel Continental. This could only have been a clandestine confrontation with a representative of either the National Liberation Front or Hanoi, or both.

There was one question remaining: had such a meeting been arranged by President Salem from Geneva? Had the announced reasons for his Vietnam tour been pretext? If so, what was to be expected from him at the critical Paris conference? What was the basis of President Salem's hostility? What private interests might he represent?

Richter had powdered the crusted blood on his chin. The secretary opened the door and waved him inside.

The Ambassador was turned in his chair, to the window. 'Sit down, Richter.'

He continued looking at the window, his lips compressed as though he found the view distasteful. Then he swivelled his chair, picked up a typewritten sheet and read from it. 'Dateline: Geneva. Eight o'clock last night. Asked about his Humanitarian Law, now being discussed in philosophical journals, Pierre Salem of the famous Geneva banking family, new President of the International Committee of the Red Cross, said: "The vision is to build a law against war and the outrages of war. A Humanitarian Law that will apply to its signatories in all circumstances. A law beyond abrogation. The flagrant abuse of the Geneva Conventions in Vietnam is an affront to civilized conscience." President Salem recently led a mission to South Vietnam where he travelled widely.'

The Ambassador dropped the paper. 'Courtesy of Reuter's,' he said. ' "*The flagrant abuse of the Geneva Conventions in Vietnam is an affront to civilized conscience."* What will this guy do next?'

Richter was shaken. 'I can't understand it, Ambassador. The Chairman will have a fit. This is a purely partisan statement.'

'Believe me,' the Ambassador said, 'something will have to be done about this guy.'

When the CIA in Washington opened a file on Pierre Salem, when the coded card was punched, cross indexed, criss-cross indexed, to buzz in the maw of computers, it became as charged with life as an acorn, germinating by its own volition into an oak of paper. Queries, coincidences, possibilities, more intricate than the human mind could imagine, were posed by the circuits.

Answers begin with questions. The computers idled on Pierre Salem's reference and waited to swallow his life.

Joseph Richter flew to Milan, the elementary dossier he had prepared in the briefcase on his knee, flushed by the importance of conspiracy. He was about to meet Milos Jelié, the world's most celebrated private detective. The CIA sometimes used Jelié's organization for personal documentation. His resources were immense, his initiative and invention brilliant, the sophistication of his electronic gadgetry beyond anything imagined for James Bond by Ian Fleming.

Richter found the restaurant appointed and looked for the bar.

'Joseph Richter?' The pleasant young man had his hand out. The recognition had been so immediate it startled Richter.

The agent smiled and looked up at him. 'You're not easy to mistake. How was the flight?'

They could talk easily enough at the table the CIA man had reserved. He was known to the management and staff, took pleasure in advising Richter on the food.

'I don't know, and don't want to know what you've got for Milos. I'm just here to make the introduction and dope you in on his operation. First thing, don't be cagey. Anything Milos wants, you give him. Milos is on our side. He's quite a guy, as you'll find out.'

The taxi stopped at a marble-faced building on the Corso Sempione, near Milan's central park. The brass nameplate read: *Mercury International Institute. Director Detective Reporter Milos Jelié.*

They rode to the third floor. Another nameplate repeated the message on a massive, polished wooden door. In the marble-floored anteroom a receptionist greeted the CIA agent, led them along a corridor striped with Regency wallpaper and hung with the originals of cover pictures from pulp novels and magazines—a motley of half-dressed women holding pistols, shrinking from monsters, dreamily stroking bare breasts, plunging knives into shadowed backs. There was another anteroom furnished in leather, glass-topped tables and magazine racks. The door off it was topped by a red bulb and a plate inscriped, *Détective Privé: Milos Jelié.*

The receptionist opened the door. The room and the furniture in it were gargantuan. Bugging devices, tape recorders, telescopic lenses and cameras were spread everywhere on tables and on the desk as big as a bed.

The man who rose to receive them was middling in height, beginning to fatten, with the most massive chest Joseph Richter had seen.

Answers begin with questions. The computers that would swallow Pierre Salem's life waited to be fed by Milos Jelié.

26

The idea of himself as a philanderer supported Ted Mitchell's conceit. He wanted no involvement other than erotic sport, the curiosity of shapes and tints of flesh. He was as interested in the variety of female architecture as an amateur musician is in instruments, as concerned to play the big bassoon as he was the violin or piccolo. It amused Mitchell to classify his women this way, to suppose himself composer and conductor. He had thought of Sarah Neveau as cymbals, resonating at a touch. But Sarah had changed and he could not place her, nor place his own need and dissatisfaction.

The halt in the affair had been her will. It was time, he had been glad of it, sensing the risks of her tension. But she had not come back to him, he had gone to her, and that irritated his masculinity. If he had pretended need of involvement as the wooden coin of indulgence, it would have been a familiar part of the game. He had thought to get back at Neveau when he telephoned.

He had been thinking about that, resentfully drunk, when Sarah opened the unlocked door. She had not crossed to him, quivering, as he expected. She had closed the door and looked hard at him. Her face was cold, preoccupied. He could sense the cold in her body.

She said, 'You're drunk. Go and shower. I will make coffee.'

She put her bag on a chair, went to the kitchen. Mitchell sat in his raincoat, holding his drink, blinking at the blur in his eyes. This wasn't the way she should have entered. If he was drunk he had reason. But he was suddenly so grateful she should be there, filling the emptiness with her familiarity, that a maudlin lump filled his throat.

He had stayed a long time in the shower, gradually cutting off the hot water, increasing the cold, until he shivered and gasped under the needling. He cleaned his teeth, put drops in his eyes, dusted himself with powder. He had called and she had come. That was it. She was pretending coldness to dissemble. They would see about that when he got her to Madame Leopard. Mitchell was already swaggering before he left the bathroom.

He had accepted the coffee, one arm casually out to embrace her. She had come into it stiffly, brushed lips, released herself to pour a drink. Mitchell took the coffee to the sofa. When the pretence was over she would join him.

But there had been no advance from Sarah. The preoccupation remained. She drank the whisky and poured another, put a record on the player. He had not seen her for two months, had forgotten the attraction of her movements. He wanted to touch her again, feel her heart race and crumple again, shiver her with the shock that was half helpless and protesting.

Mitchell said, 'I'm not going to Vietnam.'

'Oh? Did you expect to?'

'Yes, I expected to. Your bloody husband is sending Stirling.'

She inclined her head without interest. 'How nice for President Salem.'

He really didn't want the coffee, he wanted her to serve him. He held out the mug. 'Could we do this again?'

He caught her hand when she came to him. She leaned obediently for his kiss, overwhelming Mitchell in that instant with rememberance of her.

She had returned to cross her legs in the chair near the bar. To be close he took the coffee there to spike it.

'How is little Guy?'

'I hardly see him. Martin takes him about, weekends. He speaks French now most of the time.'

He saw the frown that contradicted the indifference, and was glad for the sign of nerves in the stubbing and lighting of cigarettes. He was ready for her now.

'Why did you come, Sarah?'

She had looked up calmly. 'Why did I come? Why not?'

Her manner more than her words confused him. 'You never explained why you gave me the sack.'

'Did it matter to you?'

He couldn't say no, he didn't want to say yes. In some fashion things had got reversed. Mitchell respiked the coffee. He must be beginning a hangover to let her twist him like this.

'I asked, did it matter to you?'

'Damn it, of course it mattered. It would have been decent to give me a reason. You behaved like a bloody schoolgirl.'

'Yes,' Sarah said. 'Perhaps I have been a schoolgirl. Perhaps I have always been a schoolgirl.'

All of Mitchell's earlier rage seemed to reclaim him and found focus on Sarah. 'Now that you are here for your why-not reasons, are you coming to bed or not?'

Even that did not alter her. She spoke with both distaste and wonder. 'You're really very coarse, Ted, aren't you?'

He could easily have struck her, his breath loud and uncertain. 'If I am, it's what you liked about me. You wanted coarseness badly enough.'

Sarah put out her cigarette and stood up. 'I'm not going to Madame Leopard. I can imagine those sheets. When are they changed—Friday, isn't it?'

Mitchell was helpless in his defeat. She looked beautiful in the calculated calm which so changed her. He still wanted to reach out and strike, reach out and take her in his arms. But command between them had exchanged.

Sarah took off the jacket of her suit, unzipped the skirt and stepped out of it. While he stared she undressed and stood naked.

Among the cushions on the floor, humped and sweated, he butted at her as blind and savage as a penned ram at a gate. In his rage to break and destroy her there was one instant of revelation, remembered when he woke after she had gone.

He had opened his eyes, returned to himself for a second. In a face deathly pale, the mouth grimaced, Sarah Neveau's eyes had watched him, as wide and clear and remote as a child's. Then she had closed them, and torn his back with her fingernails.

Sarah had got home late. Neveau had dined with Joseph Richter and a visiting member of the American Society. The evening had been greatly tiring, concerned with Salem's aberrations and the risk of him. A seeking, subtle discussion in which Salem was never directly named.

Neveau was in his study when Sarah returned, pained by an indigestion owed to his distaste for the table talk and the camouflage of its meaning. Neveau's loyalty to the office made it hard for him to join the growing outside opposition to the President.

'Is that you, Sarah?' He came to the door in shirtsleeves, his regular, innocuous features drawn by fatigue.

Sarah said, 'You look tired.'

'I am. Very tired. Where have you been, it's late?'

'At the cinema,' Sarah said. 'You should go to bed, Martin.'

She had never lied to him before, about anything. She put on a cap and stepped under the shower, the nipples of her breasts sore and hard. The lie was another milestone.

Neveau was too tired to go to bed, his body jangled. He drank a whisky and soda to ease the indigestion, and help him relax.

On this day, twenty-four years ago, his parents had been killed in Dresden. It was an anniversary Neveau never forgot, known to nobody else. He didn't truly know the day they had died. He kept the anniversary of the day he had been called to the headmaster's office.

He had been twelve years old, without a relative in the world, orphaned in that moment from every tie and connection, every refuge of care or love. He was as alone as the first man was alone, more alone for the others about him. He had sat alone in the lawyer's office and tried to understand.

'As trustee of your father's estate, Martin, I deem it advisable to sell the factory. There is very little liquid capital, I am afraid. Your mother made a large withdrawal before she joined your father in Germany.'

The lawyer frowned in disapproval. 'Most unwise, I must say, to travel with cash like that. Not at all like your father to permit it. A great tragedy. A great tragedy, I must say.'

He heaved a sigh. 'Terrible times. Terrible war. We must keep our spirits up. We must be brave, Martin, must we not?'

He had been brave. He had been as brave as he could. For weeks and months in the dormitory he had wept himself to sleep, strangling it into the pillow, heartbroken in loneliness and despair. Until he left school it was to be the only home he had. His father's lawyer sometimes took him on vacations. The factory had been sold. The instrument business was a small one. There were debts to pay, and taxes. There was enough money left for his schooling and a little left over for security.

It had been respectable to trade into the Third Reich. More than respectable in some quarters. Hitler had his followers among the German-speaking Swiss.

The other boys had been instructed to help Neveau, to allow for what had happened. Suitably awed they discussed it with their parents: a boy at school had his mother and father killed in a bombing raid on Dresden.

And in the playground: 'You know whose fault it is, Neveau, don't you? My father says it's the Jews. All the Jews in the world have a conspiracy to take it over. They want to get all the money. Roosevelt is a Jew.'

He couldn't understand it. He didn't know about Jews. But on that came remembrance of stopped conversations between his parents. Readings from newspapers that ceased on his entry. The Jewish question. The Jews in Cracow. Israel. The Final Solution. He couldn't understand it. It tormented him. Young Martin Neveau read as furtively about the Jews as his schoolmates did about sex.

'Well, Martin, what do you wish to do? Go on to the university? There's enough money I think for that.'

'No, Monsieur Moynier. I would like a post with the International Red Cross.'

The lawyer had showed surprise. 'Really? But you've done so well at school. I should have supposed a career. The law perhaps.'

'I would like to make the Red Cross my career. There's been enough suffering. I would like to help people.'

'Mmm.' Neveau's trustee had been unconvinced. 'Honourable of you, I must say. But a career in law, or medicine, that's helping people too, you know.'

'I would like to help more directly, monsieur.'

'Not much money in it, Martin. Not much money, you know.'

'I don't care about money, monsieur.'

Monsieur Moynier sat sucking his teeth after Martin had gone. It was, of course, because of what had happened to his parents. A great tragedy, that. The boy was bright, no doubt there. Lacking a little in force perhaps. Couldn't really see him at the Bar. Couldn't see him

194

instilling great confidence at the bedside. Perhaps he was right, perhaps service would suit him. He obviously felt a vocation for it.

The war had been ended four years when young Martin Neveau joined the ICRC as a clerk under Mick East in the Tracing Agency. The Jews and the suffering and misery of them inundated his sensitivity.

Headquarters of the Fuhrer, July 1942
Secret Reich's matter—single copy
On 7.7.42 a conference was held, object of the discussions being the sterilization of Jewesses. Himmler confirmed to Doctor Klauberg (sic) that the concentration camp at Auschwitz is at his disposal for his experiments on human beings. Moreover it should be tested preferably under consultation of Professor Doctor Hohlfelder, who is an expert on X-rays, in what way sterilization of male persons can be achieved by applications of X-ray.

'—How should I reclassify the sterilization of Jewish men and women, Mr East?'
Many of the operations were performed by a Jewish prison doctor. He was seventy years old and senile. His experiences in Auschwitz had made him a little mad. The Nazis gassed him.
'Mr East, should Dr Samuel be filed as a German doctor or a Jew?'
And in the claims for reparation:

... They had removed my right testicle, then they came for me again. I was put on a table and given a spinal anaesthetic. I said, 'Is it not enough they operate me once?' The doctor said in Polish, 'Stop barking like a dog, you will die anyway.' After a time I saw when he had my left testicle in his hand and showed it to Dr Schumann who was present ...
... There were about four hundred of us girls and women in Block 10. About one hundred and fifty were having their sexual organs X-rayed and removed for examination. The others were having caustic fluid injected into their fallopian tubes. Attempts were also being made to give cancer with mustard gas and other substances. I was made to sit down with my head between the legs of a male nurse. I screamed when they gave me the injection. I asked them to finish me because I could not stand the pain

longer. The doctor said, 'Let me finish my work, damned Jewess, and he gave me a blow on the breast...

... On one experiment Dr Sigmund Rascher exposed human subjects for fourteen hours at temperatures of −6° Centigrade, naked. Different ways of reviving them were tried. In all he experimented with about four hundred prisoners of whom eighty or ninety died. Himmler had the idea that animal warmth would be a quick method of restoring life. Accordingly he told Rascher to use gypsy women to revive the men...

Neveau was seventeen years of age then. He wanted to help people. For three years he worked in that library of horror and misery, unrecovered from his own. When he was transferred from Tracing to Administration, his first responsibility had been the Palestine refugees. Israel was being built. The Stern Gang had mounted its terror. There was no escape from the Jews.

She was so gay and frank and open. He had never known anyone like her. It had been a long time with nobody to love or to be loved by. Martin Neveau married a Jewess.

The whisky had helped. He would take an Alka-Seltzer for the indigestion. On this day, the year he left school, he had spent a month in Dresden, searching for some record of his parents, hoping to find a burial place. They had died in that bombing as they had in Hiroshima. There was no trace or memory of the Neveaus.

Neveau got up wearily and went to the bathroom. It would soon be Saturday. Guy would be at home. He was doing wonderfully well at his languages. It was a good school, Neveau's old school.

196

27

THE celebration of Tet in steel and fire struck at Salem's stomach like a blow. As the offensive overturned every hope, bared every deceit and complacency, the true drama of the meeting in the attic haunted Salem with obsession.

Because the more of us they slaughter, the more will rise up. Because they can stand booted in our blood, burn us to the earth, and we will reach up and claw at them with our fingers.

The menace of Thu, the true meaning of him, reeled in Salem's head with memories of the incinerated village.

Each day, on arrival at headquarters, Salem closeted himself with the newspapers, sending every few hours to the Telex room for new reports. All his effort had been vain, all his imaginings empty. There had never been the chance of another Santo Domingo. The steel and fire had been prepared, the date set for its explosion. Thu had offered him nothing, it had not even been a bribe. Thu had known the truce would be rejected.

Salem's anger and contempt had been unilateral. Now he ached with confusions. They were all playing with him, all of them. There was nothing but corruption and madness. Salem strode his floor, dangerously at bay, wanting to take hold of something and break it.

Neveau avoided Salem. He had become impossible to deal with. The sendings to the Telex room were known to Neveau. It worried him privately. Salem's involvement was becoming hysterical. On the occasions where he had to go to the President's office Salem would be immersed in Telex reports and newspapers. 'Listen to this,' he would always say, 'listen to this.

'BEN TRE, SOUTH VIETNAM

'At what point do you turn your heavy guns and jet fighter bombers on the streets of your own city? When does the infliction of civilian casualties become irrelevant as long as the enemy is destroyed? The decision to unleash allied fire-power—five-hundred-pound bombs, napalm, rockets, anti-personnel bombs and 105- and 155-mm. artillery—was not taken lightly, United States advisers insisted.

'About one thousand civilians were killed in the bitter fighting and a further one thousand five hundred wounded.

' "They are our friends out there," one American said, pointing to the smoking city. "We waited until we had no choice."

'Fighter bombers splashed napalm on the three-thousand-yard-long river-bank opposite the American military compound that was cluttered with thatch-roof homes. The flimsy structures were reduced to ashes.'

There was a fine tremor in Salem's hands as he read and Neveau had worried about that.

'Wait. Now listen to this.

'THAC LAO CANAL, SOUTH VIETNAM

'Child soldiers recruited by the Viet Cong lay dead beside this canal in the Mekong Delta tonight after a day of ferocious fighting. The average age of the three hundred and sixty-five dead Viet Cong was fifteen, said Major General Nguyen Van Manh, military commander of the fifteen provinces that make up the Delta.

'A United States adviser to Government troops, standing near

198

a group of dead Viet Cong said, "You put weapons in the hands of these people and they're not kids any more. The weapons equalize it."

'Another adviser said: "If they are old enough to pull a trigger and kill you, they are old enough to die." '

Salem had scarcely been able to control his voice. The report had fluttered in his hands. 'Children, Martin. Children. The children are being crucified. I told you what I saw, some of the children.'

His voice was hoarse, his breath coming hard. Neveau knew it to be shocking, it was all shocking. But one had to keep control, keep detachment. He was embarrassed for Salem, embarrassed for the unseemliness of it.

Salem said, 'I won't have it. I won't have it happen to the children. There must be an end of this.'

Neveau didn't broach his business. He excused himself and left.

After the earthquake of Tet another earthquake hit twenty-two European capitals. The demonstrations this time were not for peace. The mobs carried Viet Cong flags. *Victory for the NLF*, was their slogan.

In London twenty-four groups marched on the American Embassy. There were German, French and Scandinavian students among them. The police stopped the buses converging on London, they had information that the Embassy was to be stormed. Battering-rams, petrol bombs, water-pistols loaded with ammonia, pepper, artificial blood, were discovered and confiscated.

The timetable was arranged so that national groups could take part in each other's demonstrations. The timing came from the NLF. The instructions were given via Cambodia and the United States.

There will be more demonstrations, everywhere, hammering at the doors of American Embassies. Wait and see. Soon there will be blows and more blows that will shake them like an earthquake.

Pierre Salem could not get the attic out of his mind. Thu had been right. Thu had been right about everything.

The terror of Tet, the truth of the ghastly wreckage, collapsed the subjectives Salem had struggled against as though they had never existed. In Europe, every American effort to explain the offensive away was received with jeers, anger or despair. The American commander claimed a great victory, the enemy was at its last gasp again. The

American Vice-President was speaking everywhere at once, the allies had never been stronger.

Some of Salem's baitings, not forgotten, came home to the committee. He was wilder than ever now, and, smarting, they had to endure it.

Despite the inoculation programme, sickness and death from plague had multiplied several times. Government concern was being secretly voiced in surrounding countries from Malaysia to the Philippines.

Salem drove his point home savagely. 'What do you expect? How can the plague be controlled if it breeds unchecked in VC areas?'

The clamour coming into Geneva wiped out considerations of politics. There had to be an emergency appeal.

It was a triumph for Salem, however small.

LICROSS ICRC L/1600/17/5
To all National Societies

CIVILIAN SITUATION VIETNAM CRITICAL STOP DELEGATES REPORT FIGURE FOR NEW REFUGEES REACHED SEVEN HUNDRED THOUSAND MAKING TOTAL NOW ONE DECIMAL FIVE MILLION STOP OF NEW REFUGEES TWO HUNDRED THOUSAND ENVIRONS SAIGON REMAINDER SCATTERED STOP PRELIMINARY REPORTS SAY RECENT OFFENSIVE CAUSED DESTRUCTION FORTY FIVE THOUSAND HOUSES STOP REFUGEE CAMPS DANGEROUSLY OVERCROWDED WITH RISK EPIDEMIC OUTBREAK STOP PROTEIN CONSISTS ONE TIN SARDINES EVERY TWO DAYS PLUS SMALL AMOUNT CONDENSED MILK FOR CHILDREN STOP SAIGON GOVERNMENT PLANS TO DEAL SITUATION HOPELESSLY INADEQUATE UNREALISTIC STOP EXAMPLE IT INTENDS BUILD FLATS FOR THIRTY SIX THOUSAND PEOPLE WITHIN ONE YEAR BUT WILL SELL SAID FLATS TWO THOUSAND FIVE HUNDRED DOLLARS EACH STOP GOVERNMENT KEEPING ALL REFUGEE OPERATIONS UNDER CONTROL STOP APPEAL FOR FOLLOWING HELP PRIMO ANTIBIOTICS MULTIVITIMINS SULPHUR COMPOUNDS FOR ONE MILLION PEOPLE SECUNDO CEMENT AND ROOFING SHEETS SUFFICIENT TWENTY-FIVE THOUSAND SMALL SHELTERS TERTIO LARGE QUANTITIES POWDERED MILK AND WATER PURIFICATION TABLETS QUARTO FIVE TO TEN FULLY EQUIPPED MOBILE HOSPITALS QUINTO GENERAL PHARMACEUTICAL SUPPLIES ESPECIALLY STERILE BANDAGES SOCIETIES ABLE TO HELP SHOULD FORWARD DETAILS MONEY AND GOODS AVAILABLE TO LICROSS GENEVA STOP REPEAT THIS APPEAL MOST REPEAT MOST URGENT   SALEM

COLLINS

Janos Kisch laid out his letters as memos. There was no space wasted on formalities. The paper was headed SUBJECT: RUDOLF KLEINBERG/KRASNERDORF. Mick began to read, fumbling to pour himself coffee.

The coffee was still untouched when Mick sent again for the Agency's history book. He turned to the old cigarette packet thrown from the death transport. It had been there for over twenty years, as souvenir and curiosity. Mick touched the faded lettering of the names with wonder, the thing he had remembered, the nemesis that had waited in the album for a generation, almost unreadable now: *Betrayed—R. Kleinberg*.

There were seven names on the card. They had known each other. How many others had there been?

Simon Wiesenthal and Janos Kisch had traced a survivor. He had been in Krasnerdorf with Rudolf Kleinberg. This man had got to Israel when the camps were broken open.

Kisch had thought to have found a renegade, a helper in the medical experiments. He had found something worse.

The cruel game had been played in other camps. Shortly after Kleinberg arrived at Krasnerdorf he sought out Jews with relatives outside Germany. He had an arrangement with the commandant, he could ransom them.

Kleinberg drove the bargains, set the blood price. Kleinberg was in the room when the guard brought the dazed prisoners to write their letters, helped to work out their arrangements. Kleinberg was in the room when the prisoners got their answers, clutching at them, hardly able to believe.

When the ransom was paid the man would be given a shower and clean clothing. He would leave Krasnerdorf. The Nazis would transfer him to another death camp.

Mick poured himself coffee and decided to telephone Ted Mitchell. It would make a story for him and cheer him up: he had been getting short in the temper lately. Mick thought a good title would be *The Secret of the Cigarette Pack*, with a reproduction of it. This one would cost Mitchell a dinner.

He added the information to Rudolf Kleinberg's file and returned his attention to the North Vietnam traces which had occupied him before Kisch's letter. Three American civilians were missing, believed captured, in the fighting in Hue during Tet. Their names would be given to Hanoi with those of the new missing Allied servicemen. Hanoi would make no acknowledgment.

The ICRC had passed five thousand letters to the North from friends and relatives of suspected POWs. The score was five thousand unacknowledgments.

The traffic would continue. There was good precedent for it. Tens of thousands of queries into Russia had been ignored during Stalin's paranoia. After the Dictator's death, in Khrushchev's time, Central Tracing had been buried under co-operations dating back ten years. While the old monster lived the Russian Red Cross had not dared communicate with the West.

The Bentley turned into the avenue de la Paix, cut left and proceeded past the angular glass and steel of the Intercontinental Hotel, its national flags drooping in the still morning, into the chemin des Crêtes. The Parklands were very green, the silver beeches shining.

Salem had travelled directly from Lausanne. The idea had come to him that morning. He wanted to discuss it directly with Robert Collins. It wasn't usual for the President to visit the League. Neveau would probably not approve. He was watchful and curious about private meetings between Salem and Collins.

The Bentley parked before the long, low League building. There was more impression of bustle here than at the ICRC, less formality. Salem entered the big lobby. The young porter at the reception desk leapt to summon the elevator. Salem walked up. On the first floor photographed blow-ups of floods, earthquakes and Vietnamese refugees were displayed on the walls. The delegates' room opened off the corridor.

They greeted each other warmly.

'Pierre, should I have expected you?'

Nobody, other than Collins, used Salem's christian name. It was part of the understanding between them, a seal on their private meetings. Collins had become almost as involved as Salem in building the Humanitarian Law.

It had not occurred to Salem as the oddity which perhaps it was. Part of his difficulty with Martin Neveau was the difference of their backgrounds and breeding. He had long forgotten the colour of Collins's skin. The European patrician was fully at sympathy with the grandson of an African slave.

When they were seated Collins called for coffee. Salem wanted to get to his idea. When he had finished, he waited for Collins's opinion.

'I don't know, Pierre. I doubt that it would be productive. The

202

Vatican position is difficult. Papal calls for peace are largely a piety. They do not alter events.'

Salem had considered a Papal audience, the proposal of a joint Vatican–ICRC call for peace at the Paris conference. 'I had thought of the weight it would add to the ICRC resolution.'

'It would take months to arrange the wording, Pierre. I doubt if the Pope would dare. Most of the Saigon Government is Catholic—the educated class in almost exclusively Catholic. The Vatican's first concern in any Vietnam peace is going to be the welfare of this minority. The Catholics who did not cross to the South after the Geneva Accords had a hard time of it in the North. Most of them, you know, supported the French. They are very fearful for their privilege in the South. Short of a government victory the best they can hope for is a stable coalition. The worse could be a bloodbath. The rule of Diem is not forgotten by the NLF or the Buddhists.'

'These are political matters, Robert. The concern of the negotiators. Nothing can be resolved until honest peace talks are insisted on.'

'Ah, Pierre, you are both right and wrong.' The big Negro was gentle for Salem's idealism. 'Everything, I'm afraid, is a political matter. Do you remember how Stalin dismissed the Vatican? How many battalions has the Pope?'

Salem had felt the idea. He had not thought it out. Resolved on action in Paris, he would fortify it any way he could. The depression, which since Tet had alternated with his anger, set in and hollowed him.

He stood up and walked about the room. 'If none of our efforts alter events, what is to be hoped for at the Conference?'

'There will be eighty-nine nations at the Conference, Pierre, plus those Governments signatory to the Convention. If you get your resolution, worded as you want it, that will be power, political power.'

The emptiness in Salem left. He would fight to the last in Paris. He would pull everything down if he must.

28

TED MITCHELL stood chatting at the bar of the Press club. He was still sombre, waiting for the whiskies to lift the weight off him. He had expected to see Sarah that evening. She had telephoned in the afternoon to say that Neveau was bringing the South American delegate to dinner. Mitchell asked to see her tomorrow evening. She could not, that was Friday, young Guy would be coming home.

Mitchell had not forgotten the cold recognition in Sarah's eyes, when he had eased on her body, and he registered it for later recall. She had looked through him to a place he knew only dimly. It was cold there, and empty. The coldness and emptiness grew and troubled him. He wasn't really getting much out of life any more. He had savings, he had been shrewd about that. What else? A comfortable apartment, good clothes, a little reputation. But a man got tired of eating by himself, or watching television. He was suddenly tired too of sexual exploits, bored by the obligation afterwards to be interesting or reassuring when what he most wanted was for the girls to dissolve.

The gloomy moods that Mick East had noticed were the product of Mitchell's introspection. Soon he would be thirty-five. In a few more years he would be forty. It wasn't much of a prospect continuing this way. Mitchell considered returning to journalism, but he had softened on the ease of this job. He thought about returning to Australia, but that seemed a backwater. In his own expression, he was fed-up with everything. The fact was, he wouldn't mind settling down. The other fact was, and he had to face it, that somehow, something ghastly had happened. When he thought of settling down, he instantly thought of Sarah Neveau.

It was a bad time for Mitchell. Instead of being one among the instruments Sarah had become the entire orchestra. It sweated him when he thought about it. He was thinking and sweating when Joseph Richter joined him.

'Hi, Ted. What's new?'

I could tell him what's new, Mitchell thought. I've gone raving mad, that's what's new. He said, 'It's new I'm going to get stoned.'

'Maybe I'll join you,' Richter said. 'What's new at the big house?'

'Catastrophes. Death and decay. Starvation, cannibalism and genocide.'

'We haven't heard much of the President lately.'

'The President is out of sight in his Humanitarian Law. Bertrand Russell may come to talk to him about it.'

'Bertrand Russell? You can't mean that chap who wants to try President Johnson for war crimes?'

'The same. The great Lord Russell.'

Richter said, shakily, 'Drink up. I'll order another.'

The Ambassador put his head in his hands. Richter did not know whether he was very tired or very angry. Richter felt his own head would benefit by support. He had stayed up late with Mitchell.

The Ambassador was both tired and angry. Everything was going wrong for the administration which had appointed him. Tet had been a disaster. He had lost severely in the stock slump. A peace candidate had announced for democratic nomination. The President's credibility gap was deeper than the Grand Canyon. The *New York Times* had suggested he might walk out of office to avoid being carried out. The Ambassador liked being an Ambassador. He wasn't ready to return to Chicago. He held his head and felt unfairly persecuted.

'That Salem's nothing but trouble. Even de Gaulle wouldn't have Russell. If he comes here the Press will make a big deal of it. Can't you get with Neveau on this, Richter? We've had enough trouble out of Salem. Every burr under my saddle gets connected to him.'

'I'm going to try, Ambassador. The Chairman is hard to see just now. Everyone's tied up with the Paris Conference.'

'You get to see him, Richter. You're the one on that team.'

When Richter was leaving, the Ambassador asked hopefully, 'Have we got any intelligence yet that might explain Salem?'

Richter had heard nothing from Milos Jelié in Milan. If Jelié had completed his research on Pierre Salem, Washington had passed nothing on.

'I'm afraid not, Ambassador.'

'OK,' the Ambassador said listlessly. 'See what you can do with Neveau.'

Neveau kept the barbiturates in the top drawer of his bureau, covered by balls of socks. He was ashamed of his need and neglected the doctor's instructions to take the drug several hours before retiring. Only when hope of natural sleep had passed would he grant himself release, going softly in the dark to feel for the cold square bottle. Stiff and sore he would lie back, trying to escape from his disordered thoughts, concentrating on the loud count of the ornamental clock in the sitting-room which he had kept from his father's possessions.

When annihilation came it was usually early morning. Neveau would groan awake to the new day, propping his swollen lids by will, sour-mouthed and burdened by the unfinished anaesthesia.

Earlier in the marriage their breakfasts had been gay. Sarah woke brightly in the mornings, fully awake and mobilized from the opening of her eyes. She would tune the radio for light music while the coffee was set to perk. Neveau would walk first in the near-by gardens in recognition of his gathering weight and return aroused, pink-faced and hungry for the coffee and croissants.

He had no will or energy to take his exercise now. There was no more music, no more chatter from Sarah. Neveau desired only coffee and silence and the French cigarettes that made him cough.

His leave-takings of Sarah had become as ritualized as his evening greetings, accepting her new austerity as a further instance of his persecutions, deliberately hardening himself, contesting her self-possession. Only in the child's company was there peace and comfort for Neveau. When he spoke French and German with little Guy there was satisfaction in Sarah's exclusion. Her eyes contradicted her pretence not to care. It was a victory Neveau needed. With his son, if with nobody else, Neveau could feel himself sovereign.

At the door Sarah asked, 'Shall I expect you for dinner?'

Neveau shook his head.

'I have an evening meeting with the Conference Committee. I will eat something in the commissariat.'

'In that case,' Sarah said, 'I may go to a film.'

Neveau studied her cold calm face. 'You're becoming quite an addict. Have you nothing better to do?'

Sarah shrugged. Neveau touched his lips to her cheek.

When he had gone Sarah cleared up and sat on the balcony to buff her nails. She had heard her husband go to the dresser, had weeks ago searched out the bottle. She was past pity. He had murdered all she had felt for him. Never and never would she forgive him for alienating her child. Never and never would she forget his subtle bigotry about her origins—the chauvinism which had deadened him at the heart. He had murdered her love, and her hopes, used the child she had carried in glory as an instrument to mock her.

Sarah bent her long fingers for inspection, hard-eyed and absorbed. There was little in her now for anybody. She was voided even of her own self-respect. In cold will and defiance she lay like a whore for her lover.

A cloud passed before the sun. The balcony fell into shadow. Sarah looked at her watch and went inside to telephone Mitchell her freedom for the evening.

Neveau shut the car door and waited until the vehicle had disappeared in the morning traffic. There had been light rain, the air sparkled. It revived him a little. He crossed the pavement and entered the café. Richter was waiting at an alcove table.

'Martin. How good to see you.'

Richter put down the napkin and clumsily unfolded his length.

'Don't get up,' Neveau said.

Richter gestured at the table. 'Sorry about the mess. I've been eating breakfast.'

Neveau sat on the proffered chair and ordered coffee. He wished he did not feel so done in. He had no taste for this meeting. Events had gathered into a pattern of disaster. The twenty-first plenary session of the International would be a political battleground.

Richter observed Neveau's slumped figure from the cover of a cigarette. The man looked ghastly. He looked as if he had been dug up.

207

Richter crossed his long legs anxiously, bumping his knees on the table. 'Well, this time next week we'll be in Paris.'

'Yes,' Neveau said. 'This time next week.'

He rubbed his eyes. Richter could not bear the silence. He leaned forward and lowered his voice, coughing to clear uncertainty from his throat. 'I take it you had your talk?'

'Yes.'

Richter coughed again. He wanted to shake Neveau. He leaned farther over the table, encouraging him to speech by physical pressure.

'It's no use,' Neveau said. 'He's hopeless. Hopeless. There's nothing anyone can do. Anyone.'

Richter couldn't believe it. 'Did you tell him? Did you tell him that the American Society will not tolerate his motion? That it can't be tolerated?'

'Yes,' Neveau said.

'Did you tell him,' Richter pressed, 'that support will definitely be withdrawn? The ICRC can't afford that. He must know what that would mean.'

'I told him,' Neveau said.

Richter was lost. He couldn't accept it. This had been his trump, arranged for him in the highest places. The very future of the International was involved. The man had to be mad, possessed.

'He can't do it.' Richter shook his head, rejecting the absurdity. 'He can't do it.'

'He can. He did. He said that if any such threat is made again he will declare on the floor of the Paris conference that the American Society, by its very charter, is the political tool of its Government.'

Richter gasped. 'He's mad. It's a lie.'

Neveau at last roused himself. He lit a cigarette slowly and looked fully into Richter's greyed face. He spoke softly, almost in pity. 'There will hardly be a delegation in Paris that supports the intervention in Vietnam. You must remember that President Salem is a distinguished scholar of international law. He knows exactly where he stands. He will say that the American Society does not adhere to the principles laid down by Henri Dunant and the ICRC. The second, third and fourth principles of impartiality, neutrality and independence don't apply. How can they? The American Red Cross has its charter from Congress. In 1953 the Society was reincorporated under government supervision. Government supervision. The President of the United States appoints eight Governors, designates one to act as the principal officer of the corporation. Its fiscal reports are made to the Secretary of

Defense. Every by-law of your society confirms its inseparable attachment to the Government.'

Neveau ashed his cigarette. 'Can you imagine the outcry? The world outcry?'

Richter swallowed at the prospect. He had thought to have Salem in his grasp. Now it was the other man's fingers at his throat. One week. In one week they would be in Paris.

Neveau brushed ash from his lapel and buttoned his jacket.

In a weak voice Richter asked, 'What can we do? He will wreck the conference. He will wreck the ICRC.'

Neveau's head lifted. 'No,' he said. 'He will be stopped. I am not unprepared. Next week, in Paris, he will be stopped.'

Richter sat alone among the soiled crockery and ashtrays and wondered how he would put it to the Ambassador.

In the Salle des Fêtes, the great baroque room which is the wonder and ornament of the Grand Hotel, carpenters hammered at the glass-windowed interpreter's boxes beside the podium. On the carved marble pillars that rose two floors to the mirrored arches on the gallery, the white flag of the Red Cross confronted the French tricolour. Great chandeliers depended from the emblazoned ceiling, set in the centre by a worn oil painting. Other lights clustered on other pillars. Niched in the encircling gallery, classical sculptures posed and dreamed.

In the Café de la Paix, on the corner which projected on to the place de l'Opéra, the cellar-master inspected his celebrated bins. The Pacific Snack Bar, as baroque and ornamented as a piece of Versailles, was reviewed by the Maître d'Hôtel. It was fitting that the Hotel Grand's restaurants should be named Peace and Pacific.

Staff prepared the rooms that flanked the Salle des Fêtes for the use of the committees, and waited. Chambermaids, bell-boys and porters were given instruction, and waited. The bilingual telephonists rehearsed the special switchboard, and waited. On the great square of the place de l'Opéra taxicabs honked, and waited. On the place de la Concorde, in the Continental and the Crillon, in the Hilton across the Seine, in the great and small hotels from the Arc de Triomphe to the Ile de la Cité, managements and staffs prepared themselves, and waited.

In the last days Neveau passed beyond pride. He had to sleep. He now took the capsules before going to bed and doubled the dosage. His snored, cluttered breathing kept Sarah awake, cold with disgust and resentment.

In the last days Salem's dark eyes burned hot with anticipation. Adrenalin powered his mind and body. He walked like a man sprung and tensed to force passage through barriers.

From every country the delegations and government representatives pointed themselves towards Paris.

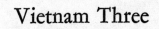
Vietnam Three

29

ADAM THOMSON's partnership in the New York practice was dissolved in the sixth month of his absence. He had agonized about it for a week. In that time he tried to extricate himself, practising it in his mind, but he was enmeshed in the suffering country.

In that week Adam was hard to talk to. The food in the mess, the stink in the wards, the sick and the wounded, all offended him. He cursed the rains and he shut his door after eating.

Sam Jarra said, 'Old Adam's got chickenshit on the liver. The slaughterhouse is getting him down.'

When he addressed and sealed the letter to his partner he lay on the bed and watched the fan limp above him. He had made the decision and it emptied him into peace. On each revolution the fan clicked before groaning, introspectively, like a small tut of worry. Adam closed his eyes and heard the words being made.

'Click! It's Jane, too, isn't it? Click! It's Jane too, isn't it?'

Adam answered wearily, 'Yes, yes. It's Jane, too.'

Then he slept.

They had kept it from her. She did not know about the killing on the promontory. Colonel Clagger had ordered Jane and Sam to the command point above the camp before the tunnel complex was searched with torches of sacking and petrol.

They had flown back to Quong Lo in the dusk. Hatton's fixed profile conveyed nothing. She did not notice the concern with which Sam Jarra observed Hatton's silence.

The tunnel had been empty. The patrol had found no weapons.

In the last month of the year the monsoon lightened. The burden of life in the Quong Lo camps eased out of the mud. Sam Jarra went on leave to Bangkok for rest and recreation. He left, threatening the ruin of the entire female population.

'That Bangkok'll be Kokbang when I get there, Adam. It's only out of pity I don't hit Saigon again. Man, this country ain't big enough. Sam's got to spread himself around.'

It was rumoured that there would be a few days' truce at Christmas to symbolize peace on earth, goodwill to men. A shopkeeper in the bazaar put a manger in his window. The infant Jesus in the crib was a sleeping doll with one eye-socket empty.

A tree was got for the Red Cross mess and dressed with tinsel and angels by Borgia. Tim Frost announced a party at the guest-house. The Quakers planned an entertainment for the child amputees.

Ton Son Nhut was mortared again, twelve civilians killed. President Thieu drew attention to the atrocity. In that week the bomb tonnage unloaded on the North and South exceeded the weight exploded on Korea and all the targets of the South Pacific war.

The bloody year weltered to a close, twelve months deeper in human wreckage.

Some of them were there for money. Some of them, the Quakers, had come to testify. Adam was there out of pity and because the reality had claimed him. Jane because she needed the involvement, the escape out of herself. They were all mixed in motive between service and self-interest and in each the one was coloured by the other.

They shared the hard life and they shared the risks but they hardly shared their thoughts. There was too much blood on the earth about them to be easy. Guilt rode the air as strongly as the stench of bodies under rubble and all of them were worried by a share of it.

214

Nothing was being won, all was being lost, more communists were being made than killed. The herded children in the camps would remember the round-eyes who destroyed and burned their villages. In them was the making of a terrible, unforgiving generation. The future retribution was being sown in the scarred Vietnamese earth like dragon's teeth.

They had all borne much in that year. The small release of Christmas was awaited with enthusiasm.

The day's duty was over for Hatton. He had showered and changed out of fatigues to collect Ho from the hospital. The dumb boy had at last submitted to his persuasions. He had made his own gesture, one evening after Hatton had been absent for briefings in Da Nang.

Sam Jarra had brought in a sick woman from the camps. He welcomed Hatton's return. They stood in the sun-shot evening and talked under the pepper tree. It was so tentative that Hatton thought an animal had brushed him. When he had to look down it was Ho, pinching at the cloth of his trousers, leaning a little on the stiffened leg.

Hatton had been about to light a cigarette. He did so very carefully. 'Yes, Sam. Go on.'

Gently he reached behind him and put his hand on the boy's head. They stood like that until a child on crutches called to Ho from the annexe.

It was characteristic that little direct remark was made to Hatton about the friendship. At his easiest, the odd force of challenge persisted. The civilians discussed it among themselves, as something to keep account of. '—I saw the Major in the bazaar with that dumb boy from the hospital.' '—There's some brass coming in from Saigon. Hatton and his mascot were out at the strip.'

The orderly room sergeant said to the corporal, 'Old Fireguts is riding about with that Gook kid again. There's nobody so young or so old or so near or so far, they can't kill you, he says. If you want to stay alive out here it's you against everything that moves. Next time old Fireguts makes the speech, I'll tell him.'

'You do that, Sarge,' the corporal said. 'I got sixty-three more days to fly my ass out of here, but for that I'm about to stay over.'

'Get poxed, Wilkins,' the sergeant told him.

Only Adam approached it, letting Hatton know he had watched and understood. 'Well, Major, you've made your point.'

He got Hatton's hard search before he replied. An almost shy smile and nod. 'He's a good kid. He's bright. I can't get him to talk though.'

215

'It's traumatic. The shock will pass. You're helping him more than we could. He's no longer afraid of the uniform.'

The door had been opened between them. Hatton had wanted to talk about the boy. It closed now on that reminder. 'Be seeing you, Doc.'

Adam watched him go. I didn't have to say that, he thought. I wanted to put him down. All the best reasons for our being here are what Hatton believes. He has had to kill and nobody escapes that except the brutes. Somewhere inside them, some day, each has to explain it to himself. How do I know what Hatton feels? What the uniform might mean to him? He's trying to keep it clean for himself, to keep it clean for us all.

The loneliness of understanding filled Adam like swallowed tears. They were all entangled. He could spend the remainder of his life here and spare less suffering than a single hour's stoppage of the war. There were small amends Hatton could make the lost boy for whatever horror had frozen his tongue. There were many little Hos. Many more would be made.

The hopelessness of it made Adam want to cry out. He wanted to turn from it. To get away into private concerns and the distance of his own country. To sit somewhere comfortable while television made it meaningless through the saving grace of commercials.

Sam Jarra once voiced his own disagreement in the way it suddenly came to him. He laid down the newspaper from home and sniffed at it. 'This guy wants to drop the big one. If the VC get the whole goddamned country they're only a thousand miles closer to this guy. What's he fluttering his asshole about? If they're going to drop any big ones, I want the hell out of here.'

Hatton checked his watch. Ho was expecting him. They were to stop in the bazaar for his Christmas present. Ho knew this was a special time, the next day the Quakers were giving a party.

For a week now when they were privately together Ho would point at himself as Hatton had taught him. 'Ho.'

And then, pointing again: 'At-ton.'

It was a start. Hatton brushed his cropped hair. It had been a good day. Everyone was borne up a little by Christmas.

The oppression of the climate had eased with the first spending of the monsoon. The air had lightened and brightened. A budding and greening arose on the earth which had seemed seared beyond resurrection. The weeks of cooler mornings and languid evenings, the return of crickets and birds, the bright new leaves on the compound trees and the sudden clear carry of voices disturbed routines, fretted habit with restless stirrings. The guns whumped forgotten. The armoured patrols clanked almost gaily out of town. The American soldiers who walked the bazaar whistled the girls in defiance of orders.

The civilians of Quong Lo raised Christmas Eve drinks and readied themselves for Tim Frost's party.

Adam rode with Sam Jarra. They both wore suit and tie. On Adam's clothing the mould traces persisted. Sam had returned in the middle of the month from his Bangkok R & R. He had entered the mess on hands and knees, claiming that his dissipations had left him unable to stand without assistance. Now he drove erratically, pulling at the chafe of collar, his long freckled face glowing with whisky.

'This is a chickenshit idea to wear a suit. An Adam's apple like I've got was never meant to be tied. An Adam's apple like this is a rarity. It's meant to run free in the world.'

The Canadian medical team had come in for the party. The pre-drinks in the mess had been boisterous. The change into suits, in which the teams had never witnessed each other, produced unexpected hilarity. Adam could not remember being so frivolously happy. In all the world that evening there was nowhere he would rather be. He wondered what Jane would wear. He had felt something like this a long time ago, going to a college prom.

Sam pulled violently at his collar, running the jeep off the road. 'For crissake, Sam.'

Sam stopped the jeep, pulled down his tie and unbuttoned the shirt. He sniffed with relief, reached under the seat and got a half bottle of whisky. Gravely he toasted the watching Vietnamese and drank. They had entered the town. It embarrassed Adam. 'Come on, Sam. You can drink all you want in a few minutes.'

'This here's an emergency,' Sam said. He corked the bottle and deposited it under the seat, sat with his hands on the wheel, frowning. 'Hey, Adam, it's none of my business, but you've had no tail here in a long time. This is going to be a big blast tonight. Why don't you get yourself a piece of this Stirling?'

Adam's face felt suddenly misshapen. He was not aware of his own chafing collar. He said uncertainly, 'Maybe she's not a girl like that.'

Sam snorted. 'There's four or five stud living in that guest-house. How do you know what she does?'

Adam had wondered about it and it quavered his stomach and voice.

He asked the question as distantly as he could. 'Have you heard something about that, Sam?'

'That's a funny thing,' Sam said, 'I ask around but nothing comes up.'

'Absolutely nothing?'

'Nothing. A fanny like she's got, it ain't natural. I get to thinking, Adam. Maybe she's got something going for you.' Sam stopped and hit the wheel. He turned to Adam on the thought. 'Hey, I know what it is. You've been there already.'

Adam laughed and shook his head. 'No, Sam. Doctor's honour. Come on, let's go to the party.'

In all the world that evening there was nowhere he would rather be.

The USAID headquarters for the province had been built opposite a pagoda on a dirt road that shortly ended in paddy. The APCs stood outside the high wall near the sheeted iron defence gates, the guarding Vietnamese crews waving greeting. Sam Jarra turned in and honked. The inspection trap opened. The armed sentinels unlocked the gates. Inside, the compound was crowded with vehicles. Sam took another drink.

'One good thing, Tim Frost is organized. I feel better with these APCs. One good satchel charge in here would take out every round-eye in the province.'

Adam felt no mortality. He chanted, 'They'll blow our asses off one day.'

'You'd better believe it,' Sam advised him. 'Where they've got us, half-way to Hatton's compound and Gook headquarters, they'll blow our asses off one day for sure.'

Adam went to the party laughing.

The chintzy sitting-room was already crowded. Jane and Frost's Eurasian secretary had strung decorations there and in the big dining-room off the corridor behind it. A table against the wall was covered with bottles. A small fan buzzed over a tub of caked ice, adding gratefully to the cooling evening. Tim Frost received his guests at the entrance with a handshake and the seasons greetings. He stared at Sam's defiant collar and turned away with distaste.

She wasn't hard to find among the men claiming attention. The dress was Italian, fiercely coloured, cut across one shoulder like a sarong. The black hair was long and loose. She wore pottery ear-rings brilliantly glazed. Her eyes were made up as Adam had not seen them. He was stunned by her. When she noticed them she crossed at once to kiss their cheeks. 'Merry Christmas, dear Adam. Merry Christmas, Sam.'

Jane took Adam by the hand. 'Come and meet some new people. We've got two Air American pilots held up by engine trouble. They had a big party planned in Da Nang tonight and are absolutely miserable about it.'

They had needed the party. Everyone was dancing. The two young Quaker women and the team leader's wife whirled with an enthusiasm that ignored puritan aspects of the faith. Jane Stirling was transformed with a force that shook the men. The sensuality of her figure and face, cloaked for months in grey hospital wraps and strained by concern and fatigue, claimed attention with a demand almost savage. All her body seemed swelled and softened. The splashed brilliance of the colour she wore heated the impression.

They were mostly men without women. The comforts of the street and girlie-bars were transactions into alien flesh. They were cheated at last of the needed thing in slanted faces that offered only submission. The men drank hard and their eyes groped on Jane Stirling.

Tim Frost stood ignored in the doorway. Darder was spinning his little Vietnamese schoolteacher. The grounded pilots were drunk. Sam Jarra hiccoughed and sniffed in a chair. Cigarette butts scattered on the floor. One of Frost's staff unsteadily swept up a smashed glass. Most of the men had taken off their jackets. The stereo had been raised to full volume.

Tim Frost barked, 'Turn that bloody thing down.'

It was without conviction. Nobody heard him. His Eurasian secretary was dancing gaily with a bearded German off the hospital ship. When she came to his rooms later, Frost would have something to say about that. She had been presuming too much recently.

The record ended and was replaced. Jane had been laughing and panting in a corner with Adam Thomson, stretching her dimpled chin at the rush from the fan. The beat rocked again in the room. She stretched her arms, hands clenched, head back, eyes closed, as though to absorb the rhythm. Then she leapt into it as though it were water.

Tim Frost watched the transformation and pulled hard on his whisky. He considered moodily that she was a sensational piece of tail. It was hard to reconcile this with the cool, aloof person she was ordinarily. He watched the soft push of breasts swelling and swinging under the silk.

Tim Frost was a tit man. His wife had a pair like Siamese melons. You could smother in them. There wasn't another pair like them in all Connecticut. He got depressed thinking about that and wondered what his wife was doing tonight.

Adam leaned over the washbowl, sluicing his face. He rubbed the back of his neck with the ice cubes he had carried to the bathroom.

'I'm stoned,' he told the mirror. 'Dr Thomson is stoned.'

She was in him like an ache and on all his flesh like a bruise. He wondered at himself as at something raw and new, leaning to stare in the mirror. All his attention had been directed outwards in these months that seemed to have become his lifetime. The return of his own needs weakened and shook him.

They had brought her back to dance again from the dining-room into which some of the party had divided. The pilots had her hands, pulling her along the passage. Hatton was inside the door, draining whisky bottles into a tumbler.

'Here she is,' someone shouted. The stereo boomed into volume.

He turned and looked at her, the measuring and challenge blurred. She took his hand and drew him to her so strongly that Hatton stumbled from the table. Her eyes were almost closed, mocking him. Again she pulled him towards her, the black hair lashing. He shook his head, jarring, the hard remote face suddenly imploring. She heard him say, 'I can't dance,' as her head came to his shoulder. Then he closed his hand on hers and squeezed until the pain shocked her still.

Hatton pushed through the crush and was gone. Jane walked shakily to the drinks table. She could not hold the glass in the hand he had viced.

'Later, chaps. I promise.' She tried to make her voice gay, to dissemble, swallowed the spirit neat, wanting it to burn her.

... She could not find him.

Sam Jarra was in the passage, carrying a glass and bottle, his eyes almost closed.

'Sam, where's Mark? Have you seen him?'

Sam rallied himself to consider.

'Sure I saw him. What I don't see is the can. They've moved the can some place.'

She almost stamped with impatience. 'Where is he, then?'

'He's gone up to the roof. Where did they move that can?'

A small moon, fronted by cloud, shone a sad pale light. He was as dark as a cut-out, leaning on the wall looking down. She took a breath for courage and stood beside him.

'Mark.'

He turned a little and his eyes were again clear and hard.

'Mark. I forgot about the leg. I'm most terribly sorry. Please forgive me.'

He said nothing, so fiercely cold, that for an instant she was afraid he might grasp her throat as he had her hand. The heat of the drink had gone out of her. She shivered with the reaction. The threat of him altered into distance, an introspection that seemed to dismiss her. Her throat filled while she waited.

'Forget it.'

He turned and felt for cigarettes, took one and offered the pack. Her hand trembled. She reached automatically but her fingers would not close. Hatton shook the pack. She took the cigarette with her left hand. He clicked the lighter, tipped his head to exhale. Then he lifted her free hand and held the lighter above it.

The long competent fingers had already lumped with swelling. The pale, translucent skin was blue with blood on the knuckles. His thumb touched over the hurt. 'I'm sorry.'

She needed the hurt now, was glad of it. 'Don't be sorry. I deserved it.'

He shook his head. The jaw muscles ridged. 'No. I'm sorry.'

The hand still lay in his. She knew the absurdity of it, but something was required. Her eyes had filled with tears. She lifted her hand towards him, made a childish voice.

'Kiss it better, then.'

He saw the tears, held her hand to his lips.

Something under her breast broke up. The roof and the sky rocked about her. He took her to him and his mouth shocked her. She held to him blindly and desperately, unable to think, her kisses shaking with sobs.

Adam had combed his hair, straightened his collar and tie. The buffet was being served. He looked for Jane to take her in.

Sam Jarra was trying to open the door of the corridor cupboard. 'Hey, Adam, Crissake man, where they put the can?'

'Last door on the right, Sam. Have you seen Jane?'

'She's gone up on the roof. Last door on the right you say, Adam?'

Adam pointed and hurried to the stairs. He felt better now, just stoned enough. The sad pale moonlight was ahead.

He stopped under the arch because he had expected a group. Chatter, laughter and glasses. Nothing moved there, it was silent. The stairwell behind him hummed with the voices and music below. Adam stepped through the arch.

They were in profile to him, against the short wall, between boxes of grenades and tear gas covered with ponchos held down by bricks. She had both arms around him, her head on his chest like a child. Hatton was fixed on the night beyond her shoulder, a hand under the loose black hair. They said nothing, made no movement. Adam had to lean to steady his trembling legs. His ears stormed. His insides had emptied, whipped by icy winds.

30

In the first weeks of January the war moved away from Quong Lo. All about them was quiet. The fighting had fiercened in the North, in the Central Highlands around Eye Corps. Ke Sanh was threatened. The big transports passed over each day, hurrying the marine reinforcements. Tim Frost sat at the dining-room table drumming his fingers and listening to the news.

Jane was too full of her own happiness to notice the change in Adam. She was quite unaware of his disorder, which others put down to fatigue. He was visibly drawn and she did not notice that, or the ache with which he sometimes watched her, the sudden avoidances and coldness of voice.

She sang about the hospital, energetic, competent, more than ever tender. Her eyes were withdrawn and musing. In the evenings she came often to the verandah, looking across the compound to the entrance.

Twice Adam made mistakes with the knife as though he had forgotten something, or had lost his way, and needed to shake himself back.

Darder said, 'Adam, why don't you take a rest? Go to Bangkok or Saigon for a few days? You've hardly had the scalpel out of your hand. I could manage here.'

He thought about it, but could not leave. The sickness of jealousy would not allow it. Perhaps he could void himself of her on others, return to perspective again. But that wasn't what he craved of her. It was the sympathy that strikes to the bone. The way she had been with Hatton, wrapped like a child against him, his hand under her hair in silence.

Neither Jane nor Hatton had known what to do or say when they remet after Tim Frost's party. He had looked at her with wonder, without challenge, asking confirmation. There, among the others, she tried to tell him with her face that it was true.

It was true. All of the past had wiped away. She was virginal. On one spin of the universe she had returned to the beginning.

Hatton tried to hold to his hardness. He was safe there. He had shaped himself that way, it was all he wanted or knew. He had hardened himself in Korea, as a kid like the new kids now. The instinct for it had been as certain as a stone inside him. When the others fell he had taken command as though by formal appointment, never in doubt of his competence, never in doubt of obedience. In the world there were men and half-men. The half-men were swill in the trough. The difference he knew to be in himself was in his spirit like flint.

He did not know what had come to him. When you needed a woman, you used one. You shaped your men and you shaped your command, and when the hard things were there you did them. The hard thing now was to get back his leg.

But something had come to him. He did not understand how or why. It wasn't her beauty, or such things as Sam Jarra remarked. She was soft to look at but there was hardness and will under that. He had hurt her and had wanted to hurt her beyond the reason for it. When he had brought his mouth down on hers it had been in revenge, to crush her with his manhood, to drive the leg out of his mind. When she cried into him out of her own hurt, delivering herself in a strange way, the unexpected thing had come to him then.

He had held her while something sad and postponed unfolded itself within him. The hand under her hair for comfort was a comfort he needed too. He had watched the night, saw the gun-flashes on the sky rim, heard the pass of airstrike targeted north. The compound was thick with the singing of crickets. He could see the dull steel of the APCs quartered outside in the road.

She had been so quiet against his chest. He was drenched with the fragrance of her hair. The hand swollen blue was on his shoulder. They had stood like that a long time and he could not account for the sadness that continued to unfold.

After Christmas was over, Hatton came again to the hospital for treatment. Jane would run out to talk. Sometimes she was there, waiting on the verandah. There was nowhere to be alone. He did not know what to offer. If the verandah was empty of others, Adam Thomson would appear to ask her assistance.

He stayed for coffee at her request. There was the surprise of an embroidered cloth on the metal table, cakes bought in the bazaar. Adam joined them, distant and quiet, Pedro Darder cheerful and hungry. The frankness of her eyes took little account of others. She was content having Hatton there to serve.

In the second week of January Hatton was called to a meeting of military advisers in Saigon. The signal was received in the morning. He got the scheduled aircraft in the afternoon. She waited that evening until the last transport had left the hospital. The next evening she waited again.

'Adam, where's Mark, do you know? He hasn't been in for days.'

Adam was aware of it. 'Hatton isn't my responsibility.'

'He wouldn't be in the field, would he, Adam? It's not his job to be in the field.'

No, Adam thought bitterly, it's not his job to be in the field. It wasn't his job to walk in on that promontory either. Why does it have to be me she asks about him? 'I don't know or care where he is.'

His mood meant nothing to her. 'If Sam comes in for lunch, would you ask, Adam? Sam would probably know.'

'Sam's been eating in the camps lately.'

'Yes, but he might come in. If he does, would you ask him?'

Adam said, 'Yes. I'll bloody well ask him.'

She frowned a little at his back, then forgot it. After lunch she would know.

Adam had gone to check medical supplies in the USAID warehouse. He was thinking about that when he pulled in under the pepper trees.

'Did you see him? What did he say?'

225

Her voice and nerves rasped him. 'What are you talking about?'

'Sam. Did Sam come in? Did you ask him about Mark?'

A shaft of pure anger went through him. He brushed whitely past her. 'Hatton's in Saigon.'

The anger stayed with him. He was worried by the low stock of medicines, humiliated in his own pride because Jane had abandoned hers.

Pedro Darder was resting that day. Adam had been checking a dressing when the wound suddenly bubbled with haemorrhage. He had finished with it and was walking to wash, his stained hands and arms held before him, almost bumped her as he turned the block. She startled and flinched away.

Anger clapped in his head. For this and for Jane and for everything. The words forced out, pulling his mouth. 'Does the blood on my hands bother you? You're pleased enough about the blood on Hatton. He slaughtered two civilians on that promontory. Did you know that? He slaughtered two civilians.'

She didn't understand. She couldn't recognize Adam's changed face. He thrust his arms at her. 'I can wash this off. I hope you can wash the blood off Hatton.'

She gasped a little, shocked by him, unable to understand. 'Adam, what is it? What do you mean?'

He spun away and left her.

Adam made a solution and dipped his arms. His breath still came hard. He had not intended to say it, but it needed to be said. He was sick to the marrow with killing. After his breath eased, Adam lit a cigarette and went to smoke it outside at the table. He felt very tired and uncaring.

It made no sense, but something shouted, Yes. She walked the verandah, stared across the compound to the Quaker annex, carried forward on confusion.

The jeep honked at her. Sam Jarra drove with one hand, drinking a bottle of beer. Jane ran to him while he lowered the waved bottle. Her hands were clenched on the metal. 'Sam, what happened on the promontory? What happened at that relocation?'

He leaned back from her, closing his sandy brows. 'What happened? We relocated a few thousand Gooks is what happened.'

'What happened with Mark? What did he do that day?'

Sam said slowly, 'You saw him.'

She shook the jeep. 'What did he do while we were away? What happened with that platoon?'

226

Sam looked across to the hospital, as though there might be hint or help there. He did not know how to answer. 'What have you been hearing?'

'Mark killed two people, didn't he? Mark killed two civilians.'

Sam tightened. 'That's chickenshit. They were snipers. They had weapons hid out some place.'

She couldn't believe the words. 'They had no weapons?'

Sam said hotly, 'They had weapons when they bust that GI's knee. They had a tunnel there that Hatton found.'

It required time. After that she was drained.

'How did he kill them, Sam?'

Sam waved the beer bottle. 'What have you got to know that for? Why don't you leave it alone?'

'I want to know, Sam. How did he kill those people?'

Sam waved the bottle again, kept silent. There was no escape. She was calm, her voice probing at him.

'I want to know, Sam.'

He was suddenly aggrieved, and loud. 'He gave them a grenade. Hatton pitched a grenade in there. If you got to know about it, Hatton gave them a grenade.'

They kept silence, Sam hot and upending the bottle.

The images of that day were as clear as photographs in her mind. Hatton tucking his helmet under the helicopter seat, laughing at Sam, two grenades on his chest. The quiet ride back, Hatton's hard profile, a single grenade clipped to his pocket.

She said, 'Thank you, Sam,' stepped back from the jeep.

He considered her and was satisfied. 'Where's old Adam? I got some new business for Adam in the camps.'

Jane said, 'Adam's inside. He's washing his hands.'

That evening, tired and waiting for transport, Jane saw Ho standing with an arm around a verandah post, near the pepper tree. He was wearing one of the bright shirts Hatton had bought him. She went and sat near the boy, put her arm about him. He leaned towards her, head bent, scratching his toe in the dirt.

Jane said softly, in the Vietnamese she had learned, 'Hatton will be back soon. He has gone on a small journey. You miss him, don't you, Ho?'

He leaned towards her again. Jane tightened her arm on the child. Her throat clotted.

227

The American Forces Network reported the first raid shortly after Christmas. Six VC had been cut down on a night attack on Bien Hoa airbase. They carried no mortars or demolition charges. The men wore loincloths, their bodies blackened. When sighted they had been among the transports that flew shuttle to the States.

Tim Frost noted it and wondered. It was odd that the raiders had carried no charges. It made no sense, and that worried him. He directed his attention to news of a massive search and destroy operation in the Delta.

Tim Frost followed the news with maps. On the wall in his office the greatest part of South Vietnam was securely pacified.

In the next few weeks there were further puzzling mentions of VC infiltrations into airfields. The oddity continued. No attempt was made to destroy the transport aircraft.

Hatton was absent for a week. In that time Jane was drawn to little Ho. He connected her to Hatton, subtracted from the thing Adam had told her.

She forgot herself enough, after the shock of his outburst to be aware that something worried Adam. Darder believed him to be worn out. She made herself close and considerate, putting out the tablecloth and bringing cakes for his coffee.

It was through Ho that Jane learned of Hatton's return. She had accepted an invitation from Adam to eat lunch in the mess and had suggested taking Ho. She couldn't find him in the compound, thought he might be in the annex. The Quakers told her that Major Hatton had collected his mascot earlier.

Jane waited out the day. Hatton was coming for treatment that evening. She would make coffee to keep him with her. It was the first time they had been alone since the night on the roof. Adam and Pedro Darder had gone to a meeting with Tim Frost to discuss the extension USAID was to build.

He walked out, buckling on the webbing that holstered the pistol. Her lips quivered a little, she couldn't help the uncertainty in her smile. 'Mark. We've missed you.'

He looked at her gravely and gently. 'I got back this morning. You look well, Jane.'

'They told me that you had come for Ho.'

'I got him a kite in Cholon. One of the big ones the Chinese make.'

It was ridiculous that this should affect her. But her throat filled unreasonably. She put out her hand. 'Come, your coffee is ready.'

Hatton took the hand, it was the one he had hurt. He held the fingers by the tips, stroked the healed knuckles. Then he smiled, raised the hand to his lips.

The shadows were dark and cool under the wall. He was standing when she brought the pot to the old metal table, gazing far away to the hills. She was close to him filling the cups.

Neither seemed to go to the other. It was as though the space between them had disappeared. She was on her toes, all her breath going out on his lips. Again and again he found her, long and deep and gentle. She laid her cheek on his chest and nothing needed saying. Her peace and happiness was like trance.

He shifted a little to ease the leg, continuing to hold her, his hand under her hair. She looked up once. The hard clean face was as still as a carving, withdrawn somewhere past the distance that fixed his eyes.

There were to be no stages between them, nothing to be grown, it had arrived fully made.

'Mark, there are things I must tell you. And something I want to ask.'

He shook his head, still focused away. 'I don't want to know.'

It was true, He did not. There was no past, for either of them.

She had thought about it. For her reasons she had to tell him. 'There is something I must ask you. I can't unless I give you something first.'

'I don't want to know, Jane.'

'I must, Mark.'

He looked down, touched his lips to her forehead. 'If you must.'

She couldn't begin. He pressed her to him as a help. 'I've been married.'

She looked up. His eyes clamped on her once, held and then withdrew.

'It doesn't matter.'

'I was very young. The boy was very young. Neither of us knew about ourselves. It was sad and ugly. After the honeymoon he was charged with homosexual soliciting. His family was very important. He drove into the country and shot himself.'

He tipped her chin and kissed her softly. 'Forget it. It's over ... Did it hurt?'

'Yes, it hurt. I was very young and alone. I did not understand.'

He said, 'It's time to forget it. Everyone has things to forget.'

'I've been wild, Mark. I've got a reputation.'

229

He held her off him and the hard look was back, searching her and giving warning. Uncertainty whitened her face. His fingers cut into her arms. He searched her a long time before easing. 'I told you, I don't want to know now or ever. The past is dead. Bury it.'

She remembered the leg, as possessive of the wound as though it were her own, knowing that it must never be acknowledged.

'Come.' She drew him to the chairs.

The coffee was cold in the cups. It seemed rueful and funny. They wanted to laugh about something.

'Have a cake,' Hatton said. 'They're about the right temperature.'

Jane went and returned bringing Darder's Spanish brandy. 'Look what I've stolen. We'll have café royals.'

She had forgotten it, or put it away, because it did not matter any more. Nothing mattered now. They sat close in the darkening, their hands linked.

Hatton said, 'What is it you want to ask? I'm not married, if that's it.'

The possibility shook Jane. It had not entered her thoughts. He smiled at her, mocking a little.

She shook her head. 'It wasn't that. It doesn't matter.'

He frowned, feeling curiosity. 'What is it, then? It seemed important.'

She was disturbed, and he saw it. It not only did not matter, it had become something to forget, to bury with the other dead past.

'Tell me, Jane. I want to know.'

'No. Please.' She shook her head. 'It really doesn't matter.'

The grasp of his hand tightened. There was something behind her confusion. He spoke the words as an order. 'Tell me.'

She had to meet him, was compelled by his eyes. She couldn't get it out unshaken. 'It was that day. That day on the relocation.'

'What about that day?'

'Oh, Mark, please. I don't want to go on.'

Hatton said carefully, 'I want you to go on. What about that day?'

'Very well.' Her own spirit rose. 'Why did you have to do it?'

He let go her hand. His throat worked. 'Who told you? Who told you about that?'

She had to protect Adam.

'Nobody told me. It was just a mention. Adam mentioned there had been an action that day.'

'Thomson,' Hatton said, with bitterness.

He came up hard, staring ahead. Apprehension of him seized her.

'Did he tell you we found no weapons?'

'No. Truly. He said nothing of that.'

Hatton turned to her. 'But you know?'

'It wasn't from Adam. I was asking later and someone——'

'You know,' Hatton said.

He remained for a long time silent. There were no words she could risk. The moonlight shone on his face.

He came to her and bent the stiff leg to take her hands. She tried to read his eyes but could not. Something there was in conflict. Hatton said, 'I don't know, Jane. I believe I did right. But I don't know. I just don't know.'

She drew his head to her breast and her eyes ran with tears. She said, 'My poor darling. Oh, my poor darling.'

31

In Quong Lo the Vietnamese got ready for the festival of Tet, the ancient celebration of the Lunar New Year. There were special cakes and sweets in the bazaar. In the little shops along the highway fireworks were put in the windows.

On that evening, before the sunset, the children could wait no longer. Fireworks jumped and banged in the town. Rockets hissed up and exploded coloured sparks in a sky too pale to display them. In the hooches of the refugee camps rations had been saved and elaborated. Old Borgia and the kitchen staff lit fireworks in the mess compound after dinner. The guard threw out a big one from the sentry box near the holed steel gate. Sam Jarra jumped and was morose about it.

Tim Frost got the first news of the offensive on the morning broadcast. The American Embassy in Saigon was under siege. The VC were all about the capital. It could not be believed. The world had turned upside-down. Tim Frost widened his eyes until they filled the lenses of his glasses.

All that day the civilians of Quong Lo hunched and dialled their radios. The reports heaped up contradictions. Radio Vietnam went off the air. Official statements of reassurance alarmed and confused them further. The offensive was being contained. The uprising had failed. It was not general.

How could it be general? What uprising? How could the VC possibly be inside the Embassy? Tim Frost snatched the signals dinned into his radio room and could make proper sense of nothing.

By late afternoon the armour was out in the town. Provincial Headquarters had announced a sunset-to-sunrise curfew. South Vietnamese troops patrolled the roads, not knowing what to expect.

Hatton got to the hospital, his jeep driven for him, two GIs with automatic weapons in the back. Grenades were clipped to his pockets. He wore a helmet.

Adam and Darder were in Reception, deciding about a man knocked down by an army truck. Hatton was directed there, took off his helmet and waited.

'Will you be through soon, Doc?'

Adam said, 'What's the news, Major?'

'They're hitting all over. For the present you had better keep to your quarters.'

'I can't do that,' Adam said. 'There are people here needing attention.'

'The Vietnamese nurses will have to manage.'

Adam shook his head. 'This man has compound fractures.'

Hatton said, 'Doc, I'm not asking you. I'm telling you. I'm closing this town down.'

Other things were between them, using this as an excuse.

'Don't give me orders, Major. I'm not in your army.' Adam was surprised by his own anger. Hatton turned away and spoke to Pedro Darder, ignoring Adam.

'You've got another hour of daylight. Can you fix your patient in that time?'

Darder gestured at Adam, not wanting to reply. Hatton continued to address himself to the Spaniard.

'There will be an escort here in an hour. Tell the Quakers. Be ready to move out.'

Adam breathed hard at the empty door. He didn't want Darder to see his face.

He found her preparing dressings, held her briefly.

233

'Mark, what is happening? There are so many stories.'

'I don't know. They're hitting all over. Jane, I'm sending an escort in an hour. I don't want you to come back here until I say so. You understand that? I don't want you to leave the guest-house.'

'Oh, Mark, is it that bad? Is something going to happen?'

'I don't know. Something has already happened. It will take a while to straighten out. I want you to take Ho. The kid's just getting better.'

It came to her with a jolt then that something could happen. That Hatton expected it. A sickness of fear for him swamped other meaning.

'Tim Frost has rules about bringing outsiders into the compound.' It wasn't that. It was something to say because he wouldn't want the other thing spoken.

'Don't worry. I'll fix Tim. Look after Ho until things straighten out.' He touched her again with his lips. 'Remember. Stay behind those walls.'

She nodded, eyes misted, and had to say it once. 'Be careful. Do be careful.'

The townspeople had their own information. Through chinked doors and shuttered windows they watched the patrolling armour. In the refugee camps and in the huts behind the shopfronts, there were those others who had waited for Tet.

The time has come. Be a patriot. The Liberation is near. Everywhere we are striking at the American invaders. In Saigon the puppet government is in flight. If our brothers come, make them welcome. Feed them if they are hungry. Shelter them if they require it. Join them if you can capture a gun.

On the second night of Tet, Quong Lo ached with waiting. The foreign civilians listened to the artillery and speculated. In the mid-mornings and afternoons, an APC and a truckload of troops escorted Adam and Darder to the hospital. When the VC had taken the town for eight hours the year before, releasing a thousand prisoners from the jail, they had made a base of the hospital, dressed their wounded there before leaving.

Window glass and mosquito screens crackled and bulged to the nearing explosions. A column of tanks from Task Force Nebraska was dispatched to the provincial capital. It was ambushed on the coast road and had to fight its way to the town. The sky was crowded by aircraft glinting on the sun-shot clouds.

In the entrenched town the waiting wearied into the fourth day of Tet. The earth was upheaving about them. They were on it as marooned as an island.

Fighter bombers and rocket ships had targeted on Saigon. In the ancient capital of Hue, the marines battled in the streets. All the South was up in flames and it could not be believed. In the mess they listened to the Voice of America's evening broadcast and switched off. The enemy was at his last gasp. Politicians were saying in speeches that the position had never been stronger. Sam Jarra got a fresh beer, yanking off the top in temper.

'I'll take another, Sam,' the team leader said, eased his paunch and sighed.

They were quiet with their thoughts. Sam yanked off the second cap and passed the bottle. He drank and sniffed loudly. 'Twelve feet long, these rockets. They're walking all over down there with these rockets twelve feet long.'

He tipped the bottle, debating it further with himself, then his voice rose.

'There's a big heap of chickenshit here. You know that? How are they walking all over the country with rockets twelve feet long? Are they invisible, and nobody sees them? We killed ten thousand already. Are they coming up out of cracks, and nobody gives us the word? Whose side are we on out here? Are we out here on our chickenshit own?'

The men did not answer. It felt like that. They were out there on their own.

The mortars slammed in at midnight. Those who had managed to sleep started up with the first concussions, hearts hammering, eyes stretched. Jane had gone to bed in slacks and shirt, Ho beside her on a blown-up mattress. For him she made her voice calm, soothing his shaking body. Doors slammed, feet ran the corridors. The building was full of calling.

In the mess they crowded into the bathroom and piled the mattresses against the door. All the town seemed to be exploding.

Sam Jarra fumbled a beer from the case he had put there in foresight, his head cocked at the blasting. 'They're mortars,' he shouted; 'mortars they can have. What I don't need is these twelve-foot rockets.'

Adam's throat was dry with excitement. He almost welcomed the crashes. He had waited for this, had lived in it for months, waiting for

235

it to happen. The disappointment that had curdled and lumped in him was gone on this strange exaltation.

Tim Frost banged on Jane's door and pushed it open. He carried a torch and carbine. 'You all right?'

Jane nodded, holding the shaking child.

'Stay here,' Frost said. 'It's as safe as anywhere.'

'Will they attack?'

'I hope they do,' he said, meaning it. 'We've got a squadron of tanks staked out for those bastards.'

Adam sat on the bath with the two Germans, chain smoking. The others were on the floor, against the wall. The team leader was seated on the lavatory, drinking beer and belching.

Another bracket of crumps shook them. Sam said, 'That lot's too close.'

Adam chanted, 'We'll get our asses blown off one day.'

They all took it up, laughing at Sam.

'You better believe it,' he shouted at them.

For three hours the mortars struck the town. Then silence lengthened and deepened. Adam's excitement ebbed. They heard the jets, distant detonations. The team leader laid down and tried to sleep, using the toilet roll as a pillow.

They were sombre now. Aware that the air stank in this confinement, that their eyes burned with cigarette smoke. Adam thought about bodies. Iron and steel had screamed in those explosions. He lowered his head in his arms and felt sick.

The sun rose weakly, as though it too had been exhausted by the night. Muddy clouds swelled the sky. Tim Frost and his staff stood quietly on the roof and watched the town shape into outline. Smoke drifted. Fires burned. A tank rumbled near by. Thinly, over the lulled violence, a wailing of voices carried.

They crowded the beds and under the beds, packed the long verandah on litters. The mulings of pain muffled under the tin roof like an outcry of a single body. Twice Pedro Darder went to his knees in the blood that dripped through the litters. The sun struck under the verandah's awning. The clouds of flies, stunned and sticky with feeding, were as loud as the sawing of timber. In the operating theatre, stained to the elbows, Adam Thomson cut and patched.

236

Mortars fell again on the town early next morning. The blows barely stirred Adam's stupor. They awoke to another clouded day and a rolling thunder in the hills.

They stumbled the work, ate when they could, drank spirits to cut the exhaustion. There was no more reality. Nothing remained clean-edged. Their eyes were as heavy as shot, turning in sockets of sand. The expressed cries of the wounded no longer had meaning. The transfers from the battles in the hills soaked red under the peppers and they had no meaning either. The world had diminished to one bloody compound and a collection of reeking sheds.

In the ninth day after Tet, Tim Frost brought in a relief team from Da Nang. Adam walked out of the hospital, legs jolting, into a violent downpour. He stood in it and turned up his face and that too was without meaning.

Again, the war went away from Quong Lo. There was no assault on the town. The mortars banged in as reminder of surrounding malevolence. VC invaded the Cao-Dai camp, tore down the plinth that memorialized a Viet Minh massacre of the co-religionists and replaced it with the head of the young camp secretary impaled on a bamboo stake.

The building and greening brought by the rains multiplied and grew. Climbing plants laid their leaves against the walls in Tim Frost's compound. The farmers went out to plant. Birds hopped the trees and were heard again. The interrupted crickets chirruped the nights.

Escorted by troops, Sam Jarra and the others got out rations to the clamouring refugees.

For two days Adam slept, waking to drink or eat a sandwich.

The war went away from Quong Lo and was fought in the hills and the road to the coast. For ten days Hatton remained in the field.

The mortar rounds were only reminders crumped into Quong Lo at night. The Quakers inspected the damaged annex, discussed it and returned to their quarters. The Quaker leader informed Tim Frost that the team would withdraw to Bangkok until there was safety to work.

The intake of broken bodies subsided. Adam directed another burning of blood-encrusted mattresses, grateful that the tremor had passed from his hands and legs.

The convoy of trucks and armour entered the town from the coast in the last colours of day. The vehicles appeared to move very slowly as they lurched the mortar craters, revved at the sucking mud. The silent, crumpled troops lolled heads in the trucks or stretched on the hulls of tanks. Hatton had roused in the jeep, looking about him for damage. The tight skin under his eyes was sooted by fatigue.

The convoy's rumble loudened as Jane and Pedro Darder walked to the Spaniard's jeep. They both stopped, querying each other, quickened by apprehension.

'What is it, Pedro?'

His eyes were screwed to concentrate. 'Armour, I think. No worry. Armour coming from the coast.'

Because she had been fearful she did not at first connect it with hopes of Hatton. It came to her as the leading tanks briefly filled the compound's gateway. She was faint with it when the jeep cut out and pointed towards them. In that light, at that distance, the figures in it were humped black outlines.

Jane whispered, 'Thank God.' She knew him as clearly as though he stood before her in sunlight.

The driver was unfamiliar with the hospital. He turned off the approach and stopped near the mortared annex.

Darder began to say, 'It's Major Hatton.'

He saw her luminous face, lashes wet with happiness. Hatton had got out to walk towards them, stiff on both legs now. His eyes did not acknowledge Darder. It was a shock to the Spaniard. He had not known or suspected. Like Sam Jarra, he had hoped Jane for Adam. In the nakedness between them Darder felt discomfited, as though he should not be there.

'Glad to see you back, Major. How has it been?'

Jane and Hatton were smiling a little at each other. 'A bit rough,' he answered, briefly including Darder. 'How has it been in town?'

Darder said, 'A bit rough.' He felt more than ever uncomfortable, quite excluded.

'I was just leaving. I'm supposed to meet Dr Thomson at the warehouse.'

Hatton nodded, directing himself for the first time to Darder, his eyes bidding him go.

'You might drop off my driver at the compound.'

Darder said, 'Can do,' and coughed. 'I'll be on my way, then.'

Again Hatton nodded. Jane touched Darder's arm.

'Would you be a dear and tell the guest-house I'm coming in with Major Hatton?'

They stood in the empty compound that filled with shadows. He gathered her in.

'Oh, Mark. I've been so worried.'

'I know. Has it been bad?'

She shuddered. 'It has been sickening.'

Hatton said, 'They tried to get in. We stopped them. How is young Ho?'

She lifted her head to smile. 'Ho is fine. He misses you. Did you know he can say your name? He says At-ton.'

Hatton was proud. 'I taught him.'

Jane said, 'Let me make you coffee. You look exhausted.'

'I am a bit. How's Darder's bottle holding up?'

'He's got a new supply. Why don't you wait in the annexe? We've been using it as the rest-room since the Quakers left.'

Hatton was surprised. 'When did the Quakers leave?'

'A few days ago. They've gone to Bangkok. They will come back when things are safer.'

'When things are safer,' Hatton repeated, and she hesitated at his tone. He had gone away from her, his eyes fixed, jaws ridging the fair down of beard. She reached up and stroked his face.

'You've got whiskies.'

He looked down. 'I've got what?'

'Whiskies. Whiskers. That's what I used to call my father's mutton-chops when I was a little girl.'

There was so much about each other they did not know.

Jane's fingers shook, lighting the primus. She was clumsy with the coffee, clumsy with the mugs and biscuits she laid on the tin tray that advertised Coca-Cola. She brushed out her hair while she waited, touched cologne to her throat.

Hatton unbuckled his webbing and laid the pistol and water-bottles on a bench. Light chinked through the shell hole in the tin roof. The explosion had chipped and flaked the plaster walls. He sat on the stretcher on which Adam Thomson had rested when the knife in his hand had blurred and the theatre seemed to tilt. After a while Hatton lay back, grunting at the easement. He put a hand under his head and stretched his aching body.

He wasn't at peace, it was too soon for that. The other things roared in his head. It was his law, and on the drops he had commanded, it truly was the only way to stay alive. In the jungles the VC had made their own for twenty years, it was you against everything that moved. But there had been no jungle in the sweeps near the coast. The country had been open, under the allied guns. The Arvin halted and took cover before the ragged fire. The arsenal of rocketships, artillery and napalm was directed on the obstructions. Afterwards, the blackened bodies of the villagers were all dubbed VC whatever their sex or age.

He didn't want to think of that, he was too full of her, but the cordite was in his nostrils. The bouquet of her skin and the stink of war clashed for attention in his mind. And it was the old way now, in his body. The dark rise, the dark need to be voided. The compulsion to lay the seed that would mean continuation, against whatever next might happen. To get the seed sown however mimed, on the bought, the barren or the contracepted.

Jane hurried across the compound, the tin tray jangling, bearing upright the pot, mugs and Darder's bottle. She stood in the doorway and could not see him. For an instant desolation struck her. He stirred on the stretcher and in the dark the burning cigarette signalled.

'Mark. I thought you had gone.' She was quite shaken. He heard it on her voice and rose to take the tray, touching his lips on her forehead.

'Haven't I been away long enough?'

She had never been coquettish, or asked the usual womanly things. It seemed to her another person speaking. 'Did you think of me?'

'Yes. I thought of you.'

She remembered the first time she had prepared him coffee. 'Come, now. Before the coffee gets cold.'

They sat at the table. The black shadows and misted moonlight enclosed them in further intimacy. There was nowhere else. There was nobody else. No war, no guns, no hospital, no past, no future. Jane was almost asleep with peace.

Hatton lifted Darder's bottle and checked the level. He leaned to clink mugs.

Jane asked, 'What should we drink to? I learned a little witchcraft in Africa. What do you want most, Mark?'

He turned his face a little away in a disturbing change to privacy. 'Want?' he said. 'I don't know.'

'There must be something you want. Tell me and I will witch it for you.'

He was still turned away. 'Tomorrow,' he said. 'Just give me tomorrow.'

The words quavered in her, and broke. 'Tomorrow?'

He looked back, the old hardness and defiance on his face. 'Yes. Tomorrow. Give me tomorrow. For you, for me and for everybody.'

She almost lost the mug that slipped in her fingers as Hatton rang the toast and swallowed the brandy. She tried to drink and could not, her breath almost gasping. 'Oh, Mark.'

He offered no help, poured and swallowed again, watching almost cruelly. Then he stood and pulled her into his arms. The sudden rise of him against her seemed to pierce her. It was not for this she had needed and wanted him. Not this. It was the last thing.

She had something now, had found something, and her instinct was fierce to keep it. To keep and hold it to her, barricaded away for ever from the place of fear and failure. She pushed back from his encircle-ment, in escape from the remorseless seeking that altered all his shape and touch into phallus. She couldn't bear the return to that mocking place, the place that pitched her to the next man.

They swayed there in light and darkness in the long, hot tin-roofed shed. He tilted her stricken face with the hand spanned under her hair. His mouth crushed at her, absent to love or tenderness. The stubbled beard was on her skin as sharp as sand. She was arched away, white and cold, when he jerked open the hospital gown.

Hatton laid her on the stretcher, drew over her hips the triangle of pink cloth that wisped so childishly. Her hair was flung, her head turned away, hopeless tears curving on the high, polished cheeks.

He sat and caressed her and his violence drained, refilling with the strange choking sadness. The swelling beauty and wonder of her body touched him with confusion and pain. Her flesh glinted where the thin moonlight touched it. 'Jane?' Hatton whispered.

She did not answer or move.

Almost absently he caressed her, looking away through the wide annex door, above the dull lights in the wards across the compound to the hills that flashed and rumbled like the brooding approach of storm. He tasted the cordite again. Jets quaked in his ears. Running figures rose off the earth and blossomed red like the opening of a rose.

Hatton came back, shaken by the sight of her, by the dark, pouted cleft drawn like a bow in her sprawl. The urgency and triumph that seized him wiped out all else.

She had waited and it was apart from time, a limbo beyond emotion, evacuated of thought or feeling. She winced and shrank when his fingers parted her, raised her eyes to his face, inhaled the musking embrace of stale sweat.

'Jane?' Hatton whispered again. His face was moonlit. There was no pride there, no challenge or arrogance. Something in Hatton had broken. The certainty which had been his force had departed and left him naked. Jane touched her fingertips to his cheek. Her breasts swelled on the beginning of a sob.

He was in her and she twisted in pain. She was closed there and afraid. Her head thrashed on the musty pillow. Her eyes were shut, teeth gritted. She did not want it and stiffened to resist her softening. Images flickered in her mind. Other places and other men, the unrelenting sterility. She was jumbled and lost, struck with panic. She could not remember this place or this man. Her eyes opened wide in confusion.

Hatton's face was very still. He saw her fright and brushed back the hair that had spilled on her cheek. Then he bent and gently kissed her.

Jane came back from where she had been as though borne up from a depth. Peace and love filled her body with unfolding. She grappled Hatton close, felt herself flood.

The moon rose farther, withdrawing its pale tilted shafts to beam through the shell-holed roof. In the free fire zones in the hills, in the incinerated wastes on which anything that moved must die, the interdiction of heavy artillery exploded in lightning flashes.

She did not hear her cries when they came. She was unaware of the hand that shuddered to her stretched mouth in an agony touched with terror. The black universe reeled in rigour, the stars and moons there expanded and burst at last in fulfilment.

32

THEY were tiny men in shorts and sandals. They carried rice around their waists in cloths. Above them the sky shook and thundered with winged death more thickly flocked than birds. They had been rice farmers, coolies, students. They walked through infernos to defy irresistible power.

Tim Frost was reduced by Tet as definitely as though by an ailment. Volume departed from his voice and body. His neck became noticeably scrawny. He kept to his office and sought for reassurance.

On a visit to the hospital he said experimentally to Adam, 'It's official now. These captured documents prove that Charlie expected a general uprising.'

Adam was preoccupied. 'What would they have uprisen with, Tim? Sticks?'

The old combativeness grew in Frost, then subsided. He had reasoned that for himself.

The offensive dissipated, the insurgents withdrew. In Cholon and Hue and in the devastated towns, the homeless picked in the wreckage. Ash and mortar streamed like dry tears on the wind. The rain beat the blackened blood on the streets and smeared the gutters with colour. Gaped walls sighed and collapsed. Refugees staggered the roads, stunned to sense of direction. The tattered hawks beaked their feathers and heard the swelling new cry, Peace With Honour.

Hatton was almost glad of the need that kept him in the field. The hot dark shed, transfixed by moonlight, shifted in his memory like worry. He had recoiled from Jane's long rigour, fearful that he had injured her or that something unknown had happened.

Against him, roused from stupor, she had whispered, 'The first time. Oh, thank you, darling, thank you.'

It could not be believed. 'How can it be? You've been married.'

He felt her lips move against his skin, as though to stifle the words, whispering shame and triumph. 'A climax. I've never had a climax.'

He sat for a long time holding her. He felt as responsible as though she had been virgin.

In the time after Tet the North Vietnamese infiltrated the Central Highlands. In the outpost of Ke Sanh the marines dug in and awaited the next blow of the hammer. Army engineers concerned with supply north scouted the Quong Lo airstrip.

In the Red Cross mess Sam Jarra dealt the cards in temper.

'Why have they got to build their chickenshit transport field here? Next thing Charlie is going to hit us, with these rockets twelve feet long.'

The team leader considered his hand and discarded. 'They're taking a thousand rounds a day in Ke Sanh.'

'We ain't in Ke Sanh,' Sam said. 'We're running the Quong Lo camps. Can you imagine a rocket in Number Three, with this new intake we just got?'

The men played their cards and did not answer.

A garrison from Task Force Nebraska sandbagged in on the Quong Lo strip. The rattle and roar of heavy equipment overwhelmed the whumps of artillery. At night, under arcs, the work continued, illuminating the pressing clouds with colour.

Hatton had been in the foothills, siting outposts to defend the new transport field. The draftees waited and sweated, three days shipped out and not yet connected, as though the velocity which had sped their bodies had neglected to transport their minds.

Hatton changed his soaked fatigues and sluiced his face. The sergeant looked through the window to the compound.

'They're getting younger every day. This lot would be too green to burn. What kind of war are we fighting?'

Hatton looked for his helmet. 'It's the only war we've got, Sergeant.'

They were very new, had come out of winter. The skin of their arms and faces white, their eyes nervous at the alien sky, the distant concussions that jumped their stomachs, the weapons suddenly stark with meaning.

'Stand easy, men.'

Men, Hatton thought. Some of them are barely nineteen. Some of these boys will die here. They shifted their eyes before him, fidgeted awkwardly in the mud.

'If you want to stay alive out here, it's you against everything that moves. There's nobody so old or so young, they can't kill you. There's nowhere so ...'

Hatton heard the speech in his head, but something in him revolted. Between him and the intent young faces the space filled with the picture of leaking litters, the crammed wounded under pepper trees, Darder slipping on the bloodied verandah, children hopping crutches, jarring on wooden pegs.

There's nobody so old or so young ...

The sergeant looked across. The Major had used that line. Hatton stopped, his eyes empty. He could feel Jane against him, her warm skin trembling on his. The draftees' faces came back: '... that they can't kill you,' Hatton finished. Resonance returned to his voice. 'You remember that. You remember it good. They're all yours, Sergeant.'

The draftees watched his back and lifted eyebrows at each other.

Ten days after the first transports terminated at Quong Lo, the strip was raided in the hour before dawn. A guard challenged and shot an old man. He wore a loincloth and his body was blackened. No weapons or explosives were found. Tim Frost worried about it as another of the attacks on transport fields which appeared to make no sense. The American Forces Network reported it as a further mystifying incident.

In the quiet provincial hospital Jane Stirling worked her duty and waited. When Hatton could, he would come for her.

Quong Lo and all the South tensed on another waiting, the expected second offensive, the assault on beleaguered Ke Sanh. It would be the last throw, the Generals said again. There were few to believe them now. The enemy that swam like fish in the waters of the people had repossessed all except a few enclaves.

Hatton dropped his field boots and grunted, lay back on the bed and closed his eyes. His hand went uninstructed to his leg. He was getting it back, but some of the meaning of that had departed. They were all somehow crippled. It was a crippled war they fought. A war without fronts or uniforms against an enemy the earth ghosted up, who hid his arms and went back to the paddy, poled produce in sampans, squatted at the roadside to cadge and wave. An enemy armoured with a hatred that drafted American boys could not feel, as natural as animals in their environment, for ever camouflaged in slanted eyes and yellow skin.

Hatton blinked against the fatigue that gritted his lids. There was nothing any more to win. The balloon Tet had punctured could never again be inflated. The wind had gone out of it through a myriad of whistling holes. They were alone out here and the monsoon mud sucked at them, crippled in a crippled war their own people did not want.

The pillow had dampened with sweat. Hatton turned it and thought of Jane. His ego tried to swagger that it had been in his arms that she had found release. But responsibility nagged him, he was bonded against his will in ways he felt and could not understand. He had to be hard, had to keep himself hard, he had to be hard to stay alive.

Hatton sat up and wiped his face with a towel. He opened the map on the table and studied the circled outposts. He did not know how long he had forgotten it when the stained map again impressed on his mind. He had been in the darkened annexe absorbed in the beauty and volume of Jane.

Adam Thomson had given himself a half holiday. After lunch he set the alarm and read himself to sleep. At five he would rise, shower and change, arrive at the hospital for coffee at five-thirty.

Darder squeaked up a window, bulged in its frame by the rains. 'Just checking on the company,' he said. 'For us I bring out the bottle. Isn't Dr Thomson smart this evening?'

He disappeared and returned to hand the cognac through the window. 'I'm going to wash. If Jarra comes in, get that bottle under the table.'

When the Spaniard had gone Adam rinsed his cup and poured a

246

brandy. 'Tim Frost wants me to go to Saigon, to check the equipment for the extension.'

Jane touched his arm. 'That's a splendid idea. You should make a holiday of it. Pedro has been worried about you.'

'Pedro is an old woman,' Adam said, nevertheless pleased. He considered how to word the suggestion he had waited for this evening to make.

'You've had no rest in months, Adam. Look what it did for Pedro.'

Adam swirled his brandy. 'Pedro had his girl with him. What would I do in Saigon?'

'You could eat properly, for one thing. Borgia's cooking is awful. You could visit the clubs, sleep late every morning.'

'The new curfew has closed the clubs.'

'No it hasn't. They just open earlier. Pedro went clubbing all the time.'

Adam said again, 'Pedro had his girl with him.'

'You'd soon find a girl. Sam could introduce you to hundreds.'

Adam emptied. He did not want that from her, abdication to other women.

'Would that be acceptable to you? A week with Sam Jarra's girls?'

She touched his arm again, sensing something. 'I don't mean that. I just want you to have a little fun. Do you remember what you told me the first day I came here? You said I shouldn't invest too much of myself. That if I did I would be unable to bear it. You've invested too much, Adam. You're a wonderfully strong man, dear. But everything has a limit. Please, won't you take a rest?'

She was so sure of herself after Hatton, almost motherly in her liberation. She left her hand on his arm, her face close and worrying for him.

Adam said, 'I suppose a stand-in surgeon could be arranged.' He inspected his drink unnecessarily. 'The Canadians offered us a saw-bones and nurse.'

'Do go, Adam. Forget the war for a while.'

'Forget the war,' Adam said. 'How do you do that? You've seen the building at the airstrip. They've put down a tarmac to last twenty years. This war isn't an interlude. The army is building to stay. The way things are going there won't be a bridge or a building left standing between the Delta and China.'

He poured again from Darder's bottle. He was worn out and he knew it. It was the comfort of Jane that had stiffened him after Tet.

He should get away and could get away. He had asked Tim Frost for a relief and a nurse.

Jane tested the coffee-pot. 'I'll reheat it.'

He didn't want her to leave. 'I don't mind it like this. Jane, you've not had a break either.' He hated himself for his difficulty. There was no reason for it. I'm out of practice, Adam thought. What is it in her that makes me so clumsy? Why now must I dissemble, put it to her like a schoolboy?

He said heartily, 'So the nurse is convinced that the doctor needs a holiday?'

'Please, Adam. You really have looked ragged lately.'

He wished that he had not looked ragged to her. 'Very well, then. The doctor will prescribe for the nurse. We will both go to Saigon and live the hell out of the place. Tim Frost can signal for replacements and we can be out of here at the weekend.'

He had got it said and was boyish with hope, suddenly energetic. It was his hand on her arm now.

She wanted to move from his touch, shaken by realization of what his welfare meant to her, how deeply she wished to please him.

'Oh, Adam, I can't.'

He was full of it now. 'Can't? Of course you can. I'll arrange it. This is an order.'

'I can't,' she said, and shook her head. 'I can't. Just now I can't.'

'But if I can get us replacements?'

'No,' her face avoided his eyes. 'It's not that. I just don't want to leave at present.'

He said, with difficulty, 'I didn't expect the suggestion to upset you.'

'Adam, don't say silly things like that. Perhaps later when things are clearer.'

'When things are clearer? What the hell does that mean?'

'I don't know. I can't explain. I just don't want to go away at present.'

Adam's voice was sharp with disappointment. 'Why don't you want to get away? I'd think you're as sick of this place as I am.'

She said, still turned, voice wispy, 'I wish I could, Adam. I truly do.'

She jumped up before Adam could speak, her face intent and concentrated, dismissing what had been between them. 'Somebody's coming. Shush.'

He heard the jeep and cursed the interruption. 'If it's Sam I'm going to get rid of him. I see enough of Sam in the mess.'

Jane said, her voice shining, 'It's not Sam. It's Hatton. He revs like that before he switches off. I won't be a minute, Adam. Tell him I'm heating the coffee.'

The gravel spread on the muddied path squeaked loudly. Adam found a cigarette.

'Ah, it's you, Doc.'

'I hope so,' Adam said.

There was only Darder's bottle on the table.

'On your own?'

'At present,' Adam said coolly.

Hatton decided and removed his helmet, scrubbing a palm over his cropped head.

'Mind if I join you?'

'Help yourself,' Adam said, without invitation.

Hatton stretched in a chair and eased his breath. 'I hear you're having a quiet time.'

'Quieter than it has been.'

Hatton grunted in understanding. 'It would need to be, wouldn't it? I hope to God it lasts.'

He looked tired, his hands cupping the helmet in his lap.

Adam's voice charged Hatton as though his was the responsibility. 'Is it going to last?'

'I don't know. Nobody knows. Nobody knows anything any more.'

The foundations for the hospital extension had begun to grow out of the mud. Hatton pointed. 'Is that going to be the new building?'

'If it's ever finished. The recommendation went in two years ago.'

'It's good to see something being built,' Hatton said.

He's as tired as any of us, Adam thought. Perhaps even he has had enough. He pushed the cigarettes across the table.

'Thanks. I left mine in the duty hut at the strip.'

'The twenty-year strip,' Adam said with disgust, and flipped his cigarette into a puddle.

Hatton ignored the inference.

'Intelligence is in a flap about last week's guerrilla raid on the transports. They've been caught on transport fields all over. Intelligence can't figure what Charlie's after.'

The gravel squeaked again. Jane had brushed out her hair, touched her lips with colour. Adam did not see the way their eyes accepted each other as Hatton indicated the extra mug.

'How did you know you had company?'

'I recognized your jeep,' Jane said. 'Didn't Adam tell you?'

They tried to talk. Adam was quiet, short when he spoke, his face resolutely set on the darkening horizon. He got up. 'It's getting late.'

Jane said quickly, 'Mark hasn't finished his coffee.'

Adam pretended to stretch. 'Haven't you paperwork tonight?'

'A little. There's no hurry, Adam.'

She would not leave, her face and voice warned him. He had to test her. 'Well, I must go. If you're coming you should get ready.'

'It's some time until curfew. I'll stay, Adam, Mark can drop me off.'

There was no help for it. He had handed her to Hatton. He couldn't sit down now.

'Very well,' he said, and acted to make his voice light. 'Keep us out of the war, Major.'

Hatton nodded. 'I'll try, Doc. Good night.'

Adam was drinking whisky, walking the room when the men came late from the camps. They jostled for cold beers and slumped to listen to the news. The enemy was at the Ke Sanh wire. A special forces camp near by had been attacked. The Ke Sanh commander had said, 'We're here to stay. These men are marines. We will hold this ground until hell freezes over.'

'You do that,' Sam Jarra advised the radio. 'We don't need any angry NVA down here.'

The team leader switched off, rattled his can in the disposal and went with the others to shower. Sam waited, watching Adam refill his glass. 'Hey, Adam. Did you hear they got plague again down in the Delta?'

'The hell with the plague,' Adam said.

Rain sounded the roof and loudened. Adam stood at the barred window and watched the puddles leaping. At the hospital they would be drenched before they got from the coffee table to the verandah. The picture gratified Adam.

He was on his bed when Sam tapped the door and put in his head. 'Call for you from Tim Frost, Adam.'

It would be about his relief. Adam sighed and pushed his bare feet into sandals. 'Yes, Tim?'

There were no courtesies. 'Have you got Stirling with you?'

'No,' Adam answered, surprised.

250

'She hasn't come in. It's after curfew.' And then, 'Hullo? You there? Hullo?'

Adam found his voice. 'It's all right, Tim. I should have let you know. She's coming in with Major Hatton.'

'You're damned right you should have let me know. There's bazaar rumour we could have trouble tonight.'

'There's always bazaar rumour,' Adam said wearily. 'I'm sorry, Tim. It's all right.'

'That's a matter of opinion.' Frost was aggrieved. 'That high-tailed broad had better keep to the rules like the rest of us.'

'I'll speak to her, Tim.'

'You do that,' Frost said.

Adam poured a drink and went to his room. He tried to sit still and could not, stood to walk the small room. The whisky fretted in him. He would wait a half hour and then check back with Frost. The rain had stopped. The thoughts that tormented him loudened in the hush.

There had been no conscious decision, only a bidding and urgency. Adam fumbled into his socks and shoes. He paused in the big room, something had to be said. 'I've a check to make at the hospital.'

They heard the armoured gate grate open, the jeep's preliminary whirrings. The team leader put up his eyebrows.

'It's well after curfew. What's going on?'

The moon had sailed clear of cloud, the shuttered town black and white in its light. Adam had cleared the bazaar when dim lights cut the road, swung at him and glared into high beam. Adam shielded his eyes and braked at the dazzle racing towards him. He was blinking at the dark when the torch probed at him.

'Would you identify yourself, sir?'

'Dr Thomson. Provincial hospital.'

The torch searched the jeep, clicked off.

'It's after curfew, sir.'

'I know,' Adam's voice was strained, 'I have a check to make at the hospital.'

'Civilians on priority missions must have an escort after curfew, sir.'

'I forgot about it,' Adam said.

The corporal was uneasy.

'I'm afraid you can't proceed without one, sir.'

'Then escort me,' Adam said impatiently.

251

'You'll have to ride with us, sir. I haven't enough men for both vehicles.'

Adam groaned.

'All right. Let's get going.'

A machine-gun was mounted on the patrol jeep. Adam swung the barrel and squeezed in.

At the compound entrance, the corporal got out. 'I'm afraid I can only give you twenty minutes, sir. We keep a schedule on the roads. Had you requested your own escort——'

Adam steadied his nerves. 'Twenty minutes will be enough, soldier.'

'I could leave a man with you.'

'I don't need a man.' Adam wanted to shout. 'Now take off, will you?'

The sight of Hatton's jeep, dark and quiet in the dark, quiet compound, slammed his stomach. Oil lamps in the wards coloured the windows dull yellow. The stirring and murmurs of the bodies inside were faint as the breeze fanning the leaves of the peppers. The office was unlit. The darkness and quiet filled Adam with foreboding. He was there because he had to be there and now he was helpless for the next thing to do.

Nothing turned him to the annex, unless it was the moonlight patching the door, a vacancy there that seemed to throb. He walked softly to the window.

The dimmed lights of the patrol jeep rocked off the airport road and pointed towards the hospital. 'He's waiting,' the corporal said, and readied his torch to light the mud.

Adam was faced to the compound wall, leaning, pierced by the images that shuddered in his mind.

Tim Frost and his staff had breakfasted early. Jane took coffee to the sitting-room and waited, preparing herself for Adam's arrival, needing to prepare as though she was somehow involved in betrayal.

Frost's Vietnamese secretary looked in. 'My goodness, Dr Thomson is late.'

The girl studied Jane and giggled.

'What's amusing, Cecile?'

'You're going to catch it from Mr Frost. My goodness he was angry last night. When you didn't come in at curfew he rang and blew up Dr Thomson.'

'Oh?' Jane said unsteadily. 'What did Dr Thomson say?'

The girl shrugged. 'He say you all right.'

A staffer had come in late and had driven Jane to the hospital. I've hurt him, she worried. Why did Frost have to telephone? Why did Adam have to know? He's so good, so good. Why did I have to hurt him?

Pedro Darder was on the verandah, directing the unloading of a warehouse truck.

Jane asked, 'Is Adam here, Pedro?'

'Adam?' Darder said surprised. 'Adam will be at the strip. He's going to Saigon. Didn't you know?'

Jane shook her head miserably.

Darder watched her go up the verandah and wiped thoughtfully at his neck.

In the next week Jane made coffee for Darder. It was the first time he had suggested it. The sky had lifted and cleared.

'The wet is about finished,' he said, 'I didn't expect to be sorry.'

Jane filled the mugs. 'I don't know what you're sorry about. Everything I have is growing fungus.'

'Better that than another offensive. I still have bad dreams about Tet.'

It was unusual for Darder to be moody. He broke a crust of mud with his foot. 'I don't know how Adam stood it. He hardly slept for a month. You've talked with him a lot, Jane. Why is a surgeon like Adam here?'

'Adam has a sense of service. He truly wants to help people. That is why he is here.'

'It's time he helped himself,' Darder said. 'He's wearing himself out on these animals.'

Jane said, 'You don't like the Vietnamese, do you?'

Darder punched the cork into the bottle. 'They stink. I look at their faces, into their eyes. Are they suffering? Are they unhappy? I don't know. I can't tell. Are they grateful for what we do? Is there an excuse for the tortures and mutilations? Is there? I don't know. For the family they will do anything. For anyone outside it, nothing. I've seen mothers weep over a child in one bed and watch a child in another choke to death without lifting a finger to help. They're animals. They stink.'

Jane said sadly, 'You mustn't think like that. They're different. We

253

can't judge them by our own standards. If that's the way you feel, Pedro, what are you doing here?'

'Learning,' Darder said. 'I've learned more in this shambles in three months than I would learn at home in three years. I've learned more than I did in America. In the beginning, yes, I felt. Then I learn about the people, too. I look into their faces, into their eyes. Nothing. Animals, I tell you.'

Darder thrust out his hands, fingers spread. 'You see that? Is there tremor in these hands? No. Why not? Because I work with my hands and keep my heart for civilized people. Can Adam do that? Have you seen his hands? Only the knife stops them shaking.'

'He's tired, Pedro. He's very tired.'

'Yes, he's tired.' The Spaniard turned on her, dark eyes set. 'And what do you do to help? Nothing. Where were you the night before he went to Saigon? I heard about it. Do you think Adam didn't know? Everyone knew. Everyone knows.'

Jane tried to speak, angry with shame that it should so be known.

Darder was glad to get it said. 'Adam had arranged for relief. Did you know that? He had asked Frost for a surgeon and a nurse. Who do you think the nurse was to relieve?'

Jane stood up. 'If you've finished, Pedro, we can go.'

'I'm ready,' he said and poured a Cognac. 'Go get your things.'

They did not speak on the drive. Darder tooted for the guard and brooded. 'I'm sorry I shouted.' His dark face was hunched in his shoulders.

'You're very fond of Adam, aren't you, Pedro?'

'Yes, I am.'

'So am I. I wouldn't willingly hurt your friend. Please believe me. I've never known a man I so much admired.'

Darder relaxed and rubbed his nose. 'I'm sorry I shouted,' he repeated.

'I understand. Good night, Pedro.'

'I'll pick you up in the morning,' Darder called.

Jane received Hatton's postcard from Da Nang, discreetly addressed in an envelope.

Hope you didn't get into trouble with Tim. Raining all day every day here. Something is on. Big changes in strategy. There's mess rumour of peace talks. Thought it might cheer you.

Yours, M

254

No love. Yours, M. The word had never been used between them. Perhaps because they feared the involvement, the implication of future. There had been no future, as Hatton had wanted no past. They had been isolated in the strangeness of the present, as unnaturally as castaways. It was strange to Jane, reading Hatton's hand, the square letters almost like printing, upright and hard, so like him. He had given her something and he remained as unfamiliar as the inked words. She had lain with him in revelation and they had never walked together or sat together at a meal.

Rumours of peace. It brought back Salem to her, Geneva, the dinner parties at the château now so implausibly distant. Salem's tall figure, earnest as he leaned to discuss his hopes. Salem sweated and blown in a helicopter. His tormented, unforgiving face when he blundered from the incinerated village. The attic, Thu and Little Flower, the silent guerrillas loading bullets into belts.

Jane sat on her bed in the bare little room, Hatton's postcard forgotten in her hand. Adam shared something with Salem. There was something in them alike.

At the end of a week Adam returned. He spent the afternoon conferring with Tim Frost and went to the hospital next morning. He looked rested. Later, in the operating theatre, he made the only reference to his leave, head down to check his instruments. Jane had followed him in.

'Pedro kept everything as you left it.'

'So I see. You were right, you know.'

'Right about what, Adam?'

'It is easy to find a girl in Saigon.' He pushed back the tray and left.

Jane served coffee at five-thirty, using the embroidered Chinese cloth.

'Coffee's ready, Pedro. I hope you've got something in the bottle. Will you tell Adam?'

Darder shifted his eyes. 'Adam left. He went a few minutes ago.'

They drank the coffee quickly, without the bottle. Darder drove Jane into town.

33

THE monsoon ended in splutters. Quong Lo was transformed by growth. In the paddy the peasants worked the bunds, slapping the beaten walls strong with mud. The green of new rice sparkled everywhere. The big-bellied buffalo soaked in their wallows, snouts tipped to snort the brown waters. In the camps every scrap of earth was gardened. Damp clothing and bedding flapped and cleansed in the sun. The latrine fields in which ordure had swilled for months crusted and became tolerable. The camp workers shed their rubber boots and ponchos and walked the settlements freely. Wading birds and wildfowl halted their migrations and stalked the paddy margins. In the cooled, twilit evenings the Quong Lo civilians cursed the forbidding curfew.

The Quakers returned, more than ever separate now in self-consciousness of their flight. The compound hopped again with crippled children. Each day was cherished as a gift. The war machine which had floundered in mud began to clank again. There were firefights in the hills, traps exploded on the road to the coast. The cleared sky shook and rumbled to the transports. Jets glinted and screamed, freighting bombs and napalm north.

Adam had spent much of his time watching progress on the new building, checking the soundness of materials, fretting at the dilatory speed and improvisations of the workmen. He stood there in the evening with Darder and watched the traffic in the sky.

'It's going to come again, Pedro. I can feel it. If Ke Sanh goes, Tet will look like a picnic.'

'It will be six weeks before the monsoon lifts in the highlands, Adam.'

'What are six weeks? This building has been in the works for two years. We can't cope with another offensive in that slaughterhouse.'

It was the first time Darder had heard him use Sam Jarra's word for the hospital. He said, 'Adam, why don't you go home? You've done enough here. We both know it's a drop in the bucket. Let these people tear each other to bits.'

'Why don't you go home, Pedro?'

'I won't stay for big trouble, Adam. Like this, it's all right. I'm learning. If there's big trouble again, I won't stay.'

Adam looked closely at him. 'You'd run out on me, would you?'

'No,' Darder shook his head. 'Not on you. On the country and the rotten mess it is. You're wasting yourself here. You gave up all you had worked for. Why don't you go home, Adam, before there's big trouble again?'

Adam studied the ground. 'I can't.'

'Why not?'

'I just can't.'

'It's Stirling, isn't it? Adam. I speak as a friend. There is something I think you should know.'

Adam looked up, tight with warning. 'There's nothing I should know. Drop it, Pedro.'

Darder shrugged. 'As you wish.'

They stood uncomfortably until Adam spoke. 'I'm going to see this through, Pedro. I'm going to build a real hospital. We're going to have air-conditioners, do you know that? We're going to have a real operating theatre in there.'

Darder laughed hopelessly and clapped Adam's arm. 'With workmen like these? Tim Frost's scrapings of the bazaar? I hope you get your real hospital. If there's no big trouble, maybe I'll stay and help you build it.'

Adam said, 'If I have to, I'll build the bloody thing with my own hands.'

They had almost forgotten the sound of mortars. The first explosions roused them up in sickened apprehension. In the Red Cross mess, the bathroom door piled again with mattresses, the men breathed hard and waited. Was this the beginning of another end? Had the VC flag gone up again in Saigon and Hue?

The team leader got up from his appointed seat on the lavatory after an hour's silence. 'I'm going to bed. That will be it. Charlie's just sending us a few calling cards.'

There were two casualties next morning. A man and wife hit by fragments. One shell had fallen in Hatton's compound, ripping the sandbagged guardhouse. The bags had split like bellies and spilled their insides like guts. The shelling was an unneeded reminder of the leashed violence that had waited on the dry. Again, there was only the now. A taut and aching vacuum that mocked the blossoms and seeding rice.

Hatton came to the hospital for Ho and spoke to Jane. He looked across to the annex and changed his hard blue gaze. 'The Quakers are busy,' he said.

And he meant, that was our place. In there we happened to each other. Now there is nowhere to go.

'They fixed the roof,' Jane said.

The moonlight had shafted there like a sword.

'Jane, if the pressure eases, I could take leave. Perhaps we could get away.'

Ho pulled at Hatton's trousers. He felt for the boy's head with his hand. 'I don't know what you want,' he told her. 'Whether you'd want to do that?'

There was puzzle in his eyes, a mute recognition of their strangeness. 'We will see, Mark.'

Darder put out his head and called. 'Jane. Adam is ready.'

She jumped a little. 'I will have to go. When will I see you?'

'See me?' Hatton said, and his eyes were lost and puzzled. 'That's all we can do, isn't it? See each other?' He pushed Ho towards the jeep. 'I can come for coffee tomorrow.'

Jane said, 'I'll be waiting for you. We could invite Ho. Would you like that, Ho?'

'He would like that,' Hatton said.

That night and next day, Hatton thought about it. If they got away together, something could be resolved. They could be together normally, dress up, drink wine in restaurants.

The rumours of peace, of coming negotiation, had revived Hatton's belief in the future. His Colonelcy had been recommended. He would outrank the Quong Lo establishment. He had pretty much got back his leg. The promotion could mean return to active command.

Once his heart would have thumped at the prospect. He had been solitary then, and safe. He was not solitary now, and his eyes puzzled to estimate the involvement. If they could get away together, learn better to know each other. Hatton's blood stirred with memory. If they could get away together he would lie with her every night.

The APC had been disabled by a mine, on the road to Task Force Nebraska. A troop truck had brought in the crew. Hatton ordered the patrol jeep readied so that he could run out and check the damage before joining Jane for coffee.

In the few weeks of dryness the coast road had already powdered into dust, a grey almost white that coated the loud green sweeping down from the hills. The patrol jeep kept to the road centre, ballooning the grey-white behind it.

The APC had lifted and slewed on the explosion, jumped sideways into grass, stopped its steel snout on a cabbage palm. The blasted track lay in the dust like a giant zip-fastener.

Hatton got out, paused to light a cigarette, considered the vehicle. In the back of his jeep a soldier peeled gum, began to chew. His companion took off his helmet to scratch.

The bullets that hit him punched through the hand raised to the short, sweated hair, expanded softened tips and burst the bared head into splinters. Scalp, bones and brain gobbeted the jeep as the dead boy screwed and fell sideways. The windscreen exploded. The jeep rocked to the fusillade that screamed on the metal. Hatton had dived for the APC, head in his arms, when the bullet struck, flipping his body in flight. He hit the grass on his back, rolled, came up tearing for the holstered pistol.

There was no movement on the green slope. Hatton rolled again, held the pistol steady on the unblown track of the armoured car, cold with futility and hatred. Something whistled in the silence. He snapped his head at the sound. It was the jeep, tipping towards the far side on expiring tyres.

The driver remained at the wheel, bent there, one arm through the spokes, dangling.

'Major. I'm hit, Major.'

Hatton swallowed the nausea watering in his throat. He thought it was the driver who had spoken, but nothing moved there, the helmeted head was turned away.

The corporal had pulled himself against the jeep, his shoulders lifted a little, his legs in the long green grass.

'I'm all dead on one side, Major. They were waiting for us, weren't they?'

Hatton edged out. It was hard to see the man the way the jeep was placed.

'Have you got your rifle, Corporal?'

The soldier pushed to raise himself, stretched an arm and searched the grass.

'I don't think I can use it, Major. I'm all dead on one side.'

'Can you throw it?'

Hatton turned back to the hill where nothing moved. They would come to loot when they were satisfied. Hatton fired into the hillside, without sighting.

'Are they coming, Major? Can you see them?'

The panic of the helpless was in the hurt soldier's voice.

'Just letting them know we're still here, boy. Nothing is going to happen.'

He didn't believe it. It was latening. There would be no more traffic out of Quong Lo. Shortly they would cut the road, using the wooded ridge for cover, attack from the open side.

The numbness was leaving his wound, it had begun to hammer and stab, sickening Hatton with pain. Blood shone on the spiky green grass. He laid the pistol on the track.

The futility and hatred blazed again, almost a loathing for this part of his body which had betrayed him a second time.

'You bastard,' Hatton said. 'You no-good limping bastard.'

It was his bad leg that had taken the bullet.

The corporal had pushed himself up with his heels. His face was dropped on his chest, panting, the M-16 across his stomach.

'Throw it to me, boy.'

He lifted his head and gulped, reached the rifle to one side and waited. A great sobbing cry came out of him as he tensed and pitched the weapon. It puffed the dust, naked in the naked space between them.

Hatton said, 'You did good, boy. You did good.'

He would have to crawl there, reach, crawl back. The wounded leg was useless. If they caught him in that naked space the boy's death would be assured as his own. It was very still, very silent. Hatton watched the hills and decided. You'll come for us, anyhow, won't you? You're probably coming for us now. He leaned back and willed his strength.

He was ready now, willed there, almost absent to his own body. 'You got a canteen, boy?'

The other's voice was low and cracked. 'I can't throw it. I can't.'

'I don't want you to throw it. Don't drink. If you're thirsty, just wet your lips. Hold the water in your mouth. Spit it out.'

Hatton got up on one knee, body propped on his fingers like a runner. There was nothing in the world but the rifle, only its length and breadth in the dust. He hit hard on his belly and the wounded leg pierced him with pain. He heaved forward again. His groping fingers had touched the sling when the silence exploded. The dust jumped. The hull of the APC clanged like a monstrous anvil. Hatton scrambled around, rolling, the rifle tight against his body.

It was still clutched there when he opened his eyes and could not believe he was alive. Exhilaration shot through him. *I made it. I beat them.* He heard the corporal cough in the returned and weighted silence.

'You made it, sir.'

Hatton panted and spat dust. 'We'll both make it, boy. Now the clips. Take your time. Be very careful.'

He breathed hard, knuckles white on the rifle. *Come and get us. Come and get us now.*

Hatton stripped the sling and made a tourniquet for his leg. Yellow berries spotted a bush. He leaned forward and picked one, sucked it in his mouth to make saliva.

The ridge was on his right. They would take the far side, run the road, come bellying through the paddy. The hot light was withdrawing. There were shadows black as sleeping in the hills.

'You all right, soldier?'

The answer was slow with stupor. 'I can't stop the blood. It won't stop.'

'Now listen, boy. They'll be coming for us soon. I'm going to back off and give you cover.'

Hatton waited. 'You hear me?'

'I hear you, Major.'

'Can you crawl under that jeep?'

261

Hatton waited again. The voice was slower and fainter.

'I don't know. I'll try.'

'You get under there. The compound will miss us soon. There's going to be armour coming up that road. Before you know it you'll be in a soft bed with a pretty nurse holding your hand.'

This time there was no answer. A cricket began evensong. Hatton tightened the tourniquet and laid down his helmet. He clasped the M-16 to his belly and stretched out. There were ants in the dust and clambering the grass blades. He watched them, so serenely busy. He would have liked to lie there for ever, watching their pointless scurry. Hatton closed his eyes and rolled, into tall grass, towards the paddy.

He had blacked out, recovered choking, coughing the brown paddy water. His face and head were slimy with mud. He laid the M-16 on the bund, switched it to automatic. This is where they would cross. If they were coming, they would cross here. He wanted them to cross with a desperation like another pain. Please let them cross, he prayed, let them cross while I can take them.

They came out on the far side of the little wooded ridge as though he had put them there by his will. Two small men in shorts and singlets, crouched behind bushes, heads prying and turning. Hatton cuddled the rifle, one elbow in the mud, as serene as the ants he had watched.

Now they would make the short, bent run. He was drawing them on invisible strings. The others would be watching on the hill. There, Hatton thought. I'll take them there. They will come together, spaced. They're so sure, so satisfied and sure. He will be almost across, the first man. There, in the rut of the road. He will hardly know but the next man will know. There will be all eternity in his knowing.

There was nothing to doubt. Hatton stopped his breath. They were coming.

The first burst exploded the guerrilla as though his clothing was filled with small bombs. The impact lifted him clear of the rut, hurled him back into the road's middle. Hatton saw the other man's face swell with disbelief as he tried to halt. In a suspension of time, lazily, Hatton elevated the barrel.

He let him stop. Let him turn. Saw his weapon drop. The man was in flight and doubled when the next burst split his back.

Bullets sprayed from the hill, hammered distantly on the APC. Hatton watched the water splash, the earth and bunds spurt about him. He

262

was untouchable now. There would be cursing and chattering on the hill.

In the rice and the mud and the water, Hatton eased himself and closed his eyes.

Jane did not want Adam to stay. She was as concerned now that he might stay as she had been previously to see him leave. His undeclared knowledge of Hatton confused her like a guilt. Ho sat on the verandah whittling with a knife Hatton had given him, looked up to smile as Jane passed. She bent to show him the sugared cakes.

'One each for us and two for Ho. At-ton will be here soon. You're watching for him, aren't you?'

He smiled, eyes big at the cakes. 'At-ton,' he laboured.

In the adviser's compound the sergeant got up from his desk and stretched. He took a beer from the freezer in the orderly room, punched the can and walked out.

'Where's Hendricks and that goddam patrol jeep?'

'He's still out, Sarge. He took the Major to check the mined APC.'

'I know that,' the sergeant said. 'It's going on sundown. They should have their asses back here.'

'Maybe Hendricks is scouting the town, Sarge.'

'Nobody asked Hendricks to scout the town. When he gets back, let me know.'

The sergeant finished his beer and went inside, punched a new can and sat with his feet up, turning a girlie magazine.

Ho had eaten his cakes, drank coffee thick with sugar. He couldn't get comfortable in the deck-chair, fidgeting expectantly at every sound. Darder corked his bottle.

'Six o'clock. I'll check the wards while you pack up.'

Jane asked nervously, 'Is there any hurry, Pedro?'

'No,' Darder said. 'Why? Are you waiting for anything? Adam has gone.'

'I thought Sam might come in.'

She couldn't tell Darder. The constraint fretted and disturbed her. The Spaniard would have chilled and walked away. It was ridiculous and she hated it.

'The hell with Sam,' Darder said. 'I want to take a shower.'

Reluctantly she packed, folded the embroidered cloth. Ho watched and lowered his head. She put her hand on his thin, bent shoulders.

'I know. Never mind. At-ton must have had business to do. Tomorrow, Ho. We will have a party with At-ton tomorrow. I will get a special cake. A big one with cream and chocolate.'

Ho picked at a scabbed knee, remote with disappointment.

The sergeant aimed another can at the waste-basket and slammed his feet on the floor. He put down the girlie magazine and sighed. The coloured nude eyed him from the cover. The sergeant doubted if he would last until his R & R. He lit a cigarette and stood on the steps of the hut, weighted with boredom.

The soldier carried his mess gear. 'He hasn't come in, Sarge.'

'Who hasn't come in? Get those sleeves down. You never heard of malaria?'

The soldier pulled clumsily at his fatigues, clashing the mess gear. 'Hendricks. He hasn't been seen. I asked the town patrol.'

The sergeant forgot his thoughts. A premonitory cold soured his stomach. He inspected the darkening sky. 'I want twelve men in the truck. The signals jeep and an APC. I want them saddled up in ten minutes. Get a searchlight in that truck.'

The soldier gaped.

'Move your ass,' the sergeant shouted. 'On the double. Move.'

In the office he buckled on his pistol and banged at the telephone.

34

Hatton had pulled himself up on the bund's earthen pillow. He was comfortable there, face turned to the road, lying on his back like a man in bed with covers of water drawn to his chest. The hills had blackened. The green and brown of the paddy flats absorbed and reflected the last light.

Hatton pinched the wounded leg. It was as stiff and dead as a wooden peg below the tourniquet. Pain pumped in the thigh like bellows. Hatton unbuckled his webbing, worked a hand into his trousers. He touched the bloody breach, and moved his hand to the inside, walking fingertips on the flesh. It was mulched there, a flayed and torn mess. Hatton lay back and smiled at the sky.

He said quite loudly to the leg, 'You bastard. You no-good limping bastard. You blew that one, didn't you? There'll be no steel pins this time.'

The leg's failure to contrive more than a flesh wound shook Hatton with amusement. It had almost got him once. He had beaten that. The leg had tried to get him again and had missed the bullet with the bone.

'You're getting old,' Hatton told the leg. 'You're getting old and sloppy.'

He dozed and woke, sweet and peaceful with dreaming. It had been a good dream. He frowned to recall it but could not, tried to get it back, gave up in irritation. He slapped the gritted water into his mouth, swallowed a little and spat. The glass of his wristwatch was scummed. He cleared it with a thumb and angled his arm for light. Soon now, soon now, he would hear armour on the road.

'Hang on Hendricks. Hang on, boy.'

He wanted to doze and dream again and gave himself permission. There was nothing to fear. Only a time of waiting to be filled.

Hatton worked his tongue. Jane would have finished coffee. Coffee was life. The smell and the scald and the taste of it. He would drink coffee soon. It would be the first thing he would ask for. He dreamed of Jane then. Her body in the dappled hut, the beam of moonlight through the roof, as fixed as something solid. It looks like a sword, she had said. Like a magic, shining sword, she had repeated, to tell him what she wanted him to know.

He would have that too. There was no more puzzlement. She was as precious to him now as his life. When this was over he would make her his to keep. One day soon it would be over. There was nothing here he wanted to win any more.

Hatton opened his eyes. The paddy was darkening in patches, like successive lights snuffing out. He didn't mind the torment of the wound. It had become part of his being.

Something nagged and he worried at it, like the dream he had tried to recall. It was connected with Jane and the coffee. Hatton lay slumped in the paddy, quite lost in concentration, searching his mind for resolvement.

It was Ho. That was it. When it was over, what would happen to Ho? Well, that's it, boy. Shake hands. Goodbye and good luck. He wouldn't cry. He would gulp his throat to make a word. He would stand there like the last boy in the world long after the aircraft had dwindled.

The image smarted Hatton's eyes. He pushed himself up and looked about. He was getting weak. It was the loss of blood. Goddam everything to hell.

The frogs croaked and creaked and he hated them. The hills were as

266

black as despair. The twilight was cold and deepening. Hatton shivered. When the armour arrived he'd have a piece of someone. He let himself drowse, and found his answer in dreaming. It was so simple, so perfect and simple. When it was over he would adopt Ho. They would all fly away together.

He woke to Vietnamese voices, jumped an arm for the M-16, still clouded with dreaming. He jammed his good heel into the mud and pushed, the weapon across his chest. The voices were clear, chattering, coming towards him across the bunds. A man and a boy shaped themselves, black in black pyjamas. Hatton sighted the weapon.

His finger was curled on the pull, the foresight covered their bodies. What were they doing, a man and a boy in the paddy, walking the vestiges of light? Why did they come, voices soft, picking across the bunds? It's you against everything that moves, if you want to stay alive.

Soft-voiced, soft-footed, they came on across the earthen walls, their shadows in the water, rippled on the rice. Sweat burst on Hatton's forehead. His brain shrieked at them to go away. He had half rolled on the smoke-blown promontory, come up with the unpinned grenade. Had they weapons hidden? He did not know. There had been no weapons in the tunnel.

'Halt,' Hatton ordered. And again in Vietnamese.

The figures stopped as though the words had frozen them, the boy backed against the man, as immobile as planks planted in the bund.

Hatton saw the man's head slowly turn, questing. The voice was low, whispering. 'Mer'can? You Mer'can so'jer?'

'Yes. American soldier.'

'OK, Joe. OK, Joe.'

The boy's voice rose thinly. 'OK, Joe. You got gum?'

Hatton held the M-16 across his body with one hand, pushed himself up on the bund with the other. He sat with his legs in the paddy.

'OK, Joe?' The man slowly raised his arms.

'OK. Walk.'

'You kill VC?' the boy asked. 'Kill VC Number One. VC Number Ten.'

Hatton rocked with weakness. He felt all his insides drain away. He lowered the rifle. They came very slowly, the man bumping on the boy, both nodding and smiling, their faces touched by last light. The boy's smile reminded Hatton of little Ho. He was very glad he had not killed them.

The machine pistol came up under the child's armpit. The yellow flame that fumed from the muzzle was the last image on Hatton's eyes as the bullets smashed his chest.

The echoes died. The frogs silenced. The man and the boy stood immobile as planks planted on the bund. Then the man spoke in a whisper. They moved slowly forward.

Hatton lay on the bund, his legs in the paddy. Blood brightened the dirty water. The man wiped the M-16 clean on his pyjamas, passed it to the boy, unsheathed the machete in his trousers. The boy squatted, fondling the rifle.

The fair hair was too short to grasp. The man pushed back the dead head with a palm across eyes and forehead. He grunted as the machete whacked into the tautened throat. The boy waited and watched, fondling his hand on his prize.

Adam lay on his bed, trying to read, with a resignation he did not feel. The Germans across the passage were playing pop music. It was ghastly enough in the original. In German it was almost unbearable. Adam punched the pillow and tried to close his ears. The villa was small. There was no acoustical privacy. He heard the clatter of the defence gates open, lowered his book in curiosity.

'Dr Thomson. Is Dr Thomson here?'

He heard the team leader say, 'Just a minute.'

The soldier stood in the doorway. Adam crossed the sitting-room, wondering at the young man's trembling. 'I'm Dr Thomson. What's the trouble?'

The soldier backed from the light, not wanting to be heard. 'We've got a casualty at the hospital, sir. There's a Medevac chopper coming. He might not last that long.'

'We only treat civilians at the hospital, soldier. Those are Major Hatton's instructions.'

'Major Hatton?' The soldier's voice cracked. He looked away, screwed at his face with a fist. The jeep had reversed, engine running. The faces staring from it were pale and stretched with nerves.

Adam asked slowly, 'What has happened?'

'There's no time, sir. Hendricks is dying.'

Something had happened. 'OK. Let's go.'

The jeep jumped before he was properly seated. Something had happened. There were Arvin vehicles on the road. A truckload of American troops turned for the Adviser's compound. Adam leaned forward. 'Is the casualty gunshot?'

'Yes, sir. Badly.'

'When we get to the hospital, let me off at the gate,' Adam said. 'Get Nurse Stirling from the guest-house. Ask her to show you where Dr Darder lives.' He grabbed to hold himself in the speeding, rocking jeep.

Adam hurried across the hospital compound. A jeep sprayed its headlights on the pepper tree. Soldiers stood there waiting for him.

Adam began. 'Where's the casualty?' and paused. The men watching him were patched with blood. 'Are you men all right?'

One of them realized. 'We're not hurt, sir. We held Hendricks on the way in.'

'Where is he?'

The soldier pointed to Reception. 'We put him in there, sir. On a litter.'

Adam leaped the steps. On the way in, the soldier had said. Whatever happened had been outside town.

Darder and Adam washed.

'What do you think, Adam? Will he make it?'

'I think so.'

Darder lit a cigarette. 'What happened? Do you know?'

Adam shook his head. 'Only that it was out of town. I'm going for a breather.'

The pepper tree was dark. The two soldiers who still waited had remembered to turn off the headlights. They stood up.

'How is he, sir? Is he——'

'He's doing fine,' Adam said.

They smiled, relief shining their faces. 'Hendricks is from my home town, sir. We did boot camp together.'

'You'll have to finish the war without him. Hendricks will be going home.'

'That can't be all bad,' the other said.

Adam asked, 'What happened to Hendricks?'

The soldiers moved uncomfortably. 'There's a busted APC on the coast road. They were out there and got ambushed.'

'They?'

'They're all dead, sir. Except Hendricks.'

Adam said, 'I'm sorry.' He supposed the others would be boys like these. Their faces not yet written on. Confused, frightened, making themselves hard, doing the best they could.

The big ward stirred and murmured. The Vietnamese nurse's oil lamp passed the windows, briefly brushing them with yellow. The sound of the wards at night always carried a smell to Adam, somehow thickened by darkness, like the body odour of a huge furry animal, crouched in jungle, licking its wounds.

He made his voice gentle. 'How many did you lose?'

'Three, sir. They were out in the patrol jeep.'

Three more, Adam thought. Killed and killing, for what? 'Were they Major Hatton's men?'

He observed their distress, the shuffled feet, the difficulty with their faces. The soldier from Corporal Hendrick's home town spoke softly, as though he himself feared to hear.

'They killed the Major too, sir. When we found him ... When we found him...' He swallowed, fists clenched.

The older boy glared, turned to Adam. 'The VC had cut off his head. The Major got two of them. He saved Hendricks's life.'

'They cut off his head,' the younger one repeated in wonder. 'They cut off the Major's head.'

Shock wobbled Adam like a blow. Hatton's blue gaze, Hatton's face, Hatton's stiffened walk, his handshake, his voice, all flashed and spun and shouted. Adam trembled. Not Hatton. It couldn't be. *They cut off his head.*

'You all right, sir?' The older soldier turned on the younger one. 'You couldn't shut your big mouth, Miller, could you?'

Adam grasped the post, fighting the annihilation of shock. He did not identify the anguished cry behind him, sobbed on the hand clawed to Jane's mouth. It might have come from one of the soldiers who so suddenly startled and leaped towards her. It was the awful slump of her fall that released Adam.

They sat at the coffee table, the Cognac bottle before them. Darder leaned on his knees, smoking. 'I wish to God she'd come out.'

'She wants to be alone, Pedro.'

'Why doesn't she cry? The English, I don't understand them.'

Adam said proudly, 'It's not her way. Tomorrow, or the next day, she will cry. We won't see it.'

'It would be better if she would cry. My God, what an awful way to hear it.'

Darder gave himself another drink. 'Animals. That's what they are. Animals.'

'What are the others. Pedro? How many napalm cases have you helped die?'

The Spaniard looked surprised.

Adam said, 'You thought I didn't know? I knew. How many innocents has our side mutilated? Hatton, at least, was a soldier.'

Darder stumped his cigarette, lit another. 'I wonder what she will do, whether she will stay.'

'Why would she not?'

Darder said, 'I think she will want to get away from this place.'

Old and new sadness muffled in Adam. 'I know, Pedro. Perhaps she will. Perhaps she should get away.'

'I think I will leave too, Adam.'

'You?'

'Yes. I'm finished here. It's strange.' The Spaniard frowned. 'In some way, Hatton is the end of something. In some way, he stood for something. It's as though with Hatton all of it is over. I can't feel any more reason to be here. It's all so bloody hopeless.'

'I will miss you, Pedro.'

'I will miss you. One day you must come to Barcelona. We will drink wine and go to the bulls.'

Adam shook his head. 'The wine, yes. The bulls, no. I've had enough blood.'

'The bulls enjoy it, Adam. They're bred for it.'

'The English say that about foxhunting. I'd like to hear it from a fox or a bull.'

Darder spread his hands. 'Anglo-Saxon sentiment. The bull dies one way or the other.'

'Everything dies one way or the other. It's the manner of dying that matters.'

The soldiers dozed in the jeep. One prodded the other. 'Wake up, Miller. Here they come.'

Adam sat in the back and tried to see Jane's face. Her lids were closed, her lips trembled, her head was bent as though for sleep.

When the gates opened, he said, 'Go to bed. I'll come in a minute and give you a sedative.'

She nodded mutely.

The horned moon was high now, a few torn clouds in the sky. Adam walked the compound. He didn't want to see Tim Frost or hear him. He wanted to be alone.

In the unlit passage he tapped the door. Jane had turned the lamp away from her. Adam unwrapped the syringe and wet a gauze with spirit. 'This will help you sleep.'

She sat up, her face curtained by her hair. Her breasts curved above the nightdress. Adam hesitated at her beauty. He withdrew the needle. 'There we are.'

Her shoulders began to shake. She tried to stop her mouth with a hand and could not. Adam put down the syringe and sat to hold her. 'I know. I know.'

She was soft, almost naked against him, her body convulsed on sobs.

'Let go. Let go, Jane.'

'Oh, Adam.'

'I know.' He held her head to him, one hand under her hair. Tears spilled silently on her cheeks. For a long time he sat and held her. At length she quietened. When he lay her back she was masked in sleep.

On the second day after Hatton's death, Jane went again to the hospital.

Darder asked Adam, 'How is she?'

'She's shaky. Just let her do what she wants. It will help her to be occupied.'

'Has she said anything?'

'No.'

'She's a brave girl. She's trying hard.'

'She's trying harder than Sam,' Adam said. 'He's been drunk for two days. Nobody can get near him. Sam was the only friend Hatton had here.'

Apart from her, he thought, remembering. The death and the hacked-off head could not absolve Adam of what he had seen in the annex.

Time, like all else, was an irrelevancy to Jane. Her hands moved to tasks ineptly, as though they had forgotten the habits of usage. All reality was distanced. She heard her own voice at a distance. She grieved for Hatton, not for herself. It had been the wrong time and the wrong way for him to die. Hatton had withdrawn his candidature for a soldier's death.

The dismemberment no longer signified horror. Her mind accepted that as symbol of the force bullets alone could not break. In dreaming she caressed the poor head.

In the days that passed Hatton's image was with her. There had been so many ways she had not known him. His face remained, hard and beautiful, his blue gaze alive. He would be with her like that for ever, dwelling in her flesh and spirit.

Imperceptibly the green of spring voided and the world began to tinge brown. Dust smoked in the bazaar. The rice in the paddy headed and was cut. Each day, calling under coolie hats, the women walked out to the threshing. The buffaloes rooted drying wallows, their hoary hides splattered with mud. The emptied fields began to crack.

At Ke Sanh, inexplicably, the besiegers withdrew. The outpost which had to be held at any cost was discovered to be redundant. Engineers blasted the bunkers in which many had bled and died. The defenders joined the relief column and abandoned Ke Sanh to the rats. A victory had been won, the Generals said. The razed earth blew in silence.

Three weeks after Hatton's death, Jane went for a week to Saigon. Adam worried about her there; rockets were bursting on the city. On the day she returned Jane had been gay, exhibiting a new percolator, pleasing Adam and Darder with impressions of past brightness. She had a parcel for Ho. 'How is he?'

Adam frowned and shook his head.

'Is he still asking for Mark?'

'Yes. He goes to the compound. Sergeant Bronski has returned him several times.'

Jane's eyes darkened. 'Poor, poor little boy.'

They sat quietly after Darder left. Jane looked to the hills, across the rise of Adam's new building.

'I asked about Mark at Army Records in Saigon. I thought there might be someone to write to. He had no kin, Adam. Nobody. He was utterly alone.'

Adam nodded, did not answer.

'His will was in favour of an army charity.'

'You should try to put it from your mind, Jane.'

'No. We must not do that. He was alone. Don't you see? There might not be anyone else to remember him.' She was quite calm. Adam shifted uncomfortably.

'He gave me something, Adam.'

His own eyes went to the hills, rested in loneliness there. 'I know.'

'No. You don't know. He gave me something. In a way it will always be his.'

Adam wondered how he could envy a dead man. 'What will you do? Will you leave here?'

She shook her head. 'There's nowhere I want to go. You're not trying to get rid of me, are you?'

Adam warmed with relief. He turned urgently towards her. 'That would be the last thing.'

She smiled. 'I was joking. We have a hospital to build, remember?'

Pedro Darder set a date for his departure and became moody. The girl he had made his mistress troubled him.

'She's talking about suicide,' he told Adam. 'Wants to come with me. She must be out of her head. I tell you, I'll be glad to see the last of these people.'

For weeks Sam Jarra drank too much at night while the others played cards and watched. On his days off he got seriously drunk, driving morosely and dangerously in the town. He couldn't forget or forgive the mutilation.

'He was something else,' was the most that could be got from Sam. 'That Hatton was something else.'

The elderly Captain posted to Hatton's compound visited the hospital and introduced himself to Adam.

He said, leaving, 'About this boy. The dumb one. Can you keep him away from the compound? We don't want to be hard on him. He's got me spooked the way he stands there watching and waiting.'

The cries at home of Peace With Honour continued to be heard. The aircraft targeted north flew out of Guam, off the carriers at sea, out of Thailand, out of Burma, out of the southern bases. The guns of the fleet in the China Sea hurled their great shells unmolested. The scrap of North Vietnam obliterated under the most terrible bombardment ever made. In the south three hundred and fifty thousand insurgents, without aircraft or armour, battled to a stalemate eight hundred thousand government troops, five hundred and fifty-five thousand Americans, forty-five thousand Koreans, twenty thousand Thailanders, twelve thousand Australians and New Zealanders.

After the cruellest devastation suffered by civilians in modern times there was hardly a secured hamlet in the country.

35

ADAM parked under the pepper and switched off. There was an Arvin jeep there, an Arvin lieutenant and sergeant on the verandah. 'What's happening now?'

He found Pedro Darder reading a letter in the office. 'Why are the Arvins here?'

'They have a prisoner. There was another of those mysterious raids on the transport field early this morning. The interrogators have him in Reception.'

'Is he wounded?'

'Leg and shoulder.'

'Who's with him now?'

'The new Captain and that interpreter you don't like.'

'I don't like what they do. I don't want it happening here.'

'He'd be worse off with the Arvins,' Darder said. 'They've roughed him up already.'

'I'm going in there,' Adam said. 'I'll give them fifteen minutes and then I'm going in there.'

Darder returned to his letter. He turned a page and whistled. 'My father has found me a practice. Listen to this, Adam.'

Darder looked up. Adam had gone.

The new adviser and his interpreter were on the verandah where the Arvins had waited.

'Here comes Doc Thomson,' the interpreter said. 'I'm going to take a walk, sir. The doctor kicks my ass.'

The elderly Captain wiped at his seamed face with a handkerchief. He had watched the Arvins beat the prisoner at the airstrip, water a towel padded across his mouth and nostrils. The Captain had fought a desk in Saigon. He wished he was back there, away from this filthy place.

He smiled uncertainly at Adam. 'Morning, Doctor.'

Adam glanced at the tall interpreter's back, slouching across the compound. 'I believe you have a wounded prisoner, Captain.'

'That's right. The other doctor, the dark chap, fixed him up.'

'Had he been beaten?'

The Captain was unsure of how to answer. He was confused by Adam's pressure, the cold hard grip of his face.

'Well, some. Not too badly. You know how the Arvins are.'

'I want you to understand there will be no beating here.'

The Captain wiped at his neck, wishing again for his desk.

'It's not in my hands, Doc. The Arvins deal with prisoners. You know that.'

Adam indicated the heavy wooden door. The Reception had once been a storeroom. His eyes paused at the bamboo cage set against the wall. Inside it something moved.

'What's that?'

'It's a cage,' the Captain said.

Adam considered him. 'The Captain had removed his forage cap to wipe at the balding grey hair. His eyes watered. He did not look well.

More gently than he had intended, Adam said, 'I can see it's a cage. Who does it belong to?'

'The prisoner had it when he was shot. There's a rat in it.'

'A rat?'

'That's right.'

Adam lifted the lashed bamboo strips. The rat humped away, red eyes malicious. Bare skin patched its back like scabs. The ridged and pointed tail was naked.

276

Adam set back the cage, his voice tight.

'Dr Darder said your prisoner was found among the transports.'

'That's right. They've been having a go at the transports all over.'

The Captain blinked against the glare. He had a touch of dysentery and wished the doctor would relax. Tense people worried him. They made his bones ache. He could feel Adam's eyes and mopped at his face to escape.

'Captain, I want to make an autopsy on this rat.'

He stopped mopping, holding the sodden handkerchief. His eyes sidled from Adam to the cage, as though that might help make sense. 'On the rat? Why do you want to do that?'

'I think the rat is infected with plague.'

'Plague?' the Captain said. 'Plague?' as though ringing the word to test it. 'What kind of plague?'

'Bubonic.'

The Captain studied the cage with revulsion. 'Sweet Jesus,' he said. 'Go ahead.' He watched Adam hurry up the verandah and felt for his cigarettes. He had not handled the cage. His plague shots were up to date. What had the VC hoped for?

The answer visited the Captain light as wings, brushing on his mind before he noticed. 'Sweet Jesus,' he whispered. And louder, 'Sweet jumping Jesus.'

Adam sat on the stool and waited, the kidney bowl beside him sprawled with stubbed cigarettes. It couldn't be true. It was too subtle, too devious, too horribly simple. He kept seeing the patient who had died during the plague outbreak in the hills. His eyes bursting, screaming vomit, flailing down the ward in rigour, the pus heaped into buboes on his groin.

And Sam Jarra saying, 'Man, if the plague hits these camps, the war's over. The whole province will be a dying-shed.'

You had to know the symptoms. You had to expect it. It could go undiagnosed at first. Before it was stopped in the hill villages it had leaped from life to life like invisible flame. It had been stopped by flame, roaring to consume the contamination. Walls of inoculation and quarantine had driven the pestilence back. How long would it take to inoculate a city? How would you quarantine New York? Who would put a torch to the ghettos and tenements?

Pedro Darder worked on the running belly, a poncho spread on the table top. Adam sweated and smoked and waited.

Darder put down the scalpel, peeled off his gloves and holding them

277

like tongs dropped them on the poncho. He lifted the corners and wrapped the mess, went to the sink and washed. He was long there and quiet. He turned and did not speak, his dark face darker.

'Well?'

'Rotten,' Darder said.

It could be coincidence. A rat in a cage. A plague rat. Adam tried to make it a statement, but his voice was weak with the need of confirmation.

Darder wanted to help, but could not. 'What was he doing with the cage? Why has there been no attempt to destroy the transports? Here, or anywhere else?'

Adam shuddered. 'How long has it been going on? Can you remember?'

Darder finished drying. 'I don't know, Adam. Perhaps nobody does. The first news report was some time ago, about a raid on the Bien Hoa transports.'

'I can't believe it. It's too simple, and it's too involved.'

Darder said, 'They made their own munitions for years. They made bombs out of beer cans and mortars out of piping. They put plastic explosives in bicycle-pumps to blow up billets and restaurants. That rat is a home-made weapon, Adam. A biological weapon.'

Adam walked, lit a new cigarette without noticing. 'We can't be sure.'

Darder said, 'There's one way we can be sure.'

Adam stopped. 'How's that?'

'That animal in reception could tell us.'

Pity and love for Adam moved Darder. It's easy to heal, Adam, isn't it? Have you got what it takes to hurt? How many sides has righteousness? How unilateral is compassion? 'Some of those transports will be flying home now,' he said softly. 'It's your country. Your people.'

Darder watched the struggle and a twinge of contempt crossed his face. The moment of truth had come for Adam. Events had handed him a shining suit and it was five o'clock in the afternoon. He was in the ring, the picadors waited. He must either fight or run.

Emotion had loosened the Captain's bowels. In the airless enclosure of the lavatory he sat miserably hunched, chewing stomach tablets. He had not handled the cage, but it had ridden with him. A flea could have jumped the distance. The Captain pulled at his shirt, searching his bony ribs and stomach. When he thought what the cage might mean, all his body sweated. Dysentery pains screwed his insides. 'Sweet Jesus,' he said, about everything.

Adam walked the verandah slowly. The interpreter leaned on the wall, smoking. He straightened when he saw Adam.

'Where's the Captain?'

'Don't know, Doc. He's around here some place.'

The door and the silence behind it was like the top of a cliff to Adam. It giddied him as heights did, the awful pull from the pit, an almost unbearable invitation to fall. He couldn't break from the wooden door.

'Here he comes now, Doc.'

The Captain's lips were white. His eyes watered anxiously at Adam.

Adam said tensely, 'I was right about the rat.'

The Captain tried not to think. 'Uh-huh.'

The interpreter looked to the wall where the cage had been. Urgency gripped Adam, a rejection of the Captain's sick green face. 'The rat had plague. It was hopping with plague fleas.'

The interpreter's slouched body stiffened, his mouth opened and shut. The Captain felt his treacherous bowels move and clenched his face in concentration.

Adam shouted into the blank of the other man's withdrawal. 'Don't you know what that could mean? Are you stupid?'

The spasm passed, the Captain eased his body. He covered his eyes, holding his fingers tightly. When he looked up his face and voice had changed. 'No, Doc. Not stupid. Getting on, perhaps. I know what it could mean. I guess I was trying not to believe it.'

His eyes were tired and frank, telling Adam that he didn't want this, that he didn't want to be here. That he knew what he had to do.

'Get down to the transports, Sergeant. I want every available man searching the area, clean into the paddy. You know what they're looking for. Keep your mouth buttoned about the rat.'

The interpreter breathed hard. 'You mean they might have—— You mean that's what these raids might be about?'

The Captain cracked his voice, 'Move your ass! That's what we've got to find out.'

He stood with his hand on the rusted door bolt and inclined his head. 'This VC has a cultivated accent. He's almost certainly an officer. It's not going to be easy. It will be up to you to keep him going.'

279

Adam's face was white. 'I know,' he said.

The Captain took off the forage cap. He took a breath and sighed it out, shaking his head at Adam. In the instant all between them was understanding.

Darder prepared the syringe and laid it on a napkin. He went to the door. Adam was alone on the verandah, walking away. He watched Adam moving slowly in the sun. At the compound gate he leaned on the stone pillar, his forehead on his arm, looking out to the browning fields.

The interpreter stood in the door, his hands on the frame. 'Where will I find Dr Thomson?'

Darder was about to answer when Adam spoke, coming up the steps. 'What is it, Sergeant?'

The interpreter wheeled, his face greasy with sweat and commitment. He said, 'You're on, Doc,' and swallowed.

Adam nodded and passed him. In the dispensary he paused to clear his sun-dazzled eyes. Darder closed the napkin on the syringe and handed it to him. Adam was almost bleak.

At the blistered wooden door, the interpreter said, 'They found two more cages in the paddy. Big ones. Empty.'

Adam hardly heard, struggling to pass through the old planking into the denial of all he had lived by.

There was barely enough light to see. Cigarette smoke pressed for escape on the gauze of the small window. A strange odour jolted Adam. The exudings of hatred and terror, the will and the want to give pain, the stink of the ravening spores of insanity embedded in each human brain. It curled in the cells of Adam's being with a savage, atavistic claim.

The man lay on a litter raised on pipes, naked except for loincloth and dressings. He was dim to Adam, only the snoring breath gurgled in his throat, meaningful and clear.

The two Arvins perched on another litter, drawing on new cigarettes, bobbing heads and smiling. The Captain had taken off his shirt, used it to wipe at his sickened face. He shook his head, 'Sweet Jesus, Doc. I can't take much more.'

Adam could hardly speak. 'Has he told you anything?'

'He keeps asking the time. That's all they can get. He keeps asking the time.'

Adam moved towards the litter.

There was no face. Karate chops had opened the flesh from the cheekbones into the mouth's corners. From closed eyes to chin, jellied blood quivered. In the fall of the burst underlip, stuck teeth shone like seeds.

Adam stabbed at the wall with his hand and leaned trembling, swallowing his gall. There was no way back, nowhere to hide. The tormented creature on the litter had passed from life into hell. He would burn and burn and burn there until all had been consumed. The Arvins chattered softly, busy with each other. Adam grasped the bare arm, knuckling the hand that held the needle to make it steady. A horror of this helpless flesh, of its texture and warmth, sprang through him. He closed his eyes and pushed the plunger.

'Doc? Is there a slug of anything in this hospital? I've got to have a drink, Doc.' The Captain's voice was hoarse, his sick face imploring. On the litter the prisoner stirred. The Arvin officer ground his tiny, polished field boot on his cigarette and leaned over. The prisoner's eyes were wide and burning, an awful confirmation of life, of shape and human meaning on the pulped and shapeless face. Agonized, he propped on the unwounded arm. The broken head went back, struck at the interrogator like a snake. The spit he had tried to make whistled in clotted blood. The Arvin shouted and drove his fist into the bloodied shoulder wound.

Adam leaned against the verandah post in the blaze of the burning sun. The Captain fumbled his shirt on. 'I need a drink, Doc. I need a stiff one.'

Outside the Quaker annex children laughed and spun a top. The pepper tree stirred vaguely. Hammers clattered on the extension. Adam grasped at the familiarities. Leaning for rest and comfort on the weathered post, offering himself to the sun to cleanse the room from his mind and body. There was no way back, nowhere to hide. The war that stormed about them had broken off in one tiny drop. The barbarism and despair of it were shut inside the old wooden door. The man on the litter was Vietnam. For twenty-five years the foreigner had torn at his flesh.

Adam said, 'A drink? Yes. I'll get you one.'

He kept his face to the sun as he walked.

'They found two more cages in the paddy,' the Captain said. 'Sweet Jesus, I need a drink.'

Adam wondered why he didn't need one. He was empty inside, dead as ashes.

Once more that morning Adam passed the wooden door, out of the sun into half-light and the stench of man's animal beginnings. Between times he sat on a stool in the little dispensary and thought about his childhood. There had been a reservoir outside the town in which the children used to sneak swims. There were carp in the reservoir, golden and silver and mottled. In the shallows he and his playmates had chased them with scoops wired to broom-handles.

Pedro Darder looked once into the dispensary and switched on the plastic fan. He closed the door gently behind him.

Before lunch the Captain knocked. He had vomited and bled in the lavatory. Inside the door, he swayed.

'It's over,' he said, and his face was as empty as Adam's. 'He's dead. The Arvins say he's dead.'

Adam nodded. 'Thank God for that.'

'He talked at the end. The sergeant said he was delirious.'

Adam nodded. It was over. He remembered the gutted rat lying on the table. The ugly stiffened tail curling out of the poncho.

'I could use another drink,' the Captain said.

Adam pointed. The bottle jittered on the glass.

'He said we came like plague. He said we came like a pestilence and crept like poison on the land. He said we poisoned the trees in the forest, the crops in the fields, the water in the wells, the milk in the breasts of mothers.'

The Captain's voice was raw with wonder, his sick-lined face twisted with the labour to understand. 'He said we came like plague and now they've sent the plague back home.'

The words fell like stones in Adam's mind, round and polished and cold, to remain there as they would remain with the other man.

'Will we get it, Doc? Will we get the plague at home?'

'We've got it,' Adam said sadly. 'We've had it for a long time.'

'That's why he kept asking the time,' the Captain said, still wondering. 'That's what it was all about: he wanted to know that those planes were in America before he died.'

He was alone and it was over. There was nothing to think or feel. He wished only to sit, commanding nothing, never again to strive or believe.

Jane listened to Darder and under her breast tenderness and pity expanded like pain. It swelled until it touched the depths, a changing realization as irrevocable as the gift she had got from Hatton.

'He will need me,' she whispered.

'Yes,' Darder said. 'He will need you. He will need help to forgive himself.'

He watched her go and lit a cigarette, then walked out to the jeep. In it he looked once about the compound, at the length of the long shabby shed, at the dusty old pepper tree. He sat remembering, flicked the cigarette away and started the motor. It's all yours, Adam, he thought. From today and this moment. Good luck, my friend.

Darder saw nothing on the drive. He was already away in his mind, escaped towards home, flying high out of the tormented country.

She was very quiet. He did not hear until she was beside him.

'Adam. My poor darling.'

He puzzled a little at her. 'You know?'

'Yes. I know.'

Adam rubbed his eyes. 'It's over. They're sending the plague back home.'

She took his head and held him to her. 'It's over,' she soothed.

He said, 'Jane? I think I'm finished here.'

'No, you are not,' she said strongly. 'You are needed. We all need you. We need each other now, Adam.'

He looked up from her arms. A smile curved her mouth a little. The etched line of her chin was tipped at something beyond her dreaming.

Adam let her hold him. Everything else dropped away.

Paris

36

It was spring. The stones of the old city, cleaned by the Gaullists of the scalings which had been their colour for centuries, gleamed new and naked in the sunlight, a return to beginnings which shocked familiar associations. Trees leafed on the boulevards. Tables and chairs swept inside by winter appeared again outside the cafés. The gendarmes on their raised platforms contested the traffic with revived spirit, gesturing batons and shrilling their whistles for pleasure.

The 21st Plenary Session of the International did not open, it erupted. Red China had sent a delegation. At an official reception there was a scene between the Chinese and Russians.

The Press was still being strident about that when a delegation from the National Liberation Front Red Cross arrived late and quartered itself in a cheap hotel near the North Vietnamese Embassy. On the day before the conference went to the floor, delegations and government representatives of Red China, Nationalist China, North Vietnam, South Vietnam and the National Liberation Front, had positioned themselves, hostile as armies.

News of the NLF's arrival was pictured and reported in the Press. A student demonstration to declare solidarity had ended outside the delegation's hotel in the traditional lifting of paving-stones and a bloody battle with police.

Mitchell stood in the briefing room of the Grand Hotel and sweated. He had not bargained for this. The room was crowded with international Press corps, littering cigarette ash and butts. Mitchell blew into the microphone testing, and was rewarded with a shriek. He clapped his hand over it: 'For Christ's sake turn this thing down. It will blast us all out of here!'

Up front a reporter shouted a question. Mitchell put up his hand.

'One minute. Just a minute.' He watched anxiously while the console was retuned, blew a smaller, experimental breath and nodded.

'Ladies, gentlemen of the Press,' he began, reading from his presentation. 'The International Committee of the Red Cross, welcomes you to this 21st Plenary Session, here in the historic city of Paris. I have been requested by President Salem, by the chairman of the League Monsieur Collins, by Monsieur Hylot the chairman of the Conference and chairman of the chapter of our host country——'

Dutifully, in boredom, shuffling and whispering, the Press corps heard him out. Mitchell ended and looked up.

'Question!'

Mitchell nodded, relieved to have completed the formalities.

'Why was the delegation from Red China invited?'

He was ready for that, having been briefed by a disturbed Neveau. 'The delegation from the Chinese mainland was not officially invited. The Standing Commission of the conference issue no formal invitations. Notice of the holding of the conference is made to all Red Cross Societies. It is customary, but not obligatory, for the societies to notify the Commission that they will attend.'

Another voice asked, 'Was such notification given by the delegation from Red China?'

'No. It is not obligatory.'

'If the Red Chinese are seated, will the Nationalists walk out?'

Mitchell made his voice careful. 'The leader of the Nationalist Chinese delegation, which is a government one, has informed the Commission of their intention to withdraw if the delegation from Mainland China is seated.'

The room loudened with interest. This was the wanted story. Mitchell held up his hand for restraint. In the medley he could not fix on a question. He settled for the nearest voice, pointing.

'What action will the conference take on this? By its charter, the ICRC is supposed to be universal, neutral and impartial. If one delegation is seated, and not the other, would it not be true to say that these principles are a paper piety?'

Mitchell smiled at the man and lifted an eyebrow. It was meant to convey that he was too old a hand to walk into a loaded question.

'No. Because these principles are far from a paper piety, but the rock the charter is built on. No such decision will be made by the Commission. Effort will be made to bring the delegations together in the humane, non-political spirit of the International.'

'Will the delegation of the Government of South Vietnam sit down with the NLF?'

Mitchell sought the new voice. He began to relax. 'As I explained in my answer to the last question ...'

Let them pitch. He had covered himself all around the bases.

Neveau was quartered in a smaller suite on the same floor as Pierre Salem. He had arranged this from the Grand Hotel's floor plan. From the open door of his sitting-room he looked obliquely across to Salem's. In the contest Neveau expected, there would be advantage in marking the President's visitors.

The arrival of the Red Chinese had shocked him. It was without precedent or warning. He could almost believe that their presence had been plotted—that Salem had arranged it. He had met with the NLF in Saigon. He had returned as obsessed as a fanatic. It could have been plotted. What other traps had Salem dug for him?

Neveau lit a cigarette and walked nervously. He tried to be calm, telling himself his imagination had become inflamed. A way must be found to get rid of the Reds. If Salem's motion for condemnation of the American action in Vietnam reached a conference vote, the voice and influence of the Red Chinese delegation would be a menace.

Neveau lifted the telephone and called his office in a room off the Salle de Fêtes. He would invite the leader of the Nationalist Chinese to discuss the problem privately, and persuade him at all costs to cease his public threats of withdrawal. Neveau asked for his assistant.

'Jeanne?' he said, and listened to the urgent voice.

'Who is pressing to see me? Dr Herman Kerut? The Israeli delegation?' Outrage swelled his throat. A pain darted in his temple. He was fighting to save the International and the Jews were at him about their cursed Red Shield of David before the conference had convened. 'To hell with them!' he shouted. 'Do you hear me?'

When he could, Neveau calmed his voice. 'I am accepting no private appointments except those I make myself. Until further notice.'

He could not remember in that instant why he had telephoned.

At their national embassies, in restaurants, cafés and night clubs and more privately in their quarters, those to be seated in the Salle des Fêtes debated and embroidered the rumour. Something was on. Something that might bring down the International. Robert Collins, the Negro chairman of the League, had leaked the information. President Salem, conceiver of the Humanitarian Law, intended to propose a motion condemning the Vietnam War. He was going to declare that the Geneva Conventions and Protocols had been set at defiance by America. Alarm, excitement and disbelief magnified the rumour. The President would not dare. Such a motion would be unconstitutional. But would it? There was the precedent of Santo Domingo and the Cuban Missile Crisis. Where did moral obligation end and neutrality begin?

Before the representatives of common humanity were met to confer together, before the issues before them had opened for debate, the power blocs and delegations seethed in argument and confusion.

Salem was alone. Alone, he had prepared himself. Alone, he had travelled to Paris. He had sat by old Rudi's bed the last night in Geneva, the beloved friend already shrinking into death, grave-grey, too weak for conversation. He had sought Salem's hand, his own as light as a child's, propped in the old four-poster in which he had slept in love all the nights of his marriage. He had dozed like that, holding Salem's hand, while his mind wandered the past. Sometimes he spoke his wife's name, or that of his children. Once he smiled. 'My most brilliant student. My best and most brilliant student.'

Before Salem gently disengaged himself Rudi roused from his dreaming.

'Remember, Pierre. The time could be seven minutes to midnight.' He closed his eyes and smiled. 'For me, it is later than that.'

When Salem went softly from the shuttered room he knew he was truly alone. Destiny had meant it so. All children were his children. All the suffering he had seen and knew also suffered in him. His was the responsibility. He embraced it as his shining white bride.

On the podium in the great room redolent with past Gallic glory, between the flags on the marble pillars, Pierre Salem and Robert Collins sat with the President of the French Society. Above them, photographers leaned, reflected in the mirrored arches of the gallery, equipment irreverently hung on the convenient arms of the sculptures. Salem looked over the crowded tables and his heart stirred in awe and excitement. The massed faces were brown, black, white, yellow, all the races of man. This was his flock. He was seated there as its shepherd.

On the aisle and at the rear, two tables remained unoccupied. Neither Chinese delegation had appeared. Each had waited to protest the other.

The mood of the conference had been set in the excitement of Salem's rumoured intention. Every eye searched his tall figure in the frank greed of curiosity.

The ceremony of opening was completed. There was to be no let or quarter. The Democratic Republic of Korea had claimed the floor. The small figure of the North Korean gestured fiercely as he spoke: 'With the illegal invitation of the representatives of Chiang Kai-shek to this conference, even though at the moment they are absent, is being realized the political plot of a certain country for the creation of two Chinas. Chiang Kai-shek, forsaken by the Chinese people and driven out...'

Charles Hylot, the French Chairman of the conference listened, shaking his neat head. For weeks he had rehearsed his wit and gestures. Hylot raised a pink palm in a mime of pained disappointment. 'No. No, no. You have no right to raise a political issue.'

The Albanian leader half stood. 'The procedure here is not right because it cannot be said that our work will be well done with the representative of Chiang Kai-shek officially here.'

Monsieur Hylot cracked his finger on the table. 'No, sir. You are not allowed to say that. It will not be included in the minutes.'

The Albanian snapped his eyes in challenge. 'Very well. I now proceed to humanism. What is the humanitarian truth? In Vietnam it is to punish the pirates of the air, sea and land who destroy hospitals, towns, villages; who sow death and suffering by fire, by napalm bombs, by deadly gas in Vietnam.'

Hylot broke in. 'I object. I shall not allow any attack against any country.'

The Albanian pressed on. 'There are provisions in the statute of our organization, Mr Chairman, which state that we are independent, neutral, impartial, and act in the spirit of humanity. What sort of humanity do we display when we have before our eyes, in our conference, the guilty party.' He flung a gesture towards the big American delegation, 'The guilty party which has been unscrupulously wiping out the lives of innocent civilians?'

Hylot thumped the table, his bald crown reddening. 'No, sir. No. You may not attack people here or delegations here. That is the last time I call you to order.'

An uproar rose from the tables. Joseph Richter rolled his eyes at the State Department members.

The Russian spokesman had risen. 'I would like to raise a question referring to the Chairman's ruling. It is not of any political flavour. It is only my intention to ask why the representatives of the Government of the People's Republic of China have not been——'

Hylot banged his gavel. 'I am afraid I must interrupt. This question is obviously of a political nature. I wish only to say this: that when the first notifications of the holding of this great conference went out to member nations, one went as a matter of course to the People's Republic of China. This was not an invitation. There are no invitations. Only notifications. I stress this because to my very great regret, I have received a telegram from Peking, full of gratuitous insults. The telegram conveyed that the Government of the People's Republic of China expected an official invitation. That is how the matter stood.'

Salem was leaned forward, his face keen. An idea had come to him. Events were playing into his hand.

The Russian continued: 'Thank you, Mr Chairman, for such a completely vague statement. Now I only wish to say that my Government supports the protests made here against the butchery being perpetrated against the people of the Democratic Republic of Vietnam, and wishes to put on record that we are, and have been, greatly concerned about the recurrent outbreaks of plague and the risk of an epidemic throughout the East.'

'Again I must interrupt. This is clearly a political matter you are raising, and as such I cannot allow it. I give the floor to the Polish delegate.'

The Pole stood, for emphasis. 'Mr Chairman. Humanity, impartiality and universality are among the fundamental principles of this organization. The performance of our duties in harmony with these high aims requires, in our opinion, that we speak out with a united voice against the illegal, unjustified aggression which is taking place at this moment in Vietnam. My Government——'

Hylot thumped harder on the table. 'No. No. No and no. Please sit down. You are continuing the political matter raised by the Russian delegate.'

The Pole continued to stand. 'My Government feels that the International Red Cross should reject political considerations in its approach to this whole problem of Vietnam, the plague and peace in the world, and concentrate with courage on our true aims.'

Hylot shrugged. 'Thank you, Mr Ambassador. I am sure we know our duty. I recognize the French Government delegate.' He nodded and smiled at his countryman, with the satisfaction of a schoolmaster acknowledging his brightest boy.

'Mr Chairman, ladies and gentlemen. The French Government delegation hopes as much as anybody that the smooth running of this conference will not be troubled by internal matters.' The French delegate paused for effect. 'Or by external ones such as the misguided demonstrations by the students. But I would remind you that the unity and universality which are the bastions of our organization will be threatened unless we take some action to prevent the difficulties in Vietnam from spreading.' He sat down.

Hylot nodded appreciation. 'Thank you. I am sorry but I do not propose to recognize the delegate from Cuba who is trying to attract my attention. Nor the delegate from Bulgaria. I am certain that our interests will best be served by terminating this discussion, reminding delegates once again that matters of a political nature must not intrude on our work. All references to Vietnam will therefore be banned from the minutes.'

The Albanian delegate jumped to his feet. In the general clamour that echoed through the Salle des Fêtes his protest went unheard.

Hylot banged and banged the gavel, his authority outraged. 'I declare this session adjourned. Sit down. I order this session adjourned.'

In the glassed boxes the interpreters removed their headsets. On the podium the seated men watched as the chamber began to clear in a racket of opinion and scraped chairs.

Hylot fussed at his papers. 'Unseemly. Most, most unseemly.'

Martin Neveau gave instruction for Mitchell to join him in his office. Quickly he pushed through the tables, hurrying to avoid those wishing to engage him. It had to be stopped. He must persuade the Nationalist Chinese to be seated. If they took the floor the chamber would be theirs by right of possession.

An ENGAGED sign had been provided above the entrance to Salem's suite. He shut the door, switched it on and went to the telephone. 'This is President Salem. Would you please get me the ICRC in Geneva?

Monsieur Bernard in the Juro-Legal section.' It had come to him on the podium. He had to be sure. He could not depend on memory.

Salem waited at the window, his hand on the red velvet hangings, and looked down on the place de l'Opéra. It was a fine point, trick of a lawyer's memory. Old Rudi would have called it naughty. Salem's lips quirked. He felt naughty.

As soon as the doors parted Neveau's attention went to Salem's suite. What was happening behind the Engaged sign? With whom was Salem plotting? Neveau watched while he waited for the National Chinese delegate.

Salem replaced the receiver and stood perfectly still, composing his next move. He must contain himself. It wasn't decent to take such satisfaction.

The first committee on the Humanitarian Law convened that afternoon. Salem sat in pride through the session. It had required an hour for the telegrams of endorsement to be read. From every nation, its most distinguished men had declared support and recognition, hailing the law as mankind's hope. The correspondents had been impressed by the messages, displayed under glass on a table in the briefing room.

He had been right. The world was sickened of choking on blood and madness. The hands of the clock that pointed seven minutes to midnight could and would be wound back.

37

In the leader's suite in the Hilton the eleven members of the State Department's representation sipped their pre-dinner drinks, whispering while Joseph Richter made his call. Below the windows that overlooked the Seine, Paris had twinkled into light. Traffic beamed on the pont d'Iéna and the pont de Bir-Hakeim. The Eiffel Tower sparkled like a Christmas tree.

Richter cradled the receiver and stood up. 'It's OK. Neveau had his session with Wong. The Nationalists will take their seats tomorrow.'

The leader handed Richter a drink, eyes intent. 'There's no doubt in this area, Joe?'

'No, sir. The delegation will arrive early. If the Reds turn up they will find egg on their faces.'

The leader lifted his glass. 'I'll go along with that as a toast.'

The men laughed and turned to each other. One slapped Richter on the back. In the renewed speculation he stood at full height, his long face warm with pleasure.

Salem's suite had emptied. Waiters and chambermaids hurried in the reception-room, cleaning and rearranging after the cocktails for the Humanitarian Law committee.

Every evening newspaper had headlined the session. In a boxed half-page *Paris Soir* had quoted from the prestigious messages of congratulation. The heading had read: GREAT MINDS IN EVERY COUNTRY JOIN INTERNATIONAL BID FOR SANITY.

It was accompanied by a photograph captioned: *President Salem Of The ICRC—Architect Of The Law.*

In the bedroom, naked, Salem was composed in a headstand. Long and pale as a lily he grew from the red-carpeted floor. In his mind there was no thought or sound. His spirit moved through the black universe of space, a tiny hot spark of being.

Salem opened his eyes, returning almost reluctantly to the flesh and temporal world. He took no more satisfaction for himself in what he was about to do. He dressed for dinner at the Élysée Palace, sat still and waited.

There was a tap at his bedroom door. His secretary announced. 'Your guest has arrived, Monsieur le Président.'

The delegate was young, with a dash of moustache, tailored in a tropical suit, his Americanized English perfect. Salem's secretary made the introduction, and switched on the ENGAGED sign as she left.

'It was kind of you to come, Mr Wong. May I offer you a drink?'

'Thank you, Mr President. I'll take a whisky.'

Salem went to the bar. The Chinese studied him, nervous and tense, one hand in the pocket of his jacket. Salem handed him the glass and smiled. 'Please be seated. Do you know Paris well?'

'I was here last year with a trade mission.'

Salem took a chair. 'A beautiful city. A very beautiful city. Please smoke if you wish.'

'Thank you.'

The bright slanted eyes reminded Salem of Thu. They flicked with the same cold attention.

The Chinese bobbed his head. 'I would like to congratulate you at this time, President Salem, on the reception of your proposed Humanitarian Law.'

Salem could not deny his pleasure. 'Thank you,' he said.

The Chinese sipped his drink and waited.

'Mr Wong, I'm sure you understand my reason for requesting this private meeting?'

Wong bowed. 'I do.'

'If possible, we wish to avoid a repetition of this morning's disorder. You no doubt have had your own reports of that.'

The delegate lowered his lids. 'My Government is very familiar with Communist tactics.'

'We wish to resolve this problem of seating.'

Wong was unsure of Salem. His delegation had discussed the rumours of the President's intention. He said, 'I have already discussed this with your Chairman, as you will know, Mr President. There is no change in our decision to be seated tomorrow.'

Salem hesitated in surprise. Neveau had wasted no time. The instinct of triumph he had dismissed as unworthy returned with this justification.

'There is a problem about that, Mr Wong.'

The delegate lowered his glass and put out his cigarette. He looked very young, too carefully glossy, to sustain the coming blow. It was there between them, undescribed. The tightened eyes and face prepared for it. 'I know of no problem. I have discussed this in depth with the Chairman of the International.'

'It is a point of law, Mr Wong.'

The Chinese said, 'My Government is agreed that our Nationalist delegation should take its rightful seat, Mr President. We intend to exercise this right tomorrow.' He waited. 'I know nothing of any point of law.' He didn't look young now. The hostility of fear had forked in his voice and face.

Salem wanted to get it over. He leaned forward. 'I want you to follow me carefully, Mr Wong. The delegation from mainland China is here as a Red Cross one. This, by its charter, the International is bound to recognize. Your delegation is present because the Nationalist Government is signatory to the Geneva Conventions. Correct?'

Wong waved a hand, his face blank.

'Now, Mr Wong, how did the Nationalist Government sign these Conventions? As the Government of Formosa or as the Government of China?'

A strain of white drained the warm skin of the delegate's cheeks.

'I am afraid, Mr Wong,' Salem continued, 'that those Conventions were signed by the Formosan authorities as representative of the Government of China. In International law, your delegation and that from the mainland, both represent the one country.'

Wong visibly trembled. 'There is but one China, Mr President, and its Government is in Formosa.'

Salem's voice was gentle. 'I understand your position. I ask that you understand mine. It was expected that at this conference the delegations representing the Government of China and the delegation representing the Red Cross of China, since they are recognized under the title of one country, sit at the same table.'

Wong was on his feet. 'It is impossible. You ask for the impossible. Never will my Government sit with those Communist pigs. There is but one Government of China, the lawful Government in exile. There is but one China, one China.'

He stopped, his breath heaving.

Salem stood. 'I am sorry, Mr Wong. It is entirely the fault of the Standing Committee that this complication was overlooked. But now it is my view that, to wilfully introduce politics into the conference arrangements would be unthinkable.'

'Your Chairman, Mr Neveau—he persuaded my delegation to be seated. He said nothing of this. There was no mention of this complication.'

'It is most regrettable. After this morning's plenary session I established the situation with my headquarters in Geneva. I can only repeat my regrets, Mr Wong.'

'This must be protested. My Government, our friends and allies, will vigorously protest.'

Salem said, 'It is a point of principle. The charter is involved. There is no alternative. I am sorry.'

Wong took a pink handkerchief from his breast pocket and touched it to his forehead. Then he bowed, a mixed military and oriental courtesy. 'I take my leave.'

Salem went with him to the door.

Alone, he stood very quietly, feeling emptiness and depression. He looked at his watch and wound it. Mauriac, the distinguished novelist, was to be host at dinner. The prospect cheered Salem. They could talk about Malraux.

He went to the bedroom and got his hat. The government car was waiting.

In a private room sparkled by glass and starched linen, in a Champs-Élysées restaurant, the leader of the State Department delegation was offering his guests Cognac and cigars when the Maître d'Hôtel called him to the private telephone. He returned in silence, sampled his Cognac in silence, and drew hard and silently on his cigar. On his right a deputy disengaged his conversation. 'Everything OK, sir?'

'Salem,' the leader said.

'What is it?'

'He has fired the Nationalists on a point of law.'

'How? What do you mean?'

The leader stopped him. 'Not now. Let's try to get out of here.'

In the Press club Mitchell's old associates ordered another round.

'He went well today, didn't he? Ted went well today.'

'Why don't you come back to Fleet Street, Ted? Bob here will find you a spot chasing ambulances.'

'You find him a spot chasing crumpet and I'll personally furnish a reference.'

Mitchell's stomach hurt. His eyes burned. He was tired, bored by the company he had used to enjoy.

'No more for me, chums. I'm going to bed. Tomorrow will be a long day.'

'The hell with that. We've got a party lined up. The highest class tail in Paris.'

'Not tonight, Josephine.'

When he got away Mitchell breathed with relief, welcoming the night chill. He decided to walk a bit before calling a taxi. They were doing the same things, saying the same things, they had five years ago. The reunion had been a failure. They were all somehow failed—fatter, balder, messed in divorces and remarriages. Talking too much, drinking too much, frenetic in dissipation. It frightened Mitchell. In them he saw himself in another five years.

He walked a little faster, hardly noticing the crowded tables on the pavement, his shoulders up. He was sick of his life, and he remembered a quote: *If you don't like your life you can change it.* Very well, Mitchell would change his life, now, before it was too late. When Sarah arrived he would ask her to marry him. He'd take her back to Australia and build a house on the water. To hell with Europe and swinging Britain and the wog Swiss and the wog French and the wog Italians. Mitchell's shoulders straightened. His eyes fixed on the pictures in his mind.

Neveau switched off the bedlamp and stared at the dark. Nerves twitched the soft flesh of his chest and belly. The Americans and Chinese Nationalists had been in uproar. He had got the head of Juro-Legal out of bed in Geneva to check the point of law. Nothing could be done. Nothing. Salem had used the charter to position himself for the declaration that could tumble it in ruins. Neveau moved on the bed and groaned. He couldn't face next day without sleep. Where had he gone wrong? At which point should he have risked everything to stop Salem? The man had gone mad, beyond reason. It had been in his eyes when he returned from dinner.

If he took the drug now he would wake hungover. If he did not there would be no peace from his thoughts. Something had to be done. He must join the Americans in a lobby. Stop Salem by vote on the floor.

Neveau began to count. He could get the Israelis by promising them their cursed Red Shield of David. The representative of the Holy See would vote against disruption. His lead would influence the Catholic countries. The Australians and New Zealanders would vote any way the Americans voted. They didn't count. The British would at worst be neutral. If he promised the Arab bloc that the Red Shield of David would not be accepted as a symbol...

Neveau lay in the dark, twitching with fatigue.

In the first murk of morning, from the suburbs, from attics and pensions in Saint-Germain-des-Prés, met over onion soup in the market of les Halles, the students moved quietly through the city towards the place de l'Opéra. Marshals on motor scooters scouted cobbled lanes, directing the growing numbers. Group leaders checked the time and communicated by walkie-talkie. Others watched from workmen's bars, swallowed their calvados and telephoned.

The student population of Paris, with support hitch-hiked in from Germany, Britain, Belgium and Scandinavia, marched to keep the appointment of place and time.

Salem had set his alarm for 6 a.m. He snapped awake at the first buzz, threw back the covers and swung out of bed. Robert Collins was to join him in a working breakfast at seven. He had an hour for a last revision before the second plenary session. Today he would stand and address them. He would demand that the twenty-first conference of the International vote to condemn American action in Vietnam.

Power and purpose filled him. He breathed deeply to still his loud heart. He would not be alone, although he would stand alone to deny precedent and procedure. He would be giving voice to the ravaged and victimized everywhere. In him righteous wrath would speak for all the world's mute and helpless.

He began to compose a letter.

MY OWN DEAR SON

On reflection it seems that all my life has been directed towards this day, this place, this purpose. By circumstance and bent, study has equipped me to conceive and lay foundation for an Humanitarian Law. By circumstance, I grew to manhood in the city that keeps the world's conscience. By circumstance, I was qualified to lead the world's one humanitarian international.

The responsibility I will discharge this day has in strange orders been destined. I will speak from a heart clean of self-interest, of arrogance of office, of conceit of person. If my voice is shaped to anger it will be the anger of outraged love. Love for all who suffer needlessly, outrage at those who permit it.

Salem walked slowly to his sitting-room, alone in the muffled quiet.

Breakfast had been served from a table in the reception room, set by the windows above the Place and the corner awning of the Café de la Paix. A warm sun in a clear sky had again favoured the day. It lit the big room cheerfully. Salem had ordered a continental breakfast. Robert Collins ate bacon and eggs.

The killing of Martin Luther King remained in Collins as a bitter hurt and anger. He wore the wound in his eyes, a grief for himself, his people and his country.

They were aware, as they talked, of the rising sound from the streets. It had introduced itself by degree, like confirmation of the day's awakening.

Collins puzzled at the windows, distracted.

Salem folded his napkin. His body ached with tension. He must find time to be alone, to prepare himself. 'Will the African countries support him, Robert?'

'I think so. I think so, Pierre. What I can, I have done.' His voice cracked in bitterness. 'There are times, few as they are, when it is an advantage to be black like me.'

In the fifteen minutes before eight o'clock the place de l'Opéra packed. From pavement cafés and bistros, from hideouts in borrowed apartments, from alleys and parks, off the avenue d l'Opéra and the boulevard des Capucins, the demonstrators shoved and hurried. In the minutes around eight, while gendarmes unholstered batons and rushed to give riot alarm, the mob voice loosened in a terrifying roar.

Salem and Collins froze. Their eyes leaped to the windows. Crockery clinked as they pushed away from the table.

By eight-fifteen the spill of bodies had halted traffic on the boulevard des Capucins. Cars and taxis in the place de l'Opéra stuck in the human aspic. Banners had unfolded to illustrate the chant of thousands of throats: Stop the War in Vietnam. Victory for the NLF.

Salem and Collins threw up a window and recoiled from the force let in. The menace of mob commitment, the violence of order defied, the wildness of glimpsed faces, shook Salem's heart. 'No,' he spoke uselessly. 'This is not the way.'

They heard the donkey braying of the Parisian sirens as the riot wagons rushed to surround the wedge of the Grand Hotel, a mad and macabre hee-hawing, a dementia in itself.

A limousine bearing the Indian delegation had arrived early to confer. It had been caught in the demonstration as it swung from the railed entrance to the Métro.

Attempt had been made to pass the Indians safely to the entrance. It was hopeless in the crush. Bodily the delegates were hoisted. Bodily, splayed and kicking, uplifted arms passed them overhead.

In the pack that crowded to the walls only the flash of faces had definition and feature. Now that began to go as those nearest the boulevard turned to meet the police.

They leaped like hounds from the black wagons, as black and forbidding as their transports. Black leather coats, black leather gloves, helmets of shining black steel, shod in steel-toed black boots, goggled in shatter-proof black-rimmed glass.

In the first clash of axe-handles and rifle butts, the clanging of black circular shields, the shouting lowered and fell. For a time the hee-hawing of further transports occupied the lull, then the massed throats opened on a new sound. A note as doleful as grieving, which thickened and clotted up from the bowels, red with the rage of combat.

Salem pushed back as Collins lowered the window. Salem remembered the Buddhists, his introduction to Saigon—it had been different there, less shocking among a foreign people. Collins remembered it had been like this, a thousand times worse, in the summer of the fire next time. There would be no let up, nothing changed. When this was over, when he had helped his friend to whatever awaited, it would be his turn, in his own country, to stand up and be counted.

In the street heads cracked, faces split, squirted and streaked with blood. Bodies thrashed under the steel-toed black boots. Among the panting, fighting men the screams of women shrilled. The limousine that had brought the Indian delegates lay turned on its side. Other cars were thrown over as obstacle and defence. A Citroen exploded, hurling burning petrol. Those about it scrambled away, beating at each other's clothing. A student with his temple laid open reeled against a wall, sobbing. Backed there, his head down, he swung a splintered axe handle into the glass of a shop window.

In the reception-room the telephone rang, startling Salem.

He said, 'Yes, Martin, cancel the session. Yes. Advise the delegations urgently. I will join Monsieur Hylot in the Salle des Fêtes.'

Collins opened the door and waited.

Ted Mitchell answered call after call. No, the riot had no connection with the seating of the Chinese delegations. No, he could not say if today's conference would proceed. No, he knew of no injury to any conference member. No, President Salem had not made a statement. No, the demonstration had no possible connection with the business of the twenty-first International.

He sat among the telephones off the briefing room, the receiver hunched in his shoulder, writing on a pad. 'Here,' he instructed an aide. 'Get the League PRO to help. Say nothing to the Press which isn't on this list. I'm going to find Salem. You got that?'

On his way out, he stopped. A few journalists were grouped about a man with a smashed camera hanging from his neck, wiping blood from his head and face with a wet towel.

'That's Bertie,' one said. 'He copped it.'

The photographer was hurt, breathing hard. 'Those bastards,' he said. 'They came out of those trucks like mad dogs. The officers were holding them back. Ready. Wait for it. Go. They just ripped into anyone in their way. I saw a woman with a shopping-basket go over. They were kneeling out there, holding their rifles by the barrel, using the butts to break people's knee-caps.'

'Just as well you got it in the noggin, Bertie. You might have been hurt otherwise.'

'You go stuff yourself,' the photographer said.

Mitchell moved, lighting a cigarette. He would have to get a statement from Salem, one from Hylot on behalf of the conference. He hoped none of the Americans had arrived early. If the mob caught one of their flagged cars there would be some mussed-up clothing.

It had to happen. Sarah was arriving on the five o'clock flight.

The fighting stopped at nine. By nine-thirty the demonstrators were dispersed. Black wagons prowled the boulevards and side streets. Tow trucks righted the upturned cars. Workmen cleared the debris. On the floor and galleries of the Sorbonne's main hall the students dressed their wounds and crowded a revolutionary teach-in. In the Latin Quarter the statue of Victor Hugo wore an NLF flag poled through the arm held to his chin in thought.

Salem met with the Standing Committee and a member of the French Government. At his representation the second plenary session was postponed. Protection was to be provided next day on the approaches to the place de l'Opéra. Police would henceforth escort the American delegation.

In the Salle des Fêtes the envoys from the civilized world gathered in speculation.

That afternoon, in disordered mood, the Health and Social Services Committee met. There was to be no peace from the great white whale of Vietnam. Its nemesis tormented the Americans as Moby Dick had tormented Ahab. As soon as business began the Cuban delegate took the floor on the issue of Vietnam relief.

Pale, determined, his voice strong with emotion, the spokesman for the American Red Cross got to his feet in reply: 'The American Government, the American Red Cross, a score of unallied aid organizations, has bent every effort towards Vietnam relief. Every practical step is being taken to assist civilian recovery. The United States of America spends three times as much on the Vietnam aid programme as on aid for all thirty-eight of the new nations on the African continent.'

The Albanian delegate broke in. 'I am glad that the American delegate has raised——'

'I am not finished, sir!'

The Albanian shouted him down. '——has raised the detail of American aid. The whole world is aware that American aid is a new form of colonialism, a means of imposing American political policy. Everyone knows that American aid is mostly a matter of strings. What are these strings in Vietnam? The Indian delegation can tell us about the conditions imposed on his country for American famine relief.'

Mick East's Indian friend, Jog Chatterji, rose and pushed on his glasses. 'I am saying something, I think so. There has been much of this. I am saying one thing and there should be no more about it in this committee. America's P-140 wheat shipments to my country were made under the Food for Peace Act. There was an insistence, not a condition, that Indian Government agree not to trade with either Cuba or North Vietnam. In Bihar last year, on that side, sixteen millions were threatened by death from famine. The Food for Peace is saving many on that side. American Government has stated that there was no intention of forcing Indian Government not to trade. It was felt that a gesture along these lines from Delhi would be appreciated in Washington. That is all about it, I think so.'

Gratefully, the American delegates extended thanks. 'May I add that at the time the Indian Government had no trade with North Vietnam? One can hardly discontinue a non-existent trade. As for Cuba, the commerce in Indian jute continues today unaltered.'

The East Germans claimed attention. 'The undebatable fact about civilian relief in South Vietnam is that the American Congress has already slashed the budget. Corruption and piracy by the puppet Government...'

Martin Neveau lit a cigarette and coughed. There was no escape from the sickening quagmire. The conference was foundering in politics as he was foundering in exhaustion and frustration. Vietnam! Vietnam! It was in everything and on everything like a putrefaction.

38

MITCHELL had booked a room and bath for Sarah in a comfortable hotel in the Latin Quarter. They were to dine in the Bois de Boulogne, a discreet enough distance away from the risk of chance meetings.

Neveau had been looking ill, thinned by the past weeks. His cheeks had sagged, elongating his face, diminishing the familiar impression of complacency. There had been a touch of wildness in his instructions, an uncertainty, a vagueness of concentration. Pity for him, a lurch of guilt, surprised Mitchell. Contempt for the cuckold was briefly replaced by understanding. When a man's down you don't kick him. He reminded himself that you don't get sentimental either. When you want something, need it like Mitchell did, you can't take it bleating. Neveau had had his chances with Sarah—years and years of chances. He was Swiss to the backbone, dull to the backbone, smug to the heels of his boots.

In the telephone-room he called the hotel again. She must have arrived by this time. She should have answered a half hour ago. He twiddled on a paper-clip.

'Yes? Who is it?'

Mitchell filled with peace. Her voice went through him and eased him like the effulgence of a strong drink.

'Sarah? It's Ted. When did you get in?'

'Just now.'

'Do you like the room?'

'It's very gay. One could wash a horse in the bath.'

'I've been anxious. Where have you been?'

'I stopped off to do a little shopping.'

It discontented Mitchell that Sarah had not gone to the hotel directly, hurrying to wait for his call.

'Ted, I bought a newspaper. What on earth has been happening?'

'A riot. I'll tell you about it at dinner. Can you be ready in an hour?'

'I'll be ready. Was anyone hurt? The paper says the Indian delegation lost their limousine. Was Martin there? Is Martin all right?'

Mitchell bleakened. 'Yes, he was there. Yes, he's all right. Can you see your Swiss husband getting caught in a riot?'

Sarah gave a doubtful laugh. 'I suppose not. Where are we going for dinner? I hope it's a quiet place.'

'It's to hell and gone out in the Bois. You'll be seen by a few ducks and Frenchmen.'

'In an hour, then.'

'In an hour.'

Mitchell put down the telephone. In ways he could hardly define, Sarah always managed to disappoint him. He had wanted to hear her excitement. He had wanted her to consider nothing but him.

In the Hilton the State Department leader introduced Joseph Richter to the CIA representative and the Information Services chief from the Paris Embassy.

'Joe works out of Geneva. He has special knowledge of the ICRC and has worked with Neveau and Salem. If you want a personal rundown on these guys, Joe might be able to help. All right, what do we have for openers?'

The CIA man brushed cigarette ash off his knee. He was deeply tanned from a ski-ing holiday. 'It's not that we didn't know something might come off, we didn't know when or where. This was a buttoned-up deal. The demonstrations here and in other capitals are more than a few students goofing off. This is organization, disciplined all down the line. They work them to a timetable. There were hard core here from four or five countries. Next time it will be maybe Amsterdam or Berlin.'

'Right now it's Paris,' the leader said.

'That's the name of the game. This one was timed for the conference. It hasn't ended with this morning.'

'How do you estimate the intention?'

'One: intimidate the delegates. Two: influence the delegates by demonstrating NLF support among students, workmen, men in the street.'

'This morning was purely students, wasn't it?'

'Mostly. It's spreading. There's word about a big lock-in brewing at the Renault works. We can't place this Salem. The word is that he's going it alone. Maybe you know something, Joe?'

It wasn't a secret. Everybody knew the rumour. Richter wanted to convey that his information was privileged. 'The position here is that Salem is out of control. He and Chairman Neveau have been fighting a stand-off. We know that Salem deliberately inspired that Press blow-up about the plague. Every move he has made controverts the neutrality of his office. The International Committee in Geneva is split. They've got ghosts in their heads about the use in Vietnam of nuclear tactical weapons. You know—the old powder-keg syndrome? Neveau got close to getting the committee behind him. He knows that Salem could wreck the International. There wasn't enough time. He couldn't get the committee to a vote of censure.'

The CIA man was careful. 'You can take it that today's nastiness was organized out of Cambodia by the NLF. We're not in doubt about that. There is some reason to believe that President Salem made contact with the NLF in Saigon. Question: is this guy committed, is he tied into the action, or has he got a bat in his belfry?'

'Joe?' the State Department leader prompted. Richter was careful too. He wasn't sure if the CIA man was informed about Milos Jelié. 'There's not a great deal known about Salem's interests. He inherited a bank. He has been active academically. His private life's clean. We've got nothing there. I think maybe your people might be digging deeper.'

'The Jelié inquiry?'

Richter nodded. 'Yes. Anything come up on that?'

'We're waiting for Jelié now. The agency has an analysis on Salem's movements in Saigon. If there's anything sinister we want it quick.

308

Would Neveau act if we could hand him something?'

Richter looked grave. 'You can depend on it. Right now I'm helping Neveau put together an anti-Salem lobby.'

'Where does Robert Collins stand?'

'Negative,' Richter said. 'Collins is playing the other side. He's one jump away from black power.'

'I see.' The agent tapped his cigarette. 'We can't expect anything there, then.'

The leader scrubbed his face, got up to freshen his drink. 'What I want to know is whether we're going to be embarrassed again. Headlines like today's are hard on the administration. We're working in a hostile climate at this conference.'

The Information Services chief looked thoughtful. 'I've got a few travelling scholarships left in my grant. Maybe they can be used as a come-on among the leaders of the responsible student element.'

The agent nodded. 'Maybe. You have to be real careful in that area. You can't fart in this town without the lefties smelling a reactionary plot. The thing is, the lid will be slammed on the entire quarter around the Grand. The instruction came from the top. When Long Charlie speaks you'd better believe it.'

The State Department man was grey and decent and wearied. 'It's got to where nothing we do is right. You know and I know that these demonstrations around the world, the attacks on the Embassies, the hostile Press, the Bertrand Russell movement to try LBJ for war crimes, the petitions from scientists, the pressure on the dollar, the dissent at home, it all gets back to that goddamned war. There's a world-wide conspiracy to put the administration over a barrel. Sometimes I wonder if we've got any friends left anywhere. Sometimes I wonder how long the administration can hold out.'

It was too frank. Richter looked at the CIA man in embarrassment, coughed and lowered his eyes.

The agent said, 'I understand your delegations are to be provided with police escort.'

The leader blew smoke, looking through the window to the river. 'I've asked the Ambassador to kill that. It would make a great news picture, wouldn't it, our cars needing police protection? Every goddamned paper in the world would print it.'

He put down his glass. 'Well, gentlemen, I'm grateful for your information. If you'll excuse me I have to change. Stay on and kick the ball around. Joe will fix you a drink.'

The restaurant was quiet, romantically placed on the river, countrified and middle-class. In the weekends the burghers of Paris brought their families, fed the ducks, fished the river-bank in waistcoats. On other days and evenings it profited by the discretion of location, a place of middle-aged men and younger women, low-voiced and intent.

Mitchell poured the Champagne. Sarah was flushed with wine, her eyes bright. She was good like this. Tonight he could get her drunk. For the first time they were free of Neveau and the need of pretence.

She leaned forward, amused, and touched Mitchell's moustache with her finger.

'What's that for?'

'Grey hairs, my dear. You're getting old.'

Mitchell frowned and brushed at his lip. He hadn't noticed them. It confirmed his worried feeling that life was getting away.

Sarah left him to powder her nose. He watched her go, the soft round of her hips and tail, the strong shapely legs and quick carriage. She was beautifully made, more beautiful than could be guessed at in clothing. Women like Sarah wore well. She would keep her girl's figure.

Mitchell sighed with satisfaction. It was going to be a great night.

Later, blurred a little by the second bottle, he caught the meaning in her eyes. They're all bitches he thought, they thrive on deceit as naturally as a man does on food. He'd been a bastard himself, but there was no indecency, no brutality, no deadness of consideration, that a woman could not serenely perform for her own gratification. He thought of Neveau, sweating away there in the rooms and corridors trying to hold something together. He'd be grey and sick and making his fight for something outside himself. Just now he'd be able to use a little love and support. You've got it, Neveau, Mitchell thought. You've got it where the chicken got the axe.

Sarah snapped her fingers. 'Where are you? What are you thinking about?'

'Women,' Mitchell said. He lifted his glass. 'To women. The only opposite sex we've got.'

Sarah covered her glass with her hand. 'Ted you'll have me tipsy.'

'Drunk is the word. Maiden aunts get tipsy, and what does it matter? This is one night you don't have to go home. In the Australian idiom, I propose to get as full as a Wellington boot.'

'Something's worrying you. What is it?'

'You.'

'Me?'

'You! This conversation sounds Chinese. Let's dance. Can you dance?'

'I'm a very sexual dancer.'

Mitchell got up. 'That figures.'

They danced for a long time, dreaming with the other couples. It was a good feeling between them, the music gay and Gallic. Mitchell was already tight, filling with emotion at the hold and touch of her. He stopped.

'Now, what is it?'

'Let's sit down. I want to talk.'

He ordered brandy and coffee, silent until they were served. Sarah shook her hair, lifting it off her neck. Her skin glowed. She lit a cigarette. 'You're funny tonight.'

'I'm funny, all right. I'm a scream.'

'Ted, what is it? Are you sorry you asked me to come?'

'Hardly.'

'Why on earth are you so jumpy, then?'

'I've been thinking. About us. Right back to the beginning. I've been thinking that if you could do what you've done to Neveau, you could also do it to me.'

Sarah changed. Her eyes darkened. She ground out the cigarette. 'I'm sorry you had to say that.'

'Would you? Would you do the same thing to me?'

Her voice was cold. 'It hardly arises, does it.'

'It could arise. I want to marry you.'

Sarah's astonishment widened and widened. All kinds of words tumbled now into Mitchell. He swallowed them down.

'Have you any idea what you're saying?'

'I'm saying I want to marry you. I want to get out of Europe and take you with me.'

She shook her head in disbelief. 'Ted, I've got a son. I've got a home, a husband.'

'You haven't got a son. He's Neveau's son. If you cared a damn for your husband you wouldn't be here.'

Sarah's thoughts were incoherent. She was moved, faintly triumphant that Mitchell had come to this. She looked at his well-featured face, swollen with wine and feeling, the lines of indulgence and self-concern. 'You're not the marrying kind, Ted. No, my dear, this is an impulse. It will pass.'

He had got it said. It had filled up in him until it spilled. He couldn't bear the prospect of rejection. 'Sarah, I love you. I can't make it any more with other women. This isn't an impulse. I've thought of nothing else for months. You've got no life with Neveau. Nobody knows that better than you. For Christ's sake marry me, I'm sick of my life.' He waited, bent forward, watched her face sadden with understanding.

'You're sick of your life, are you? You want to change it for yourself, and I'm convenient. That isn't love, Ted. Love is wanting something for someone else.'

'Sarah, I mean it. You've got to believe that. We're suited to each other—we're great together. Jesus, you wouldn't know yourself if you got off the chain. You'd be crazy about Australia. We could get a house on the beach.'

She touched his hand. 'You mustn't tempt me. I haven't the character for it.'

Mitchell tried not to sound desperate. 'Give it time. Give yourself time to think about it. You've got a nothing life with Neveau. We both need to change. We could make the change for each other. Neveau doesn't need you, Sarah.'

She looked away, gone to a great distance. 'He used to.'

He had to break her from that. It frightened him. 'Come on. Let's go back to town. I'll buy you a drink in an Arab place I know.'

Mitchell left Sarah's hotel for his own early in the morning. There had been a wonderful difference in her love-making, a deeper, truer giving. Mitchell thought of it as wifely. That was the way it could be. And she couldn't have meant it. She couldn't have meant it would be over between them when she returned to Geneva. She had said that before. She had come back to him, stepping naked from her clothing in the hotel bedroom, overwhelming him with her predatory will. He remembered her eyes when he had spent himself and opened his—the hard, mocking reflection, seeing through him to the nothingness inside.

Mitchell was frightened. He was cold and shaken and frightened. He had somehow lost his rule over Sarah. Somehow, he must win it back.

39

On rising, Salem switched on the engaged sign. He breakfasted alone, worked for an hour, and lay in his dressing-gown on the bed. He had prepared himself at this time yesterday. The violence of the riot, the day-long confusion, the meetings and discussions at night, the shouting headlines in the Parisian Press were all in him as confirmation. Among the delegations and committees he walked alone. They opened to make him passage, conjecture in their eyes. Their voices closed behind him like water over dropped stones.

He was alone and among them alone. They waited for him to make it happen. Salem closed his eyes and stilled his breathing, as he did in the void of the headstand. His long arms stretched at his sides, palms up. His mind darkened and sought for peace.

Monsieur Hylot laid down his gavel. The interpreters tensed in their boxes. In the galleries under the baroque ceiling of the Salle des Fêtes photographers shuffled and lined the balustrades. The auditorium silenced. They were black, brown, yellow and white. All the races of man. The hush on the massed floor was like an aching. Slowly, Salem raised his head. For a long minute, graven, he held there under the mesmerizing eyes. The joined breath in the great room came to him ruffled like a wind in trees.

He gave himself no command to rise and stand alone, rehearsed no word or sentence. He was as impelled in his body as in his mind.

'This great International which Henri Dunant founded was conceived in compassion and horror one hundred and six years ago on the awful battlefield at Castiglione. Henri Dunant was one man, a simple man, wearing a white suit. In him, on that day, was mysteriously realized the charity and brotherly love which has contended with man's bestial inheritance since the beginning of civilization.

'Today, one man like Henri Dunant, I stand to ask this great congregation to reaffirm with me the beauties of love, the godliness of compassion, the future hope which without these must vanish together with man and all his works in the last conflagration.

'Do not suppose that I ask this in meekness and supplication. I ask and demand it in the righteous wrath of all men outraged by evil. I demand it for all those whose voices can never be heard, who needlessly suffer at the hands of madmen reasoning the world to its grave.' Salem stopped and swallowed. A vein swelled and beat in his temple. Below him the tilted faces were as fixed as a photograph.

'In every land the beast walks paramount on the earth. In every land indifference, self-interest and complacency are joined to bigotry, hatred and savagery. In every land the cry of the starving and imprisoned and mutilated beseeches us to be heard.

'The force of those weapons of mass destruction which have become the crown of man's achievement, the nuclear bombs whose cataclysm involves the deepest secret of nature, the diseases and gases and poisons laboured over in laboratories by scientists, the spy satellites that orbit space, the bombing platforms to be put there, are terrible evidence of a species become insane.

'There are those in the world who believe that the time is already seven minutes to midnight, that the slavering ape in the brain of man has devoured all opposition, that by accident, or intent, all mankind's agony and aspiration will be cancelled and made for ever fruitless.'

At his table Martin Neveau stared up, oblivious to all except the words. Seven minutes to midnight. It was this that Salem had meant.

'Those who deny the disappearing margin which connects our children to the future are liars. Those who excuse atrocity in the name of ideology, politics, nationalism are the monsters men become when they maim their own humanity. We cannot plead lack of instruction. A generation ago in this city, across Europe and into Russia, millions died in ovens for an accident of birth or were strangled on butcher's hooks for their courage.'

Again he stopped. Again they waited, scarcely moving.

'I am not unaware that the request I will make will be considered unconstitutional by many. I am not unaware of the risk to the stability of this International, or of the opposition which will confront me. It will be four years before this great parliament gathers again. Events cannot wait another four years for condemnation to be raised, for help to be promised the helpless, hope revived in the hopeless, the boundless possibilities of the future returned uncorrupted to our children.'

Salem's voice hoarsened. 'In all the carnage and mess of the world one adventure prevails as a horror without present parallel. Vietnam!

'The mightiest nation in the world has concentrated there the most awful arsenal of weapons ever seen. The flesh of men, women and children is put to the torch of phosphorus and napalm. Water is poisoned in the wells. The crops of the field and the trees of the forest are withered to the earth. Thousands of hamlets and villages have been consumed by flame in the relocations, their people herded into camps, their land and the tombs of their ancestors blackened into the cinder of free fire zones.

'In this dreadful place even civilized pretence is abandoned. The protocols and conventions built by man for his own restraint are abrogated and derided. Torture of prisoners and their summary execution has become routine. For every North Vietnamese or Viet Cong soldier killed, three and perhaps five civilians die.

'The conscience of the world is involved in Vietnam. The meaning and significance of this International, the great humanitarian responsibility of the charter, is as much on trial in that sad place as is man himself.

'I am told that this International can only exist by fierce allegiance to its neutrality. I reject this with scorn and passion. There must be an end to mute neutrality where there is no other collected voice to speak.

'Men of the civilized world, add your voices to mine. There is no place so distant that our outcry will not be heard. The war in Vietnam must be condemned. On behalf of all I demand it!'

Salem stood in the echo of his words, alight with the force of his passion. In the boxes the interpreters stared through the glass, as captured as the crowded delegates. Painfully, the waiting continued. It was as though they required his permission to break silence.

'I thank you. I thank you all.'

In that release the first groups began to applaud. Others came to their feet, shouting. The uproar became turmoil. On the floor of the Salle des Fêtes the procedure of order collapsed. Debate and contention flamed between the tables. On the podium, white-faced and ineffective, Hylot pounded and pounded his gavel, shrilling unheard into the microphone.

Neveau took his head in his shaking hands. A century of reason and order and neutrality was to be laid waste by one man's intransigence. He pushed himself up. 'Stop it. Stop it, stop it.'

Flashlights exploded on the galleries. Photographers pushed to the floor.

Hylot was on his feet. 'Adjourned. Adjourned. Come to order. Adjourned...'

He turned to Robert Collins, waving the gavel about his head. 'Clear this podium. President Salem, clear this podium. I order this podium cleared.'

Collins stood behind Salem's chair. 'It would be best, Pierre. When they see we have gone they will become quieter.'

There was no answer from Salem. He was drained, disorganized by the reaction.

'Pierre, do you hear me?' With his fingers on Salem's arm the big Negro walked him to the exit in the wing.

Behind them Hylot flourished his gavel and then with fine temperament tossed it from him. Joseph Richter and the American delegates began to shoulder from the room.

Collins pulled the door shut, switched on the sign and expelled his breath. He went to the bar and mixed two large brandies. 'Here. How do you feel?'

Salem smiled a little, took the glass. 'Grateful for this,' He drank. 'I believe you're worried about me, Robert.'

'Not worried. Concerned. I didn't anticipate such an effect. We've left an all-out fight down there.'

'What will happen?'

'There will be a lobby to kill the motion. A lobby for a vote of censure. A lobby to remove your address from the minutes. The constitution will be invoked.'

'I am prepared for that. There is provision in the constitution for initiative in the service of peace. Our work in the Cuban missile crisis provides a further precedent.'

Collins smiled at his friend, comforted and a little surprised by the calm and strength that armed him. 'Pierre, you will have no peace until the session resumes. There's going to be a line outside your door and mine. I must go now. I will do what I can. Try and eat something before we reconvene. If you want me, ask for the bedroom extension or send a message.'

Almost together both telephones rang, jumping their nerves like a starting signal.

Collins waved. 'There. It has begun. Good luck, Pierre.'

Salem inclined his head, almost formally. 'I am ready. I have been ready, Robert, for a long time.'

Mitchell held the telephone and waited to be connected, checking the statement he and Neveau had dictated. It said, without detail, that President Salem had proposed a motion pressing for peace negotiations between the hostile forces in Vietnam. The motion would be debated in the afternoon's plenary session.

When Sarah answered, he said, 'Look, I'm sorry, I won't be able to join you for lunch. Salem blew his top his morning. No, I can't go into it now, I'll tell you about it this evening.'

He cupped the telephone and looked up. 'What is it?'

'The Press is waiting, Mr Mitchell.'

'I'm coming. Get off my back, will you?'

He waited until he was alone. 'Sarah, have you thought about what I asked you last night? I want you to know I meant it. I never meant anything more.'

He didn't want to let her go, needed her voice to reassure him. 'Until this evening, then. Think about it.'

In the Salle des Fêtes, separated into groups the delegations dealt and argued. Emissaries trafficked between the executive suites, rode the elevators and negotiated in the corridors. In the Café de la Paix and the Pacific the regular clientèle arrived for lunch to discover themselves crowded out. Flagged limousines hurried between the Hilton, the Majestic and the Crillon. In the American Embassy the Ambassador made a priority call to the State Department.

In the last minutes before Monsieur Hylot reopened the session with a heated admonition, banging his gavel as punctuation and emphasis, Salem received Martin Neveau.

In the conflict between them, something had remained. Now, in crisis, it was evidenced. Neveau looked desperately haggard, patched beneath the eyes, his blue shirt bagged and uncared for. Salem was moved by sadness that their courses had been so irreparably opposite. 'I was expecting your call, Martin. Come, take a chair. Have you eaten? Will you join me in a sandwich and coffee?'

Neveau shook his head. 'Thanks. No. I've had coffee.' He lit a cigarette and coughed. 'I'm tired. The last four days have been greatly tiring. You know why I'm here, President?'

'Yes, Martin. I think so.'

'It's not too late—it's not too late to withdraw your motion.'

Salem said, 'Martin, Martin, you don't understand, do you? Even now?'

'Understand? It is you who doesn't understand. You've never understood. If you gain this motion, the American Society will withdraw from the League. Collins is aware of that, he has been given warning. It will be America's moral and legal right to do so. Their allies in Vietnam will follow. Australia, New Zealand, Thailand, South Korea. It will be the beginning of the end.'

'If the war in Vietnam continues, Martin, it could be the beginning of a much more terrible end. You know and I know that the Pentagon recommended the use of an atomic bomb to relieve the French at Dieu Bien Phu.'

Neveau put up his hand. 'That is not our business. I don't want to hear. If this motion is moved, the administration in Washington will be forced either to announce an initiative for peace or be pilloried as criminals by the world's one humanitarian International. The position would be intolerable.'

Salem said, 'I'm sorry, Martin.'

'Sorry! If you don't rid yourself of this folly you *will* be sorry. You've let yourself become obsessed, President. You can't see beyond your obsession.'

Salem hardened. 'I want nothing for myself, Martin. I have taken this stand for others.'

'For yourself?' Neveau became excited. 'Do you think I am fighting for myself? I am fighting for others. Fighting to save this International and its great work for others. I joined this movement as a boy, as a boy, to work for others. I know what war means. My parents died under bombing. What do you know about that? I was an orphan, an orphan, at twelve.'

Salem went sadly to the bar and poured two brandies. 'Here, Martin. Join me.'

'I don't want it.' But he took the glass, sipped and swallowed the measure.

'Are you going to rescind this motion?'

'I cannot, Martin.'

Neveau straightened and shook a finger at Salem. 'Then you must be stopped. Whatever it takes, I must stop you. Whatever.'

Salem said, his voice soft, 'I'm sorry, Martin. I am truly sorry that it has come to this between us.'

At the door, Neveau turned, his lips quivering. 'Remember. I tried to reason. I warned you. Remember that.'

Salem stood, his eyes on the slammed door. He put down his drink, untouched.

40

HYLOT finished, banging the gavel.

'This is the last warning the chair will give this conference. Now let us proceed. I recognize the delegate from Australia.' In the negotiations this had been agreed with Hylot. He sat back and folded his neat hands.

'Mr Chairman, the motion proposed in this chamber this morning by the President of the ICRC is an outrage, to use his own favourite word, of all precedent and procedure. It is overt introduction of politics, in defiance of the constitution. In the first plenary session the chair forbade political discussion and ruled that the Albanian delegate's hysterical words be struck from the minutes. Will the chair exercise a like discipline in the matter of its distinguished president?'

A growl of agreement and dissent rumbled the assembly.

Hylot leaned over his microphone and pinched on his glasses. 'The President has provided the chair with a legal argument. Attention is drawn to Resolution Ten of the twentieth International conference. I quote: All Governments are urged to settle their disputes by peaceful means in the spirit of international law. President Salem contends that this resolution provides his motion with a constitutional base.'

Hylot banged the gavel as warning. He waited for quiet before continuing. 'Further, the conference is reminded of the precedent of the Cuban missile crisis in which the ICRC agreed to be involved on a score of special urgency in the immediate threat of nuclear war.

'It is President Salem's submission that present risk, associated with the abrogation of Conventions and Protocols and the breaking of international law, has created a situation in which his motion is justified by both precedent and Resolution Ten of the constitution.'

Hylot paused importantly. 'The Chair has given concentrated attention to this submission and has consulted on it with Chairman Collins of the Red Cross League. It is the ruling of the Chair that this conference should debate President Salem's motion.' Hylot banged his gavel in self-congratulation and pinched off his glasses.

In the cover of raised voices, Joseph Richter turned to the State Department delegation. 'Collins,' he said. 'Mark that. Collins is backing Salem.'

As Salem rose, the Salle des Fêtes stilled. He waited until the great room was almost silent, putting the passion of the morning from him, using the tone and voice in which he lectured the faculty of international law.

'Mr Chairman, delegates. I submit that the points we should debate are these: The unequalled and unjustified suffering of the civilians in Vietnam, the illegal torment and torture of war prisoners, the illegal use of chemical weapons contrary to the Geneva Protocols and the storage in Thailand of bacteriological weapons of mass destruction.'

Immediately the Thailand delegate rose, protesting. 'There is no proof of this. There is no connection with the South Vietnamese people's struggle to be free. I demand the withdrawal of any discussion based on rumour.'

Hylot banged his gavel. 'Sustained. Nothing will be discussed that has not been proven.'

Salem nodded. 'The Chairman's ruling is noted. When the question of bacteriological weapons arises, all necessary proof will be furnished. May I now return to the matter of civilian suffering in Vietnam?'

He held up a document. 'This morning I made mention of a technique of ground clearance which the Americans call relocations. In brief, this involves the arbitrary removal of up to six thousand villagers from their homes in a single operation. These villagers are then rehoused in refugee camps at some distance from their ancient settlements, together with all their portable belongings. This forcible wrenching of hundreds of thousands of civilians from their homes, villages and property, the subsequent destruction of everything that stands, of the wells, the crops and the buildings, is without punitive excuse. There is not and has never been claim that these villagers are active VC. The NLF characterize themselves as fish that swim in the water of the people. The relocations are based on the theory that if the water of the people is removed, the VC fish will die.

'I refer this conference to the Universal Declaration of Human Rights, decreed for international celebration in this year by the body of the United Nations. There is hardly a declaration in this great instrument which the relocations in Vietnam do not most barbarously offend.

'Article 3: Everyone has the right to life, liberty and security of person.

'Article 12: Nobody shall be subjected to arbitrary interference with his privacy, family, home or correspondence, nor to attacks upon his honour or reputation. Everyone has the right to the protection of the law against such interference or attacks.

'Article 17: No one shall be arbitrarily deprived of his property.

'Article 19: No one shall be subjected to arbitrary arrest, detention or exile.'

Salem had recited from memory. He let the report drop from his hand.

'Unhappily, there are many other articles in the Declaration of Human Rights from which I could quote in this context. I ask you to read the facts of the Vietnam relocations and to ask yourselves by what right every fundamental law of life and place and property should be thus consumed and obliterated there by foreign armies.'

In the stir on the floor Salem waited for a challenge. Again it came from the Australian delegation. 'Does the President pretend that these relocations are not aimed, at least in part, at the protection of civilians from VC terror?'

Salem spoke with contempt. 'Does the delegate from Australia pretend that the burning of living places, the forced detention of farmers and fishermen in barbed wire reception centres, the destruction of gardens, fields and solid structures by artillery and airstrike, the declaration of these areas as free fire zones on which anything that moves is a target for killing, that all of these acts of savagery are committed in the name of protection?'

322

The Australian sought firmer ground. 'I didn't say that. This rhetoric confuses the point. I simply said——'

Salem ignored him.

'The deliberate making of refugees is separate to the desperate situation of the civilians killed and wounded by air and ground fire. It is to this I direct your attention. I know of no conflict in which the ratio of bloodletting between civilians and troops has been so terribly and consistently disproportionate.'

Again the mixed growl of agreement and dissent interrupted Salem's address. Again he quietly waited.

'I believe that there has been conspiracy to conceal the magnitude of civilian casualties lest an outcry go around the world. Repeated requests to United States official sources for these figures have met with equivocation and evasion.'

The growl loudened and persevered. Richter looked to the State Department delegation's leader. He shook his head, white and tense.

'I have obtained through special sources, estimates of this ratio that vary between three and five civilians killed—not wounded or maimed, gentlemen, but killed—for every Viet Cong or North Vietnamese soldier.'

He held up his hand. 'No. Wait. The American Dr Spock has stated from his investigations that one million Vietnamese children have been killed, wounded or burned.' Salem's voice roughened and shook. 'Children, gentlemen. Helpless, innocent children.'

In the disturbance that rose again, Salem composed himself. 'If the official American count of enemy dead is multiplied by three and five, this would give the range of civilian casualties. The Pentagon figure for enemy killed since 1961 is two hundred thousand. Thus, by this multiplication, we arrive at a sum of civilian casualties of between four hundred thousand and one million.'

Richter received his signal and leaped up, dominating the seated delegates under his height. 'My delegation utterly rejects this hearsay figure and the convenience of President Salem's mathematics. We are witnessing here this afternoon a spectacle that must be repugnant to every responsible delegation and Government. The spectacle of the President of the International, the last person of whom it would be expected, engaged in a scurrilous attack on a member nation whose contribution to the cost of Red Cross works is sufficient testimony to its charity and generosity.'

Cries of 'Hear, Hear!' rose in support. The Cuban delegation began a slow clapping. Hylot banged his gavel and called for order.

'What is not in debate is the twenty thousand civilians murdered by the VC. The police chiefs, schoolteachers and political cadres, those leaders of free opinion who stood in the way of Communist subversion and terror. It is to planned, selective and ruthless massacre like this that President Salem should bend his attention. It is unfortunate that there is no official figure of civilians killed or wounded accidentally in allied actions, but there is a great moral difference between accidental hurt and the cynicism of selective murder.'

The Albanian and Russian delegates were up shouting, before one deferred to the other. 'Does it make any difference to the million children killed, wounded and burned, that they suffered by accident?'

'What is accidental about the relocations?'

The leader of the NLF delegation spoke for the first time, waving his arms, using French. 'The puppet Government inside Saigon represents nobody but racketeers and landlords. Those executed were traitors and enemies of the people. I deny the American pirates' figure of twenty thousand. There have been millions of civilians murdered by the allied gangsters. Here I have figures——'

Monsieur Hylot clattered his inescapable gavel, his small face congesting. 'Order. I demand order. There will be no repetition of this morning's display. Unless the floor comes to order immediately this session will again be adjourned.'

Gradually, the disturbance subsided. Salem addressed the chair. 'May I continue?'

Hylot waved, mollified.

'When I began this address I proposed to the conference that I would make certain points for debate and that, where necessary, I would provide substantiation of these terrible claims. In the matter of Vietnamese civilians killed and wounded there is unarguable testimony enough. I will provide this to you later and it will not be convenient mathematics as the American State Department representative has suggested.

'It is common knowledge that torture and mutilation of prisoners is practised by both sides in this barbarous war. None of the Governments involved, foreign or indigenous, has made any serious attempt to deny this. Press reports and news film have clearly depicted the sadism. In the library of the ICRC, which for reasons of its neutrality makes no public release of its reports, there is film record of these tortures. One segment shows NLF prisoners confined in a steel box in which they can neither stand nor stretch. The box is in an open space, positioned to receive the full blast of the tropical sun.

'An NLF agent taken prisoner in Da Nang, cut out his own tongue so that he could not be made to talk under torture.

'Article 5 of the Universal Declaration of Human Rights affirms that no one shall be subjected to torture or cruel, inhuman or degrading treatment or punishment.

'Today, in a world in which all civilized values are set at naught, it is our inescapable responsibility to cry halt and warning.

'On my return last year from South Vietnam, shocked by what I had seen, I appealed personally to a high American official. His reply gave me no great comfort. It said, in part, that those involved in aggression against the Republic of Vietnam rely heavily on disguise and disregard generally accepted principles of warfare. From the outset it has therefore been difficult to develop programmes and procedures to resolve fully all the problems arising in the application of the provisions of the Conventions. He said that continued refinement of these programmes and procedures in the light of experience will thus undoubtedly be necessary.'

Salem laid down his notes. 'He concluded his message with these words: "The United States Government will co-operate fully with the ICRC in its traditional humanitarian mission in Vietnam."'

At his front seat Martin Neveau rose slowly. He stood and waited. The murmur that began in the delegations about him spread across the floor. Neveau was looking directly at Salem, his knuckles on the table.

Hylot said uncertainly, 'I recognize Monsieur Neveau, Chairman of the ICRC.'

Neveau turned a little, to include both the floor and the podium. 'I did not expect to find myself in contention with the distinguished President of the International. However, that is as it may be.'

He sounded dull and wearied. 'The world movement has done all that can be done to alleviate suffering in Vietnam. There is neither point nor product in this afternoon's rhetoric. It only divides us and exacerbates political passions. Politics and levelling blame are not our business. Let me remind this conference of what has already been done in Vietnam.

'Bearing in mind the many photographs showing the abuse of prisoners, I long ago took this matter up in my capacity as executive chairman. This was before the International was to benefit by the devotion to humanitarian principles of our present distinguished President. Long before that.'

Neveau had addressed himself directly to the podium. He resumed his former position.

'By way of reply the Government of South Vietnam furnished the ICRC with a file of atrocities attributed to the NLF. It also invited the committee to investigate the plight of prisoners held by the Democratic Republic of North Vietnam. We took this matter up.

'The Government of North Vietnam and its Red Cross replied that they did not consider the American captives as prisoners of war and that consequently the third convention did not apply. The Government holds that the bombing attacks on the north constitute a crime for which these prisoners will have to answer in courts.

'All requests by the ICRC to the Red Cross of the NLF and the Red Cross of North Vietnam, to return lists of prisoners held and to authorize correspondence with their families and the receipt of food parcels and medical comforts have been met with total rejection.

'The ICRC's efforts to offer the NLF assistance through its representatives in Prague, Moscow and Algiers have evoked no response. Similarly, the offer made to provide medical teams for their sick and wounded was also ignored. These contacts were broken off by unilateral NLF decision.

'Let me turn your attention to South Vietnam. All members of the armed forces of that Republic have been given instruction in the application of the Geneva Conventions. The Red Cross of that country has had the third and fourth conventions translated and distributed to army commanders.

'There is no provision in our great charter for the coercion of members of Governments. Those signatory to the Conventions and Protocols are involved only in conscience. Everything that can be done in Vietnam is being done. President Salem's insistence here is both dangerous and irrelevant.'

Neveau stopped and took a deep breath. 'I hereby declare, to every member of this parliament, my opposition. I declare it both individually and as Chairman of the International Committee.'

Hylot made no attempt to still the outburst on the floor. He was looking at Salem's strained face. Collins leaned over to Hylot and whispered. He nodded and banged the gavel.

'This session is adjourned for one hour of free discussion. It will resume at four-thirty.'

Salem gathered his papers and walked to the exit in the wings. On the floor Neveau was trying to free himself of those milled about him. At Joseph Richter's table the State Department men huddled heads.

41

TED MITCHELL slammed his office door and took a bottle of whisky from a drawer. After the fireworks of the morning and afternoon the second plenary session could continue until any hour. He would have his briefings to make, hand-outs to distribute, questions to answer. It could be late before he finished. He had told Sarah to expect him at seven. To hell with everything.

He needed to see her. He had been too intense last night, should have played it with a lighter hand, and prepared her better. Perhaps he could get away after adjournment for a half-hour. Meet for a drink, be gay and off-hand, confuse her by pressing nothing. Mitchell was trying to think of somewhere close and safe when his door opened.

'Chairman Neveau wants you in his suite right away, Mr Mitchell.'

'Thanks for nothing,' Mitchell said, imagining Neveau's dull badgering voice, the look and manner of him so like a seedy schoolmaster. How could she live with a man like that? What could she possibly owe him? To take her away would be an act of charity.

Mitchell swallowed the whisky and went grimly to the elevators.

At four-fifteen Robert Collins cleared his suite. He would be with President Salem, he told his aide. He would accept no more calls before resumption of session.

Salem let him in. He was quiet, suppressed. 'Have they been at you, Pierre?'

'I haven't had a call. What does it mean?'

'The lobbies are being lined up. It's in the open now that Neveau has declared his position. There's a good deal of excitement, Pierre.'

'I expected there would be.' Salem put his coffee on the bar, his back turned. 'It isn't every day that a division within the committee becomes the stuff of public debate.'

'Neveau is very determined, Pierre. The American influence gives him massive support. If you have any doubt, any regret, you should consider it now.'

Salem remained turned. He spoke as though to himself. 'I walked in the embers of a village, Robert, in which every soul had been incinerated. I've seen hatred of the white man so implacable it terrifies. I've seen rent bodies jammed into hospital sheds that reeked like charnel houses. I've seen the despair of the old, the agony of children, the hopelessness of the helpless.'

Salem turned. 'No, Robert. I have no doubt, although it is human to have regrets. Somebody must accept the responsibility. I have chosen to do so. I owe it, if nowhere else, to those who gave me office. I promised it to old Rudi and the others when they came to me in the fear of what they knew.'

The Negro lowered his voice. 'Pierre, I must tell you something. Rudi is dead. This morning. I had a call from Geneva asking me to tell you.'

Salem's eyes filled. He shut them.

'He died in peace, Pierre.'

'In peace,' Salem repeated. 'In peace as he had lived.'

'I didn't want you to hear it from anyone else.'

'Thank you.'

Salem was looking away, the tight planes of his face waxen. 'You go on down, Robert. I will join you in a few minutes.'

Collins nodded and softly left the room.

In the resumed debate the lines to be drawn by the lobbies and power blocs clarified on the conference floor. Hylot reprimanded the Polish delegate and recognized his associate and countryman.

'It is undoubted that the escalation of the war in Vietnam has led to indiscriminate military action that cannot help but take a special toll of the civilian population. The Pasteur Institute in Dalat was destroyed at a time when plague vaccine was vital. The United States should be asked to make every effort to avoid the bombing in North and South of buildings protected by Red Cross markings. This is not political. It is humanist and neutral.'

The South Korean delegate jumped up. 'Rubbish. This is rubbish. Where is this French neutrality? In November two Russian ships loaded supplies for North Vietnam in the French ports of le Havre and Marseilles. A delegation of two thousand, headed by a French Communist leader, with Russian and North Vietnamese Embassy officials, welcomes these Russian ships. This is French neutrality? When the ICRC asked North Vietnamese Government for permission, what did they get? No reply.'

On the podium Salem hardly heard. He was remembering himself as a student, listening to Rudi lecture, full of fire and humour then, an old scarf about his neck in the winters. It was always an old scarf. He seemed to come by them like that. *My best and most brilliant student. Always my best and most brilliant student.* He had worn an old scarf on his death-bed in the big twilit room.

The Cuban delegate stuck out his beard.

'Listen, we all know why the ICRC can't do its duty in Vietnam. This debate is hot air. It can't do its duty because it depends for financing on the foreign aggressors in Vietnam. How can the ICRC get tough with America when the Yankees are its biggest contributor outside Switzerland? When, apart from that, the Yankees provide a million and a half US dollars to support the disaster programmes?

'Chairman Neveau has tried to tarbrush President Salem's motion. Why? Because Chairman Neveau is a money boy and the Yankees have him in their pocket.'

Salem roused at his name. He had not been listening and did not know what had prompted the protests.

It was almost midnight. Neveau knew he would take no pills tonight. His exhaustion had passed beyond that.

He poured a whisky, face wry with the strength of it, wincing against its violence. His eyes ached. There was trembling in his legs. He thought of his son, the handsome little face bright and smiling, the thick hair that shone like a polished helmet. He needed very much to see him. Neveau touched a hand to his own wisped hair. The boy had taken after his mother, he had his mother's eyes, his mother's sparkle. Neveau sighed. He had never been able to sparkle. It was a help in the world to be handsome, to move lightly, to have a personality people remembered.

He stilled, hearing noise in the passage. The voices passed the door. Neveau trickled more whisky into his drink.

People remembered Sarah. He had used to be very proud of other men's envy. When she had laughed and romped in those first years, walked in their rooms brazenly naked, he had swallowed and looked away. But he had been proud too, and unbelieving that so much beauty and style should be his. Neveau pressed his eyes. The shock of her being Jewish had troubled him. Not that it mattered, really. It was simply that he had not known. Something had happened between them. Perhaps he had let himself become too engrossed in his work.

He was dozing, almost asleep, when the door-bell startled him upright.

Richter collapsed his height and felt for a cigarette. 'I won't keep you long, Martin. I came as soon as I could. I've been talking to the Egyptians.'

Neveau waved him to a chair and sat forward, blinking the sleep away.

'We can depend on them, Martin.'

Neveau nodded.

Richter touched his tongue to his lips, nervous. 'How does it look, Martin? How do you judge the voting will go?'

Neveau spread his hands. 'It is indeterminate. The President has made a deep impression. The Communist countries will vote for him. The Western bloc will vote against, with abstentions and doubtful neutrals such as France. There are seventy votes in the Afro-Asian bloc. Half of these are for, half are apathetic. It is among these unaligned countries that influence could be critical. It is here that your delegation must use maximum persuasion. Tomorrow the President is going to raise the question of plague. I need not tell you what an emotional issue this is. He will report on the ICRC's drive last year against the plague in Vietnam, the dangers of its spreading. I have seen plague—as a young man I helped fight it in India. If one has seen plague, one does not forget.'

Richter moved an arm, his long face seeking comfort. 'He can't tie that in against us, can he? For Christ's sake, he can't blame America for the plague.'

'It will be implied. The war makes it hard to deal with. There have been cases in the countries surrounding Vietnam, in the Philippines and Indonesia. The dangers are real, very real.'

Richter needed help, could find none. 'What are we going to do? Are you saying he can't be stopped? Is there nothing the committee can do?'

'The President has received a censorious letter from the committee. He has chosen to ignore it. There is no existing machinery by which he can be summarily dismissed from office.'

Richter rose, agitated, remembered Neveau and reduced his height. 'We've got to stop him.'

'Yes. He must be stopped. Tell your people to make every effort with the Africans. I must retire now, I am very tired.'

Richter pushed the elevator button. Now it was the plague. Jesus, he didn't need it. He had been sent to the conference because of his pipe-line to Neveau. They looked to him as the special appointee out of Geneva. If no way could be found to stop Salem, Richter would be remembered for it. The circumstances which had so advanced his career would become the cause of his downfall. Joseph Richter, special appointee: failed. The thought wobbled his insides.

The evening had chilled early. When they got back to Sarah's hotel after eating late, Mitchell had turned on the heat. The room was comfortably fuggy. The traffic on the boulevard Saint-Germain came to them dully. Lights flashed on the drawn blind, emphasizing the sense of privacy. Mitchell smoked, an arm behind his head, one leg between Sarah's. She lay on her side, cheek against his shoulder.

'Is it absolutely necessary to go back on Friday? Couldn't Guy stay the weekend at school?'

She moved drowsily. 'How would I explain that? He would tell Martin.'

'Let him tell Martin. I will tell Martin. To hell and gone with Martin.'

'You're being silly.'

'Suppose he found out. What would happen?'

Sarah turned on her back. 'Light me a cigarette, will you?'

Mitchell lit a cigarette and passed it. 'What would happen?'

'He's an idealist. He'd kick me out.'

Mitchell lay and thought. 'You don't love me, do you? You like me. I'm something you can use.'

'You haven't exactly made me feel exclusive.' Sarah reached over and grasped him.

Mitchell said, 'Fair go, Sarah. It takes ten minutes. You haven't answered my question.'

'I could love you. It's just that everything's against it.'

'Why did you want me in the first place?'

'You're fun. It's easy with you. Martin takes everything so seriously. He's got the world on his shoulders just now.'

'And you want to play and muck up?'

'Is there anything wrong with that?'

Mitchell got up on his elbow and filled the champagne glasses. 'It's not entirely desirable in a wife and mother.'

'I've told you. When Martin gets back to Geneva we've got to stop all this.'

'Not even a quickie now and then?'

Sarah rolled away. 'That's a horrible expression.'

'It's the truth, isn't it? That's what you've been doing for months. Any time, anywhere. Find Ted, and get your pants off.'

Sarah smoked and drank the Champagne. 'If you're going to talk like that, I'm going home tomorrow.'

Mitchell swung his legs and sat on the bed. 'Then why the hell don't you?'

'Because it will be our last night in Paris. Because I hate Geneva and everyone in it and everything it means. Because it's wonderful here and I want our last night together.' Suddenly she was crying, a slightly drunken hysteria.

'What is it, Sarah? What's the matter?'

She rolled on to him, sobbing, 'I'm so desperately miserable. I don't want to go. I'm going to miss you so much.'

Mitchell covered her. She threw her legs wildly apart.

'Not that way. This way.'

She took him as she desired.

42

THAT afternoon the American Ambassador to France returned from an audience at the quai d'Orsay. For the second time in three days he used the scrambler telephone to Washington. Within hours of his call, following a White House meeting, a special envoy flew out of New York.

The Parisian Press, obedient to government wishes, reported the third plenary session of the twenty-first conference on small type on inside pages. The brief notices read that President Salem had drawn attention to the need of exceptional care in the storing of preventative chemical and biological weapons with particular reference to the deposits in Thailand. The adjective *preventative* was used in the captions.

Between eight o'clock and twelve that night, the members of the International Committee met at the Geneva Headquarters in an unprecedented confrontation.

The issue was a vote of no confidence in the Presidency. At eleven-thirty the Judge who had been one of the secret deputation which had waited on Salem at Château Malraux, asked permission to read from part of a document. It was old Rudi's last will and testament. In it he bequeathed to his friend and President, Pierre Salem, his love, respect and understanding, in both this world and whatever lay beyond. The codicil said that if ever, for whatever reason, the committee should meet to terminate the President's term of office, the deceased willed Pierre Salem his vote.

The high disturbance and emotion caused by this voice from oblivion upset at a stroke the fierce division of the committee's extraordinary meeting.

When the ballot was cast and counted, the result was equally divided. Old Rudi had returned from his own midnight to speak a last time for his friend.

Salem and Robert Collins had dined at the Swiss Embassy. The Ambassador was known to each of them. There had been no discussion of the conference upsets. They had talked of the student riot, the work on the Humanitarian Law. Salem had been refreshed by the evening, although the unspoken curiosity of others burdened him with restraint. Pleading work, he left early.

The weather had been variable. Sunshine in the morning, showers in the afternoon, now a clear warm night with moon. On the boulevard des Capucins Salem dismissed the car and walked.

He needed this anonymity, the sight of other faces, the spilled life that dawdled the bars and restaurants, chattered under striped awnings at pavement tables. In the glint of shop windows and shoving traffic, the neon lit cinema foyers, the bundled old women offering flowers, he eased in the normality of ordinary concerns.

Salem moved slowly, his hands in the pockets of the black topcoat, brown felt turned up and worn squarely. He thought again of old Rudi. The funeral at which he would be absent. Rudi would understand and forgive.

A touch of the old desolation returned to Salem in the love and loneliness for his lost friend. He had thought to be rid of it. It was in his flesh. It would abide within him all the days of his life.

The girl marked Salem coming, dropped a coin on the table and went to the traffic lights, brightening her eyes automatically, rehearsing her hips and shoulders. He didn't look French, too tall. He could be American or English.

Close to Salem in the waiting she tipped her pretty young face, placed herself against him. She looked up at him then and stopped at the distance and pain she saw, the stoniness her soft body pressed. The lights changed. Salem crossed to the place de l'Opéra. The girl watched. Then she frowned and shivered a little.

Joseph Richter slept restlessly, his big feet splayed bare on the dressing stool he had added to the length of the inadequate bed. When the telephone rang he jumped and grunted, found it and blinked at the dingy early light. 'Joe? This is Stevenson.'

'Yes, Mr Stevenson?'

'Can you get up here?'

Richter sat up, awake. 'I'll come right away.'

Richter looked at his watch. It wasn't yet six-thirty. Apprehension dried his mouth. Why would Stevenson want him at this hour? What had happened now? In the bathroom he stooped to the mirror and hurriedly shaved, jangling with surprise and worry.

The State Department leader opened the door, wearing his dressing-gown. He waved at the other man in the room. 'You've met McCredie.'

Richter nodded to the agent who had briefed the delegation after the student riot.

'Joe,' Stevenson said. 'Mac has got something hot. It came in with the night bag.'

It wasn't trouble. They were too keen for that. Richter untensed with relief.

'It's Salem,' Mac said. 'We've got the rundown.'

Richter saw the stiff yellow sheets on the table.

The CIA man picked up the papers and read from them: 'Subject: Pierre Salem, President of the ICRC. Source: General Agency sources plus a commissioned investigation by Milos Jelié, Milan. Remarks: Report originally requested from our station in Geneva. Skeleton dossier on file under heads international organizations. Expanded and updated at Geneva request. Personal evaluation added by State Department, ref. RICH/SAL/ICRC 1035. Identification: Male, Caucasian. Born Geneva 17/9/1919. Medical/physical: Subject enjoys general good health. No history communicable diseases. No major——'

'Come on,' Stevenson said. 'Get to the gravy, Mac.'

'Subject suffers from psychosomatic impotency directly attributable to irreversible azoospersia contracted following an infection of mumps at age seventeen.'

Stevenson said, 'Explain azoospersia.'

335

The agent directed himself to Richter. 'Dead spermatozoa. Male sterility. The stuff's there, but it's useless.'

Richter swallowed. The agent continued.

'Subject was treated for psychosomatic impotency in the years 1949–50 at the Rona Clinic, Gabriel Metsustraat, Amsterdam, and at the Royal Bethlehem Hospital, Kent, England, as an in-patient.

'Records in the files of Dr Dimitri Rona detail a series of hypnosis sessions which also failed, although this treatment diminished the subject's pathological depression.

'In the course of the Jelié investigation a contact was made with the subject's housekeeper, Signora Cenci, in Geneva. From her the contact learned that subject keeps a record of letters written to a purported son. Neither housekeeper nor husband, in fifteen years' service, have seen this son or heard mention made of him. Jelié's report is emphatic that no traceable evidence exists that subject ever fathered a son, in or out of wedlock, and medical evidence is conclusive that subject has been incapable since age seventeen.'

Richter said, 'Jesus!'

Stevenson was thinking of his own two boys. 'Spooky, isn't it? The poor bastard. Cut the rest of it, Mac. Give him the clincher.'

The agent turned the sheet. 'The subject's family fortune has depended since 1853 on the Bank Salem, Geneva, founded by his great-grandfather, the first Pierre Salem. It is privately known that the condition of inheritance, established in perpetuity by the founder, is conditional on there being a male heir of direct line to receive it.

'Personal: Inquiries led to the locating of Mrs Edwinea Lovillia, wife of Dr Bruno Lovillia, of *Il Popolo*, a Rome daily newspaper. Mrs Lovillia was formerly married to subject. They obtained a Mexican divorce in 1951, after a period of residency. Mrs Lovillia confirmed her past marriage to subject but would furnish no further comment or information.'

'Leave it there,' Stevenson said. 'The rest doesn't matter.'

Richter was trying to collect himself. To relate this clacking skeleton to Salem's power and person. Psychosomatic impotence. Male sterility. An imaginary son. Salem, the man with everything. Salem, the man they had been unable to stop. It was too much to manage at once.

Stevenson was ordering coffees and Cognacs. The agent looked at Richter. 'Well. How does that grab you?'

'What does it mean? Where does it get us?'

'Come on, Richter, wake up. It means that your President Salem's a nut. He's got a ghost boy in his head. He writes him letters. He's round the bend because he can't father children. Salem's a sexual dud. All he can do is piss through it.'

Stevenson sat and lit a cigarette, rubbing at the greying stubble on his chin. 'The poor haunted bastard. All that other stuff there from Saigon about his low threshold on the Vietnamese children. It all comes back to his sterility. The children he could never have himself.'

Richter asked, 'The bank? This business about the male heir. What happens to the Salem Bank?'

'That must really have got to him,' the agent said. 'It goes to a trust for charity. Salem's the end of the line. After Salem, nothing.'

It was too new, too private, too strange an area for Richter. He kept seeing and hearing Salem. The handsome head. The passion of his first plenary address. He couldn't match that figure with the tormented creature in the dossier. He said, 'I don't follow. You don't have to be impotent because you're sterile, do you?'

Stevenson leaned his head back on the chair, crossed his pyjama'd legs. 'A proud and introverted man like Salem, a sensitive man with a line to maintain, well, he could take it as a personal shame and failure. First there'd be the trauma when this azoospersia thing was diagnosed. Then there'd be his wife. Maybe she wanted children as much as he did. Then there could be a crippling disgust about this deadness inside him. Maybe a horror about putting it into a woman.'

Richter had a spasm of revulsion. 'Jesus!'

Stevenson sighed.

'In a way, yes. He's trying to be Jesus. The question is, do we crucify him?'

The waiter knocked and rolled in the trolley. Croissants, butter and jam were served with the coffee and Cognacs. In the interruption Richter interpreted Stevenson's remark. His face blanched.

They sat in silence. The Cognac expanded in Richter's empty stomach. He swallowed, holding his breath to keep from coughing.

Stevenson put down his glass. 'Well?'

It had to be faced. Richter tried to make the effort. It was what they needed. It could ruin Salem. It was a break beyond anything expected. All Salem's intransigence, his demonstrated irresponsibility, could be read into those stiff yellow pages. Richter floundered and wished it had never happened. They had looked only for some evidence of bias, something political, perhaps a student association, membership in some organization, anything breaching neutrality—an adult relationship contrary to rule and law. But this other thing. The clinics. The letters to a son who had never existed.

'I don't know, sir,' Richter said. 'I don't know how we would go about it. I don't know the law on a thing like this.'

Stevenson poured the remainder of his Cognac into the coffee. He dropped in a sugar-cube and slowly stirred it. 'There's no law, Joe. There's a moral law, but they don't put those on the books. What we have here is an instrument of blackmail.'

He looked directly at Richter. 'How would Neveau feel about that? You've told us often enough that the Chairman says Salem must be stopped whatever the cost.'

Richter said, 'How would he explain it? He couldn't produce the dossier, could he? Where would that put us? Salem's an authority on international law. He might pull the house down.'

'Balls,' the agent said.

They both looked at him.

'Balls. There's nothing he could do in law. This thing could be re-written—remove the sources and keep the dirt. Neveau could have come by it in any way. He's not obliged to explain that. There's no law in this, moral or otherwise. This guy's got us in trouble. We either win, or we lose.'

Stevenson nodded. 'That's about the strength of it. Salem has got the administration in a corner. If his motion goes through there will be world publicity. The penguins at the Pole will hear about it. Things are divided enough at home, God knows. With an election coming up it could blow the lid off. The Department is flying in a special Envoy this morning. That's how seriously this thing is being taken.'

Richter knew and dreaded the answer. 'Who would put it to Neveau?'

'You would, Joe,' Stevenson said. 'You're the Chairman's boy. That's why you're on this team, isn't it?'

Richter glanced at the yellow pages. They seemed to have enormous weight and volume. His lips were dry. He used the coffee to wet them. 'When?'

Stevenson said, 'It's seven-fifteen. How long will it take to rewrite this material as you suggested, Mac?'

'I could have it back in an hour.'

'Do that. The next session is scheduled for ten a.m. You've got time to move about in, Joe. You had better set up an appointment with Neveau now.'

When they had gone Stevenson sat a long time over his coffee.

Absently he rubbed his face and remembered he had not shaved. In the bathroom he lathered and picked up the razor. His eyes in the mirror looked strange. He hesitated there, examining himself. Two years to go. Two years to retirement. It was lousy luck to draw one like this for last.

'The poor bastard,' he told himself aloud. 'The poor haunted bastard.' He slashed the razor down the lather.

43

RICHTER took off his coat and lit a cigarette. He began to pace the small room, thinking. It came easier now. He was getting used to it. If Neveau would play, Salem was done for. Neveau would play. He would have to. It was the gift Neveau needed. If necessary he could go back to the committee. Those good and careful Swiss. They would scream in horror. Salem would be yanked back to Geneva. A no-confidence vote in the President due to diminished responsibility. A hushed-up agreement followed by resignation.

Richter lengthened his stride and straightened. It would be a coup. His coup. Joseph Richter, special appointee: brilliant success. When he asked to be connected to Neveau his voice shook with excitement.

Naked, Salem prepared for his headstand. Soon it would be over. Soon the conference would vote. There was no more need to stifle the passion that shouted inside him. He would pour fire and brimstone on the forces of anti-life when he rose to make his final appeal. They were there from all the world's nations. They were all the races of man. He would speak to them, and for them, and for all the humble who suffered at the hands of others. The righteousness invested in him would crumble opposition, as Samson crumbled the temple pillars.

Salem balanced and closed his eyes. He let himself slip into the peace of Nirvana.

Mitchell worried about the time. The taxi-driver had not kept off the boulevards, and now they were caught, held in by crawling metal. He had breakfasted with Sarah under grape vines, in the courtyard of a restaurant on the Ile de la Cité.

In the past days of being together, in the freedom and intimacy of the involvement, unbroken by returns to her husband as in the past, Sarah had truly been his lover, absorbed in him. She had hardly spoken of Neveau. If his name had to be mentioned, Sarah used it with derision. She required his faults as the excuse and reason of her betrayal.

But she held fast that it must stop between them after the return to Geneva. Mitchell wasn't much worried. She would try, but the pattern had been set. They would meet. A glance would pass between them, perhaps under Neveau's nose. Her eyes would darken, her breath would thicken. She would come to him as compelled as a sleepwalker.

It wasn't what he wanted. He wanted to marry her and get out.

At the Grand Hotel, as he paid off the taxi, he saw Richter going in ahead. Salem had the Americans up early. That meant there would be more fireworks today. Mitchell thought of Mick East—he was right, it was all a load of old codswallop. Look after Number One. Mitchell would do that. If he had to force Sarah to make the break he could tip off Neveau anonymously.

Richter stood in the elevator, holding his portfolio with both hands. He could feel the stiff envelope with its string seal, through the polished calf. He rehearsed his words again. 'Martin, something has come up. A document that concerns President Salem.' Unzip the portfolio. 'I thought you should see it right away. You'll want to read it in your own time, Martin, so I'll just leave it and go. If you want me, I'll be waiting near the telephone in the Café de la Paix.'

Stay near the door. Get it said. Get out.

Richter took a breath and pushed the bell. Neveau answered. He was in striped flannel pyjamas, unshaven, his sallow face blackened by beard, eyes red.

341

He had taken a pill late, having tried to sleep without it. He had slept again after Richter's call, and the bell had wakened him. The drug was like a weight behind his eyes and on his limbs. He put Richter's envelope on the table and went to shower. First hot water, then cold. Strong black coffee and aspirin against the headache.

Neveau wondered what it was all about. It wasn't easy to think yet. A document concerning Salem. Perhaps something to do with the lobby. His mind jumbled, calculating the votes. In his drugged dreams it was always this. Dealing, persuading, bribing. Trading one delegation against another. He had the Jews. He had promised them their cursed Red Shield of David, more money for the Sinai refugee camps. The Jews had no ethics outside self-interest.

Neveau braced himself. The cold water hit him like a violence, choking his breath with protest. He forced himself not to step out. He turned his face to the nozzle. The numbness on his mind and body loosened under the icy pelting.

Neveau refilled the coffee cup and took it to the table. It was odd of Richter to have telephoned so early. And he had been odd at the door, excited. Now that he could think, Neveau faced it. He picked up the envelope, unwound the string and withdrew the file of yellow paper.

Subject: Pierre Salem, President ICRC.

Neveau stared. His eyes picked over the page. He felt for the chair and let himself down, his heart racing with surprise.

He stumbled when he dropped the sheets at last and backed away from the table. All his body trembled. He lit a cigarette, fumbling it from the packet, breaking matches. He couldn't believe it. Where had Richter got such a document? A son. An imaginary son. It couldn't be. A mistake had been made. It couldn't be reconciled with Salem. His person, his privileges, his power. But he had been married. He had been divorced. He lived as aloof as a monk. Again Neveau picked up the pages. Again the irrevocable words dinned his mind.

How had Richter got information of such searing privacy? It was horrible, indecent. Why had Richter wanted him to know?

Neveau sat smoking, his eyes on the file, hearing and rehearing the words. He had been jealous of Salem. Not because of the office which he had hoped for himself. Not for the losses and frustrations he had suffered at Salem's hands. For himself—his tall handsome figure. The distinction of his mind and person. His money, his château, his background of family. The French shirts and English tweed suits.

It was meaningless, a grotesque façade. It was Neveau who had everything. Salem had nothing. He lived in a cave blown by winds of desolation. It was Neveau who had everything. A beautiful, vivid little boy. A wife other men looked at. A loyal, beautiful wife.

He stilled his thoughts. Why had Richter been so urgent that he must know?

Neveau jolted. Realization roared through him.

Richter shook out another cigarette. The piled ashtray embarrassed him. He moved down the bar and ordered a glass of soda. He had not eaten, expecting Neveau's call. The soda tasted clean, cold and alive. What was Neveau doing? It had been more than an hour. Had he gone directly to Salem? Richter butted the cigarette and lit another, unaware of the action.

'Your caller is on the line, sir.'

Richter's long arms flapped absurdly. He got off the stool and buttoned his jacket. 'Richter speaking.'

'Will you come up, please?'

'Sure, Martin. Right away.' He left money beside the glass and hurried out of the café.

Neveau opened the door. He gave no greeting. Pushed the door shut and stood there, his hand on the knob. The yellow envelope and papers lay on the table. He lifted his eyes to Richter, his face set.

'This document. That thing. I don't want to know where you got it, or how you got it. I don't even want ever to hear it mentioned again.'

Richter crouched. 'It was just routine, Martin. You know? Just a routine check.'

Neveau ignored his words. 'I want to know if it's accurate. If there's any possibility of faking.'

'None, Martin. I promise you. I wouldn't be party to anything like that.'

'Very well. That's all I wanted to know.'

Richter said, 'The thing is, the President's not well. I mean, he's not responsible. You had to know, Martin. Someone has to stop him.'

Neveau opened the door. 'That will be all.'

'But, Martin—what are we going to do? I mean, we've been fighting this thing.'

Neveau said, 'Richter: if I ever hear, anywhere, from anyone, the faintest hint that this document has been shown to others, I will personally petition the President of the United States.'

343

Richter gasped. 'But, Martin, don't get me wrong. I don't under-stand your attitude. I mean——'

Neveau said, 'You can depend on that. Depend on it. Now please leave me.'

Richter blundered down the passage, hardly knowing where he was going.

Deliberately, once again, Neveau summarized the struggles of the last hour. Then he put the sheets in the envelope, opened the door and crossed the passage to Salem's suite. The secretary answered.

'Is the President in?'

'Yes, sir. He's dressing.'

'Please tell him I'm here. Then leave us, if you would.'

Salem came out. His smile was a little puzzled. 'Well, Martin. This is a surprise.' He puzzled further at Neveau, unable to account for his silence, the strange examination, the strange set of his face. Salem waited.

'Pierre, I've come to ask you, to plead with you, this one last time, not to force this dreadful division.'

Pierre. Neveau had never used the christian name before.

Salem said gently, 'I'm sorry, Martin. I must.'

'Is there nothing I can say? Nothing I can do?'

'Nothing.'

'You know that if you succeed it will almost certainly pull down the International?'

'I'm not convinced of that, Martin.'

'You know that it would be a betrayal of your office, of your trust, of everything the movement is founded on?'

Salem said, 'I see it differently. It is to my trust that I'm bearing witness.'

Neveau began to labour. 'That's your last word?'

'My last word, Martin.'

'I have to stop you. You know that?'

'Yes. It is according to your rights.'

'Pierre. I want you to know. I want you to know.' Neveau stopped.

'What is it, Martin? What's troubling you?'

Martin shook his head, and extended the envelope. 'I want you to read this. When you are ready I'd like you to call me and tell me what you decide.'

344

Salem took the package. 'Very well, Martin. If it's that important to you.'

Neveau pushed past him to the door.

The windows were open over the place de l'Opéra. The sun shone there pale and cheerful. Pedestrians stared at the arriving delegations, the pomp of national flags and chauffeurs, the exotica of skins and national dress. Gaps remained unrepaired in the paving where students had prised up blocks during the riot. Salem watched, appreciating the hopeful morning, speculating on Neveau and his visit. How strange that he should have used his christian name.

Salem returned to the table where he had laid the yellow envelope, inspected it and undid the string.

In the Salle des Fêtes the congregation became restless. Monsieur Hylot spread his hands first at Salem's empty seat, then at Robert Collins.

'Irregular. Most irregular. There is much business to be done this morning.'

It was ten-fifteen.

Collins decided that Salem must have Neveau with him—it would be more than coincidence that Neveau too, was absent from his table.

Collins said, 'Perhaps we should begin without him, Monsieur Hylot. The President must be delayed importantly.'

Hylot huffed. 'In such a circumstance I would imagine that the President would notify the Chair. He rapped his gavel, greatly offended, opening the fourth plenary session and apologizing for President Salem's unavoidable absence.

At the State Department table Richter heard and slumped. Stevenson looked across and nodded. On the uneven podium the President's empty chair seemed to occupy a vortex.

Stevenson looked away. The poor bastard. What a lousy assignment to draw on the last lap.

The sunshine had entered the room. It lay neatly shaped by the windows on the pastures of carpet. Salem's head was bent to his breast, his arms across the table, surrounding the yellow sheets. 'No. For God's sake, no.'

His clenched fists rose. He stood there as he had stood shuddering before Jane Stirling in Saigon, his arms agonized above his head.

In his suite Neveau waited, face dropped into hands.

44

Betrayed—R. Kleinberg. Mick East had opened the Tracing Agency's history book at the cellophane-covered cigarette packet pushed from the Jewish transport. It had been the only memorial to the names blurred there in pencil. A group headstone on a tablet of cardboard, a last despairing cry, falling at the feet of a Polish farmer from the boards of a train of cattle trucks.

His own trace on Rudolf Kleinberg, increased by the documentation forwarded by Janos Kisch's Jewish Research Bureau, was opened beside the history book. Mick drank from a fresh flask of coffee and Cognac, polished his glasses and read.

Something had happened. Kisch had telephoned at mid-morning from the War Criminal Tracing Bureau in Vienna. He was flying into Geneva late and had asked East to wait for him at the Agency.

Across the long slope of green grass a few lights lit windows in the headquarters building. East wondered if the committee was to meet again. The day had been excited with gossip about last night's emergency session. It was speculated that it had to do with Salem's carrying on at the conference. It didn't much touch East's curiosity. He thought it all a dustbin load of old codswallop.

'Something has come up on Rudolf Kleinberg.'

Janos had sounded happy. He was always happy when he got the scent. The damnedest things would come out of him, laughing! 'I don't believe in justice. I don't believe in mercy. Everything in life has a price. I've paid a heavy price. Now I am an instrument of vengeance for my people. Vengeance is the purest, most liberating of all emotions. An eye for an eye is a beautiful law.'

Mick East read, shaking his head in appreciation. That Janos. He could smile a man to death. He and Simon Wiesenthal had dossiers on twenty-five thousand Nazi criminals yet to be arrested. Every Jew in the world was their field worker. Give old Janos a finger hold on vengeance and he wouldn't let go until he got his hands around a man's throat.

An eye for an eye. Look after Number One. They understood each other. Codswallop was for nits like Salem.

The headlights struck across the window. Mick East opened it and looked out. A taxi had stopped in the headquarter's parking lot. The driver went to the boot for a suitcase. Janos Kisch stood in the light, glancing down to the Tracing Agency.

They met at the entrance.

'Well, Janos, good to see you.'

'You are looking well, my friend, as always. It was good of you to wait for me.'

They sat at his table at the end of the main filing room. 'Coffee, Janos? Or a hard one?'

Kisch laughed. 'For me your coffee is enough hard.'

He nodded at the open history book and file, touched the old cigarette pack with a finger. 'Strange, no, how the inscriptions we make outlast us? One does not think of a pencil as an instrument of nemesis.'

Mick said, 'That's why I never write to women, Janos.'

They both laughed, calculating each other.

'Well, Janos, what have you got?'

The Jew frowned, rubbed his moustache. 'A strange thing. I have a strange story to tell you.' Kisch presented his information this way, telling it as though it were a tale, to be enjoyed without involvement.

East asked, 'Betrayed—R. Kleinberg?'

347

'Yes, yes. Betrayed—R. Kleinberg. Your coffee, as always, is excellent. On the flight it was cold and horrible.'

Mick sat intently. The paper chases he pieced together in this room were the absorbing interest of his life.

Kisch lifted his eyebrows, ordering it in his mind. 'We will begin, as they say, at the beginning. A good story has a beginning, a middle and an end. Not so?'

'Just so long as you get on with it, Janos.'

Kisch tipped his head and laughed, smacking his palm on the table.

'Ah, my friend, you would have to learn patience to do my job. One learns to wait. Waiting makes everything taste better.'

He sat forward. 'So, I will not torment you. Now, you remember the SS informer who sold Simon Wiesenthal the Hermann Harz story?'

'Yes. One cent for every Jew Harz had killed.'

'Seven hundred thousand lives. Seven thousand dollars. You will also remember that Rudolf Kleinberg's name was mentioned?'

East nodded.

'Now, it was you who remembered that cigarette packet,' Kisch pointed. 'Very good, my friend. You have an instinct for the craft.'

East said, 'From you, Janos, that's a compliment.'

'True.' Kisch smiled happily. 'So, what next? I trace a survivor from the list of betrayed, a schoolteacher in Israel. One of the victims Rudolf Kleinberg promised to ransom.'

He held out his mug.

'A little, please, to warm it. I see I have aroused your hunting instinct, yes?'

East said, 'Go on.'

'So. Now we know the meaning of "Betrayed—R. Kleinberg". We want that man. Does he live? Is he hiding somewhere, fat and prosperous like thousands of these animals? Search, I tell my people. Check every record and document for the name Rudolf Kleinberg.'

Kisch waited. 'What did you find, Janos?'

'A strange thing. In the file on Dr Heinrich Müller, chief of the medical experiments, whom we have just now traced to Chile, we find the name Kleinberg, a forced worker in that section. After the name Kleinberg, comes Rudolf.'

Kisch pointed his finger. 'After the name Kleinberg, Rudolf, what do we find? We find, alias Rudolph Neveau.'

Mick East put down his glass.

348

Kisch continued to smile but his eyes were hard with bitterness. In the organizations dedicated to vengeance the renegade Jew had terrible priority. Mick East played his job as the greatest game, an abstraction on paper which he won with a rubber stamp: *Closed*. When Janos Kisch put *Closed* to a hunt, a man suffered or died.

'If he's alive, Janos, I wouldn't care to be him.'

'I want that man to be alive,' Kisch eased and smiled again. 'I want him alive and happy.'

That Janos. The neat moustache, the dimpled hands, the unalterable *bonhomie*. The dark, watering eyes, that all the smiling never touched. If Kleinberg lived and they found him, the eye for an eye that he'd pay would be a terrible summary and private judgment. East looked away.

Kisch took a cigarette from a gold case. 'That finishes the beginning of my story. Now we come to the middle.'

East felt he was being played for some purpose. Kisch was watching him like quarry.

'We turned to the documents captured when the Americans opened Krasnerdorf. We find this entry.

'*Rudolf Kleinberg, alias Rudolf Neveau. Male Jew, 48, born Munich 21/3/1894. German citizen travelling on Swiss passport. Accused of trading faulty aircraft instruments. Arrested with wife Eva Kleinberg.*'

Mick East had an instinct to avoid the other man's eyes. Premonition chilled him. Mick kept his face empty, said nothing. Kisch blew smoke, then continued.

'We check Eva Kleinberg. Gassed Auschwitz, 23/10/42. So, who knew Eva Kleinberg at that time? A survivor in Sydney, Australia. They slept on the same rack that year.

'What does she remember? She remembers that Eva Kleinberg told her that after her husband's arrest in Dresden, she was contacted at her home in Geneva.' Kisch paused. 'At her home in Geneva,' he repeated, 'and told to bring ransom to Germany to save her husband from the camps. After she delivered the money, Eva was arrested. She never saw her husband. It happened many times, no?'

It had. There were many such stories in the Tracing Agency's records. Mick East was not thinking of that. A pattern was whirling on his memory, thumping his blood and shortening his breath. He said, 'So you checked here with the Magistratbeilung.'

349

It wasn't a question. Kisch lifted his eyebrows and smiled. 'Good. Very good. You see, I said you have a talent. Yes, we check at the Magistratbeilung.'

They were concentrated on each other now. Kisch was leading him, timing it and leading him relentlessly. Mick knew what had to come, calmed himself to ask the question. 'What did you learn, Janos?'

The Jew put out his cigarette, 'The registered change of name, 1934. Rudolf Kleinberg to Rudolph Neveau. With him his wife, Eva Kleinberg.'

Now he looked up. It was over. Only the formality remained. Mick East took a drink. It had been he who had started this. The cigarette pack in the opened book seemed to crackle and blaze on the page.

'And with the wife, Eva?'

Kisch nodded. 'The son, Martin. The son, Martin, aged four years.'

Mick opened a drawer and poured from the Cognac bottle. 'For you?'

'Please, no. A little more of the coffee.'

Mick was making effort to get it straight. Martin Neveau was a Jew. His father was a Jewish renegade. His mother had died in the ovens. Martin Neveau was a Jew.

He said, '*Our* Martin Neveau.'

Kisch spread his hands. 'Possible. Who knows? His parents? Rudolph and Eva perhaps?'

'Yes. He believes them killed in the Dresden bombing. That was what the Swiss Embassy had been told. My file on them has never been deactivated.'

'His age? Approximately?'

'The age is right, Janos. Do you know what this could mean?'

'Specifically?' Kisch asked.

'Specifically. The end of the Executive Director's career with the International. He is not a natural-born Swiss. You know the unbreakable rule. Neveau is a committee member.'

'I am sorry for that.'

'You're going to tell him?'

'Yes. If Rudolf Kleinberg is alive there could have been contact between them.'

Look after Number One. East knew it was not Neveau's philosophy. 'No, Janos. If Neveau had known he was not Swiss, he would have resigned from the committee. Neveau goes by the rules, whatever the cost. Why don't you leave him alone?'

Kisch smiled and shook his head.

'Ah, my friend, that is not in my grant. There are blood debts to be paid. There must be retribution if Rudolf Kleinberg lives. It is owed to the murdered millions. It is owed as warning to the future. One waits. One strikes. It must be. The sins of the fathers are visited on the sons.'

The bleak eyes in the cheerful face struck East with further knowing. One waits. One strikes. With awe and wonder he considered Janos Kisch. 'You've waited for this, haven't you? You've had this information some time.'

'Some little time, yes.'

'You waited to get him at the conference. You waited to get him off balance.'

Kisch shrugged. 'There are techniques. One looks for the advantage. If Martin Neveau knows anything about his father we must get it as best we can.'

East said, 'Janos, you frighten me.'

Kisch laughed and rose.

'You know nothing of fear, my friend. Nothing. Come, I will give you dinner.'

Mick East flew out next morning. For the first time in ten years he had not gone to bed and immediately slept. On that occasion the secretary he had got pregnant had threatened him with a paternity suit.

He would have to tell Ted Mitchell. The article he was writing around the cigarette packet had come home in devastation. East couldn't get Neveau off his mind. They had all thought him the architypal Swiss. He looked so Swiss, acted so Swiss, the repository of every Swiss pride and snobbery. He was as Swiss as the cuckoo clock.

He was a Jew. A Jew out of Germany. His mother had died in the ovens. How would a man cope if his identity was wrenched from him? How would he ever again know himself, or the stranger within his skin? Mick rubbed his face in alarm. It would be like himself waking up as a Hottentot or a Hindu untouchable.

Everything Neveau accepted, every image he had of himself was mirage. All in which he took sustenance and pride was a counterfeit inheritance. He was a Jew, skullcapped and unclean in a ghetto. His mother had died naked in a sealed room packed with the others who screamed and scrambled or prayed as the cyanide hissed from the roof vents and vomit and excreta ran from them.

'Jesus' sake,' he whispered to the sky in the aircraft's window.

What did it mean then? What did patriotism and national pride

351

mean? The flags, the anthems and the slogans, the rest of the tawdry, cheating pomp? It all came down to a notion. The whole codswallop lot was in the head. If a few words and a few scraps of paper could amputate that from a man, turn his guts inside out and make him a ghost, it was time somebody shoved it up all the Presidents and Prime Ministers and all the flags in the world.

Janos would take his time, smiling. Today or tomorrow he would be in Paris. Neveau would receive his telephone call or find him waiting cheerfully in his suite. Another thought jarred Mick East. The little boy. Little Guy. The Swiss apple of his father's Swiss eye. Little Guy was a Kike.

Cloud slid grey and damp past the window. Mick had hoped for a good time in Paris. That had gone out of him now. There was one chance for Neveau, if Janos Kisch left him his sanity. He had one chance if he just shut up and pretended to be what he thought he was. He could make it and hold together if he just looked after Number One.

45

In the Salle des Fêtes Salem's empty place on the podium continued to distract Richter's attention. The debate had continued for more than an hour, less acrimoniously than in previous sessions as though those lettings had weakened emotion, or perhaps because of Salem's absence. Richter hardly followed the arguments. His imagination kept putting Salem there, seeing the tall, tweed-suited figure cross the podium to his chair. He wouldn't dare. Not now. There would be an announcement of illness. The President had withdrawn from the conference. Without Salem's influence and impression the floor would remember its own interest. Neveau's lobby would crush the motion before it got to a vote.

What was happening between the two? Anxiety and tension wound Richter like a spring.

Neveau's secretary entered without knocking, the morning cables from Geneva in a folder. 'I beg your pardon, Mr Chairman. I thought you were in session.'

Neveau removed his hands from his face. The girl put the folder on the table. 'I hope you're not unwell? Is there anything I can get you?'

He looked at her vaguely, shook his head. 'No, thank you. I'm perfectly well. Until further notice I won't take any calls.'

'Very well, sir.'

She looked back at him, huddled again in the chair, his eyes fixed on nothing. He wasn't well, she could see it. He had not been well for weeks.

Neveau checked his watch. Salem had been alone for over an hour. Alone, exposed, naked. Helpless and alone. He had warned him. Until the very last he had laboured with Salem for reason. He had to stop him, Salem had left him no choice.

It was hard for Neveau to comfort himself. He felt soiled to the ends of his body. The cigarette packet before him was empty. He turned to the table and opened the folder. It was something to do and he was grateful. The top cable was headed, *Received from ICRC Delegate General, Saigon*, and marked URGENT.

It read:

AMERICAN AMBASSADOR REPORTS VIETCONG SMUGGLING PLAGUE-INFESTED RATS ON STATEBOUND AIRCRAFT AND LODGES URGENT PROTEST TO ICRC CLAIMING BREACH GENEVA CONVENTIONS ARTICLES FOUR STROKE FIVE STOP AMERICAN GOVERNMENT INFORMED BY PRIORITY STOP DISEASED RATS AUTHENTICATED BY AUTOPSY AND STATEMENT DOCTOR ADAM THOMSON CHIEF MEDICAL OFFICER QUONG LO PROVINCIAL HOSPITAL STOP PROCEEDING QUONG LO SOONEST TO INVESTIGATE AND INTERVIEW DOCTOR THOMSON STOP PLEASE INSTRUCT.

All other concern went from Neveau. He filled with fear and disgust. The stink of death entered the room. He could see and smell the smoke-smudged sky burning to the horizon with gasoline-soaked bodies.

The rheumy-eyed sun hammered the earth. The vultures left the plague-struck dead and ran croaking before the hygiene teams, jumping and clashing their wings, too gorged to get off the ground.

The wind blew and the black death blew on it, finding out every hut and hamlet, leaping unseen from the dying to the living with a venom that multiplied with its victims.

He had been young then and he saw himself as he had been on that landscape, slim with thick brown hair, a Red Cross band on his arm, fighting the pestilence that slaughtered like an invisible, proliferating army.

Neveau got up. All the weight of the International's censure must be cabled to Hanoi and the Liberation Front. When the Delegate-General had reported from Quong Lo, verified the facts, the League and the ICRC would protest the atrocity to the world. He had seen plague.

Neveau straightened and stilled. He was letting his mind slip. They were here, those delegations. They sat below him now in the Salle des Fêtes, waiting to inherit Salem's motion.

The dossier, the envelope, remained spread on the sitting-room table. Salem lay on the made bed, as unnaturally as a corpse, waistcoated and tweed suited as he had dressed for the morning session. The highly polished shoes pointed neatly upwards. A dark tie was knotted loosely into a stiff white collar. His arms were at his sides, hands clenched, the shirt cuffs starched and gold-linked.

He lay as though an undertaker had prepared him, cold and hard and waxen, only the jump and flicker of the blue-veined eyelids reminding the body of life.

He had travelled like that far and long across the grey pumice of his desolation. He had wandered there, cut his own old tracks, the crumbling cairns in which hopes had been buried. The ruin of his love, the castles he would have built in it, lay in that place like grey grains.

They had searched him out and found him. They had split him open with a knife. He could feel and see them inside him, ransacking his shame, picking at the locks he had closed, spilling his pain and privacy over a poison of yellow paper. Salem began to compose:

My Own Dear Son,

How clearly I sometimes see you. How many beautiful images you have.

I saw you last night as I walked on the boulevard. Was that a school blazer you wore? You appeared so grave, watching from the balcony. What did you think behind that small, still face?

I saw you in Saigon, your shoe-button eyes, your shamefully dirty feet.

We were secret to each other. Now strangers know about us. They seek to use you against me, unable to understand.

Because I could not get you born they think you can't exist, a little boy who for ever changes.

I am supposed to forsake you **now**. They took my pride for ransom. When the worst was over I was humbled, wanting only to hide. I had no pride.

A strange, strange thing happened then.

A warmth more wonderful than anything I have known, aroused and broke free in my body. It burned and expanded inside me like sun, blinding my eyes with revelation.

It was my pride, my pride which had crippled me. Taking that, they had returned me all.

Salem's chest heaved. A smile awakened his face. He lay like that briefly, his eyes opened, his body melting out of rigidity.

Neveau had telephoned Geneva a cable to be beamed on the ICRC frequency. The Saigon Delegate-General was instructed to substantiate the facts of yesterday's message by the most urgent priority and to report in full directly to the Chairman in Paris.

He was at the telephone, listening to his scribbled message being read back when Pierre Salem knocked and entered. He stood inside, eyes calm, direct, both hands before him holding the big yellow envelope.

Neveau gripped the receiver as though it might support him. The droning voice in his ear passed from meaning. He was mesmerized by surprise at Salem's figure, his exuded calm, the peace that was almost withdrawal. The radio operator's voice spoke several times before Neveau heard it.

He said, 'Yes. Thank you. That is correct. No, that is all at present.' He couldn't bring himself to put down the telephone. It was refuge while he held it.

In the silence Salem spoke. 'Am I interrupting you, Martin?'

'No, President.' He still held the instrument, lowering it.

'I wish to return your papers.'

'Not my papers. Not mine, President.' Sweat shone his scalp.

'Whosoever they might be, then.'

'I had nothing to do with it. Nothing. It was brought by others.'

Salem walked to the table and laid the envelope there. 'I don't doubt you, Martin.'

Neveau remained at his distance, struggling. 'What are you going to do?'

'Do?' Salem asked.

'Are you going to stop? Stop this mad obsession?'

'For what reason, Martin?'

'For that reason.' Neveau jabbed his finger at the table. 'I told you I had to stop you. I pleaded with you to stop.'

'How can that stop me, Martin? Everything in there is true.'

Neveau lurched, uncomprehending, his face and voice disordered. 'But they will circulate it if you don't stop. It will be my duty to bring it to the committee.'

'*They?*' Salem asked.

Neveau did not hear. 'You're finished, don't you see? If you don't stop you're finished.'

Salem said, 'Then finish me, Martin. Do what you must.'

He was at the door when Neveau shouted after him, lost to all control. 'I will. I'll finish you. You're a madman. I'll finish you.'

The door closed. Neveau leaned on the telephone table, panting.

It was twenty minutes to the close of the morning session. The leader of the English delegation was completing a summary of compromise. Most of the others were considering private dealings or lunch. Richter noted a point from the Englishman's address, for advantage in the afternoon.

Alongside him a State Department man pinched his fingers into Richter's arm. Startled, he looked up and turned. Pierre Salem had entered from the wing, crossed to take his chair. The English speaker halted, went on. The chamber rustled. Richter stared in disbelief, his long jaw sagging. Across the table Stevenson folded a note and passed it.

Richter: Now what the hell has happened? Where's Neveau? Get to him in the break.

On the podium Salem leaned towards Monsieur Hylot. The Chairman listened and nodded, granting the apology. Big Robert Collins observed Salem's face and smiled.

As soon as Monsieur Hylot had adjourned the morning session, the emissary from the American Embassy pushed through the retiring delegates. Stevenson and Richter were leaving the room when he stopped them and handed the State Department leader an envelope. Stevenson went to a corner. Richter waited miserably. The reception he had got from Neveau that morning did not encourage a further approach. What had happened? What could possibly have gone wrong? He seemed to be riding a maddened pendulum.

Stevenson put the envelope in his pocket. 'I'm wanted at the Em-

bassy. Get to Neveau. Don't blow this one, Richter. When you've
found out what went wrong wait for me at the hotel.'

Richter decided to give himself a drink before looking for Neveau. His
earlier nausea had returned to quake him. Why did his big chance
have to be such a mess?

Don't blow this one, Richter. Jesus, he hadn't blown anything. He
had done as well as he could. Stevenson was looking for someone to
blame. If the buck was passed, Richter knew who would get it. He
swallowed on that, the castles he had built tottering in prospect.

Ted Mitchell had a Press briefing to give, mostly for the correspondents of the wire services. It would be lengthy and tedious, a résumé of
the many subcommittees. He had hoped to fit in a lunchtime drink
with Sarah, but had to abandon that in the preparation of hand-outs.

He was eating a sandwich in his office, checking copies, when the
door opened and Mick East's plump face appeared. 'Wotcher cock.'

' 'Ow are yer mate, orright?'

They grinned for each other.

'When did you get in?'

'About an hour ago. How's it all going, then?'

'It's been a bastard. Compared to this one, Istanbul was a picnic.
What's new in the sacred city?'

'Not much. We heard that Salem went a bit bonkers. The committee had a meeting about him.'

Mitchell said, 'The bastard has had us all up early and late.'

East sat down. 'King of the nits, that's Salem. What have you got
lined up for us, Teddy boy?'

'I've been pure, Mick. I haven't had time.'

'Codswallop,' East said. 'Since when have you been that busy?'

Mitchell had to be careful, at least until Sarah left. 'Give me until
tomorrow. I've got a lot on my plate.'

Mick East looked disbelieving. 'You're up to something, Teddy boy.
You didn't smuggle something out of Geneva, did you?'

It caught Mitchell. For an instant he thought East might know. He
asked, 'Coals to Newcastle?'

East cleaned his glasses. 'How's Neveau?'

The question put Mitchell further on guard. 'Neveau? How should
he be?'

'That's a good question,' East said. 'I don't know how he should
be.'

358

Mitchell mistook the meaning. If East knew, who else knew? How would Sarah react?

He pushed the sandwiches away, leaned back. 'If you've got something on your mind, Mick, get rid of it.'

East said, 'You're a prickly bastard this morning. Get out of bed on the wrong side?'

'What have you got to say, Mick?'

East frowned. 'I don't know what you're upset about. But I do have something to tell you. For this one you'd better button your seatbelt, cock.'

The Embassy stood on a corner of the rue Gabriel. The Ambassador's big room looked over the park to the Seine.

He rose when Stevenson was announced. 'Ah, Stevenson. I believe you have met our distinguished visitor. He is here as the President's private envoy.'

Stevenson was shaken. He had not expected this famous old man. The envoy nodded.

'How do you do, sir.'

'Well enough, considering the times and tribulations.'

The Ambassador was youngish, a veteran of Kennedy's administration.

'Stevenson, I must tell you that as far as the Press is concerned our visitor is here on a private vacation. A statement to that effect was made at the airport this morning.'

Stevenson nodded. 'I understand.'

The Ambassador addressed the envoy. 'How do you wish to handle this, sir?'

The envoy adjusted his glasses and folded his hands. 'Stevenson and I will chat.'

Stevenson had not recovered from his awe. The pale old eyes that contemplated him had looked down Khrushchev at the United Nations. He had been in the administration section of the Manhattan Project which had birthed the atom bomb, Ambassador to France, and the Presidential envoy who had nearly achieved peace in the Middle East.

His voice was thin, cultured. 'The present circumstances are not usual ones. You will be told as little as possible and would be well advised to forget what you hear. Now, have you heard any mention of a protest lodged to the ICRC by our Ambassador in Saigon?'

'No, sir. Nothing. A protest of what kind?'

The old man said to the Ambassador, 'Perhaps it is too early yet.'

359

He looked back to Stevenson. 'No rumour of anything at all?'

'No, sir. Discussion in the delegations has been exclusively about the President's motion.'

The envoy considered. 'So far, so good, then. Now, Stevenson, somewhere in the ICRC machinery there is a message, which at all costs must not be publicized. This matter is of such importance that it could cause national panic at home. Perhaps civil disorders, which could be difficult to control.'

Stevenson tried not to appear overwhelmed. The envoy appreciated his confusion.

He said, 'If you wish to smoke, by all means do so.' The old man adjusted his glasses, drew papers towards him. 'I will read to you in some detail from a summary. This is an extract:

'"The outbreak was first reported by the Registrar of the Watts County hospital. Plague is a notifiable disease and once it has been diagnosed the hospital was under legal obligation to report it to the Los Angeles Public Health Department.

'"A Negro male was admitted. He had a temperature of one hundred and four degrees, muscular rigours and bloody sputum. The interne had not seen plague before and it was not until he got a laboratory report the following morning that *Pasteurella pestis* was established. The patient was a city employee and worked in the refuse disposal section. He died of cardiac failure."'

The old man raised his head. Stevenson's cigarette burned untouched.

'"The report was made to the Public Health Department at nineteen a.m. By three-fifteen p.m. there had been two more reports. A special epidemic team from the Public Health Department moved into Watts, traced all the contacts of the cases, and injected sulphadiazine. This took until eleven p.m. that night.

'"Meanwhile the department had contacted the Health Department in Washington, asking for a supply of vaccine. Most of the vaccine was under army control and it took twenty-four hours to get it to Watts. Meanwhile the third case died. This man was a civilian employee of the army working in a labour detail unloading aircraft returning from Vietnam.

'"The base was immediately sealed off, but by noon of the third day there were another sixteen cases. All flights from Vietnam to anywhere on the American mainland were stopped. The authorities were in a difficult position. Every contact of every case had to be discovered and isolated. The most efficient way of doing this would have been by mass media. This had to be weighed against the panic such an announcement could cause.

' "The decision against publicity was taken at the highest level. Instead, every hospital and general practitioner on the West Coast was circulated with a list of symptoms and instructed to report in secret to the public health authority the moment a case was suspected. A security blanket of the utmost severity was generally applied.

' "There have been several hundred reports. It is now thirty-two days since the first case in Watts. The situation could precipitate a national emergency." '

He pushed the papers away.

Stevenson said, 'Good God, sir. How did it get into the country?'

'Until yesterday that was unknown. The President received from the Ambassador in Saigon, later confirmed by the Commander in the field, a notification that the enemy had been apprehended placing plague-infested rats aboard States-bound aircraft. We don't know how long this has been going on, or where outbreak might occur next. The Ambassador unfortunately lodged a protest to the ICRC. He had no knowledge of the state of affairs at home. The administration, in turn, had no suspicion that the enemy had activated this ingenious form of germ warfare.'

The Ambassador said, tense, 'You can see how it is, Stevenson. If the ICRC publicizes the protest, in view of what is happening at home, and what may yet happen, as well as this motion of Salem's and the plague warnings he has repeatedly given—well, the situation could become extreme.'

The old man's eyes were lidded. 'In your estimation, Stevenson, how will President Salem act when the protest reaches his notice?'

'He will use it, sir. I have no doubt he will use it.'

'Would reasonable council not prevail? The welfare of a member state is concerned.'

Stevenson was thinking of his wife and sons. They were in Los Angeles.

'I have heard him speak. He appears prepared to risk anything. He is concerned about only one member state—for President Salem that state is all people, everywhere.'

The old man looked to the window, across the park to the Seine. He touched his fingertips together. Age blots showed on the backs of his hands. 'It is most unfortunate that it should occur at this particular moment in time. Most complicating and unfortunate.'

The thin voice conveyed neither urgency nor emotion. His words

361

were spoken as flatly as something read off a page. 'Thank you for coming, Stevenson.'

Was that to be all? Why had he been brought before the President's envoy? 'Is there nothing you wish me to do, sir?'

'You might establish if notification of the protest has been received by the President or Chairman.'

The Ambassador nodded dismissal. 'Inform me here if you will, Stevenson. I don't need to remind you about discretion.'

Stevenson went from his Embassy, white. It was inconceivable. The summary had noted thirty-two days since the first case in Watts. When had the summary been dated? How long had it been known? What was the flash-point for plague epidemic? Somehow, at any risk, he must get word to his wife.

When the door had closed the old man continued to think. The Ambassador waited for him.

'Most unfortunate,' he ruminated, 'at this particular moment in time.'

'It's rough,' the Ambassador agreed.

'I believe I must meet with President Salem.' He was here for that, if necessary. That, and other things.

'How much will you be able to tell him, sir?'

'Enough to convince him that the administration has decided on an initiative.'

The Ambassador wanted to ask, and finally dared. 'Is it hopeful?'

'Oh yes. It is hopeful. Nothing immediate, of course. There will be the formal observances, for allies and political advantage. Demonstrations of toughness about venue. Proposals and counter proposals, for face. Their side has already accepted Paris in principle. De Gaulle has been a great help.'

It was the assurance the Ambassador had hoped for. If it happened, he would be in the thick of it.

The old man said, 'I will not be reluctant to meet President Salem. I believe he would make an interesting bridge opponent.' Bridge and chess were the old man's games.

362

46

In the Press room the correspondents moved impatiently and decided that Mitchell must be hungover. He was making a balls of the briefing. In the section on the Humanitarian Law he had distributed a report from the Social Services Committee.

Sarah had tired of her confinement on the Left Bank, had taken a discreet bus tour into the country. Mitchell was so compelled that if he had known where to find her he would have hired a car and given chase.

Mitchell was sure her resolve of fidelity was sham. A failure of courage to face the facts, the inertia of married habit. She had cuckolded Neveau with the deliberation that passes mending. She had altered herself as implacably as she had altered the faith of her marriage. The wound of the wanton was in her now, as palpable as the horns she had put on her husband. Sarah would cut and run. She'd already left Neveau in all but fact.

Neveau was done. His career was done. The Swiss boorishness he had used to torment her lacked even the excuse of validity. Neveau was an Izzy, a Hun to boot, with a wanted criminal for a father. Maybe the old man did what he did on a trade to save his wife, as Mick East had suggested. Maybe he had deliberately sold faulty instruments. Maybe he had just been unlucky enough to be recognized from the old days in Munich. None of that changed anything for Janos Kisch or Wiesenthal.

Mitchell knew she had found it hard enough to bear things as they were. She would never submit to this. There might even be a hell of a scandal. He had her now. She would come to him like a homing pigeon. Where else did she have to go?

After the adjournment Robert Collins arranged his own interviews and followed Salem briefly to his suite.

'What happened, Pierre? Was it the committee?'

Salem shook his head. 'Not yet, Robert.'

'Wasn't Neveau with you? He wasn't on the floor.'

'Yes, I had a visit from Martin. He has learned something out of my past. A dossier was provided him. How strangely some people gain their ends.'

'A dossier? On you, Pierre?'

Salem touched his friend's arm. 'A personal unhappiness. Nothing lurid, Robert.'

Collins put down his curiosity. Whatever it was could not have been important. 'I was concerned when you didn't appear.'

Salem said, 'I expect to be removed, Robert.'

'Removed? You can't mean it.'

'Yes. The material in the dossier, innocent as it is, provides the committee with a reasonable excuse.'

'But, Pierre——'

'There is nothing I can do. It is in Martin's hands now.'

'But your motion, Pierre. Everything you worked for.'

'I don't expect to make my speech tomorrow.'

The telephone rang.

Salem said, 'Very well, thank you.'

Collins could think of nothing to say. Salem had changed. He seemed intent on some inner wonder, was somehow ghosted away. The rage that lay suppressed like a load in the big Negro rose and shook free. 'I won't let them do it. Not this way.'

'It is not in our hands, Robert. Now your visitors are waiting. The English are here to see me.'

'You've got to fight. Can't you fight it?'

'I don't know. While I can, I will try.'

Richter sat in Neveau's reception-room, piling the ashtray with cigarette ends. He had waited an hour. What was Neveau doing? His secretary said he was alone. *Don't blow this one, Richter.* He uncrossed his long legs, lit a new cigarette unsteadily. Stevenson was probably waiting for him at the Hilton now.

Neveau finished his call and lodged another number, making a tick against his list. He had more than a quorum now. The committee would be waiting when he got to Geneva. The sweat that raised so easily on his scalp shone under the sparse hair.

Salem was finished. When the committee rose this evening Neveau would be free of the sight and sound of him. He wanted Salem crushed. He wanted him crushed to the ground. God Almighty Salem, his English suits and French shirts, his sickening superiority, his whimperings to an imaginary heir.

The new arrival thanked Neveau's secretary and sat on the couch, holding the big briefcase on his knees. He smiled cheerfully at Richter and nodded. Richter nodded in return.

'American?'

'Yes,' Richter said.

'Here for the conference?'

'Yes,' Richter said.

'You appear to be fortunate in the weather, no?'

Goddam the man. 'Yes,' Richter said.

The secretary put her head in. 'The Chairman is free now, Mr Richter.'

Richter put out his cigarette and rose. The secretary said to the other, 'The Chairman has your card, sir.'

In her own room she telephoned a message for Ted Mitchell. The Press Officer had asked to be informed should Janos Kisch arrive.

Stevenson looked again at the time and made himself another drink. He needed it. The plague, Sweet Jesus, the plague. Imagination tormented him. If the plague got established in the black ghettos...

Stevenson was Presbyterian, a good churchman. He had been bred in the fear of God. That awakened in him now. Vietnam, the bloody quagmire. It was like a horrible judgment. He would have to get his family out of Los Angeles, find some reasonable excuse. He wouldn't move until the call he had booked came through.

Stevenson answered the door. Richter entered, walking at full height.

'What kept you?'

'Neveau was engaged. I had to wait.'

'Richter, have you heard of any protest to the ICRC lodged out of Saigon by our Ambassador?'

'No, sir.'

Richter was too exalted to be distracted. He looked down on Stevenson. 'Well, I had a successful talk with Martin. We agreed that the time has arrived for firm action. He is flying out late this afternoon to meet the committee in Geneva. You know, of course, what that means. He's taking the CIA file.'

Neveau had given Richter a cold reception. He had informed him of the facts and shown him out.

'I don't think we should rest on our oars,' Richter finished. 'I would suggest we concentrate on the African lobby.'

He waited for Stevenson to relax, to congratulate him with a drink, perhaps offer him a quick lunch. The other man said nothing. He wasn't eased, he was tensed.

'You and Martin agreed on that, did you?'

Richter slumped a little. He had overdone his entrance. 'It's over, sir,' he said, reducing his voice. 'We've won. There will be no Presidential wind-up tomorrow morning.'

Surely Stevenson understood. He couldn't be that obtuse. It was over. They had won.

'I'm glad to hear it,' Stevenson said, and paused. 'Now, Richter, I want you to go back to your buddy the Chairman and find out if the ICRC has received any kind of protest from our Ambassador in Saigon. If so, what action is to be taken. Telephone me here. I'm going to cut the afternoon session. This is important, Richter. Discuss it with nobody except the Chairman.'

'Go back to him?' He couldn't go back to Neveau. The man was in a state. He could hardly make himself civil. Richter sagged with dismay. 'What protest? I don't understand, sir.'

Stevenson sat down and rubbed his eyes. His voice was dull. 'Neither do I,' he said. 'It seems that every day things become harder to understand. I don't know what we've gotten into.'

He sighed and took a breath. 'Sorry, Richter. I'm a bit jumpy today. I can only tell you that it is of the utmost importance to know about

366

this protest. The Ambassador is expecting to hear from me this afternoon.'

Richter swallowed. 'The Ambassador?'

'Yes. The Ambassador. The Ambassador and another very important personage. See what you can get, and telephone me here. And, Richter, be discreet. Don't blow this one.'

Richter went from the room hardly seeing. The pendulum he rode had gone insane. He felt that his brain would explode. *Don't blow this one.* For the sweet love of gentle Jesus. What were they trying to do to him?

The afternoon was latening. There had been bitter debate immediately following adjournment. In the glass boxes the interpreters were hoarse with fatigue. Isolated in their earphones, smoking and sipping drinks, the representatives of one hundred and three nations deliberated the outcome.

Tomorrow morning Chairman Hylot would sound his gavel a last time. The man on the podium would rise. Pierre Salem, President of the world's single humanist International, would demand in the name of that humanity an unprecedented declaration to the world.

If there was to be a beginning of the way back, the beginning could be here.

Salem sat unmoving, waxen.

The Reverend Dr Luigi Fregosi, representative of the Holy See, was speaking about the need to protect the Catholic minorities in the North and South of Vietnam.

Before the plenary session closed, Joseph Richter telephoned the State Department leader at the Hilton. He had been unable to see Neveau.

The worried secretary had said, wondering, 'I'm sorry, Richter. The Chairman hasn't answered the telephone since his last visitor went in. You must be tired of waiting. Is there anywhere I could call you?'

Richter looked at his watch. 'When does the Chairman's plane leave?'

'He's booked from Orly at six o'clock.'

It was four-thirty.

Richter asked, 'Is there a private telephone I could use, please?'

'I'll bring you one.'

She returned with a set and plugged it in, closed the door behind her.

Stevenson listened. 'What is he doing? Who has he got with him?'

'Somebody named Janos Kisch. He's not listed among the delegates.'

'Chrissake, Richter. Can't you get through to him on the line?'

'I tried, sir. He's just not answering calls.'

Stevenson sounded his exasperation. 'What's coming off? Are they all nuts on that committee? The Ambassador's waiting to hear from me!'

Richter was at his rope's end. 'I've baked my ass here all afternoon. If he won't take a call, that's it. I can't hammer his door in.'

Richter patted his forehead with a handkerchief, corrected himself. 'I'm doing all I can, sir.'

There was no answer.

'Sir?'

'All right, Richter. Stay with it. If you have to, ride with him to Orly. Call me back in a half hour.'

Richter sat down and held his stomach. He had not had a bite of food all day. Whatever happened in his future career couldn't be worse than this.

Stevenson asked nervously for the Embassy. His call home to Los Angeles had not come through. The house number wasn't answering.

The taxi had becalmed in the evening traffic before it got off the boulevard des Capucins. Mitchell gripped the grab strap and groaned. He had become unused to the fret of big cities. Geneva might be a comfortable morgue, but a man could get from point to point without having the nerves plucked out of his body.

He stopped himself from wondering how Neveau had borne up. Thinking about him and Janos Kisch made his skin creep. What he had to think about was how to put it to Sarah. Provide the manly shoulder, the future.

He had a handshake coming from the do-gooders. He had lived off his expenses for years. If he wanted, he could sit on his arse in the Bahamas for six months, drink planters' punch and have Sarah peel his grapes.

Mick East was right. A man had to look after Number One.

'Bonsoir, Monsieur Mitchell.'

'Is Mrs Stone in?'

Sarah had used her maiden name. The clerk checked the key rack. 'Oui, monsieur.'

Mitchell took the stairs.

The door had been ajar. She looked out of the bathroom, holding a

368

lipstick. 'You're early. I'm just putting on a new face. Give yourself a drink. I won't be a minute.'

Mitchell poured a whisky. 'How about you?'

'Mmm. Lovely. Make me a brandy dry. There's ice in the bucket.'

He would have to give it to her without quibbling. This wasn't a thing to break gently. He called to the other room. 'How did it go today?'

'It was lovely in the country. I had the most delicious meal in the most unlikely place. Do you know, Ted, I get by quite well in French? I think I have more confidence away from Martin. He just won't try to understand.'

She came through the door, head tipped, brushing her long blond hair. Electricity zipped in the nylon bristles. She stood wide on her shapely legs, leaned back, the light silk moulded on her pelvis.

'How was it with you today?'

'Bloody.'

'You say that every evening. What shall we do tonight? Aren't you going to change?'

Mitchell was aware that he was crumpled. The shirt collar was sticky on his neck.

'I came direct from the conference.'

'You promised me something special for our last night. Here am I all bathed and powdered, dressed in my best, and you look as though you've walked through a hedge.'

She was very striking. Very total and happy, intent on the coming evening. She bent the brush to the back of her head. 'Please?'

'Please what?'

'Do go and smarten up. I'll wait for you at our café.'

Mitchell said, 'Sarah, I've got something to tell you.'

'Oh? Won't it wait? It's much too lovely an evening to waste indoors.'

Mitchell couldn't get started. Sarah sat on the bed, still busy with her hair. 'What is it? You look funny and flustered.'

'I am flustered,' he said, and turned to enlarge his whisky.

'Hurry up, then. What is it?'

He handed her the drink and said, 'You'd better get some of that into you first.'

Her smile was uncertain, wondering. 'Very well.' She toasted him and drank some of it off. 'There, now.'

'Sarah, this is going to be a hell of a shock. It's going to sound like something you've dreamed or read about. Before I start I want you to

369

know that there's no question of doubt. It's been checked out backwards and forwards. The other thing I want you to remember is that I want you.'

Her voice came small and frightened. 'What is it? What do you mean? What in the world are you trying to say?'

Mitchell said, 'It's about Neveau.'

It was all in him now, watching her face. He wanted to give it to her. He wanted to smash everything. 'Neveau isn't Swiss, he's Jewish. Neveau isn't his real name, it's Kleinberg. His father changed the name by deed poll when Neveau was a little boy. His people weren't killed at Dresden. The Germans put them in concentration camps. Mick East got it all from Janos Kisch of the Jewish Research Bureau. Kisch thinks that Neveau's father is alive. They want him as a renegade criminal.'

The glass had spilled on the covers. One hand was knuckled there, the other on her mouth. Her eyes seemed to be bursting. Her head shook.

'It's true, Sarah. Here's how it happened ...' Mitchell continued to give it to her, straight.

Several times her whimpered voice rejected him. 'No ... Stop it ... What are you saying?'

'It's true. You've got to accept it.'

Mitchell began to walk, telling the story. He didn't want to look at her face. He finished. 'That's about it, Sarah. There wasn't any other way to tell you.'

All her body was in rigour, dry-eyed.

She whispered again, 'No ... No ... It can't be.'

'It's true. It means the end of Neveau.' Mitchell splashed neat brandy in a glass, sat and took her shoulders. 'Here, drink this.'

The spirit ran on her mouth. Mitchell felt for a handkerchief to wipe her chin.

'Does he ... does he know?'

'He will by now. Janos Kisch was there this afternoon.'

'He ... knows?'

'Finish your drink. It will do you good.'

Sarah brushed away the glass, breasts heaving. Mitchell spoke again. Her eyes were glazed. She did not appear to hear or see him. The cry she gave frightened Mitchell. It was torn out. 'Martin. Oh my God. Poor Martin.'

She pushed up wildly, eyes and mouth distorted. 'Martin,' she cried again.

She was running from the room when he caught her, spun her back by the shoulder. 'What do you think you're doing? Where are you going?'

'To him. I'm going to Martin.'

'Are you mad? How can you? He doesn't even know you're here.'

She lashed her head, pushing at him. 'Let me go. Let me go.'

Panic lurched in Mitchell. He shook her hard. 'Get a grip on yourself. Sit down.'

'No ... let me go.'

It had gone wrong. How could it have? He held her almost grappled to him. 'You're not going anywhere. Don't you know what this means? Neveau is finished with the ICRC. There could be a scandal. Anything. You don't have to put up with that, Sarah. We can clear out. Do anything you want. I've got enough money to be independent.'

Slowly she stopped shaking. Her voice became more normal. She was looking at him now. Mitchell eased his hold.

'Clear out?'

'Anything,' he said urgently. 'Anything you want, Sarah.'

'Is that why you told me? Is that why you hurried here?'

'No ... yes ... I don't know. You had to hear it from somebody.'

Her eyes and face darkened. 'Let me go.'

'If I do will you sit down? We've got to talk this out.'

She did not answer, her breath suppressed and heaving.

'Sarah. Do as you're told.'

'Are you going to let me go?'

Mitchell began, 'Not until you come to your senses. Not until——'

He neither saw nor sensed the movement. Her clawed hand knocked back his head. The lacquered nails raked his cheek with fire, streaks that leaped beaded blood.

Mitchell recoiled, his hand to the wound, eyes shut against the shock. So quickly did she move, snatching her bag, that she was gone before he recovered.

'Sarah! Sarah!' Holding his face, Mitchell rushed to the stairs. He had one glimpse of her, heels clicking the lobby. He took away his hand. The palm and fingers were red.

'You bitch,' he sobbed, 'Oh, you bitch. You rotten bitch.'

Salem and Robert Collins left the elevator together. At the secretary's room they looked in. 'Has there been communication for me from Geneva?'

'No, monsieur le Président.'

The Negro smiled. 'In a half-hour, then.'

'In a half-hour, Robert.'

Collins was hosting a cocktail party. He crossed the corridor and entered his suite.

Salem's secretary said, 'The American Ambassador called. He asked you to telephone him at the Embassy.'

'The Ambassador?'

'Yes, sir. He called in person. I've never spoken to an Ambassador before.'

'How very courteous of him,' Salem said.

The taxi pushed towards the place de l'Opéra. Sarah's eyes were bright with tears, her lips apart, tremulous. She touched fingers to her breast for the pain there, the strange pain that was also fulfilment.

She had forgotten Mitchell, forgotten the details he had told her. She was going to her husband. In all the world only she could heal him. In all the world he had only the refuge of her love. She would take his poor head to her breast, make his pain her own. She would absolve him in her flesh, dress his wounds with love.

In her mind an older image returned. He was there as he had been at the beginning. Young and thin and shy, realized in her and through her. She had been in a place dark and ugly. In it she had lost him, lost herself. Now she was returned into the light, washed clean by the love and compassion swelling her heart like pain.

He needed her. Now he needed her. In all the world she would be all he had.

Sarah gave no care to her being in Paris. That would come later, if it must. Now all that mattered was what she had to give. That Neveau would not have to be alone. Now, or in the future, whatever waited.

In the ancient city looped by dark river, a new moon and stars domed cloudless over the dazzle of light and life. The music of accordions sounded in cafés and bars. Butter hissed in copper pans over spirit stoves alongside dining-alcoves. On the Champs Élysées elegant women strolled their elegant dogs. Students on the left bank drank their beer and calvados, ate in the horsemeat restaurants, shouted and kissed their girls.

The boulevards had quietened and emptied when Salem rode back from the Embassy. He saw and heard only his thoughts.

The old man had asked him, saying goodbye, 'Do you play bridge, President Salem?'

'I never learned the game.'

'Ah. What a pity. Farewell, then. We leave each other in hope.'

In hope. In hope. He did not know what might await him next morning. What Neveau might do or had done. He had been delivered into the other man's hands on sheets of stiff yellow paper. He waited for others as they waited now in America for the pestilence come home.

In the attic Thu had said, 'We are used to plague. The French lay on our country like the plague for one hundred and fifty years.'

Man's inhumanity to man is another kind of corruption, Salem thought. Each man carries the plague within him.

The old envoy had promised him peace. It could be long in coming but it was enough. He had helped win the battle, no matter what Neveau did to him now. Salem's law, the Humanitarian Law, would one day vanquish the ape.

My Own Dear Son

If I take my place to speak tomorrow it will be in more gentle and hopeful words than I had thought to be possible...

He stopped. Faintly, a smile curved his face. He turned to the car window and saw the lit streets, the throng of life at peace. It was enough. There was no more need of letters.